CW00550260

# Wild Thing

# Wild Thing

*Ted Darling crime series*

*'a chilling cold-blooded killer'*

**L M Krier**

# Contents

Chapter One                                     1

Chapter Two                                      9

Chapter Three                                   19

Chapter Four                                    30

Chapter Five                                    40

Chapter Six                                     49

Chapter Seven                                   59

Chapter Eight                                   69

Chapter Nine                                    79

Chapter Ten                                     89

Chapter Eleven                                  99

Chapter Twelve                                 109

Chapter Thirteen                               119

Chapter Fourteen                               129

Chapter Fifteen                                139

Chapter Sixteen                                150

Chapter Seventeen                              160

Chapter Eighteen                               170

Chapter Nineteen                               181

Chapter Twenty                                 192

Chapter Twenty-one                             203

Chapter Twenty-two                     213
Chapter Twenty-three                   224
Chapter Twenty-four                    234
Chapter Twenty-five                    245
Chapter Twenty-six                     256
Chapter Twenty-seven                   267
Chapter Twenty-eight                   279
Chapter Twenty-nine                    290
Chapter Thirty                         301
Chapter Thirty-one                     314
Epilogue                               324

# About the Author

L M Krier is the pen name of former journalist (court reporter) and freelance copywriter, Lesley Tither, who also writes travel memoirs under the name Tottie Limejuice. Lesley also worked as a case tracker for the Crown Prosecution Service.

The Ted Darling series of crime novels comprises: *The First Time Ever, Baby's Got Blue Eyes, Two Little Boys, When I'm Old and Grey, Shut Up and Drive, Only the Lonely, Wild Thing, Walk on By, Preacher Man.*

All books in the series are available in Kindle and paperback format and are also available to read free with Kindle Unlimited.

# Contact Details

If you would like to get in touch, please do so at:

tottielimejuice@gmail.com

facebook.com/LMKrier

facebook.com/groups/1450797141836111/

https://twitter.com/tottielimejuice

For a light-hearted look at Ted and the other characters, please consider joining the We Love Ted Darling group on Facebook.

# Discover the DI Ted Darling series

If you've enjoyed meeting Ted Darling, you may like to discover the other books in the series:

The First Time Ever
Baby's Got Blue Eyes
Two Little Boys
When I'm Old and Grey
Shut Up and Drive
Only the Lonely
Wild Thing
Walk on By
Preacher Man

# Acknowledgements

Thanks to all those who helped with this  book in the DI Ted Darling series., beta readers Jill Pennington (Alpha) Emma Heath, Kate Pill, Alison Sabedoria, Christopher Nolan, Jill Evans.

Thanks, as ever, to the people of the Stockport Memories group on Facebook for reminders about the town in which I grew up.

*To Emma,*

*Small, Medium and Large*

*Thanks for all the help*

# Chapter One

'Cold cases, Chief Inspector,' Superintendent Debra Caldwell, universally known as the Ice Queen, began formally, as she put two fresh coffees on her desk, one for herself and one for Detective Chief Inspector Ted Darling.

'Now, I know you already have a lot on your hands with the new mobile unit. But since you've had a promotion and associated pay rise, the powers that be want to get even more for their money out of you. Speaking of hands, how is yours now?'

Ted lifted his scarred left hand and moved the fingers over an imaginary keyboard. The thumb still showed some reluctance to join in.

'Almost as good as new. I could be a concert pianist, except I can't play a note.'

'Excellent, I'm glad it's improving. So, back to cold cases. Your clean-up rate is outstanding to date. We want to profit from that, and from your newly expanded team, to start mopping up anything still on the books, even from some time ago. Is there anything recent still outstanding?'

Ted took a gulp of his coffee before replying. The high-quality ground coffee she served was the best part of his meetings with the Ice Queen, although her attitude towards him had thawed somewhat since he'd been promoted to just one rung below her on the rank ladder. They even occasionally lapsed into first name terms, but it didn't come naturally to either of them. They had spent too much of their early time together walking on eggshells.

'There's still the stabbing in Hallam's Passage, from a couple of years ago now. We've never abandoned it, it's just stalled and we've not made much progress.'

Seeing her look of surprise, he hastened to add, 'Nothing to do with our DS Mike Hallam. It's the name of a ginnel that connects the A6 at Heaviley to Bramhall Lane and Cale Green. I think most of the reports at the time said the attack happened on Bramhall Lane, but it was actually in the passage.'

The killing had taken place before the Ice Queen had transferred to Stockport, replacing Ted's former boss and great friend, DCI Jim Baker, now a Detective Superintendent in another division. Ted summed up the broad outline of the case for her, although she'd doubtless read about it in the press at the time and, knowing her, had studied all the files on it when she took over the division.

A black teenager, Luke Martin, just seventeen, had been walking home through Hallam's Passage, on his way back from a music lesson. A talented musician, tipped for an easy scholarship to the Royal Northern College of Music in Manchester, once he'd finished his sixth form studies. He was attacked whilst walking through the ginnel, a single, deep stab wound to the abdomen. Nothing was taken, apart from some loose change from his pockets. His mobile phone, a cheap, older model, was broken but left. The only item of any value, the violin which he was carrying, had been pulled from its case and smashed to pieces.

Despite his injury, he had managed to crawl to a nearby street looking for help. A couple later admitted having seen him, lying in the road and vomiting, but had assumed he was drunk and had not gone nearer to check on him. It was dark and they were too far away to see that he was actually vomiting blood from the stab wound which cost him his life shortly afterwards.

No witnesses to the attack had ever been found and there was no CCTV anywhere close to where it happened. Despite countless hours of house-to-house enquiries, as well as appeals via the local papers, radio and television, there was still no suspect and the case was listed as open and ongoing.

Superintendent Caldwell knew that it was not for want of trying on the part of Ted and the team. He was one of the most diligent officers she knew. He was also a rarity in that he never had to be chased for paperwork and his enquiries were almost always scrupulously run by the rule book, so it was rare for any of them to collapse in court.

'A tragic case,' she responded. 'Always devastating to lose one so young, but to lose talent like that …'

'Talking of teens, how is Justin?' Ted asked.

The Super's elder teenage son had recently given his family a scare after falling into a coma from trying a so-called legal high at a party. Two of Ted's team, DCs Maurice Brown and Dennis 'Virgil' Tibbs had been doing the rounds, putting out the word that legal or not, such products were not welcome on their patch. Anyone found selling them, especially to youngsters, could find themselves in for an uncomfortable time.

'Better, but still grounded until hell freezes over, according to his father,' she smiled, suddenly showing a glimpse of the human side of her which was mother to two teenage boys. Then she became her serious and formidable work-self again in an instant.

'Keep on with that case. I know you're already doing everything possible, but let's see if we can finally get some justice for that young man and his family.

'I also want you to put someone onto digging into all the historic cold cases on the patch, see if we can't mop up a few of them. I'm talking about before your time here, of course, as I know you have very little outstanding. You tell me that DC Brown is methodical and dogged, so it would seem to be an ideal task for him. Never forget that we are both under constant pressure to justify our personnel budgets. Even though I can now attest from personal experience to his excellent hand-holding qualities, I would need more than that to put the case for his continued place on the team, if it ever came to that.'

Despite appearances to the contrary, Maurice Brown was a kind and sensitive man who could help anyone through a crisis with complete discretion. A lot of officers in the station had experienced him in 'daddy hen' mode, dispensing comfort, compassion and hot chocolate, in equal measure. It had been him Ted had sent to the hospital to be with the Ice Queen when her son was in a coma and her husband was away from home.

'You have two computer experts now, plus a very expensive piece of kit for your CFI, so let's make good use of them. With all the advances lately in forensic science, especially with DNA, we're in a good position to get ourselves some extra Brownie points by wrapping up some files from the past. From a purely PR point of view, ask DC Brown to begin with any cases where the prime suspect at the time is still alive and could still be brought to court.'

'Océane and Steve are currently busy helping Sal on the Sabden House file. We're still trying to make a watertight case against our dodgy councillor friend. I could leave Océane on that, as some of it is more within her area of technical expertise than Steve's, but he can certainly work with Maurice on cold cases.'

'Good,' she responded brusquely, with an air of finality.

Ted half expected her to follow it up with 'Make it so,' from the second Star Trek series, but suspected her taste in television was not quite the same as his. He took his cue and drained his coffee.

As he rose to leave, she added, 'Of course serious and serial crimes remain your personal priority, and that takes precedence over anything else. But any down-time at all, for you or your team, please use it for clearing up some cold cases. I look forward to some early results.'

Ted decided to look in on his opposite number in uniform before he went back upstairs. The two men had a good working relationship, which in no small measure accounted for the high clean-up rate in the division. Ted tapped briefly at the office door before he went in.

Inspector Kevin Turner was desk-bound behind piles of paperwork but looked up, snapped an ironic salute and greeted Ted with a 'Morning, guv'nor.' He enjoyed teasing Ted about his recent promotion to one rank above him.

'Idiot,' Ted smiled good-naturedly, taking a seat. 'So, what's the word on the street? Anything going on I should know about?'

'Usual Monday morning in Stockport. We've spent the weekend locking up the dangerously drunk and those who've been busy knocking seven bells out of one another after a few too many bevvies. Oh, and something I hope is going to turn out to be nothing at all, but we've got a small kiddy gone missing from his back garden this morning, first thing. His mam let him out to play, got distracted by a phone call, then when she looked again, the garden gate was open and there was no sign of him.

'I've got every available officer out there now looking. He probably just trotted off to find a friend to play with, but we've not got him yet. He's four so he could have toddled off quite a way already, or he might be hiding somewhere in a neighbouring garden, thinking it's all a huge joke. The mother's distraught, though, says it's not like him. He's a quiet little lad, always getting teased about his carroty hair, she says, so he tends to keep to himself.'

Ted nodded.

'Keep me posted, won't you? Too early to think of dogs yet?'

'Oh, I think so, at this stage. It's barely been a couple of hours, although I don't like to leave anything to chance, not with a little 'un. I know how frantic me and the missus always used to get if we lost sight of either of our two lasses for even a few moments. Sad that we need to feel like that these days, eh?'

'If there's anything we can do to help, Kev, just shout. Meanwhile, we're on cold cases in a big way now. And another big push on the Luke Martin case. I know we've been down every avenue we can think of to date but if any of your team can come up with any angle we haven't covered, do let me know.'

Ted had already briefed his team for the day, before going to see the Ice Queen. Several were out of the office on assigned tasks, but the ones he really needed to talk to were still in. DI Jo Rodriguez and DC Megan Jennings were additions to the team since the Luke Martin killing, so they could bring fresh eyes to the case. DS Mike Hallam and DC Jezza Vine also joined after the murder, but had been following the case so far. Ted and the older team members had been over and over it, but sometimes, even after all their work, someone could still pick up on something they'd overlooked. He hoped so. It disturbed him that they had so far made no progress on the case.

He outlined for them what he needed them to do. Mike Hallam, who shared an office with Jo Rodriguez, was out, so he, Ted and Megan could shut themselves away in there to concentrate. Once Ted had set them on their task, he went to find Maurice Brown.

'Cold cases, Maurice. Finish whatever you've just started then confine yourself to those until further notice. The top brass want to raise the clean-up rate from the past. They're especially after serious cases where the prime suspect is still in the land of the living and could be publicly hung out to dry, if we can crack the case with newer technology.'

Maurice groaned.

'Does that mean I've done something wrong, boss? This is my punishment for some dire sin I've committed and can't even remember?'

Ted grinned at him.

'It's a special present for you from the Super. She asked for you by name. You've clearly made a big impression on her. Do a good job for her and she might bake you a chocolate cup cake, with her own fair hands.'

Ted had been on the receiving end of the Super's grateful thanks in the form of an attempt at home baking. She was a highly skilled officer in many areas including, like Ted himself, being a former firearms expert. A contender for Masterchef she was not and her efforts, although kindly meant, had proved to be inedible, even when Ted was trying to be polite.

'If that's a present, I hope I never get to see what she'd give me as a punishment,' Maurice grumbled, shuffling papers around on his desk, though his tone was good-natured enough.

'Oh, and Steve,' Ted looked across to where Acting DC Steve Ellis was sitting as close as was decently possible to their recently-recruited civilian Computer Forensic Investigator, Océane, and her expensive all-singing, all-dancing new computer. 'You're with Maurice on this. Anything he needs, you get it for him. I want you to find me a case we can sink our teeth into, preferably by end of play today, so I have something to report back to the Super. The idea is that this is something the team can get on with when next I have to go chasing off to another far-flung corner of our little empire.'

He didn't miss the way Steve's face fell at the prospect of being parted from the new colleague he clearly held in high regard, and not just for her computer skills.

Ted went back to his office, put on his reading glasses and pulled up his own notes on the Luke Martin case. There had to be something they were all missing. It was just possible that they were looking at a random, motiveless killer, the hardest of all to track down. But Ted was still optimistic that fresh eyes on the case would finally turn up the link they had so far overlooked.

He spent much of the day going over old ground. He was starting to know some of it word for word by now, but he stayed optimistic. He had to. If there was a needle anywhere in the haystack, he was determined to find it.

It was the middle of the afternoon when his desk phone rang and it was Kevin Turner. His voice was solemn.

'Just to update you, Ted. Two of my team have just found the little lad, after we got a phone call. Well, found his body, anyway. In the river.'

'Very sorry to hear that,' Ted said sincerely. Despite all his time in the force, he still felt deeply the loss of any life, especially a young one. 'Accidental drowning?'

'We won't know for sure until the post-mortem, but there's a possibility that this is one for you and your team. From what we know so far, we're treating it as a suspicious death. SOCO and a pathologist are on their way, and I imagine you'll want to go yourself, as soon as possible.

'He was ...' There was a catch in his voice and he had to take a moment. Kevin may have been a good, seasoned copper, but he was also a father and soon to be a grandfather. 'Ted, his trousers and underpants were missing. We might just be looking at a murder with a sexual connection.'

# Chapter Two

It wasn't the first time that Ted had been called to view a body on this river bank, though not in the same place. The last time had been the mutilated corpse of a young woman. This time it was possibly every copper's worst nightmare – the body of a child.

Ted tried not to jump to any conclusions on the short drive over. There may have been a simple explanation for the missing clothing and he fervently prayed that was the case. The possibility of another paedophile case on his patch held no appeal.

He'd pulled Jo off the Luke Martin files to go with him, together with newly-promoted DS Rob O'Connell. Jo, a father of six, was unusually quiet and sombre. The death of a child was always hard for any police officer. For one who was a parent, Ted couldn't begin to imagine how difficult it would be. He carefully checked his pockets to make sure his Fisherman's Friend lozenges were there to offer what comfort they could when he arrived on the scene.

Uniformed officers were already taping off access to the river bank when they got there. For form's sake, Ted held up his warrant card, although every officer in the station knew and respected him. The three men ducked under the tape and followed the constable's directions, through the trees and down a slight slope to the riverbank.

The body had been carefully recovered from the river and laid on the bank. It would by now have been photographed *in situ*, exactly as it was found, from every possible angle, and a detailed initial examination carried out.

Ted was pleased to see that the attending pathologist was Professor Elizabeth 'Bizzie' Nelson herself. He knew there was no safer pair of hands for finding out what had gone on. He was also aware of the amount of respect and concern she would show for the body of the little boy. He and Bizzie had become friends outside work since she'd taken over the post of forensic pathologist.

Ted saw Jo's jawline tighten at the sight of the body as he slid the first of his lozenges into his own mouth. It was going to be a difficult one for all of them.

'Professor,' Ted greeted formally. 'What can you tell us so far?'

'Good afternoon, Chief Inspector,' she replied in the same tone, nodding to the other two. In private, they were on first name terms, but never in public, in a work setting. 'With the age and the distinctive hair colour, I think we can be fairly certain that this is, sadly, the wee boy who went missing earlier today.

'I'm not able to give you anything conclusive at this stage, of course, but the reason it's been signalled as suspicious is that my initial examination has shown me two things. The first is that he very probably drowned, and the second is that, from these marks here, on his neck, it would appear that someone held him face down in the water until he did so.'

She was indicating as she spoke. Ted didn't get too close, so as not to compromise a possible crime scene, but he could clearly see red marks on the scrawny neck which protruded from a Batman T-shirt, under a hoody, the only items of clothing on the body.

Jo and Rob had already moved away, talking to the first responding officers, finding out what they knew, going about their routine work with no need to be told what to do.

'The only crumb of comfort I can offer you at the moment is that so far I can see no sign of any sexual activity, despite him being naked from the waist down. There is no evident indication of penetration or anything else, but that, of course, is something I will only be able to confirm for you once I get him on my table.'

Ted nodded his thanks, his experienced eyes wandering along the bank looking for tell-tale signs of the presence of a third party or parties.

Bizzie Nelson noticed and told him, 'I've been careful where I've planted my big Welly boots but I have noticed, as you doubtless have, that there are footprints about. Quite small ones, too. The Crime Scene team can start in detail once I've finished with this poor little lad and had him taken away.'

'Thanks, Bizzie,' Ted slipped into informality now that it was just the two of them. 'I know you'll look after him. When will you be able to do the post-mortem for me, please? I'll take this one myself.'

'First thing tomorrow morning, Edwin, if that suits you. The sooner I give you everything I can, the sooner you can start getting justice for this little chap.'

Ted nodded his agreement and turned to follow Jo and Rob to talk to the other officers on the scene. The two uniformed constables greeted him politely. His fairness and courteous manner made him popular with everyone, not just his own team.

'Assuming it is the missing boy, which seems almost certain, what's his name?'

'Tyler Bradbury, sir. Inspector Turner's sending someone round to the house now to inform the mother,' one of the officers told him, then added, 'It's not going to be easy for her. She's a single mum; Tyler was an only child.'

They were all quiet for a moment, taking in the full implications, trying to imagine the impact the news would have on her. Then Ted switched back into professional mode as he asked, 'Who called it in?'

'The two lads over there, with mountain bikes,' the same

constable nodded in the direction of two teenage boys. 'They're a bit shaken, naturally enough, but also worried because they'd clearly come down here to smoke a bit of blow and sink a few cans, sir.'

Ted nodded his understanding.

'Right, Jo and Rob, take one each, separate them and get initial statements. You know what to do. Let them know we're not remotely interested in under-age drinking or smoking weed when there's a possible murder to deal with. Make sure you thank them for having the guts to stay and call it in.

'Any sign anywhere of the missing clothing?' he asked, turning back to the first responders.

'Nothing yet, sir, but we haven't looked very far so we didn't contaminate the scene. Inspector Turner is sending reinforcements.'

Ted got out his mobile phone.

'I'll get a dog team; they can help with that. They may pick up a trace of whoever's done this, at the same time. Professor Nelson thinks it's a deliberate drowning but hasn't yet seen anything to indicate a sexual motive. At least that's something positive to hold on to, as long as it's confirmed.

'The Professor will do the PM tomorrow and I'll take it. But we need to let his mum see him as soon as possible. I can't imagine what it's going to be like for her, but the uncertainty of not knowing must be worse than even the harshest reality, surely?'

His next phone call was to his partner, Trevor, to warn him that he would be late back. He seldom discussed his work in much detail at home, but he did mention that it was the death of a small child.

'So sorry, Ted. Are you all right?' Trev's concern, as always, was for his long-term partner.

'I will be once we get the bastard who's done this.'

As Senior Investigating Officer on the case, Ted was responsible for coordinating everything about it. Although he wouldn't get confirmation until the PM that this was a deliberate killing, he trusted Bizzie Nelson enough to start the case as if it was. If he was wrong, his budget would take a clobbering in terms of lost hours and he would have some explaining to do. But if it was murder, an early start could be invaluable in terms of wrapping it up swiftly.

Ted was particularly anxious to be present when the little boy's mother made the formal identification. It didn't bear thinking about, but he knew there was a high statistical probability that the killer was a family member, or at least closely connected, and he needed to rule out the mother early on.

He put through a call to DC Megan Jennings to be on standby to go with him to the hospital when the mother arrived for the ID. Ted felt himself inadequate to deal with grief on the scale of a parent losing any child, let alone one so young. DC Jennings had a son herself, Felix, who was eight. He knew she would be a comforting and reassuring presence for this little boy's mother.

He was also interested in what Bizzie had said about small footprints at the scene. He'd called Jo over and asked him to check the shoe sizes of the youths who had found the body. It would have been a monumental bluff if they had been involved in the killing and had coolly hung around for the police presence, having reported it. But they would need to be eliminated, as they had clearly been sufficiently close to the river to spot the body in the water.

He'd been lucky enough to get an early response to his request for a dog team to attend, to help locate the missing clothing. Ted wasn't good with dogs, but he recognised how vital they were in police work and knew they were well trained and sociable. It didn't stop even the least imposing ones from intimidating him. He had no idea why they worried him so much. He made himself a mental note to ask his mother if she knew, now she was back in his life.

He was relieved when he saw a dog handler coming down the bank with a small liver and white springer spaniel pulling enthusiastically on its lead. The man was looking round for the officer in charge, so Ted stepped forward to greet him. With his small stature, Ted looked far from an impressive figure of authority. People often dismissed him, finding it hard to believe he was a policeman at all, let alone a DCI.

'You were lucky, sir. We'd just finished up a case not far away when your call came through to the unit. What do you need us to do for you?'

Ted briefly outlined the details they had so far then added, 'The boy's trousers, underpants and shoes are missing and we really need to find those asap; they could give us a early lead. Can you do that for us, please, Constable?'

'Well, I can't, sir, but Ricky certainly can.'

Ted let it go. He knew it was not disrespect, either to him, or to the enquiry. It was just a typical copper's dark humour, the thing which got them all through the hardest of the cases.

'Also, when you've done that, can you backtrack to find how the boy got down here? What direction he came from?'

'Different dogs, different specialities, sir. Ricky will find the clothes for you easily enough. The rest of it he's not quite so hot on. But you're hopefully our last shout of the day, so we can certainly give it a go for you, especially if, as I understand it, the trail is still quite fresh.'

'Thank you, Constable,' Ted said, then looked down at the dog, whose entire body, not just his tail, was wagging frenetically in his eagerness to get on with the work he was trained for, which to him was just one marvellous game. 'Thank you, Ricky.'

The dog handler went on his way, grinning to himself. He'd never worked with Ted before but he had heard how polite he was. It was the first time an SIO had thanked him before he'd even achieved anything, and Ted was certainly the first, in all his years in the force, who'd thanked his dog by name.

Once Bizzie had finished with the boy's body at the scene and it was on its way to the mortuary at the hospital, Ted headed back to the station in his own car to pick up DC Jennings. Two officers from Uniform had gone to collect the mother and would meet them there for the identification.

'I'm sorry to lumber you with this, Megan. I know it won't be easy, and I'm trying hard not to sound sexist when I say I'd feel happier with a woman officer present. I know you're a mum and that must make it harder for you, but you'll certainly be better at it than I would by myself.'

'It's part of the job, boss, what I'm trained for,' she assured him. 'When it's over, I'll just be glad to get back to Felix and give him great big smoochy cuddles, which he'll hate.'

Ted thought he'd better not voice that he was planning something similar with Trev, as soon as he could get home. Trev was his rock. He dreaded to think how he'd get through his job without him.

He'd arranged to meet the uniformed officers bringing the boy's mother to identify him at the discreet side entrance, which gave direct access to the stairs down to the mortuary, in the bowels of the hospital building. He could see that she was sitting in the police car, parked close by. One of the two constables was waiting for him by the door.

'We left her in the car until you got here, sir,' she told him. 'She's in a real state, almost shell-shocked, you could say.'

'Genuine, do you think?'

'I would say so, sir, but you'll be able to judge better for yourself when you see her.'

'Is she Mrs or Miss, and is anyone with her?'

She shook her head in reply.

'She said there was no one she knew who'd come with her. She's not long moved to the area, doesn't know anyone well, yet. She's a Ms, but said we should call her Helen.'

Ted went over to the car. The driver got out and opened the door for the white-faced woman in the back seat. She looked young and fragile, thin and anxious. She'd probably thought waiting for news of her missing son was going to be the hardest day of her life. She was about to have to confront her worst fears as reality.

'Ms Bradbury? I'm DCI Darling, I'm the Senior Investigating Officer dealing with this matter. I am so sorry for your loss.'

'Are you sure it's Tyler?' she asked, desperation in her eyes, wanting him to say there had been a mix-up, some grotesque administrative error that meant it was not true.

'I am very sorry, but from the detailed description you gave earlier, and the photos you provided, it seems likely that this is Tyler. I need you to make a formal identification, and I'm sorry to have to ask you to do so. Would you please come with me and DC Jennings?'

He held the door open to allow the woman and Megan to go through first, then guided them down the stairs to Bizzie's domain, a place he had visited many times, without it ever getting any easier.

He showed them into a viewing gallery which overlooked the mortuary, currently curtained off. Only at his signal would the curtain be drawn back to reveal the small body.

'Please take your time, but let me know when you're ready to see him. DC Jennings is here to help and support you in any way she can.'

'I need to see him, as soon as possible. I need to know.'

Her eyes sought his, clearly desperate for a last-minute reprieve, any possibility that what she most dreaded being true was about to confront her.

'I need to. Now, please.'

As the curtains parted, the three of them looked through the window at the body on a table in front of them. It seemed tiny, defenceless, the bright red hair showing up vividly against the stainless steel of the table and the white sheet which covered everything below the chest.

'Tyler!' The sound ended in a choking sob. 'Oh, Tyler, what happened to you, love?'

She held out a shaking hand, her fingers clawing at the glass as she tried to reach out to her child.

'Can I touch him? I want to hold him. He looks so alone. And so cold.'

'Ms Bradbury, I'm so sorry, we can't let you touch him yet,' Ted explained, as gently as he could manage. 'We haven't yet finished our examinations. There is a strong possibility that this was no accident. We need to find traces of who might have done this to him, if that is the case. As soon as we have, I promise that you will be able to do so.'

She nodded in response, looking at Ted, trying to comprehend what he was saying to her, clearly not yet taking everything in. Then a look of panic came over her face and she looked back through the window.

'Where's his flying Batman? Has he got it with him? Did you find it? He needs it. He can't sleep without his Batman toy.'

'I'll do whatever I can to make sure that it's found for him. My team and I will do everything in our power for Tyler, please be assured of that.'

It was late before Ted finally got home, tired and emotionally drained. He'd made sure that the boy's mother had somewhere she could go so she would not be on her own at such a time. She'd spoken of a sister with whom she'd fallen out. A phone call from Ted was all it took for her to be welcomed there. He arranged for her to be driven over to the house and seen to be in safe hands.

He'd driven Megan back to the station, and they'd both been in agreement that there had been nothing in the mother's behaviour to arouse any suspicion. Then he'd been to catch up with both the Ice Queen and Kevin Turner with the broad outline of the case so far. Both parents themselves, they were clearly affected by what had happened.

When Ted got back home, Trev had just finished eating his pudding and was siding his plates away to the worktop. He'd never got as far as learning to rinse things or put them in the dishwasher. It was always Ted who cleared away the inevitable clutter he left behind him. He may have been an excellent cook but he certainly needed a kitchen porter for the cleaning up.

He greeted Ted with a warm hug and said, 'I wasn't sure what time you'd be back and I was starving, so I ate while I was waiting. I've kept yours warm; it's ready whenever you want it.'

Ted shook his head.

'I'm honestly not hungry. It was an upsetting one, for all of us. All I really want is a long, hot shower and an early night.'

'I could scrub your back for you? Maybe give you a massage?'

Ted smiled gratefully.

'I think I'd really like that.'

# Chapter Three

Early morning post-mortems were never Ted's favourite thing to start the day. He was less enthusiastic than usual about the current one. A life snuffed out so early was always tragic. The likelihood of foul play made it ten times worse.

He'd told Jo to set the team on to anything ongoing but to be on stand-by for a full briefing on the Tyler Bradbury enquiry as soon as he got back from the PM with further details. Jo could make a start, checking things like CCTV footage anywhere between where the boy disappeared and where he was found, although from his local knowledge, Ted couldn't think of where there might be any that would be of use to them.

If there was no forensic evidence to help them, it could be a hard case to solve from the start, and he desperately wanted to get whoever had done this, as soon as he could.

He changed his clothes, made sure he was well armed with his menthol lozenges, and went into the autopsy suite to join Bizzie as she was just preparing to begin her work.

'Morning, Edwin. This is a bad business. I'll try to give you anything and everything I can. Do you have any initial ideas?'

She was already working swiftly and efficiently as she spoke. Ted had to look away as she made the first incision into the body. It was a part he never enjoyed. With such a young victim, it was nothing short of obscene.

'We don't really know very much at all yet. He went missing from the back garden first thing yesterday. We had officers out looking for him as soon as his disappearance was reported, but they didn't turn anything up. Then we got the call to the station that he'd been found in the river.'

Bizzie was already deftly removing the lungs for closer examination.

'We took samples of river water from the site. So one thing we can do for you is to confirm - if it is a definite drowning, which is looking more and more likely - that the water in his lungs matches that of the river. That will at least rule out the possibility that he was drowned somewhere else and his body merely dumped in the river, to make it look like a possible accident.'

'The missing clothing bothers me at the moment. If there is no sexual motivation, and if someone wanted it to look accidental, surely they would have left him fully clothed? I'm having difficulty imagining a little lad like this toddling off all the way to the river by himself to begin with. But I'm beggared if I can see why he would take his kecks off before getting in the water. It would have been cold, for sure.'

Bizzie was bending over the table, peering intently at the organs which had kept the boy's small body supplied with oxygen, until someone had seen to it that they were filled instead with cold river water, robbing him of life.

'If it were not so tragic, this would be fascinating. Deliberate drownings are really quite rare, except in children. We'll come to those marks I showed you in due course. But for now, the lungs are telling me that this is a definite drowning. There's a fine froth in both them and the air passages, which is what I expected to see. That's consistent with similar froth that I noticed around the mouth and nose yesterday, which gave me the early indication. The lungs are quite water-logged.'

'Would it have been quick? Would he have known much about it?'

Bizzie lifted her gaze from her work and looked directly at Ted. Although normally bluntly-spoken, she could be surprisingly sensitive when the occasion called for it.

'I won't lie to you, Edwin. Drowning is not a particularly quick or peaceful way to die, as the body's primeval instinct is to fight against it, to try desperately to get vital oxygen. So, sadly, he would probably have been very frightened and struggled. It takes a particular type of person to hold someone, especially a child, under water until they die. It's not physically easy to do, for one thing, unless the killer is much stronger than the victim.'

Ted reached for another lozenge before he had even finished the one already in his mouth, biting down on it hard. He needed something, anything, to focus on as he took in her words. He had his own bad memories of the terror provoked by near drowning. He couldn't bear to think of what the boy had been through in the final minutes before his death.

'Was he abducted from his home?' the Professor asked as she continued with her work.

'We're not really sure yet exactly what happened. I'll know more when I've spoken to his mother in greater detail. It seems he may have wandered off out of the back garden while she was on the phone, but whether that was alone or with someone, we don't yet know. The garden backs on to the park, so anyone could have been passing.

'It would help a lot if you could let me know roughly how long he was in the water. Kevin Turner's beating himself up that he didn't call in a dog team sooner than he did but I don't think anyone was expecting this outcome, certainly not his mother. I hope, in a sense, for Kev's sake, that it wouldn't have made much difference.'

'My initial examinations showed he'd been in the water for perhaps six hours, if that helps? Although as I am repeatedly telling you, it is actually very difficult to pinpoint the exact time of death from autopsy findings. Sadly, any degree of exactitude only happens in books and on television.'

'That suggests that he was killed not long after he went missing so yes, it probably means we'd have been too late, even with a dog team. I doubt if Kevin could have got dogs there in that time, unless he'd fallen lucky, like I did yesterday with Ricky. So it probably wouldn't have changed anything, except that we may have had a better lead on the killer, if Tyler been found sooner. At the moment, all we have to go on is whatever the footprints tell us, and anything you can give me from the marks on his neck.'

Bizzie was already carefully positioning the body so they could both get a more detailed look at the finger marks on the neck, still clearly visible against the delicate white skin.

'Any chance of finding the killer's DNA from those?'

'Highly unlikely, Edwin, given the length of time the little chap was in the water. I'm not ruling anything out at all, though, and we will try for any trace we can give you. I can tell you immediately, as you can see for yourself, that the hands which did this are small. Another child, perhaps?'

She again looked intently at Ted who returned her gaze, his face showing his mounting horror as he exclaimed, half under his breath, 'Dear God, I hope not.'

'There is precedent though, in the UK,' she reminded him. 'Children as killers of other children.'

He nodded, his mind racing with the prospect of what it all might mean.

'There was Mary Bell in Newcastle, in the sixties, I think, and Thompson and Venables, on Merseyside, in the nineties. Their victims were other children. Can you give me as much detail as you possibly can on the hands? I don't know why it makes it any less horrific but somehow I almost prefer to think of a small adult doing this than a child killer on my patch.'

'There are some rather interesting marks here near his hips, too,' the Professor said, pointing them out to him. 'They look rather like scratch marks. There is some sign of scratching on his neck, as you can see.'

She turned her attention back to the boy's hands, examining the fingers and nails in detail.

'This is nothing very scientific, I'm afraid, just my best guess. It looks as if someone was pulling down his pants, and their nails, possibly their thumb nails, caught his skin and left marks. He doesn't have long enough nails for it to be likely that he did it himself. If your killer keeps their nails quite long, that would explain both sets of scratches. I'll do a more detailed analysis of the scratches later, take some swabs, see if we can find anything.

'So now I need to do a detailed rectal examination and take samples from there and the genital area, so I think the phrase might be look away now, if you prefer.'

Bizzie didn't often make light-hearted remarks during her examinations, but Ted was grateful for the warning and needed no second bidding. Some parts of the PM process he always found harder to deal with than others.

The Professor worked quickly and silently, while Ted kept his eyes averted, looking around the suite, trying to distract his thoughts. The spotlessly gleaming walls reminded him that he needed to give the kitchen at his home what his mother would call a good 'bottoming'. Trev's latest baking session had yielded its usual delicious outcome but rather a lot of cake batter had insinuated itself into the grouting on the tiled splash-back.

'Well, I'm satisfied that there was definitely no sexual assault involved,' she said finally. 'I realise that it's not very much comfort, in the greater scheme of things, but it is at least something. I've now done all that you need to be here for, I think. I need to get the various samples tested next, and I'll email you my findings in detail as soon as I can.'

Ted hadn't had anything more than his customary green tea with honey before the PM. He generally preferred to face the horrors on an empty stomach, to save embarrassment. He'd expected to be hungry, having given his supper a swerve the night before, but he still couldn't face any food. To go through the motions, he stopped to buy himself a sticky bun for a sugar boost, which he'd eat later, when he felt more like it.

He greeted the team, told them he'd be with them shortly, then headed for his kettle to top up on tea before he began. He checked his emails and messages while he gulped down the hot drink, and gave the Ice Queen a quick call with the details so far.

'Oh, dear heaven I hope not.'

Her response was exactly like his own.

'Whatever you need, in terms of personnel for this one, you've got it. To hell with budgets. The death of any child needs to take priority, but the prospect that the killer is also a child means you pull out all the stops and you wrap it up as quickly as you can.'

Someone had already written the name Tyler Bradbury on the white board, with the basic details they had so far, when Ted went back to the main office for the briefing. It looked like Rob O'Connell's writing. He had really stepped up to the mark since his promotion to DS.

Ted quickly filled the team in on all they had to date, ending with the news that, because of the size of the footprints and hand-marks, they could be looking at another child being the perpetrator. There was a shocked silence from all the team members at the news.

'Right, initial thoughts, everyone. The mother, first, clearly. She's not a suspect at present, but we need to check her out in case. Megan, if it's all right with you, you and I will take her again, now she at least knows us by sight. We'll talk to her informally first, at the sister's place, with her present. Can you phone and set up a meeting, preferably later today, please?'

As Megan nodded, Océane put in, 'Boss, do you want me to check for anything similar in other areas? Free the team up to do the routine groundwork? I can break off for now and do that, if it would help?'

Ted went quiet for a moment as the implications sank in.

Their first experience of a young offender being the killer would be bad enough, but if they had struck before and were still at large, going on to kill again, it was the stuff of nightmares.

'Yes, great, thank you. But let's not get hung up on our killer being a child just yet. It could be a small adult. We'll get a better idea when we have full details of the footwear and the hand prints when the Professor's report comes through. So, what else? Other possible lines of enquiry?'

'Do you want me to check kiddy fiddlers on the patch, boss?' DC Maurice Brown asked. 'Even if there was no sexual assault, it might have been the intention and the killer just got interrupted.'

'Sex offenders or paedophiles, DC Brown,' Ted corrected him. He wouldn't allow disrespect in any form from his team, especially during a briefing, even towards convicted offenders. 'But yes, thanks, get on to that. Can someone also check if we have any young persons on the patch with a history of anything at all like this? Any type of assault or attempted assault on anyone, especially on younger children.'

'I can take that, sir,' Steve Ellis put in. 'Is it worth checking with local schools, and perhaps even children's homes, about any particularly nasty bullying incidents lately? Especially towards younger children?'

'Good idea, Steve. Do that, please. If I get time to go to the self-defence club tomorrow, I can ask some of the children there. After all, a lot of them come because they've been victims of bullying in school so they may know what's going on.'

Ted and Trev ran the club for local children, an initiative they'd started to help combat bullying, which they'd both experienced when they were younger. It was a huge success, always well attended.

'Do we know who the boy's father is yet, boss?' Jo asked. 'We'll need to eliminate family and close friends early on.'

Ted shook his head. He didn't yet have that information but it was something he would find out when he and Megan went to interview the mother.

The handler and his dog had found the missing clothing for them before they'd knocked off for the evening so that had been sent for testing in the faint hope it might give them some sort of a pointer. It was a slim chance as, like the boy himself, it had been found in the river. After six hours in the water it was unlikely to yield much information.

'Boss, this isn't meant to sound flippant but, babysitters. I know some of the child carers I get for Tommy freely admit to feeling like strangling him sometimes when he's being particularly difficult, so it might be worth checking out.'

Jezza's younger brother was autistic and could be difficult. Talking of throttling him was just a figure of speech for most people, but it was something that might lead them somewhere, and with a case like this, they needed any line of enquiry they could find to start on. If the boy was used to a particular babysitter, he might well go off happily with them, but not with a stranger.

'Boss, stating the obvious here, but it would help to know if the little lad went off by himself or if he was deliberately taken,' DS Mike Hallam put in. 'I know you'll have more detail after you've spoken to the mother, but when we start house-to-house, we could ask if he'd ever been seen going off on his own. Do you want me to organise that?'

'Thanks, Mike, yes, that would be a big help. He was four, would he have started school yet?'

Mike and Megan answered almost in unison, both parents.

'Depends on when his birthday was.'

'Find out from the neighbours; you might get an earlier lead, depending on when Megan and I can see the mother. If he was, check the school, of course. If not, is there somewhere else he might have gone to? Pre-school, or whatever they call it?

'There's another thing, while I think of it. It may be nothing. His mother said he had some sort of flying Batman toy which he always carried with him. He couldn't sleep without it. I don't think it's turned up yet, so keep an eye out while you're round and about the area. I'll also make sure Inspector Turner knows to tell his Uniform officers that it's missing and needs to be found.'

Oceane's long fingers were, as ever, still flying over the keyboard as she spoke up.

'Boss, this may be crazy, but I'm just looking at those toys now online. You put Batman onto a sort of launcher, pull a cord and off he flies. What if he flew out of the garden and the little boy went looking for him? Then just bumped into his killer by chance?'

'Anything is worth looking into as a starting point, Océane, thank you. In fact, can one of you get one of those toys for us? I'll sign an expenses form for it. If we don't get any other indication of why he might have gone off, we could do worse than try the theory for ourselves. I know the early information from the mother was that he never went off by himself, and certainly never with strangers.

'Right, this one takes priority for now, but I don't want to drop the ball on anything else. So, Maurice, once you've checked sex offenders, back to cold cases, please. Sal, stick with the Sabden House case for now; I want that wrapping up tight.

'Has anyone had chance for a fresh look at the Luke Martin file, and do we have any new ideas on that?'

'I had an idea, boss, but it may be way off.'

'Let's hear it, Jezza. I'll take anything going on that one; it's been an ongoing case for far too long.'

'Well, I know all his friends, schoolmates and people who played in orchestras with him were spoken to at length. But what I didn't see mention of in the files was who actually got the scholarship after he was killed? I mean, it was taken as a given that he would get a place. But was there strong rivalry for the places? Enough competition for someone to want him out of the equation?'

Ted looked at her appreciatively. Jezza was definitely a thinking outside the box sort and could often bring fresh new ideas to a case. He and the team had thoroughly investigated all those close to Luke Martin. The angle she'd suggested had not been gone into, and he mentally kicked himself that he'd not thought of it before.

'Good, Jezza, you follow that up, see what you can find out, please. But it will need some tact and sensitivity. We can't just go barging in accusing a promising young musician of having killed their rival for a scholarship, without something solid to go on.'

'Boss, you cynic, are you suggesting I can't do diplomatic?'

Ted smiled, despite the seriousness of the situation. He didn't mind a bit of banter. The job was hard enough to get through, without keeping it serious all the time.

'Right, you all know what needs working on, please get on with it. I'll let you know as soon as I have the Professor's report in full, with details of shoe sizes and any other results.'

Before he did anything else, he was anxious to go and have a word with Kevin Turner. Kev looked up expectantly when Ted went into his office.

'What news from the PM, Ted?'

'Definitely a deliberate drowning.'

'Shit. Shit, shit, shit. I should have called a dog team in sooner. We might just have been able to save him. By the time I did call the dog section, all the handlers were tied up and we had to wait. I made a bad call.'

'Kev, the PM showed he was killed within a couple of hours of disappearing. Even if you'd called in the dogs as soon as he was reported missing, it would probably have been too late. And there's no guarantee a team would have been available earlier on. You know we can't always get one when we need one. Not your fault, don't blame yourself.

'Something very unsettling showed up, though. The killer had very small hands and feet, so we're looking at either a small adult or ...'

'Oh, bloody hell, Ted, no. Not that. Not on our patch.'

# Chapter Four

'Shall I get your official car, boss?' Megan Jennings asked as she and Ted were getting ready to go and interview Tyler Bradbury's mother. 'And I could drive, if you like? That is, unless you object to being driven by a woman?'

Ted opened his mouth to protest at her implying he might be sexist, then saw from her smile that she was teasing him. He liked that. It showed she felt relaxed in his company. Knowing her previous senior officer, it must have made a pleasant change for her.

'I'll just suck on my menthol sweets if you scare me too much. I'm nearly ready. If you go and get the car, I'll come and find you in a couple of minutes. Oh, and Megan? That funny stick thing between the seats is what you use to change the gears with,' he grinned back at her.

Kevin Turner would be pleased. He was always going on at Ted about using the car he'd been allocated, pointing out that designated cars were getting like hens' teeth with the never-ending round of budgetary cuts.

'Use it, or lose it,' was his endless refrain.

Ted hadn't made any changes since his promotion to DCI; he just carried on as he always did. He had his own ways of getting respect from the officers under his command without relying on turning up, chauffeur driven, in a big, official car.

He wanted a quick word with Jo before he left, putting him in charge in his absence.

'That poor young woman. I can't imagine what she must be going through. My six can be a proper handful at times, especially when they all start fighting between themselves. But I've no idea what the wife and I would be like if anything happened to any one of them. You don't seriously suspect her for it, do you?'

Megan asked the same thing as Ted slid into the front seat next to her and made a show of fastening and double-checking his seat belt, like a nervous passenger. It was not an enviable task which lay ahead of them. Any note of humour they could inject without being flippant would help both of them.

'You know the statistics as well as I do, Megan. Murder by random strangers is mercifully rare, so we have to start with immediate family and work from there. We wouldn't be doing our jobs properly if we didn't.

'I don't want to disclose too much detail at this stage, for obvious reasons, even to the mother. I wondered if you could have a glance at her hands and feet, and the sister's too, see what you think about sizes. I'm still waiting on exact details of the footwear - size and make - but Professor Nelson said at the scene and at the PM that whoever held him under the water had small hands and feet, and possibly long nails.'

Tyler Bradbury's mother was staying with her sister in Romiley. The house was a small semi-detached, not far off the main road. The sister came to the door to let them in, her arms full of a wriggling small child, another toddler clinging to her leg, peering warily at the strangers.

She led them into the first room off the narrow hallway, a modest-sized sitting room, the floor strewn with toys. Helen Bradbury was sitting on a low, squashy sofa, staring vacantly into space. Dark smudges under her reddened eyes pointed to a lack of sleep. Her fingers clung to a small pyjama top with a Batman logo, occasionally kneading it, lifting it to her face to inhale what Ted and Megan immediately realised must be the last lingering smell of her child.

'Helen, love, the police are here,' her sister told her then, turning to the officers, 'Shall I make some tea or something?'

Ted nodded. The woman they'd come to interview certainly appeared to be in need of a warming drink. She looked frozen and her hands, still absently caressing the fabric, were trembling.

The room was open plan, leading through to a compact kitchen at the rear of the house. The sister went through, the two little ones still clutching on to her. Too small to understand anything, they were still sensitive enough to pick up on the almost palpable sense of tragedy surrounding them.

Ted and Megan had agreed that he would do the questioning while she took notes. His ability to talk to people was one of Ted's greatest strengths. Quietly spoken and mild-mannered, he inspired confidence and appeared to present no threat. People often told him more than they intended to, simply because he seemed so innocuous.

'Ms Bradbury, could you please tell me, in your own words and your own time, exactly what happened yesterday, when Tyler first went missing?'

It seemed to take a long time for Helen Bradbury's eyes to come into focus on Ted's face, as if she had been somewhere far away. Ted had seen the same reaction before, too many times, in those who had lost loved ones.

'Please,' he said quietly, his voice full of sympathy. 'Anything at all you can remember which might help us.'

'We'd finished our breakfast. Tyler had Coco Pops; it's his favourite. Then he wanted to go into the garden to fly his Batman toy. Have you found that yet?' She looked hopefully from Ted to Megan as she asked. 'He'll not settle until he gets it.'

'I have officers looking for it now, Ms Bradbury. What happened next?'

'I said he could play in the garden, but not to go anywhere else. He knows that, he's very good. I work from home and he'll play for hours by himself, with Batman, without getting bored or interrupting me. He's a good little boy.'

Her sister had parked the children in a playpen in the corner of the sitting area while she made the tea. She hadn't asked anyone what they wanted but reappeared with three mugs, each with a teabag in the hot water, which she plonked in front of them, then came back with sugar, spoons, and milk in the bottle.

'What sort of work do you do?' Ted asked, helping himself to milk and sugar.

He looked around for somewhere to put the teabag. Not finding anywhere, he left it in, the tea darkening to a real builders' brew, not how he normally drank it.

Helen Bradbury was absent-mindedly adding sugar to her mug, clearly not keeping track of how many spoonfuls. Without a word, her sister took the spoon away and helped her to lift the mug to her lips. She was still gripping the pyjama top in one hand as she drank.

'I type stuff for people. Transcripts, from a voice recorder, that kind of thing. And a bit of proofreading.'

'And yesterday? After breakfast?' Ted's quiet voice gently guided her back on track.

'I got a phone call. Would I do a short survey. I could win a load of shopping. I know these things are just rubbish. Even if anyone does ever win, it wouldn't be me. But then I thought I'd take a chance. I was thinking of all the Batman stuff I could buy for Tyler, and it would only take five minutes, they said.'

She broke off as her throat tightened and her voice caught. Her sister, who had sat down protectively next to her, carefully guided the mug to her lips once more.

'I looked through the window to check on Tyler. He was playing nicely, flying Batman. He didn't even notice when I waved to him. I think the survey took quite a bit longer than five minutes. I got a bit distracted. When I looked again, he wasn't in the garden. The back gate was open onto the park.

'I ran out to look for him but I couldn't see him anywhere. I ran and I called him but there was no sign of him. There weren't many people about. I asked anyone I saw but no one had seen him. I searched and searched. Then I ran back to the house, in case he'd gone back there and I hadn't seen him.'

Tears were running down her face now, her hands wringing the fabric, which she lifted to bury her face in, drying her tears on the cotton.

Ted hated to press her but he knew that any information he could get from her now would be vital. Her grief appeared to be genuine, and he'd already noticed that her feet were not unusually small. Her hands, although slim, had long fingers, the nails well kept, apart from the left thumb where it was bitten down almost to the quick. He wondered how recently that had happened.

'What can you tell me about Tyler's father? Is he still in contact?'

The sister gave a scornful snort which appeared to indicate what she thought of the man in question. Ted wondered if that opinion was part of the reason the two sisters had fallen out.

Helen Bradbury shook her head, a weary gesture as if she was already tiring of the questions.

'He's never been involved, right from the start. It was a mistake, a one-off. He was married, with kids of his own; he didn't want to know.'

'Did he ever see Tyler?'

'Only the once. He refused to believe Tyler was his, so I showed him his son. Then he couldn't deny it. They had the same hair, the same eyes.'

Ted looked from her to her sister.

'And, forgive me for asking, was that the reason the two of you fell out? Something to do with Tyler's father?'

The sister answered for her.

'I'd no time for him at all, that's true. But no, we fell out a couple of years ago over money. Our mum died and left us the house. I wanted to keep it and let it out, Helen wanted to sell it and split the money.'

'I needed it so I could move away from where I was and make a new start. I don't earn much and I'm renting. I needed money for a deposit.'

'So would the father know where you and Tyler had moved to?' Ted probed.

'I think he could probably find out easily enough. He's in the police.'


They'd been given the name of the father, Lewis Chase, a PC in Tameside Division. Ted had made a phone call and arranged to go straight up to Ashton to talk to him. He was being called in from duty but, at Ted's request, not given any details of what it was about, other than that a DCI from Stockport needed to talk to him about a case on his patch.

An interview room had been made available for them. When Ted and Megan arrived at the station, signed in and got their visitors' passes, they found the constable sitting there, patiently waiting for them. The first thing they both noticed was the hair colour. Tyler's mother had said her son was teased about his carroty hair. PC Chase's was much darker than carrot but still decidedly ginger.

He looked up as the two officers came in but made only a half-hearted attempt, for form's sake, to stand.

Ted waved him to resume his seat, then introduced them both. Again, he would do the talking while Megan took notes. It was not, at this stage, a formal interview. He just wanted to get a feel for what, if anything, PC Chase, knew about his son. Ted had no grounds on which to suspect him at the moment, especially as the man sitting opposite him was tall, large-framed, and had big hands with thick fingers.

'Thanks for agreeing to see us, PC Chase. I'm wondering if you can help with an ongoing enquiry. Does the name Helen Bradbury mean anything to you?'

The man looked genuinely puzzled, his lightly freckled

face creasing as he appeared to search his memory for the name.

'Bradbury? I don't think so, sir. Can you tell me what it's about?'

'What about a Helen? Do you know anyone called Helen?' Ted persisted, ignoring his question.

The man coloured slightly as he replied, 'I did know a Helen, briefly. Not the proudest moment of my life. Sir, what's this about? Should I have someone with me? A solicitor? Or my Federation rep? I'd prefer not to answer any questions without knowing what it's about, if it's all the same to you.'

'You'll probably have heard that we're investigating a murder which happened yesterday in Stockport. A little boy of four, Tyler Bradbury. Helen Bradbury was his mother. She says you are his father.'

It was brutal, but Ted needed to see the man's reaction at the news. He didn't at all fit the profile they had so far of the killer, but he wanted to know if he was involved somehow. The way the constable's face drained of all colour and the look in his eyes told him all he needed to know.

'That little lad was mine? I heard about the case, of course, but I didn't make any connection. I only saw him the once. Knew he was mine, as soon as I saw the hair. The poor little sod. And his poor mother. What must she be going through.'

'Did you have any other contact with Helen, after you saw your son?'

The man shook his head.

'Like I said, sir, I'm not exactly proud of myself. It was a stupid thing to do. A quick drunken knee-trembler in a ginnel behind a pub. Helen and I were both there for the same party. I can't even remember what it was or who it was for. We'd both had a lot to drink; we were both well up for it. You know how it is, sir.'

Ted had to bite his tongue to stop his response. He didn't know. He'd never been into one-night stands, certainly never drunken ones as he was teetotal. He tried to keep his expression neutral, to allow the other man to continue, without breaking his train of thought.

'I'm a married man, two kids of my own. It meant nothing; it was just a drunken act.'

'How old are your children?'

'They're fourteen and sixteen now, sir, so they were quite young when all this happened. That was one of the reasons I didn't want any of it to come out when she told me. I didn't even give her my phone number, just my first name, and I only ever knew her as Helen. She must have got my details from someone else at the party. She got in touch a few weeks later to tell me she'd fallen pregnant and it was mine.

'I didn't really believe her. I couldn't believe she'd got pregnant just like that. I don't even remember much about it, if I'm honest. But I didn't want the wife finding out, so I offered to pay for a termination. She refused point blank, said she was going to have the nipper and keep it. I said I wanted nothing to do with the kid. I couldn't take the risk to my marriage. Apart from meeting her to see the kid and giving her a bit of money to help, that's the last contact I ever had, I swear.

'Christ, this is awful. The poor kid. And poor Helen. Sir, do you think I should get in touch? Go to the funeral or something? Could you give me the contact details?'

'Honestly, PC Chase? I think I would leave well alone. I strongly suspect you might be the last person she would want to see there.'

'Bloody men!' Megan grumbled as they got back in the car. 'No disrespect, boss, but I get fed up of hearing this sort of a tale. You don't think he had any hand in the murder though, do you?'

'It doesn't seem likely, at this stage, Megan, but we needed to cover all bases. One thing I do think we do need to look into though, tactfully. He has teenage children. Is it possible that they got wind of any of this and would that be enough of a motive for one of them to kill a rival sibling?'

'Christ, boss, I hope not,' Megan said fervently. 'This case gets worse, the further into it we go.'

Trev was looking pleased with himself when Ted got home. He was busying himself in the kitchen, humming happily but totally tunelessly as he worked. Whatever he was cooking smelled appetising and Ted realised that he was ravenous. He kissed his partner then went to the fridge for some apple juice. Trev already had a glass of wine on the go.

'You sound as if you've had a better day than I have.'

'Sorry, has it been dire? Are you hungry? I've made comfort food.'

'I've been interviewing the little boy's parents. Not exactly a barrel of laughs. I'm glad your day was better. What's put you in such a good mood?'

'Apart from playing with bikes all day and drawing a salary to do it?' Trev laughed. He was a partner in a motorbike dealership and loved every minute of his work. 'But I'm extra excited because I've got the chance to go to the south of France for a few days, if you wouldn't mind?'

'Of course I don't mind,' Ted said, trying fervently to mean it. He relied so heavily on Trev to help him through his darkest cases, but he didn't want to be selfish enough to stop him from having fun.

'Willow and Rupe have got a shoot there and they asked me to go along for the ride. It would be for about ten days, but I'm not yet sure of exact dates. Is that ok?'

Willow and Rupert were friends of them both, top models who enjoyed the sort of jet-setting lifestyle Trev adored. Ted moved closer to give him a hug.

'Just promise me you'll phone whenever you can. And be careful, hanging around with the Beautiful People. Don't do any funny stuff, all right?'

Trev laughed and kissed him.

'Oh Ted, honestly. Yes, of course, it's going to be nothing but drink, drugs and debauchery. I can't wait.'

# Chapter Five

Even though Ted arrived at work early as usual the next day, Professor Nelson's PM report was already waiting in his email inbox, having been sent an hour before. Ted knew Bizzie was a night owl who often didn't sleep. She was frequently up and about when most mere mortals were still in their beds.

He read the report through carefully himself then made copies to share with all the team members at the morning briefing. It gave him the details of the shoe sizes and those of the hand prints, which was what they were waiting for to help them to advance the enquiry.

'The trainers are a popular brand and a small size. 33 European, Professor Nelson has put. Does that give us any help?'

Océane was clicking away on the keyboard as he spoke.

'That is small, boss, it's a ladies' Size 1, in old currency, or a child size. And those hand measurements – well, those hands couldn't stretch to even an octave on a piano.'

'I don't quite follow you?'

'Sorry, that's irrelevant really. I was just thinking about musicians, after what Jezza said about the other case. It got me pondering on musical instruments. I'll shut up now. Except to say that a lot of the sites I'm looking at here don't do ladies' shoes that small. There's only a few specialist ones that do.'

'Trainers, though, that could easily be a child or a small teen,' Megan pointed out. 'They're a pretty universal item of footwear these days. I suspect most of us have a pair.'

'I'm not a trainers sort of a bloke,' Maurice Brown put in,

raising a smile from the rest of the team. Even since he'd started taking better care of himself, in particular with his diet, all of them had a hard time visualising him out jogging, playing sports or even power-walking.

'The other thing we now have from the PM report is a small trace of what appears to be nail varnish in one of the scratch marks on Tyler's hips. According to Professor Nelson, a very dark purple colour, almost black. It's gone off for further testing, just on the off-chance they can get anything more from it for us. It would be a minor miracle if they find a DNA trace and it's one that's on record, but we live in hope.'

'Nail varnish? So the killer's a lass, then? With small feet and painted nails?'

'Maurice Brown, remind me how you can possibly be my best friend when you're such a sexist pig,' Jezza told him, although her tone was good-natured. 'Anyone can wear nail varnish, it doesn't necessarily mean a female killer.'

'Boss, just a thought. Jezza's right, it could be a male or a female. But varnish that dark could possibly be a Goth thing, and Goth lads might wear nail polish, as part of the get-up. They usually wear black but possibly the dark purple is a new thing,' Megan Jennings suggested. 'Do we have any tame Goths we could ask, in case they know of anyone?'

'Right, Goths, anyone? Not something I know much about. Are they any more likely to kill than anyone else? Who knows where they hang out, and who can go and talk to them? Jezza?'

'Give me time to nip home and change and I can out-Goth any of them, boss. I'll see what I can find out. Though as far as I know there's no sinister child-drowning ritual linked to them. There's no particular link to the occult; they just tend to like the dark side of things.'

With her drama training, Jezza could take on different appearances to suit various circumstances. Ted didn't doubt that, dressed the part, she'd succeed in getting somewhere, if any of them could.

'We also need to be tracing any older children or small adults who may have come into contact with Tyler. Megan, can you look into the father's other children, as discreetly as you can, just in case? What else have we got? Any CCTV anywhere around?'

Ted knew that CCTV footage had been a big help in the Merseyside case involving the murder of a little boy by two ten-year-olds. He didn't think there were any cameras covering the area where Tyler went missing, or where his body was found, but they may just pick something up from the surrounding area.

'Negative on that, boss,' Jo told him. 'This is going to be a shoe leather case – we just need to get out there on our various sized feet and start talking to people.'

Ted's mobile phone rang as Jo was talking. He checked the screen then said, 'I need to take this, it's the Big Boss. Jo, can you allocate tasks and I'll catch up with you shortly.'

'Morning, Super,' Ted began as he went back into his own office. To his surprise, Jim Baker didn't respond with the rest of their usual joke.

'Ted, I want you to get over to South Manchester straight away. There's something strange going on there. An old lady's been run over by a bus and killed. The driver is swearing blind he saw someone deliberately push her into his path. He's clear on the breathalyser and his driving record is clean as a whistle. I need you to assess whether we should open a murder enquiry on this one.'

'Why don't I send Jo and Rob over to start initial enquiries while I'm dealing with the Tyler Bradbury case? They're both perfectly competent.'

'Dammit Ted, don't start getting bloody uppity with me. You're Serious and Serial and if you know anything more serious than deliberately shoving an old granny under a bus, I'd like to know what it is. Get your backside over there and find out what's going on. And take the bloody car I got for you, with someone to drive it. I hear you're hardly using it and we'll lose it from our bloody budget if you don't. Start acting like a DCI, for God's sake.'

'Yes, boss, sorry, boss,' Ted said meekly, although his tone was ironic. Then, after a pause, he asked, 'What's wrong, Jim? I'm sensing you're not your usual sunny self this morning.'

There was another silence, apart from a long exhalation at the other end of the phone.

'Sorry, Ted. I was just in the mood to rip someone's head off and piss down the soggy end and you happened to be in the line of fire.'

'Want to tell me what the problem really is?'

Another sigh.

'Bella and I had our first row this morning. A really heated one and she flounced off out. It wasn't even my fault. Apparently I was talking in my sleep last night, pretty passionately, from what she said. Only the name I kept mentioning wasn't hers.'

Ted suspected it was not the right moment to chuckle, although he felt like doing so.

'I tried pointing out I'm not responsible for what I dream. And that I don't even know a bloody Monica, as far as I'm aware. But that seemed to make things worse. I'm not quite sure what to do next. I've tried phoning her but she won't answer and she's ignoring my texts of apology.'

'Flowers and a meal out usually works for me, with Trev.'

'But what sort of flowers? I don't want to get something else wrong.'

'It's always a single red rose for us. It's an in joke between me and Trev. Why not ask a florist? They must have some sort of grovelling scale for bouquets. And don't worry about it. Every couple has arguments, it's only natural.'

'You and Trev don't.'

'We're the exception that proves the rule. Right, I'd better get over there, in the official car, with a driver and do DCI sort of stuff to find out what's going on. I'll update you as soon as I know anything.'

'Thanks, Ted, and sorry, once more. I know you'll look at it from all angles, screw a guilty person to the wall but not let an innocent man go down for it. That's what we need on this. What's left of the old team there, even with a strong new DS, hasn't got your skills, which is why I want you there in person.'

Ted went back out of his office, in search of Mike Hallam. With any luck, he could sort things out up in South Manchester in an hour or so and get back to the Tyler Bradbury enquiry. He didn't much like the idea of someone deliberately pushing an elderly woman under a bus, especially not on his extended patch. If he could just set things in motion, he could probably safely hand the enquiry over and concentrate on the other case.

'Mike, you and I are needed up at South Manchester to check something out. I've just got a few ends to tie up, so please can you go and get my official car and I'll meet you in the car park in five minutes.'

Mike laughed.

'You're taking it out twice in a week, boss? You'll wear the tyres out.'

'I'm under increasing pressure to use it or lose it. And just for your cheek, you can drive and I'll sit in the back seat, like a proper SIO.'

He didn't, of course. He wouldn't dream of it. He sat up front with Mike and told him all he knew so far about the incident they were going to investigate.

'They've got a good new sergeant there, and just two DCs now. You possibly know her? DS Rakale?'

'Leona? Yes, I know her. Very good. She'll bash that shower into shape if anyone can.'

Ted had been instrumental in an enquiry into police corruption in the division which had seen the former DS leave the force by mutual consent, and had left a DC on remand for perverting the course of justice.

'I would have said Leona would be more than capable of handling this one on her own, even if it does turn out to be a murder enquiry, boss,' Mike went on.

'Orders from the Big Boss, Mike. He wants me to oversee it. Ours not to reason why.'


The DS was waiting for them in the CID office once Ted and Mike had signed in. She was the only one in, and stood up to greet them. Most other officers towered over Ted's small frame but she was exceptionally tall and dwarfed him. Ted hadn't met her before but had heard good things about her.

'Hello, sir, it's nice to meet you. Mike, good to see you again,' she greeted them, then indicated chairs so they could sit down together while she told them what they had so far.

'The deceased is a 78-year-old local woman, Mrs Joan Murray. She was walking home from the shops. The bus was being driven by Owen Arnold, who's been doing the job for twenty years without incident and has a completely clean driving licence. He was interviewed and breathalysed at the scene. Breath test was clear, but he was brought here for questioning pending more information.

'I've spoken to him briefly myself. His story has never wavered. He claims to have seen a teenager in a hoody deliberately push the old lady straight into his path and he had no chance of avoiding her. Traffic are still investigating and measuring up but their sergeant told me that, from the initial marks on the road that he's seen, the story checks out.'

'What news of the alleged killer?'

'Had it away on his toes, sir, according to witnesses. I've sent DCs Winter and Eccles out to start getting witness statements, with extra help from Uniform. And the good news is that there's CCTV just higher up the road from the incident site. So if he ran off that way, which is what we've been told so far, we might well have some footage of him.'

'Definitely a male?'

'That's what everyone has said so far, sir, and we have quite a few to question. There were several passengers on the bus, some of whom had to be treated for mild shock, some passers-by and a few passing drivers who stopped. Everyone so far says a young male, like a teenager, wearing jeans and a hooded top with the hood pulled up, so there's no description of his face at this stage. I'm organising the CCTV for you. It should hopefully be here by the time you've done your initial interview with Mr Arnold. If it comes in earlier and shows anything you should know about immediately, I'll come and find you.'

Ted was impressed. She'd been picked because she was a strong DS who could build a solid team out of what was left from the cull. She certainly knew her job.

She showed Ted and Mike downstairs to an interview room where Owen Arnold was waiting patiently, then left them to it.

Ted introduced himself and Mike as they sat down opposite the driver. He was cradling a cup of tea, his hands shaking slightly, but he appeared calm and composed, though pale.

'Mr Arnold, at this stage you're not under suspicion of any offence; you're a key witness to a possible one. I'd like you to tell me, in your own words, exactly what happened in the moments before the bus you were driving came into collision with Mrs Murray.'

'I've already gone over it with the other officers, twice. But I'm happy to do so again if it'll help you catch the person responsible. It's a terrible thing. I knew the lady by sight, I'd often pass her on my rounds.

'I know the route and the road conditions well. I've been driving it for twenty years without incident. I saw the lady coming along the pavement towards me. I'm always careful, always well within the speed limit, and keeping an eye out for possible hazards.

'I saw a young lad jogging up behind the lady, who was pulling a little trolley. I was going slowly, in the bus lane, so I could see quite well that the lad seemed to grab something from the trolley. Then just as he got alongside her to go past her, he gave her a real shove with his shoulder and she just fell into the road, right in front of me. I hit the brakes straight away, as hard as I safely could, but there was nothing I could do. She went under the wheels.'

'Did you see what happened to the youth?'

'Inspector, I had a bus half full of passengers, on a busy road, with an old lady under my front wheels. I was doing all I could to prevent the accident being any worse by losing complete control and the bus perhaps mounting the pavement and hitting other pedestrians. I'm afraid watching where the lad went was the last thing on my mind.'

'And from what you did see, you're sure that this was a deliberate action by the youth?'

'It all happened very quickly, the whole thing. But in a sense, I think I realised what was going to happen by the way he positioned himself alongside her. I'm pretty sure I was already hitting the brakes when she started to fall. I'm only sorry there wasn't more I could have done to prevent her being killed.'


'Genuine, do you think, sir?' DS Rakale asked Ted, when he and Mike went back upstairs after talking to the bus driver.

'I'd put money on it. Any news of the CCTV or any other witness statements?'

'I'll arrange to get the tape sent to you. Are we treating this as a murder enquiry then, sir?'

Ted nodded.

'I think we have to, based on what we've got so far. If you think Traffic will confirm what the driver says, he's in the clear. And if we can find any other witnesses who saw this young lad, especially anyone else who saw him push our victim, then we need to go from there. I just need to phone the Super to let him know where we're up to. We'll start with some media appeals for more witnesses. A cup of tea wouldn't go amiss, if that could be arranged, before we go back.'

Mike and Leona went off to make tea and catch up, as they knew each other of old, while Ted put his call through.

'Jim, you were right, this looks deliberate. Are you all right with me leaving DS Rakale in charge for now while I go back to Stockport? She's going to send CCTV over and we'll have a look at what we've got, but I just want to touch base with the other enquiry.'

'Run it how you see fit, Ted. You don't need me to tell you how to do your job. I was behaving like a complete dickhead this morning, but all is now back to normal. Bella's been in touch, I'm taking her out to dinner tonight so all is well with the world once more.

'Just keep me in the loop at all times, but it's up to you how you handle things. If you want to take one case and leave Jo on the other, or head them both up, that's up to you. Just don't spread yourself too thinly. We need some quick results, if you can do that. What's our killer looking like for this one?'

'Too early to be sure, but possibly a teenage lad.'

'And the Stockport one is another teenager or a small adult? You don't think there's a connection?'

'I'm not ruling anything in or out at the moment, Jim, but on the face of it it's improbable, I would say. I'm going to shoot off back to Stockport now and leave Leona in charge here. I want to get to self-defence tonight and see if any of the kids there can help me with the Tyler Bradbury case. If anyone knows about older kids bullying younger ones on our patch, it's likely to be one of them.'

# Chapter Six

Young faces in a semi-circle looked at Ted as he spoke, taking in everything he said. The boy Philip, known as Flip, was particularly rapt. He was a big fan of Ted, so much so that his stated ambition was to become a policeman himself.

Ted spoke quietly, requiring them to pay attention. It was a trick he found useful when talking to coppers other than his own team. It forced them to listen to what he was saying. He was talking to the youngsters about a subject most of them knew too much about from personal experience – bullying.

A lot of the children who attended the self-defence classes were there because they'd been picked on at school. Ted suspected that a couple of the teenage girls were simply there because they fancied Trev, as they spent a lot of time gazing adoringly at him and giggling when he spoke to them. Ted often wondered what they would think if they knew that it was his bed which Trev shared every night. The two of them made no secret of their relationship but they always tried to tone it down in front of the youngsters. Some of their parents were reluctant enough to let them attend the club. There were still those who might stop them from attending at all if they knew they were in the company of two gay men.

'So if any of you hear or see anything at all, especially where older children seem to be bullying younger ones, it's fine to tell someone about it. It's not telling tales; it's helping to stop someone getting hurt and being made to feel their life is miserable.'

He uncrossed his legs and moved to a kneeling position.

'Right,' he said, 'let's get started. Make you all a bit safer.'

He bowed formally, mirrored by a chorus of heads dropping towards the mat. Then they were on their feet and Ted and Trev were moving among them, showing them defence techniques, stressing that the best line of defence was always to run away where possible.

'This case has got to you, hasn't it?' Trev asked as they walked home after the kids' club had finished and they'd enjoyed their own judo session. 'With the little boy, I mean. I know the drowning aspect makes it especially hard for you. Do you want me to cancel the trip to France, so I'm here for you?'

'No, don't be daft, you're really looking forward to it. It's a kind offer, but you go, have some fun.'

'Well, if you're sure ... Because if I'm going, it's going to be this Friday evening. But only if you really don't mind.'

'So soon?' Ted felt a sudden grip of panic. He relied so much on his partner to bring some stability to his life.

Trev reached for his hand in one of the spontaneous gestures of affection which came naturally to him. The slow, suggestive smile Ted knew so well spread over his face as he broke into a slow jog, pulling Ted with him.

'We've got tonight. Who needs tomorrow?'

Ted's response was under his breath so Trev didn't notice it, as he added the next line from the country song.

'Why don't you stay?'

Ted had barely got through the door of his office the following morning when his mobile phone rang. Jim Baker.

'Morning, Darling.'

The voice was certainly much more cheerful that it had sounded the previous day, so Ted completed the old joke.

'Morning, Super.'

'Ted, you're bloody brilliant. If you ever get fed up with CID, never mind going to join that lot in Complaints, you should become a marriage guidance counsellor. Seriously. A big bunch of flowers, a posh restaurant, and things are back to where they should be between me and Bella. Better than ever. It was certainly her name I was shouting when things got passionate'

'Whoa, Jim, have to stop you right there. This is quickly descending into the realms of Too Much Information,' Ted told him with a laugh.

As far as Ted was concerned, sex lives were private, kept behind closed doors. He never talked about his to anyone. As it happened, he'd spent an amazing evening with his partner, which made the prospect of him going away even harder. He was pleased Jim was in a better humour but he really didn't need to know the details.

'Well, I just wanted to say your advice worked so I owe you a drink or something. Keep me posted on the cases.'

Ted wanted to catch up with the Ice Queen before morning briefing. He knew that she was always in early, as he was. It was a good excuse to start the day with a decent cup of coffee. The South Manchester case wasn't on her patch, but as a courtesy, he'd keep her in the loop in case it took him away for any length of time.

'We need to launch a press appeal for witnesses in the Tyler Bradbury case,' he told her, 'and I need to do the same for South Manchester. Do you want to arrange a press conference for our case, or shall I just talk to Alastair for now?'

'We'll do both. Like I said, no stone unturned for this one. Talk to your friend as soon as possible. You seem to have something of a working relationship of late, so build on that. Let him know he's getting an early lead. I'll talk to the Press Office and organise some wider coverage. We certainly do need the public's help on this if we're going to get an early result.'

Ted thought calling the local reporter, commonly known as

Pocket Billiards, his 'friend' was taking it a bit far. But he had been useful to them of late, so he made a mental note to force himself to meet him during the day and buy him a pint of his favourite lager top. He hoped he could avoid eating with him, which was always guaranteed to kill his own appetite. But he was prepared to do whatever it took to bring the little boy's killer to justice.

True to her word, DS Rakale had sent over the CCTV footage which briefly showed the hoody, the prime suspect in the killing of the elderly woman, sprinting towards the camera then running on past. The face was obscured and shadowed by the large hood so it didn't tell them much. After they'd all watched it through a couple of times, Ted asked for observations.

'It's not easy to see much, but he certainly looks short and slight,' Virgil Tibbs observed.

Jezza had been watching more attentively than anyone, bending forward for a better look at the image, which was not clear.

'Boss, I don't think that's a he. I think it's a she.'

'Really?' Ted was surprised. All the witness statements he'd seen so far had suggested the figure in the hoody was male. 'Are you sure, Jezza?'

'Well, the last time I checked, I was a woman, boss. I also work out and do kickboxing with other women. And I'm pretty certain that figure is female, not male. It's the way they move.'

'You can't tell for sure from just that blurred clip, surely? The figure's not got any … well, it's not the right shape for a girl, is it?'

Maurice Brown, trying to be tactful, raised a small chuckle from the rest of them. Even Ted smiled.

'I'm not that sure, Jezza,' Megan Jennings put in. 'It's really hard to tell.'

'I looked like a boy until I was in my teens,' Jezza put in. 'Some girls are quite androgynous, and some even stay that way. I just don't think we should get hung up too much on the gender thing.'

'Give me a bit of time and I'll see what I can do to enhance the image, see if that helps at all,' Océane put in.

'I agree with Jezza. At this stage, let's just concentrate on what we can tell for sure, even if it's not a lot,' Ted told them.

'Small and slight, and we can't tell skin colour,' Sal voiced what they were all thinking. 'It doesn't really get us very far, boss.'

'Anonymous baggy clothes,' Megan continued. 'They hide the figure effectively, and there's no logo visible on the hoody.'

'So if this is a female, boss, is there a link between the two cases? Is that what you're thinking?'

Ted shook his head.

'Far too early to be jumping to conclusions like that, Mike. We're not taking this case on, unless we do find a definite link. It'll stay with South Manchester and I'll oversee it. I just wanted your input, to see if anyone could come up with some suggestions, and you have.

'So, now back to our own case. Tyler Bradbury. What's new there? Goths, Jezza?'

'Goths, boss. I spent a pleasant couple of hours with some of Stockport's finest. And I have to say, they were an intelligent lot, artistic in the main. I don't know if they're representative or not. They had heard about the case, of course, and seemed genuinely shocked and disgusted by it. They didn't know of anyone amongst the local Goths who could fit the profile of someone wanting to kill a little lad, and they're a close-knit bunch. They all know everyone. When you stand out as much as they do, it's easier to flock together.

'They were also dismissive of purple nail polish. For them, it's black or nothing. They don't know of any self-respecting local Goth who would wear purple; they say it's more of an Emo thing.'

Seeing blank looks from some of the others, she explained,

'Emos are a bit like a punk wing of the Goth culture, sometimes with brightly-coloured punk hairstyles. It's also worth mentioning that the whole Goth style thing leans towards the feminine and a lot of Goth males wear eyeliner, for example.

'We all know, too, that Goths are sometimes victims of hate crime themselves. There was that murder of a Goth teenage girl in Lancashire a few years ago. That's why they're a pretty tight-knit community. Anyway, I gave them all my number and they'll contact me if they get wind of anything.'

'Do they know you're a police officer?' Ted asked, out of curiosity.

'Oh yes, I wanted to be level with them, to get them to trust me. But they're cool with that. They were a nice bunch. Genuine, I think. If they hear of anything, they'll get in touch, as much to protect their own image as anything else.'

'What else? What do the neighbours say about the mother?'

'I've been talking to other young mums in the same road, boss,' Megan began. 'They all said pretty much the same thing. She hadn't been there long; they didn't see a lot of her, just going out to the shops with Tyler, that sort of thing. But working from home, on her own, with a little boy, I doubt she had time to socialise much. They'd have got to know her a bit better when he started school, no doubt.

'They did say they would see her taking him into the park for a bit of a run about whenever the weather was right. He always had his flying Batman with him. Oh, and none of them had ever babysat for her. As far as they knew, the ones I talked to, she didn't go out.'

'What about people using the park? Have we covered that yet?'

'It's on our To Do list for today, boss,' Jo told him. 'I've been liaising with the CSOs. They've not heard of anyone hanging round the park behaving suspiciously, and they're usually the first to hear anything like that. If the weather forecast is accurate and it stays fine, we'll try the park today.

No point in going if it's siling down, there'll not be enough people there to ask.'

Ted nodded his satisfaction. The Police Community Support Officers had good contacts in their areas. They'd have heard if there had been anyone in the park recently who stood out for any reason.

'Good, we're on the right lines, just keep on with it, until we get the break we need. Oh, and Jo, have a word with Inspector Turner to see if Batman has turned up yet. I can't help thinking we might learn something from that missing toy.

'Mike, you and I need to whiz up to South Manchester again just to see how things are going there, and to feed back Jezza's suggestion that the suspect may not necessarily be male. Can you get the car while I make a phone call? I need to fix up a meeting with my favourite journalist.'

Ted was early for his meeting with Pocket Billiards after his trip up to South Manchester. He made sure he had a drink ready in each hand – a Gunner for himself and a pint of lager top for the reporter – when he arrived. Ted always tried to avoid shaking his hand, never knowing quite where it had been or what it had been doing before he touched it.

'Thanks for coming, Alastair. Lager top, isn't it?'

'Thanks, Ted, I was ready for this, I'm spitting feathers. I've not eaten yet, either, and I could eat a scabby donkey,' he said hopefully.

Ted sighed to himself. He should have known he wouldn't get away without putting his hand in his pocket. He'd taken the precaution of grabbing a sandwich himself earlier, never relishing the prospect of having to eat in the journalist's company.

'No problem, have what you fancy,' he told him as Dave, the landlord, grinned at him from behind the bar.

Dave was well aware of Ted's real feelings towards the reporter, and had also witnessed his less than charming eating habits himself on too many occasions.

'I'll have a hotpot, Dave, then I can decide which pudding I want after that.'

Ted led them over to a quiet corner table where they sat down with their drinks. The first half of Alastair's disappeared without seemingly touching the sides and he sat back with a loud, satisfied sigh, followed by a belch.

'Right, then, Ted, what have you got for me on the little kiddy? Is it true you're looking for another kid as the killer?'

Much as Ted disliked him, he had to concede that he was a good journalist, with his nose to the ground and plenty of contacts. He was always well up on what was going on. Ted doubted his sources came from within the station, since he was widely avoided, not least because of the way he sponged off people and never stood a round himself.

'It's too early to jump to that conclusion.'

Ted was anxious to avoid any such assumption appearing in the media too soon. It wouldn't help their case, and it might actually delay the enquiry if the public were fixated on the idea of the killer being a child.

'We'll be holding a press conference soon, but I just wanted to let you have what information I can give you first, before anyone else gets it. You've helped me in the past, so I'm trying to keep up my end of the bargain.

'We don't yet have a lot to go on. What we do know so far is that the killer has small feet and hands. They were wearing trainers, a ladies' or child's size 1, European 33. We don't yet know if the little boy was taken from the garden or went off by himself. I'd be really grateful if you could avoid calling it an abduction at this stage. That might cause panic, and it might not be true.'

Ted was speaking quickly, keen to impart all the information he had as fast as he could so he could hopefully get out of there before Pocket Billiards began to eat.

'The other thing you might be able to help me with is

Tyler's Batman toy. He had one of those flying ones and we've not yet been able to find it. I've put all the details down for you, with a link to the kind of toy I'm talking about. It would be very useful to trace his toy; it could help us a great deal.'

He put a couple of sheets of paper on the table, then his heart sank as he saw Dave coming across with a steaming hotpot. Dave caught his eye and winked at him, knowing full well Ted would have appreciated a longer delay before the food arrived.

The reporter grabbed his knife and fork, tucked his napkin into his collar and fell on his food like a starving dog. He crammed more into his mouth than he could comfortably close his jaws around but, undeterred, he started talking, spitting out bits of crust as he did so.

'And what about this case you're on up the road? Is it true you're looking for a teenager for that one?'

Ted wasn't surprised he'd already heard about the South Manchester case. He dropped his eyes to his glass, seemingly fascinated by the mixture of ginger beer and lime. Anything to avoid having to watch the reporter chewing with his mouth open.

Alastair swallowed noisily and, to Ted's surprise, began to sing.

'Oh, ye canny shove yer grannie aff a bus
Naw ye canny shove yer grannie aff a bus...'

Ted winced involuntarily at the bad taste of the old Scottish song, in the circumstances.

'Not of interest to you though, is it? A bit off your patch?'

'But I can just see the headlines, Ted,' he said, raising a hand with a still dripping fork in it to draw an imaginary banner in the air. 'Manchester kids on a killing spree. Have the police lost control?'

Ted groaned inwardly, wondering who would be more

likely to kill him first, Jim Baker or the Ice Queen, if he didn't do something to prevent such catastrophic press coverage.

'Let me get you another drink, Alastair. Would you like a short, perhaps? And I'll get the dessert menu, see what Dave has on the Specials board today.'

# Chapter Seven

Ted hardly dared look at the local news website the following morning. The weekly paper wasn't out for a few days yet but the reporter had promised to get a piece up online soon after his meeting with Ted. He'd update it later, after the press conference which was scheduled for mid-morning. The Ice Queen had insisted that Ted must be present in person as SIO on the case. He hated such occasions, never comfortable in front of cameras and microphones. But in a case like this, he was prepared to do whatever it took.

'Jo, anything new from the park?' Ted asked to start the morning briefing.

'No reports of anyone conspicuous hanging about, boss, but Virgil picked up something interesting.'

He looked across at DC Tibbs to supply the details he'd discovered.

'May be nothing at all, boss, and may not even be related. I got talking to one of the maintenance crew who look after the park. There's been a few strange incidents there lately, he told me. A load of ducks on a pond were poisoned, deliberately, it seems. They found bread with slug pellets in it. And a kitten was hanged from a tree. Like I said, it could be unconnected to our case, but I thought I'd flag it up.'

Ted nodded.

'You did right to. We need to know everything we can about what's been going on in the area. As you said, it's maybe not related but they're both pretty sick things to do.'

'Boss, I could ask Sally if the RSPCA have been involved

in anything like that in the area.'

Sally was Rob O'Connell's fiancée, an RSPCA inspector who'd helped them before on another case.

'Good, thank you. What else? What's everyone working on today?'

'Boss, I'm going up to the music college this morning, just doing a bit of digging on the Luke Martin case. I can change it, though, if there's anything specifically you need me on here? But there's one thing in that file that puzzles me, that I picked up on from the case notes.'

'Go on, Jezza, and it's fine to work on that for now. That's still an open case and I'd dearly love to see it wound up.'

'I was puzzled by the notes so I went and checked all the evidence bags to be sure. Luke's violin was smashed at the scene, and it was a valuable one. But the bridge was missing. It wasn't found with the rest of the pieces, it wasn't in his personal effects and as far as I know, it's never been traced. Is there any significance to that, I wonder?

'Anyway, I'm just going up there for a chat with a tutor, doing my tactful best to find out who filled the scholarship place Luke would almost certainly have got. Then I can at least have a look into them and their background.'

'Well spotted, Jezza. Not sure how that was missed or what it signifies. He was just walking home from a lesson – could he have broken it while playing?'

'Not really sure yet, boss, but it's something I'm planning on asking about when I go to the college.'

'Anything else?'

'I was going to go to Ashton this morning, boss. I have a friend in Tameside. I've arranged to meet her for a coffee, see what I can find out about Lewis Chase and his family. If that's all right?'

Megan always sounded so hesitant for anything she did off her own initiative. The legacy of her former boss cast a long and unpleasant shadow.

'Good idea, Megan, thank you. I'd prefer to get some background on him before we go wading in. If he and his family are unconnected in any way, it might be better to let the past lie. No sense in tearing two families apart if it's not absolutely essential to the enquiry.

'Right, I've got this press conference later, and you all know how much I love parading in front of cameras. So get out there, do your stuff and see if you can find anything, any crumb, that we can throw in front of the press pack to show we really are doing our best on this.

'Oh, and shall we all meet up in The Grapes at the end of the day? It's a tough case, it might be nice to unwind at the end of the first week.'

He didn't add that it was as much for his own benefit as theirs. Trev would have left for France by the time he got home and he wasn't looking forward to rattling around an empty house with just the cats for company for ten days.

'I can't this evening boss, sorry. I'm going out and I need to get Tommy sorted and settled before I go.'

'Another hot date with Nat, Jezza?' Virgil asked. He'd introduced the two of them and was pleased they seemed to be getting on well. He laughed as he chanted teasingly, 'Jezza and Nathan sitting in a tree, K.I.S.S.I.N.G.'

'You just remind him that if he doesn't treat you right, I'll break his other leg,' Maurice growled menacingly, always protective of Jezza.

The briefing was breaking up now as they all went about their work so Ted let it go, even when Jezza made a kickboxing feint in Virgil's direction as she went to get her things and head for the door. They were a good team, they worked hard. He wasn't the sort of senior officer who was forever jumping on them. He didn't need to.

He spent some time on his never-ending paperwork, then went over all the notes they had so far on the Tyler Bradbury case. He didn't want to be caught flat-footed at the press conference by a question he couldn't answer.

Kevin Turner was also under orders to attend. The Super wanted to reassure the media and the public that they were taking the murder of a small child seriously and using all their available resources. Kevin and Ted had been summoned to her presence in good time for their own briefing on what would be presented and who was saying what.

'I know we need to disclose the small hands and feet to get any news of potential suspects, but I don't want to dwell too much on the possibility of the killer being a child at this point,' Ted said. 'I think it might cause alarm and it might not be so. It could still be a small adult.'

'I'm still finding it strange having a killing on our patch and no call from Honest John. I never thought we'd miss him. I suppose someone will fill his shoes in time,' Kevin Turner said reflectively. Their former serial confessor had himself become a victim in a recent case.

'And the missing toy?' the Ice Queen asked, topping up their coffees. 'Do you want to go public on that?'

'I think we should. There's always an outside chance that the killer has kept it as a trophy. It wouldn't be the first time that happened. If we can find Batman, he might lead us to the killer.'

'On the other hand, if we make it public, it may possibly alert the killer so they get rid of it. But I agree, on balance, it's worth a shot. The killer may not have it, it could simply be lost. So now, gentlemen, are you ready to face the fray?'

She rose majestically to her feet, her uniform and turnout immaculate as ever. Kevin Turner was also looking his smartest, hair carefully slicked into submission. Trev had supervised Ted's wardrobe for the occasion. The Super insisted he was always suited and booted, when he preferred more casual wear. He'd been careful to do up his top button and pull up his tie to cover it. She looked him up and down critically and for one awful moment, he thought she was about to straighten his tie and smooth his lapels as she might do for one of her teenage sons. But the moment passed and she swept out of the room, the two men trailing in her wake, to face the press pack.

The press conference passed off reasonably well. Pocket Billiards was at his most odious, constantly wheedling to try to get the angle of a potential child suspect. The Super was in her element, deftly fielding all his questions, a ready answer to everything. Ted contented himself with sitting scowling and mentally using his martial arts to inflict a slow and painful death on him.

The ordeal finally over, Ted headed back upstairs, loosening his collar and tie as he went and heading straight for his kettle. He'd just made himself a welcome mug of green tea when his mobile phone rang. Megan Jennings.

'How did the press conference go, boss?'

'Good job I'm not a Catholic. I think I just sinned by thought, wanting to kill a certain reporter of my acquaintance. But I think it went well. The Super handled things smoothly, as usual. What have you found out?'

'Something interesting, I think. I was just chatting to my friend off the record, girl talk, a lot of it, about people we both knew. It wasn't hard to get the conversation round to Lewis Chase. Apparently he's known as a bit of a dog who can't keep his trousers zipped, so I think him saying it was a one-off with Helen Bradbury might be bending the truth a bit.

'Anyway, my friend knows him, but not like that, and was able to tell me he has two sons, both big tall lads, like him. So they don't sound likely as suspects. But she did tell me his wife is tiny. Like a little bird, she put it.'

'Did she, now? Right, I think we need to talk to PC Chase again, find out a bit more about this wife of his and if she could possibly have known about his love-child. I'll call the nick, arrange a time, then can you meet me there, please?'

PC Chase was looking more than a little ill at ease at his second visit from an SIO on a murder case involving a child who had turned out to be his son.

'Do I need a solicitor, sir?' he asked bluntly, as soon as Ted and Megan went into the interview room and sat down opposite him.

'You are not at this stage under suspicion of any crime, PC Chase. I just wanted to ask you some further questions, following information which has come to my attention. You're not obliged to answer, but clearly it would be helpful if you did and might therefore be in your own best interest.'

Ted's formal tone clearly rattled him. He wiped the back of his hand across his forehead, suddenly beaded with sweat.

'Tell me again, PC Chase, is there any possibility that anyone in your family might know that you are the father of an illegitimate child? I'm assuming there is only one, although information which has recently come to my attention suggests that might not necessarily be the case.'

Chase opened and closed his mouth a few times before he found his voice.

'All right, I sometimes get a bit carried away. Don't most men? But the missus doesn't know, I swear, and I'd like to keep it that way.'

'What size shoes does your wife take, PC Chase?' Ted's calmly-posed question, seemingly out of the blue, took him by surprise.

'She's, er, I'm not sure, sir. Small, I do know. About a Size 3, I think? I know she's always complaining she can't often find the styles she wants in the right size.'

'It may be necessary for us to interview your wife, PC Chase.'

Now he looked horrified.

'But she knows nothing about this, sir. She doesn't know I had a kid with Helen. Even I didn't know it was my little lad who was murdered. If she got wind of any of this, it would wreck our marriage. She can be very jealous.'

'PC Chase,' Ted said coldly. 'I am investigating the particularly nasty murder of a little boy. One who just happened to be your illegitimate son. Your sensibilities and the state of your marriage are of absolutely no concern to me. Be under no illusions, I will do whatever it takes to find out who did this. Are we clear on that?'

'Yes, sir,' he replied miserably. 'Can I at least talk to her first?'

'Absolutely not. You must surely understand why. Now, where can we find your wife?'

Ted had driven up in his own car which he left at the station and went with Megan on the short journey over to where PC Chase and his wife lived. Chase had told them that his wife worked mornings so was likely to be at home that afternoon.

There was no car on the driveway but there was one parked outside so they had to park a short distance away and walk. There was a long pause between Megan ringing the doorbell and the front door opening.

The woman who stood there was certainly petite. About five feet two, Ted judged, comparing her to his own size. She looked a little flushed, her hair untidy, her clothes clearly thrown on in haste.

Both officers held up their warrant cards for her inspection as Ted introduced them both.

'I'm sorry to disturb you, Mrs Chase, but I wondered if we might come in and have a word. It's to do with a case we're conducting in Stockport. It's possible you may be able to help us with a line of enquiry.'

She looked decidedly uncomfortable and Ted didn't miss the anxious glance she threw towards the stairs as she stood aside to allow them in, then led the way through to a sunny kitchen at the back of the house, with a minuscule conservatory outside it.

'Erm, do you want a cup of tea or something?' she asked uncertainly.

'No thank you, Mrs Chase. It's just a few questions.'

'You'd better sit down, then.'

She indicated chairs at the kitchen table and sat down opposite Ted, still straightening her clothes.

'Do you know anyone called Helen Bradbury?'

She looked from one to another of them before she replied.

'I don't think so. The name doesn't sound familiar. Who is she?'

'Ms Bradbury is the mother of the little boy who was murdered in Stockport on Monday.'

Ted spoke bluntly, watching for a reaction.

The woman's hand flew to her face and her eyes widened as she replied, 'Oh, God yes, I saw that on the news. That poor woman, what she must be going through. But I don't understand. How do you think I can help with the case? I don't know the woman at all, or the poor little boy. I would honestly help you if I could. Anything to help catch the sort of sick bastard who could do something like this to a defenceless little child.'

'You've seen the photos of Tyler? Did anything strike you about him, when you saw them?'

There was silence for a moment as she looked in bewilderment from Ted to Megan and back again.

Then, 'Oh, bloody hell, no. Not that. The bastard! The little lad was Lewis's? Did he know that? So, what – you think I found out and decided to do away with the child for some reason? Believe me, I'd be far more likely to kill Lewis than harm one hair of any child's head, even his bastard.

'So I need an alibi, do I, for the day it happened? Well, you tell me when, and I'll give you an alibi. Bloody hell will I give you an alibi.'

'Let's start with Monday, Mrs Chase. Can you tell me what you were doing on Monday?'

'I was at work in the morning, as usual. I'm a part-time clerical assistant for a solicitor. I'll give you their contact details. They can vouch for me for the morning. And as for the afternoon ...'

She rose to her feet and went to the doorway to the hall and stairs, sticking her head through the gap and calling, 'Barry! Get your arse down here. I need you.'

They heard light footsteps coming down the stairs then a man appeared through the doorway, barefoot, tucking his shirt hastily into his trousers. His eyes widened and he gaped as he saw Megan.

'Hello, Sarge, long time no see,' she said, smiling at his discomfort. 'This is DCI Darling. Have you met?'

'Bloody hell,' was all the DS could manage before he pulled himself together. 'Sorry, sir. DS Barry Stephens. We've not met, I don't think. Look, this is all a bit awkward.'

He pulled a spare chair out and sat down next to PC Chase's wife.

'Are you meant to be on duty at the moment, DS Stephens?'

'No, sir, I'm on a day off.'

'Then I'm not concerned with what you do in your spare time. Can you tell me where you were on Monday afternoon? Say from lunchtime to about four o'clock.'

The man grimaced.

'Now that really is awkward. I was here, with Tracey, and I should have been on duty for part of it. Are you going to tell my boss, sir?'

Ted threw him a look of contempt.

'No, DS Stephens, you are. I'm not remotely interested in your grubby little affair, I'm busy working on a murder case. But if I find out later that you haven't told your DI, and that you haven't put an end to your personal life interfering with your work, then you and I will talk again.'

As they walked back to the car, Megan chuckled.

'I'm glad there is some natural justice in life sometimes. Chase thinks he's the big caveman, running after the women and all the time his wife is sleeping with a DS. But I would say that probably rules her out, doesn't it? And her feet are the wrong size, even if she didn't have a pretty good alibi.'

# Chapter Eight

Megan dropped Ted off to pick up his own car, then they drove back in convoy to their own station. They both had loose ends to tie up and reports to write before they could finish for the day and relax over a drink in The Grapes. Maurice and Steve would be babysitting for Jezza, as usual, so they wouldn't linger. Jezza still didn't know why Nat would never come up to the flat to collect her if Maurice was there when they went out, preferring to wait outside for her to go down. She would have been furious if she'd known of Maurice's physical threat to him, the first time they had gone out together.

Ted wanted to call DS Rakale at South Manchester, to make sure she felt her team could cope if they started getting inundated with calls from witnesses after the press coverage and had to start checking out anyone they mentioned.

Since the team there had been streamlined, there was only her and two DCs, Graham Winters and Charlie Eccles. Ted had high hopes for DC Winters who'd shown himself to be capable of good work, with the right direction. As far as he was concerned, the jury was still out over Eccles, who had a long way to go to make any kind of a good impression.

'I'm working over the weekend, and I've got Graham on tomorrow and Charlie on Sunday, sir. We've already had a few calls as there was a brief mention on the lunchtime news, so you know what it's like. I can get all the help I need from Uniform now, though. Things are quite harmonious between us, now the old guard have gone.'

The former DI there had always ridden roughshod over the

Uniform branch, treating them like his personal lackeys and bending rules all the time. There had been no love lost between uniformed officers of any rank and the old CID team.

'I'm on call any time for anything you might need. And I do mean anything. Don't hesitate. I'll probably drop in briefly on Sunday, in any case, to see how you're getting on. I'll also send you some reinforcements on Monday, to help with the legwork. You don't need another DS; you strike me as more than capable, but you can have DI Rodriguez, Jo, and I'll send you a DC. Don't forget though, just call me if you need anything.'

It was nice to relax with the team after a long and difficult week. The first round at the pub was always on Ted, yet another reason he was so popular. It was a time to forget talking shop and just chat like any other office workers at the end of the week.

Gradually, those with families and partners waiting started to drift away. Jo seemed to realise that the boss needed a bit of company so he stayed on a while longer and got another round in. It was good to talk, to spend some time together away from work. Ted didn't really know all that much about his new DI yet and it was the ideal opportunity to get to know him a bit better.

When they finally parted, Ted picked up a takeaway on his way back, knowing he wouldn't feel much like cooking for himself. The cats gave him a hard time when he arrived home, swarming around his legs and claiming to be starving, although he could clearly see that Trev had given them plenty to eat before he'd left. Even with six affectionate cats, the house felt quiet and empty without Trev's presence.

Ted tried to settle down to watch some television, but couldn't concentrate. He was planning to work through the weekend, just for something to do. He hated being apart from Trev. He knew he would miss him the whole time he was gone, but tried to be happy for him, having a wonderful time in the south of France.

It was late before Trev finally phoned. Ted had gone up to bed and was reading an Ian Rankin crime fiction book, though he found himself starting the same page over and again, subconsciously worried until he heard that his partner had arrived safely.

'Ted, you should see it. We're staying on a luxury yacht off Cap Ferrat. You could honestly fit most of our downstairs into my bedroom. It's amazing!' Trev's voice was full of enthusiasm.

Ted knew he would be loving it. He would hate it himself. It highlighted the difference between them. Even after so many years together, he couldn't believe his luck in having Trev as his partner, nor profess to understand the chemistry which kept them together. He always made a joke of it, trotting out a quote from his favourite film, *Blazing Saddles,* 'What's a dazzling urbanite like you doing in a rustic setting like this?'

'I'm glad you're having a good time. Go and enjoy your jet-setting, while you can. Take care though, won't you?'

'You make sure you eat. Remember you're invited to your mum's for lunch on Sunday. That way I know you'll get at least one decent meal while I'm away. Oh, and don't over-feed the cats. I'll call you when I can. Love you.'

Then he was gone.

Ted decided to go and do his own investigations of the park and the area around Tyler Bradbury's home the following day. He knew his team would have done a first rate job and wouldn't have missed anything vital. But Ted liked to see things with his own eyes, on his own, if he could. He would sometimes pick up things or get ideas that way which were useful in solving a case. Working like that, with no one to distract him, it gave him a chance to get inside the head of victims or suspects, often with surprising results.

Away from the station, he could dress as he pleased, so he

opted for his comfortable walking trousers, a polo and light fleece jacket, with his fell-walking boots. He wouldn't look out of place wandering around the park dressed like that. He'd collected the Batman toy Steve had ordered online for him and tucked it carefully inside his fleece. There was only a light drizzle and his jacket was shower-proof, so he decided to walk the short distance to the park.

He hadn't bothered to track down the keys to Helen Bradbury's house. He was more interested in the garden and the area around it. He'd worked out roughly where the house backed on to the park and made his way there from the gates.

There was nobody about. Clearly the park held no attraction to anyone fairly early on a damp Saturday morning. He found the back gate to the property, high enough that he could just see over it if he stood on tiptoe. It was locked, as he'd expected, but he was fit and it presented him with no problems. He glanced around. There was no sign of anyone, even in the neighbouring houses. If anyone did happen to see him, he had his warrant card in his pocket to explain his presence there. He hoisted himself up easily, swung over and dropped lightly down the other side into the small garden.

He stood perfectly still for a moment, letting his eyes travel round, taking in everything. The garden looked unkempt. The lawn could have done with some attention and the uninspired planting of shrubs to either side showed a lack of any pruning in recent times. He remembered that it was a rental property and it looked it. No one loved it and cared for it as their own.

He walked up to the house and looked in through the back window. It was frugally furnished but looked comfortable. A table by the window clearly served as Helen Bradbury's workstation, so she could keep an eye on her little boy, playing in the garden. The back door was frosted glass and he couldn't see in, but through the window he could look into the kitchen, to the side of the living room, where there was a telephone on the wall. He could see that it was not a cordless model. He'd need to go in at some point to check if the mother could see into the garden while she was on the phone, or if she'd had her eyes off her son for long enough for him to disappear.

Next Ted turned back to the garden and took Batman out of his jacket. He needed to find out if it was possible to launch the toy high enough for it to fly out of the garden. He fitted the figure into the launcher and tentatively pulled the rip cord. Gotham City's favourite hero certainly reached some altitude, to his surprise, but didn't move far away, coming to land not all that far from where Ted was standing.

He tried experimenting with the angle at which he held the launcher, quickly finding out that a safely lock kicked in and prevented the launch taking place if the angle was too great. Now he was talking quietly to himself as he experimented.

'So, you went a bit further down the garden, a bit nearer to the back fence, did you? What happens if I launch him from here? No, still not right. What about from here, with more of an angle? Ah, right, there you go, Batman, on your way to freedom. So what now, Tyler?'

He looked at the gate and discovered a bolt above the latch, which would have been out of reach of a small boy.

'Now what?' He was still talking to himself, half under his breath, as he looked around, noticing a plastic garden chair, lying a short distance away, on its side. 'You get the chair to stand on? Mam's told you never to go out of the garden. But you have to get Batman back. And you'll only be gone a minute, so it doesn't really count. So you stand on the chair and pull the bolt open. Then what? You put the chair back because you know you're not allowed to climb on things. Clever boy.

'Now the gate's unlocked, so you can go out and get Batman back before your mam even notices. So who do you meet when you step out through that gate?'

As he spoke, he pulled back the bolt, lifted the latch and opened the gate, then nearly jumped out of his skin at two voices, both shouting at him at the same time.

'Police officer! Stand still! Don't move!'

'Taser officer! Don't move. Taser! Taser! Taser!'

Ted gaped in surprise at PC Susan Heap, taser drawn and pointing straight at him, and a young officer he hadn't seen before, standing with one hand on his baton, the other holding a CS spray which was also pointing towards him.

Ted calmly lifted both his hands, aware as he did so that he was still clutching the Batman launcher and hoping that Susan Heap didn't think it was a firearm. He didn't fancy being tasered.

'It's a fair cop, guv, I think is the standard phrase, but it's me, PC Heap, so please don't taser me.'

'Sorry sir,' the constable said contritely, immediately putting her taser away, 'but we got a call from a neighbour to say someone was acting suspiciously and had made a forced entry to the property. Given the address and knowing what happened here, we were sent straight over.

'Sir, with respect, wouldn't it have been a good idea to warn the nick that you were coming here? You know better than anyone that resources are in short supply and Gavin and I have had a wasted trip out here. This is Gavin Jackson, by the way. He's only just joined us.'

Ted reached cautiously into his pocket and pulled out his warrant card to show to the young officer, once he'd lowered his spray and no longer looked likely to use it.

'DCI Darling,' he told him. 'Nice to meet you, PC Jackson, and don't worry, I don't make a habit of house-breaking. I was just trying out a theory.'

He turned back to Susan Heap and continued, 'You're absolutely right, of course, PC Heap. I should have done and I apologise for wasting your time. I didn't see anyone about, or I would have explained myself. I consider myself thoroughly told off. Now please may I have my toy back, officer? Out of interest, how far did he fly?'

PC Jackson was looking at Ted as if he not only doubted

that he was a senior officer but had concerns over his sanity. He'd obviously decided it was best to humour him.

'Just over there, sir. Shall I get him for you?'

Ted looked to where he was pointing. He was impressed. Batman had made a respectable flight this time.

'No, it's fine, thank you, Constable, I can manage to retrieve him. And because you're clearly thinking I've lost the plot, I'll just point out that this was by way of a scientific experiment. A successful one, I think.'

Susan Heap looked interested now. She knew that, despite being different, in a good way, from most of the other senior officers she'd encountered, Ted was a good detective, with an excellent track record.

'Tyler's mother said he was a good boy who never went out of the garden. But she also said he couldn't bear to be parted from his Batman toy. I've just proved that Batman is capable of flying out of the garden, and I've found how a little lad like Tyler could manage to let himself out of the garden, despite the gate being bolted. Now all I need is a break in finding who he met when he came out of the gate and why he went off with them.'

'I think I can work that out for you, sir,' Susan Heap told him. 'The why he went with them, at least. Shall we go and get Batman?'

Ted looked puzzled but went with her. As they got near to the toy, she bent down, grabbed it, and sprinted off at high speed. Ted watched her for a moment without following and saw her disappear from sight round the corner of a hedge surrounding the last house in the row. Then he smiled to himself as he jogged after her, PC Jackson trailing behind.

She appeared, grinning, back round the corner of the hedge as Ted caught her up.

'Just a suggestion, sir, but could that be why he went with whoever it was?'

'Brilliant, Susan, thank you. That's something else I owe

you for. Sorry again to have inconvenienced you.'

As the two PCs were walking away, Gavin said to her, 'I can't believe you told a DCI off, and he took it from you. I thought he was the original Kung Fu Panda? He doesn't look all that impressive.'

'I wouldn't let him hear you calling him that. He has four martial arts black belts, none of them in Kung Fu, and he's a stickler for detail. And I can get away with murder because I probably stopped him bleeding to death when he got knifed. He's very good at what he does and he's one of the nicest senior officers you could ever meet. Just don't ever underestimate him. He'll solve this case, because he won't rest until he does.'

As the officers walked away, Ted returned to the gate and stood there, looking round, thinking things through. He continued talking to himself.

'So, Tyler, who would you run after, if they picked up Batman? Not a bigger kid, surely, unless you were very brave. You might get thumped.'

Ted knew all about bullying. As a child, small and slight – 'runty' he always described himself as – and called Darling, he'd known his fair share of playground bullies, until his dad had paid for the martial arts lessons. No matter how much Tyler loved his toy, Ted was having difficulty imagining a small boy running after a bigger one, or possibly more than one.

As he stood in the increasing drizzle, a small, shaggy, white dog came trotting down the path and stopped in front of him. Ted couldn't read dog body language like he could cat and human so he wasn't sure if the fact that its mouth was open and showing a lot of sharply pointed teeth should worry him or not.

'Nice dog,' he said warily, by way of greeting.

An elderly lady was walking up the path behind the dog. Shorter even than Ted and quite stout, with a waterproof coat and a folding plastic rain hat.

'Good morning,' she greeted, her voice well-spoken. 'I hope Bobby isn't bothering you. He's just wondering if you have a toy or something you could throw for him.'

Ted looked at the dog with renewed interest. It appeared to be grinning at him, its short tail threshing the ground as it willed him to produce an object to throw. It looked hopeful for a moment as Ted reached in his pocket for his warrant card, which he held out towards the woman.

'Good morning. I'm a police officer. Would your little dog pick up a toy if he found one on the ground, Mrs...?'

'It's Miss. Miss Dean. I can't actually read that without my glasses but it certainly looks official enough. But you don't look tall enough to be a police officer,' then as Ted smiled, having heard the comment so many times before, she added hastily, 'Oh dear, that was very impolite of me. Do excuse me, officer. I'm sorry, I couldn't read your name.'

'It's Darling, Detective Chief Inspector, and yes, I've heard all the comments about that, too. I'm quite used to them. But please tell me about Bobby.'

'Yes, he would most definitely pick things up. He's always doing it in the park. Are you here about the little boy? So very tragic. I used to see him in the park sometimes, with his mother. A nice little boy, very polite. He had some sort of a toy which flew. Bobby tried to catch it a few times so I had to put him on the lead when I saw them.'

'Did you happen to see the little boy or his mother at any point on Monday?'

'We didn't come to the park on Monday. I had to go to the doctor's. I so dislike going on Monday mornings, it's always crowded.'

'Are there any other dogs who come to the park who might pick up a toy and run off with it?'

'Oh yes, we often meet dogs out by themselves and they sometimes try to take Bobby's toy. Luckily all the ones I've met so far have been quite friendly. You look as if you could probably throw a ball very well. I can't do it much these days; arthritis in my joints. But if you would be kind enough to throw Bobby's, he would be your friend for life.'

She took a much-chewed ball out of her pocket and handed it to Ted. He was no cricketer but he made a respectable overarm swing which saw the ball fly off into the distance, with the ecstatic small dog in hot pursuit.

'Thank you, Inspector, that was very kind of you,' the woman said as she walked off after her dog.

'And thank you, Bobby. You've given me an idea,' Ted said to himself as the pair wandered off.

# Chapter Nine

Ted's next port of call after the park was the station. He often went in at the weekend, to keep on top of things. With Trev away, his office was his refuge from the empty house. He'd been up early, as usual, and had seen to the cats before leaving. They would complain, but he could safely leave them until much later in the evening if he needed to. He'd given them enough dry food to cover emergencies.

Sal and Steve were on duty in the main office, Steve on the phone, Sal just finishing a call.

'Morning. Plenty of calls coming in?'

'No shortage, boss,' Sal told him. 'Unfortunately most of them appear to relate to people who saw Tyler in the park with his mother on other days. Nothing much for Monday yet.'

'I'm just going to make a brew before I start. Do you two want one?'

Even after his recent promotion to DCI, Ted didn't consider himself above brewing up for his team members. He usually remembered what everyone drank and how they took it, too. Sal nodded his thanks as he picked up another call. Steve hadn't reacted so Ted made the universal drinking motion in front of him and Steve raised a thumb, going pink, as he generally did when the boss had any kind of contact with him.

When he came back with the drinks, Ted perched on a desk until there was a lull in the calls allowing him to ask for an update.

'We're noting everything for checking later on, but nothing so far that's of much use from the calls I've taken. I think

Steve's have been the same?' As Steve nodded, Sal went on, 'It seems Tyler and his mum were often to be seen in the park together and people are getting mixed up about days, I think.'

'I'm almost certain the mother had nothing to do with it. Her reaction appeared too genuine. I've been at the house this morning and I think I can see why Tyler left the garden. I do need to check out the positioning of the telephone, and I want to get details of incoming calls to his mother on Monday. I'll start the ball rolling for that. I need to know if she really was on the phone when she said she was. I'm going to look stupid if I don't check her alibi and it turns out she was involved.

'As long as the caller number wasn't masked, we should be able to get it traced. Do these cold callers keep a record of the calls they make, I wonder? Might someone remember speaking to an individual for any reason?'

'Not sure, boss. I imagine they're on some sort of piece rate, or performance related, so they must keep some kind of record. They probably get a lot of people who just hang up on them so they may remember one who actually agreed to do their survey, or whatever it was.'

'Especially if the mother suddenly broke off the call saying something about her little boy having disappeared, sir,' Steve suggested. 'That might have stuck in someone's mind. Although they may not have heard anything about the case, if they were from an overseas call centre.'

'Good point, Steve, I hadn't thought of that. I'm being particularly dim at the moment, not thinking of a lot of things I should. I also want to check out all of the mother's family and other contacts. I don't want to overlook anything that could be staring me in the face.

'Right, I'll be in my office, buried under paperwork, but shout if you need me for anything. Oh, and if anyone's going out for sandwiches at some point, please let me know.'

Ted wanted some quiet time to go through all the witness

statements on both cases. He was particularly intrigued by Jezza's assertion that the figure who pushed an old lady to her death under the wheels of a bus was female. He respected her judgement and had learned to trust her intuition, but she was the only person so far to suggest that, as far as he knew. He wanted to go through the statements for himself to check on that.

With no real risk of disturbance, he could spread papers about, make himself notes, litter statements with Post-Its. Ted's methods may have been a little old-fashioned, but he found they worked best for him. Above all, he was trying to get some idea of motive in the two cases. A child abduction ending in death was sadly not all that rare, but there was usually an obvious motive, often sexual. Without a 'why' in the Tyler Bradbury case, it would be hard to work back to the 'who.'

He was similarly baffled in the South Manchester case as to motive. Another sign of the times in that purse-snatching was not all that rare. But what could have prompted the thief to go a step further and, having robbed Joan Murray, to callously shove her into the path of the bus, almost certainly knowing it would be fatal? He made himself a note to check with Leona Rakale if there was any record of what had been stolen from her trolley.

He broke off to join Sal and Steve over sandwiches. Steve had been sent out to get them, while Ted once again brewed up for all three. Steve wasn't going as far as the deli, so Ted couldn't have his usual bagel.

'Get me a cheese and tomato then, please, Steve. No, tuna. Tuna and tomato. Or cheese and tuna?' Ted realised he was burbling, not able to make a simple decision. It wasn't like him. 'Surprise me,' he said, taking out his wallet and giving Steve enough to cover them all.

He always enjoyed down time with his team members. It helped them work better together, and emphasised that he was approachable. Both were off the following day, Sunday, so he asked them about their plans.

'Shopping with the girlfriend then a meal with her parents for me.'

'Getting serious, then, Sal, meeting the parents?' Ted asked.

'Oh, we've met before a few times. They seem to approve so yes, I think it might be.'

'What about you, Steve? What have you got planned?'

'Gaming, sir, MMORPGs,' Steve told him, always uneasy about dropping the formalities with the boss.

'I'm not sure I even know what that is,' Ted confessed with a smile.

'Massively Multiplayer Online Role-Playing Games. Things like *World of Warcraft*.' Steve's face lit up with clear passion as he started to speak about his interest. 'They're online games. Players take on a role and can play with other people from anywhere in the world.'

'So this is all online, you never actually get to meet up with the people you're playing with?'

Steve blushed furiously as he replied, 'It can often be like that, sir, but sometimes people do meet up in real life too. I'm actually meeting another player tomorrow.'

'Is it someone you actually know, or is this a bit like blind dating?' Ted was genuinely intrigued by how the young man spent his off-duty time.

'Sometimes you don't know the people you play with, but in this case, it is someone I know.'

He was looking decidedly uncomfortable, so Ted decided not to press him further. He kept a lot of his own private life to himself so he didn't want to intrude on Steve's.

'Well, I hope you have an enjoyable day off, both of you. Right, now I'm going back to my paperwork, but don't forget to shout if you need me for anything. And please keep me updated on any sightings of Tyler with anyone we can't immediately identify from the description.'

The afternoon appeared to fly by and it didn't seem long before Sal was tapping on Ted's door and putting his head round to tell him that he and Steve were done for the day and heading home. Ted had compiled himself a To Do list for both cases. It wasn't much to show for his efforts, but it felt like some degree of progress.

He was looking forward to talking to Trev later that evening. They'd arranged between them that Trev would always be the one to call. Ted didn't want to cramp his style by interrupting him when he was enjoying himself. He was imagining his partner's reaction when he told him about almost getting tasered. He could almost hear him laughing, just thinking about it. Trev was always quick to laugh, often collapsing in giggles at the most banal things. His laughter was just one of the things Ted missed about him.

The call came earlier than Ted feared it might. He moved senior cat Queen off his lap to take the call, not wanting her loud purring to monopolise the conversation. Trev was sounding even more enthusiastic, making Ted feel almost envious with mention of the warm sunshine they were enjoying.

'I got into a bit of a pickle today...' Ted started to say, then he heard a voice in the background calling something.

'Ted, look, I'm really sorry, I can't talk now,' he said, then, clearly to someone else, '*Oui, j'arrive. Deux minutes.* We're going to a beach barbecue and I literally daren't miss the boat or I'll have to swim ashore. Tell me all about it when I call tomorrow. Love you.'

Ted was left forlornly saying 'Hello?' into the silence.

Jezza and Megan were on duty together on Sunday. They'd be manning the phones, in between doing their own paperwork, still hoping for a reliable witness sighting of Tyler in the park on Monday, with someone other than his mother. The phones hadn't yet started ringing and they were taking advantage of the lull before they started to catch up with one another.

'So, how's it going with you and Maurice?' Jezza asked.

'He really is a lovely man, so kind and caring. Not at all what anyone would expect. He's brilliant with my Felix, and his own girls. We've had some great times out together.'

'I'm sensing there's a big but coming?'

'It's always us with either all the kids, or with Felix. Never just the two of us. I'm starting to think he doesn't fancy me.'

'Of course he does! I'll tell you another unexpected thing about our bonny lad Maurice. He really is a great big softy who's afraid of making the wrong move. I practically had to rip his clothes off him. He's not the caveman he looks as if he would be.

'Look, here's an idea, why don't you bring Felix over and leave him with me and Tommy one evening, when Maurice hasn't got the twins with him, then get him to take you out, just the two of you? Then I'll reclaim the favour one evening when I want to go out with Nat. Maurice is a bit possessive and I'm starting to think Nat is secretly afraid of him.'

Megan was about to answer when the door opened and the boss walked in and asked if there had been any more calls from potential witnesses.

'Nothing much yet, boss, it's perhaps too early on a Sunday morning for most people,' Jezza told him.

'If you get chance, can you start to draw up some sort of priority list of people to talk to further. It doesn't sound as if Sal and Steve had anyone much worth following up, but have a look through all the calls, see if you can pick up on anything. I'm just on my way to South Manchester to catch up with things there, but don't forget, I'm on call if you need me.'

As the boss headed back down the stairs, Megan smiled across at Jezza and said, 'You're on. It sounds like a fair trade to me.'

It would be the first time Ted had seen DC Eccles at South

Manchester since having had to deal with him on an earlier case. He and Leona Rakale were both working at their desks when he went in. To his surprise, Eccles greeted him with a fairly civil nod and a muttered 'sir'. DS Rakale was clearly already having a good effect on turning around what was left of her team there.

'How are we getting on after the press appeal?'

'Still getting calls, sir, all still saying pretty much the same thing. A young lad, grabbed something from Mrs Murray's trolley, shoved her with his shoulder then ran off.'

'Do we know yet what was taken?'

'We're going on the assumption that it was her purse, sir, as none was found either on her or in the trolley, and she had clearly just been shopping.'

'Good, thank you. Can we just be a bit wary of any kind of assumption, though. Make sure we check everything out carefully, although I agree, a purse would seem to be the most likely. Are all of the witnesses saying the suspect is male?'

DC Eccles looked up from his notes in surprise.

'Are you saying they might be female?'

'As I've just said, I'm trying to avoid assumptions. We've had one person who's seen the CCTV footage who pointed out that it could conceivably be a teenage girl.' Then, remembering his previous experience of Eccles and his former team-mates, he added, 'But I do not want that idea planting into the head of any potential witnesses. No leading questions, no suggestions. Is that clear, DC Eccles?'

'Sir,' Eccles' tone turned surly at what he perceived as a reprimand. But Ted couldn't afford to take chances. He'd had witness testimony spoilt before by a former DC who had worked closely with Eccles. He wanted to make sure everything was done by the book.'

'Good, thank you.' First the reminder, then the praise. It was how Ted always liked to work. 'DS Rakale, is there somewhere we could have a quick catch-up?'

'There's the old DI's office, or, if you fancy a brew, we could go to the rest room?'

Ted had seldom been known to refuse tea so he went willingly with her into a small kitchenette down the corridor, where she put the kettle on and started opening cupboards for mugs and the makings.

'Sir, if I call you boss, will you call me Leona?' she asked, waggling a packet of tea bags at Ted, who nodded.

'Yes, I'd like that. I just don't like to presume. So, how are you getting on with DC Eccles?'

'He's not too bad, really. He just needs a bit of house training. He got very sloppy, working with the old team and their dirty ways, but he's coming round, slowly. How are you getting on with the little boy's murder? That must be so hard for everyone to work on, especially any parents on the team.'

'Do you have children, Leona?'

'Yes, boss, my wife and I have a little girl, Ellie. She's two and she is unutterably gorgeous. I would rip out the eyes and the heart of anyone who touched a hair of her head.'

The way her face changed when she said it made Ted fairly sure they were not just empty words.

'What about you, boss? Do you have any?'

Ted laughed as he shook his head. 'I'm not always good at being a grown-up, between you and me. I'd be hopeless as a parent. And my partner, Trev, is just a big kid. We content ourselves with cats.

'Now, tomorrow I'll be sending you over Jo Rodriguez, and a DC, although I don't yet know who will be best to send. Do you know Jo?'

It was Leona's turn to laugh as she replied, 'Only by reputation, boss, and of course he will be wasting his time with me. But I don't mind a bit of harmless flirting, I'm not going to start screaming sexual harassment or anything. I'm sure he'll be a great help.'

Ted drained his mug. 'Right, I'd best get going. I'm on the

end of the phone if you need me for anything, don't forget, and good luck with Jo.'

He was on his way to have lunch with his mother, then had promised to take her for a run out to Roman Lakes. It was a place of fond memories for both of them, so the damp and drizzly day wouldn't be too much of a deterrent to their enjoyment.

She'd gone to a lot of trouble, as usual, to cook his favourite meal. Ted had to admit to himself that it was nice to have some company, and some good home-cooked food. He still wasn't completely at ease in his mother's company. The conversation tended to be light and centred round the time when he was a small boy, before she'd left him and his father.

Although Ted didn't like to talk about work, his mother was keen to ask him about the case. She felt an affinity with any mother who lost a child, through any circumstances.

Ted remembered to ask her if she knew why he was so afraid of dogs. Her expression was guilty as she replied.

'Oh, Teddy, *bach*, I'm so sorry, that was my fault. We were out walking together when you were just a little *twt*.' She still slipped into her native Welsh for odd words, sometimes without even noticing it. Ted was surprised at how many he still remembered when in her company.

'We were walking along the pavement, down Dialstone Lane, and a great big dog came bounding out of a garden, barking. He was bigger than you. I found out afterwards that he was a big softy, just trying to be friendly. But it frightened you so you jumped out of the way right into the road and nearly got hit by a car. I grabbed you and scooped you up. We were both a bit hysterical. The dog's owner came out, all full of apologies, and wanted you to pat the dog to see that he was really gentle but the whole thing had frightened you half to death and you were always scared of dogs after that.'

They were strolling round the waterside when Ted's mobile phone rang. He checked the screen then smiled, 'It's Trev, not work. Do you mind?'

'Of course not! I'll go and look at the ducks. Do give him my love.'

He appreciated her discretion in letting him talk privately. He hoped that, during the afternoon, Trev might have a bit more time to talk to him. He did, and he was still full of enthusiasm.

'The weather's fabulous. I'm getting a bit of a tan already. It's gorgeous here, we've had a trip out this morning looking at some of the locations for the shoots.'

Ted was picturing him already turning golden brown, showing off his sculpted form to perfection. It all sounded right up his partner's street. Ted wondered if Stockport would be enough for him when he got back. He wondered if he would be enough for him.

# Chapter Ten

Unusually, Steve arrived at the last minute for morning briefing on Monday. Even more surprisingly, he was not dressed in his customary shirt and tie. He was wearing washed-out jeans, with a Star Wars T-shirt and a bomber jacket which had seen better days. He looked as if he'd been dragged through a hedge backwards, more than once.

Ted didn't mind how his team members dressed, as long as they did their jobs. It was the Ice Queen who was the stickler for a strict dress code. Steve's gaming had clearly developed into something else. Ted wondered if he was the only one who noticed Océane trying to stifle a yawn as she sat at her computer. He was surprised by that development.

'Oh dear, look what the cat dragged in,' Maurice laughed, nodding towards a carrier bag he'd left on Steve's desk. 'I brought you a change of clothes and your wash bag, you dirty stop-out. You look as though you need it.'

'All right, everyone, settle down,' Ted called them to order as Steve blushed more furiously than ever. 'Some of us have two briefings to get through this morning, so let's make a start. Jo, I need you over at South Manchester today, helping out there. Who else is free to go? Sal? Could you hand Sabden House over to Océane for the day?'

'Fine by me, boss, if Océane's all right with that? I'd welcome a break from it, to be honest.'

This time Océane's yawn was more noticeable as she nodded her agreement, and Ted could see from the broad grins that most of the others had made the same deduction as he had.

'I met a little dog in the park on Saturday,' Ted began conversationally, his voice quiet, so they had to concentrate. 'Bobby. He was very helpful. He gave me a new insight into why Tyler might have gone off away from the garden, when he knew he wasn't supposed to. My experiment showed me that Batman could indeed fly out of the garden, but not far enough away to explain Tyler disappearing. Bobby showed me one possible explanation for that.'

He told them about his experience with the flying toy. He also admitted his brush with Uniform. He knew Susan Heap wouldn't spread it around but he didn't yet know about the young officer, Gavin Jackson, who might think that a juicy bit of gossip about a senior officer was good currency for someone new to the station.

'What I want you to factor in now, when you're following up all the witness calls, is to try and find out if Tyler was ever seen playing with other children, or with a dog. Now, I've reminded the South Manchester team for their case, so it's only right that I remind all of you, too, although I don't need to. No leading questions. I don't want the idea planting in anyone's mind. I want you to find it out without suggesting it. I just can't imagine a little lad like Tyler running off after bigger kids, even if they had his toy. But maybe after a dog, especially one he knew, which might just have taken him further away than he meant to go and that might have led him straight to his killer.

'Right, I'm heading up to South Manchester. I'll take my own car, Jo; you and Sal get yourselves there, then I'm independently mobile to come back here. Don't forget, I'm at the end of the phone if any of you need me. Mike, over to you. Oh, and Steve, make yourself presentable before the Super sees you looking like that at work.'

Ted didn't really need to go to South Manchester again. Jo was always reliable in charge of an enquiry and Leona seemed to be on top of the case. She was clearly handling the team well. It was just that Ted really didn't like murders on his patch. He took them as an affront, so that solving them became as much a personal mission as a professional one.

No officer enjoyed dealing with the killing of a young child, but Ted was equally appalled at the seemingly casual murder of a vulnerable elderly person, harmlessly doing their shopping. He wanted to give each case equal attention and was optimistically hoping for an early result on them both, despite the lack of any significant leads to date. Someone, somewhere, must know something. It was only a matter of time, and methodical police work, before they had their suspects.

He tried to avoid the negative thought that he'd been telling himself the same thing on the Luke Martin case for two years now. But at least Jezza was looking at some different angles on that one, which always gave hope.

Leona and the two DCs looked up expectantly as Ted went into their office, flanked by Jo and Sal. He made brief introductions. Sal had experienced some of the old team before but they were new to Jo. The dynamics had changed completely with the suspension, then sudden death, of the old DI, Cyril Foster. Under him, the team had been exclusively white and male. Anyone outside that profile had barely lasted five minutes. Now that the small team was being headed by a black woman sergeant, Ted hoped things would be different.

'Any suspects yet?' he asked. 'Anything from any of the witnesses, or from your own local knowledge, that's putting anyone in the frame as a possible?'

'A few familiar names have cropped up, boss. Graham and Charlie and I have been going through them, trying to prioritise. I thought we'd get out there and start checking alibis, then we can look at hauling in anyone who doesn't have one, for further questioning.'

'Names that jump out at you?'

'I've not yet been here long enough to know all the likely ones, boss. Charlie's been here the longest of us, he's got good local knowledge.'

'There's a couple I would say could be likely contenders. Especially one. Jake Dolan. Proper little scrote, he is. Nothing as serious as this so far, but it wouldn't surprise me. Nasty little sod. I could have a word with him, get him to tell me what he knows?'

Ted considered him carefully. Bearing in mind the bully culture which had reigned in this nick before, he wasn't sure how much of a threat was implied by what he said.

'Just so everyone is completely clear, I don't want suspects intimidated in any way. Any questioning must be done by the book, and do it in pairs. I don't want to be in the position of losing the chance of a conviction because of dodgy procedure. Clear, everyone?'

There was a chorus of 'sir' from everyone, including Jo, but excluding DC Eccles who sat looking mutinous. Ted knew he would have got away with anything under his old boss. He was going to have to learn that his new one wouldn't stand for anything out of order.

'Clear, DC Eccles?' he repeated pointedly.

'How are we going to make any progress if we can't lean on the local pond life?'

'My team and I manage quite well, and our clear-up rate isn't too bad,' Ted told him levelly. 'Perhaps you should watch and learn. Jo, could you go with DC Eccles to have a chat with the young man in question? Show him how we like to do things down in Stockport.'

'This isn't just some meek kid who'll tell us all he knows,' Eccles protested. 'Like I said, he's a nasty piece of shit. We'll need to send in the Wood...' He stopped himself, just in time. He had at least remembered Ted's dislike of the derogatory term Woodentops for uniformed officers. 'We'll need Uniform, with stab vests and probably spray to get him to come quietly.'

'Why is he known to CID? What offences?'

'He bottled someone in the face. There was a ruck in the

street and he waded in. Couple of years ago now.'

'Gang related?'

'No, he's a loner, doesn't mix with any gangs, as far as we know. He deals a bit of skunk, small-time, so it might have been related to that. Only we couldn't get a positive ID on him, so we couldn't bring a case.'

'So he allegedly bottled someone. Young person? Is he in school?'

Eccles snorted. 'He probably turned up to school once, decided it wasn't for him, and hardly ever went back, from what we do know of him. Yeah, still a juvenile, maybe sixteen, by now.'

'So he'll need an appropriate adult present to be interviewed. Who's that?'

Again, a scoff of derision.

'Good luck with that. His mother, Kathleen, is a smack-head who's on the game to fund it. She'll be either off her face or working to earn enough to get that way.'

'We'll need to alert the Youth Justice Team, then, when he's found and brought in. Right, DC Eccles, million-dollar question. Do you like him for this, as you're the one who knows him?'

Eccles looked surprised to be asked for his opinion.

'I wouldn't put anything past him, the little gobshite.'

'But it would seem to me, on the face of it, to be one thing to attack someone in the heat of a pitched battle, albeit somewhat brutally with a bottle. But to go from that to something as cold-blooded as pushing an elderly lady to her certain death under a bus ... That seems a bit of a leap, to me. Especially as there appears to be some doubt as to whether he did do the bottling.

'Leona, can you liaise with Uniform, please, about getting him brought in. Then make sure the custody sergeant sorts out an appropriate adult. Let me know when he's here, please, and I'll decide who interviews him first. In the meantime, can you and Jo sort out interviewing the most likely of the witnesses to start with. Find out if anyone saw enough of a face to do an E-fit. Perhaps the driver? If this Jake Dolan doesn't have a reliable alibi, and if we get any sort of a likeness, then we can start to think about VIPER for a solid ID. But just remember, all of you, we don't want to be wasting what resources we have chasing after the wrong suspect.'

The use of Video Identification Parade Electronic Recording was helping to cut the number of wrongful identifications, but still required a likeness to work on, to find people similar to a suspect.

Ted had, as usual, been perching on a desk. He stood up to go, waiting for an acknowledgement that the team had understood. Again there was a general chorus of 'sir', but nothing from Eccles. Ever patient, Ted stood waiting expectantly, looking directly at him. Eventually, he got a grunt of assent.

'Thank you, DC Eccles. Your local knowledge has been useful.'

Eccles' brow furrowed as he turned the remark over in his brain, wondering whether it had been sarcastic, but Ted was already preparing to leave.

'Jo, walk with me to the car, will you, please.'

As they went down the stairs together, Ted continued talking.

'Keep a close eye on Eccles for me. He's clearly set in the old team's way of finding a likely suspect then wasting time and resources trying to pin a case on them. I don't want to go down that route again; it slows us down too much. Leona's excellent, I have no complaints there. I just think it might be diplomatically easier for her if you come in as the heavy to keep him in order.'

Jo chuckled.

'I get to be bad cop, then? That's fine by me, boss. Don't worry, I'll keep him to heel, and I'll let you know if we track down this Dolan lad.'

Ted was just about to get into his car when his mobile phone rang. It wasn't a saved number, nor was it one he recognised so he answered neutrally with, 'DCI Darling.'

'Hello, Ted, it's Sally, Rob's fiancée.'

Ted knew all his team members' partners through the Christmas drinks parties he and Trev hosted every year and was always on first name terms with them once they got to know one another.

'Rob said you were interested in any cases we've had recently in the park or the area around it. Could we meet up, today, if you have time?'

'We could meet at The Grapes at lunchtime, if that suits you? I need to eat, anyway, and I assume you do, too. I'd be happy to stand you lunch.'

'Ted, I'm not being funny, but I'll be bringing some files to show you which are strictly your eyes only. I wouldn't want to have them out in a public place, just in case anyone caught sight of them.'

Ted's mind was already boggling, wondering what was in store for him.

'Come to my office, then. What time suits you best? Any time either side of lunchtime, or during, works for me today.'

'I'm not trying to be melodramatic here but if we meet before, there's a strong possibility you won't want to eat. If it's after you've eaten ...'

Feeling increasingly apprehensive, Ted opted for a time shortly before what would normally be his lunch break, if he allowed himself the luxury of one. He was hoping that, however bad the files were, he might have recovered his appetite enough by the evening. His mother had sent him home with the leftovers from their Sunday lunch to heat up for himself for supper.

Several of the team were out chasing up witnesses when Ted arrived back. He noticed that Mike had sent Steve out into the field. It was probably a good idea to separate him from Océane for a bit, if their suspicions were well founded. Ted didn't like to interfere in private lives, but nor did he like any relationships to spill over into the workplace and interfere with ongoing enquiries.

He headed for his kettle as soon as he got back to his office. Green tea and honey seemed to be a good idea to face whatever Sally had in store for him.

As he sat down, there was a brief tap on the door and Maurice came in. He was also carrying a file.

'Take a pew, Maurice. Do you want coffee?'

Maurice shook his head as he sat down.

'No, thanks, boss, I just finished one. What about our Steve and Océane, then, eh? Mucky little bugger. I would never have thought he had it in him.'

Ted wasn't going to get drawn into office gossip, but he couldn't suppress a smile.

'As long as they both do their jobs,' was all he said. 'So, what have you got for me?'

'While I've been wading through the cold cases, with not a lot of success so far, it has to be said, I thought I'd take a look at any ones which are still unsolved and which happened around the park.

'Shadwell Drive. Down the other side of the park from where Tyler lived. There was an arson there, four years ago. You might well remember. It's still an open case. We never got anywhere with it. I just thought I'd flag it up, in case there's any connection. Cover all bases, if we're starting to look for things going on around that area.'

He pushed the file across the desk to Ted, who glanced at the details on the cover. He did remember the case. A middle-aged man with learning difficulties, living on his own and managing, just about. The butt of a lot of teasing and name-calling locally, especially from children, for some of his eccentric habits. He'd had a huge collection of garden gnomes in front of his home, which had singled him out as something of a target.

One evening, as he was eating his supper in front of the television, someone put a lighted firework through his letterbox. By the time he'd reacted, it was too late to get out and he had died in his burning ground-floor flat.

Extensive enquiries had led them nowhere, only to the assumption that local children had been playing a particularly unkind trick on him which had gone tragically wrong.

Ted's desk phone rang just as Maurice was leaving. Bill, on the front desk.

'Does Rob O'Connell know you have a date with his fiancée? Only she's down here, waiting for you.'

Ted went down to meet Sally and get her signed in. She was clearly on duty, in the uniform of an RSPCA inspector. He showed her up to his office and invited her to take a seat. She had a briefcase with her, which she put down and opened, taking out several files which she placed on the desk in front of her.

'Tea? Coffee?'

Ted topped his own tea up while he had the kettle on and made the 'coffee, black, as strong as you like' which Sally asked for. That, too, filled him with a sense of foreboding.

'We've been keeping a tight lid on these cases,' Sally began, taking a sip of her coffee. 'We're investigating them, of course, but we don't want the information to get out for fear of it giving someone else the same sort of sick ideas.'

She started opening the files, pushing them towards Ted. He thought he was hardened to most things, handling the kind of murder cases he did. But these were a whole new level for him. What he was looking at appeared to be systematic animal torture, pure and simple.

'How long has this been going on?'

'About five years, and each one seems to get worse than the previous one. You can see from the photos. Not many cases, mercifully, but they are grotesque. Really sick. They're the worst I've seen yet in this job. Our own theory is that this is someone who's experimenting, almost testing themselves to see how far they can go, what they're capable of.

'Ted, I really hope that this is in no way connected with your current enquiries. Because if it is, you're dealing with a seriously disturbed individual, someone who appears to have absolutely no concept of the boundaries between right and wrong.'

# Chapter Eleven

It was late afternoon before Ted got a call from Jo to say the potential suspect, Jake Dolan, had been brought into the station at South Manchester for questioning.

'Youth Justice Team?'

'Someone's on their way now, boss. We're waiting for someone to arrive before we start questioning him. He's been offered refreshment while he waits. All by the book and above board.'

'I know you can handle it standing on your head, Jo, but I think I'll come over myself. I'd like to work with DC Eccles a bit, see what we can do with him, or if he really is a lost cause. Tell him to be ready to sit in with me for the interview. If Leona is happy to carry on without you, why don't you and Sal come back here to wind things up while I come up there and see what we can get out of this young lad? What's he like?'

'Small, skinny and the dad in me would have said scared rather than aggressive, but you can never tell. We've not yet told him why he's been brought in.'

'Good, keep it that way until I get there, please. If the YJT representative is wanting answers, just say we think he might have been witness to an incident we're investigating. Although I'm sure they can both put two and two together if they've seen the press and TV coverage.'

Ted smiled to himself as he steered his own car back north of the Mersey. Small, skinny and scared about summed up a lot of his younger years, until his dad had paid for the martial arts lessons which put an end to all kinds of bullying and abuse.

Now Ted wasn't scared of much. Except dogs. He was definitely scared of dogs and now, at least, he finally knew why.

He passed Jo and Sal on the way, exchanging a wave and a flash of headlights. Once Ted arrived, he went to find DC Eccles and led the way into what had been the old DI's office before the team was drastically reduced. He wanted a pre-interview briefing with him, so he could make it clear what his role was to be.

'I want you to sit quietly and observe, please. Say nothing. Just give me your thoughts afterwards. I also need you to pay attention to your own body language. No scowling at him, nothing aggressive. No folded arms. You can lean forward slightly, arms on the table, but I don't want anything which could be interpreted as threatening.'

Eccles didn't quite roll his eyes and sigh but Ted could tell that he would have liked to. He was clearly not used to the gentle approach in handling suspects. Ted found it often worked well for him. There was nothing intimidating about Ted, with his small height, slight stature, and quiet, level way of speaking. His appearance often encouraged both suspects and hostile witnesses to say more than they had intended to.

There was a young woman sitting next to their suspect when the two officers entered the room. Ted introduced the two of them to the suspect, Jake Dolan, and to the woman from the Youth Justice Team. He wanted this interview to be text book, for Eccles' benefit. So he began by cautioning the youth, mentioning only the lesser charge of theft, without going into specifics, and set the tapes running.

Jo was right in his description. Small, skinny and scared about summed up the youth sitting opposite them. But he certainly had some spark, as he sneered, 'Darlin'? What sort of a poncey name is that?'

Ted smiled at him. He found it was disarming, something unexpected, which often caught a suspect off balance.

'It's my name and I make the best of it, although it always takes some explaining. Now, Jake, you've been brought here because I want to ask you a few questions. Can you tell me where you were on Wednesday morning?'

'I didn't do it.'

'What didn't you do?'

'Whatever it is you lot are trying to fit me up for this time. I didn't do it last time but the filth still tried to fit me up. And whatever it is this time, I didn't do it neither.'

'If you could tell me where you were on Wednesday morning, that might just help with our enquiries. And it would mean that we could let you go much sooner.'

'Morning? I was in bed, innit. No point getting up when I got nothing to get up for.'

'Can anyone confirm that? Your mother, perhaps?'

'Fuck, no, she were off her face, as usual. There's no one else, just me and her.'

'Jake, I'm an old-fashioned sort. I'm not keen on swearing, especially in front of ladies. No offence,' he added to the woman opposite in case she took it as sexist or patronising. Instead, she smiled at him, pleasantly surprised by his attitude.

'So, Jake, you have no alibi for Wednesday morning?'

'Don't need none. I didn't do nothing. So now I suppose you lot will just knock me about until I confess to summat I never did, like you did last time.'

He was glaring directly at Eccles now. The officer shifted in his seat and opened his mouth to speak, but Ted held up a hand to silence him.

'Jake, let me get this straight. Are you accusing this officer of assaulting you on a previous occasion?'

The youth continued to stare hard at the DC opposite him, then he said, 'Nah, not him. It were another pig. A tall one. He slapped me about a bit, trying to get me to say I bottled someone. But I never.'

DC Coombs, Ted thought to himself. The ringleader when

it had come to rough stuff in the old team. He wasn't surprised.

'Thank you, Jake, I appreciate your honesty. So, back to Wednesday morning. You may have heard that an old lady was robbed and killed.'

'That weren't me neither. I don't rob no old codgers. They ain't got enough money to be worth it.'

'How do you make a living, Jake? Are you on benefits? Jobseekers?'

'You must be kidding, mate. Waste of time. There's naff all work round here for the likes of me. An' I ain't going down the Job Centre for some snotty piece to 'ave a go at me if I'm two minutes late for an interview.'

'So what is your source of income? You must have financial support of some sort?'

'This an' that,' he said evasively. 'I ain't tellin' you about most of it. I'm not saying it's all on the level. But I don't rob no old folk, and I never shoved an old granny in front of a bus, like they said on the telly someone did.'

'Do you like animals, Jake?'

Ted's sudden complete change of direction seemed to confuse the youth for a moment. He looked warily at Ted, trying to work out what hidden meaning there was behind the question. His face was pale and thin. He looked as if a few square meals would do him some good. He looked even smaller in his oversized hoody and baggy jeans. He shrugged, his expression wary.

'I like dogs, as it goes. I make a few quid sometimes, road walking some greyhounds for a trainer a mate of mine knows.'

'And you've no alibi at all for Wednesday morning?'

'Don't need one,' the youth repeated defiantly. 'I didn't do nothing, and I don't have to prove that. You have to prove that I did.'

Ted looked down at his notebook, where he'd made a few jottings, to hide a smile. He quite liked this cocky kid; he had something about him.

'In which case, thank you for coming in to talk to us, but you're free to go now. We may want to question you further at some point. And Jake, things have changed at this station now. I'm in charge, and no suspect ever gets slapped by a police officer under my command, I promise you.

'Here's my card.' He slid one across the table as he spoke. 'If you remember anything about Wednesday, or you hear anything that might help us, please feel free to call me at any time. And before you say it, I know you're not a grass. It's just that expect you don't think much to someone who would kill an elderly person in such a callous way. You don't strike me as the type.'

Dolan was studying Ted's card in detail. Given his lack of formal education, Ted wondered if he had literacy problems. He looked up at Ted's final words, surprise on his face and something like a smile flickering there for an instant. Ted noticed that his eyes were a vivid green, like a cat's. Another reason for him to be singled out as different.

He looked almost pleased at the words, but he hid the fact behind a sneer as he said, 'Darlin', though, eh? Bloody silly name.'

Ted stood up, shook hands with the woman from YJT, then led the way back upstairs, heading for the rest room.

'Right, Charlie, let's you and me have a debrief over a cuppa,' he said, surprising Eccles with the informality, then surprising him further by asking, 'I'm brewing up, so what's your poison?'

'Tea. NATO standard. Thanks.'

'Ex-forces?' Ted asked him conversationally as he made tea for them both.

'Army brat. My dad was in the Engineers. We moved about a lot.'

As he said it, the DC wondered why he was telling stuff about his personal life to the bloke he had been determined from the start not to like, and not just because of his sexuality, which was an open secret.

Ted put the mugs of tea on the table and the two men sat down facing one another.

'Tell me what you think of young Jake. Did he do it, do you think?'

'Definitely, I'd say. He's got the form, he's got no alibi.'

'Now I'd have to disagree with you there, for two reasons. The form isn't proven. As for the alibi. Well, Jake might not have had much schooling, but he's smart. Streetwise. If he really had killed Mrs Murray, and he knew from the telly that the police were looking for someone whose description matched him, don't you think he would have made sure he had an alibi? Even if he's a loner, he must know someone he could have persuaded to lie for him.

'And there's another thing. I think he's basically pretty honest.'

Eccles' eyes widened and he opened his mouth to protest.

'Hear me out,' Ted told him. 'He had the perfect opportunity, back there, to drop you right in it. He could have claimed you assaulted him. It would have been his word against yours, and I would have been obliged to pass the allegation on to Complaints. He strikes me as sharp enough to know that, too. You've already had an encounter with Superintendent Fletcher, so you know that being interviewed by him is not a pleasant prospect.'

The DC shifted uncomfortably in his chair at the memory of being questioned by the ex-Guardsman head of Complaints and Discipline.

'So why let you off the hook that easily? Why not lie, say you hit him, and take the pressure off himself for a time? Tell me what you see when you look at him.'

Again, Eccles looked surprised by Ted's methods.

'I see a typical little thug. Hard case. Cocky. Aggressive.'

'I see a scared little lad who's used to being bullied so hides it behind that attitude. D'you know how I spend my Wednesday evenings, Charlie?'

Now the DC's look was almost of horror. He had a bad feeling the DCI was suddenly going to share some intimate detail of his personal life, which Charlie definitely neither wanted nor needed to know.

'My partner and I teach self defence to young kids just like Jake. The ones who get bullied at school and wherever else they go. We teach them some martial arts basics, show them how to look after themselves. Give them some self-confidence which helps boost their self-esteem. I see the same fear in Jake that I see in those kids when they first start coming to the club.'

The DC gave a cynical grunt.

'I bet you a tenner he did it.'

'It wouldn't be appropriate to be gambling on a potential suspect in a case. But I'll tell you what. If you're right, I'll buy you a pint. If I'm right, you owe me a drink. You won't be surprised to hear that I drink ginger beer.'

Ted drained his tea and stood up to go.

'When did you last do any update training on interview techniques, Charlie? Cognitive interviewing, for example?'

This time there was a snort of derision.

'All that new-fangled stuff? It was never the boss's thing so none of us did it.'

Ted wanted to say that it showed, but didn't. He hadn't yet given up on DC Eccles.

'I want to talk to the driver again tomorrow. There are some techniques which might help him to remember more than he has done so far. More than he might realise that he knows. I'd like to explore those with him. I'd also like you to sit in on that interview. It might be helpful for you.

'Can you please contact him and set up an interview, here, if he doesn't mind, sometime tomorrow. Then give me a ring and let me know what time. See you tomorrow, Charlie.'

DC Eccles surprised himself still further by responding, 'See you, boss,' which had Ted smiling to himself as he went out to his car.

Having interviewed Jake Dolan, Ted didn't for a moment think he was guilty, but he couldn't go off his instinct alone. When he got back to his office, he went through all the phone calls from witnesses claiming to have recognised him or those saying it sounded like the sort of thing he would do, the transcripts of which he'd had emailed to himself. Some were anonymous, inevitably, so could well be rival small-time skunk dealers. Even small fry like Jake could pull trade away from other dealers and they might see the appeal for information as a golden opportunity to get him off their patch.

He also went carefully through every witness account and every description they had received about the person who had pushed the elderly woman off the pavement. It didn't amount to much. Short, slightly built, male, youthful, wearing a hoody with the hood up and, from varying accounts, either jeans or tracksuit bottoms. Significantly, all the witnesses mentioned the hood and there was not one who was able to state the skin colour of the assailant.

The bus driver, or one of the passengers, would have been the most likely by far to have got a glimpse of the face under the hood. Ted had a trick or two up his sleeve which he intended to try the following day on the driver, to see if he could help him to jog his memory, without leading him in any way.

The rest of the team had gone home for the evening, so Ted took advantage of the quiet to go over the notes of any new developments in the Tyler Bradbury case. There were precious few of those, either. They desperately needed a break to advance their ongoing cases.

Ted only realised how late it had got when DC Eccles phoned him to say that he had arranged for the bus driver to be at the South Manchester station at ten o'clock the next day. Ted thanked him, noticing the time showing on his mobile phone, and knew he was in for yet another a hard time from the cats when he got home. He'd left them with plenty of food, as usual, but they were used to Trev's more regular hours and would be demanding attention. He knew he could ask his mother to go round to see to them at any time, but he didn't like to impose.

Queen, the senior cat, was sitting in the middle of the kitchen table, glaring reproachfully at him when he got in. The rest were milling around the floor, pointedly ignoring several bowls still full of the morning's offering of dry food.

Ted carefully side-stepped the headless body of what might have been a mouse, dumped in the middle of the kitchen floor, and went in search of clean bowls and pouches of tasty morsels in sauce.

'Sorry, everyone, but you really aren't starving. Far from it. Stop looking at me like that. I miss him, too, you know. And Brian, is that you leaving bodies about again? What have I told you?'

Only after all six cats had been stroked, fussed and fed did Ted start sorting out heating up his leftovers from the day before. The microwave had just pinged when his mobile phone went again. The call he was eagerly awaiting. Trev.

'Hey, you.' Trev's voice sounded happy, full of laughter, and something else besides. There was loud music and lots of noise in the background.

'Are you having a good time?'

'Blissful!'

Ted smiled indulgently. He knew his partner so well he could detect the slightest change in the timbre of his voice.

'And are you stoned?'

A great shout of laughter.

'Guilty as charged, officer. Ever so slightly. I'm having a wonderful time, though. I'm getting up to all sorts of stuff I wouldn't dare do with you around. But I miss you. Ever such a lot. And I'm behaving, most of the time.'

'I'm glad. The cats miss you, too. They've been giving me a hard time as I worked late.'

'I wish I was there to give you a massage. Oh God, that's making me feel horny now. And I've got the munchies, as usual. I'd better go and eat. I'll call tomorrow. Love you.'

Ted was smiling to himself as Trev ended the call. No matter how bad a day he'd had, Trev could always make him smile. With him away, it just emphasised to Ted how much he relied on his support.

# Chapter Twelve

'So how do you think you're going to get more out of the bus driver than anyone has so far?'

DC Eccles was interested, in spite of himself. He didn't see himself ever being pally with the DCI like he had been with the old DI. He knew it wasn't PC these days and he had to keep his feelings to himself, but he just couldn't get past the mental image of him in bed with another man. But he had a good reputation and a better clear-up rate than the old boss by a land mile.

Maybe he could learn something from him. Perhaps even make progress towards that promotion the missus was always nagging him to go for. They'd been married forever, since they were nothing but kids, really, and she was always wanting more. Bigger house, newer car, fancy holidays, private lessons in this and that for their two kids. Why not? DS Eccles had a ring to it. It had never seemed much of a possibility with the old team and their sloppy ways.

'I might not,' Ted admitted. 'I just have a few more techniques I would like to try, to see if he can remember more than he thinks he can. I splurged a bit of my budget on update training, so I'd better make the most of it.

'One of the things I'd like to do at some point is to take him back to the scene of the incident. I came up in my official car, so I'd like you to drive, while I talk him through what I want him to do. Are you happy with that?'

The DC couldn't get used to a senior officer asking his opinion and approval all the time. He was used to being given orders and being expected to get on with them. Ted was certainly not like any officer he'd served with before, and not just because he was on the other bus.

He nodded his agreement and Ted went on, 'Other than that, I'd just like you to sit quietly and observe once more, plus take notes of anything he says, please, then write them up as soon as possible. So, let's go and see if Mr Arnold knows anything of value that he's not yet told us because he's forgotten it.'

Ted's opening gambit, whether he was talking to suspects, witnesses or anyone indirectly connected to an enquiry was always to make the interviewee feel relaxed in his presence, off guard even, disarmed by his appearance and quiet voice.

'Thanks for coming in, Mr Arnold. I know you've been over all this a few times, with me and with other officers. I just wanted to take you through everything once again, in case anything else has come to you in the intervening days. What I'd also like to do, but only if you're comfortable with it, is to take you back to the scene. That's simply to find out if being back in the context of the incident might jog a buried memory.

'So, first of all, please tell me, in your own time, everything you can remember about what happened last Wednesday.'

Calmly and methodically, the driver went through his version of events, which was almost identical to the last time. Ted had no reason to doubt what he was saying. He just needed to use various techniques to find out if there were any details tucked away subliminally, which could be teased out of him.

'Thank you, Mr Arnold. Now I'd like you to go further back, before the incident. You'd driven, what, about two hundred yards down the road before the collision took place? Had you made a stop already on that road? Where was your first stop, in relation to where the collision occurred?'

'I was just coming up to my first stop on that road. Another twenty or thirty yards, perhaps. I was going quite slowly all the way, because I like to be careful, but I was also slowing down, getting ready for the stop.'

'You've described seeing the youth coming towards you. Can you go back from there. Go back to the first moment at which you became aware of the youth.'

Ted was being careful to use gender-neutral words and phrases in relation to the suspect.

'I think he came out of a shop lower down. Perhaps the newsagent, there's one just near there. No, hang on, wait a moment.'

His brow was furrowed with the effort of remembering, then he looked surprised.

'Well, bugger me, that's strange. I hadn't remembered that until now. Just briefly, when I first saw the figure coming out of the shop, I thought to myself, that looks like Beryl's lass, from round the corner to me. Then as it got closer, I could see it was a lad, not a lass.'

'You're sure? It was definitely a male figure walking towards you, who pushed Mrs Murray?'

'I'm sure it was a lad. In any case, a girl wouldn't do something like this, would they?'

'Don't worry about that aspect for now, Mr Arnold. Just concentrate on the figure you see walking towards you, and anything you can remember about it. Did you see the face at all, at any point?'

Again, the look of surprise.

'I didn't think I had but I must have done because now I have an image of a white face. Not pale, I mean white, not a black person. Is that the right way to say it? It doesn't sound racist?'

'That's fine, Mr Arnold, I understand what you're saying. Is there anything else? Any other feature you can remember, no matter how insignificant it might seem?'

He thought hard for a moment, then shook his head.

'And going back to that first moment you saw the suspect. Are you able to say what it was about the figure that made you think it could be female? Concentrate on that moment. Close your eyes, if you feel it might help you to see it more clearly.'

The driver looked from one officer to another, suddenly a bit wary. He probably hadn't been asked to close his eyes and imagine anything since his days in junior school, Ted thought. After a pause, he did close them, or rather, screwed them up in evident concentration. Then he opened them again, shaking his head.

'I can't just pick out what it was. Something about how they moved? But then, these young teenagers, they do all look alike in baggy clothes and just slouching about. When he came walking towards me, he had his head down so the hood fell forward and I couldn't see anything about him, not even his colour. He had his hands in his pockets, walking along. Then I saw a hand dart out and grab something from the old lady's trolley. It was windy and the flap on top was blowing about, like she hadn't fastened it properly. Then he shoved her and I was braking as hard as I could and trying to control the bus so I didn't see anything more of him, just that he'd run off.'

He took a steadying drink of the cup of water which had been provided for him, obviously still shaken every time he thought about what had happened.

'Thank you very much, Mr Arnold. That's been very helpful, and I know it's hard for you to have to keep going over it. So now is it all right with you if we go and visit the scene? Have you been back there since it happened?'

He shook his head again.

'I've been avoiding it, to be honest. But I have to go again some time. I'll be going back to work next week and I might be on that same route again, so I have to face up to it eventually.'

'Very good, thank you. DC Eccles, can you go and bring the car to the entrance, please. It's a black Ford.'

He handed the keys to the DC as he asked their key witness

if he needed a break or any refreshment before they went. He didn't, so they followed DC Eccles down and waited at the entrance while he brought the car round.

Ted installed the witness in the front passenger seat and sat in the back himself. Eccles drove carefully and meticulously through the morning traffic to where the incident had happened. Ted wasn't sure if he was normally such an exemplary driver or if it was his presence, or that of a professional driver in the vehicle, which made him more careful than usual.

As they turned into the road they were heading for, Ted could see ahead that the area where the incident had happened was still taped off. It was, of course, a police crime scene, as the death was being treated as a murder enquiry. He made a mental note that Mr Arnold's estimations of distance were accurate. It always made for a more reliable witness, to know that there were no wild guesses involved. It's what he would have expected from someone who had driven for a living for many years, with a clean licence.

'If you could just indicate to me the point at which you first became aware of the figure, please, and DC Eccles, could you please pull up just before the tapes.'

There was still a uniformed presence at the scene. A Police Community Support Officer was standing near the tapes, keeping an eye on things. Ted had asked if that could be done, aware that sometimes a certain type of killer would return to the scene of their crime for some sort of gratification.

As soon as Eccles pulled closer to the kerb and slowed down to a crawl, the officer moved quickly forward. Ted lowered the window on his side.

'You can't stop there, mate, it's a crime scene. We don't want any bloody rubber-neckers.'

Ted produced his warrant card and held it out of the open window. He kept his voice quiet, so it was not easy for the two men in the front to hear what he had to say.

'What about the SIO on the case? Is he allowed to rubber-neck?'

'Sorry, sir, I didn't know who you were.'

'Precisely, so I would like to think that you would address any member of the public with a bit more respect than that.

'Now, I appreciate this is restricted parking, but we're just going to stay here briefly, to do some context reinstatement with a vital witness. You're doing the right thing in discouraging onlookers. Just please try to be a bit more courteous about how you do it.'

Ted had tried to keep his voice down but Eccles had clearly heard everything and started to chuckle.

'That's enough, DC Eccles,' Ted told him sharply. 'Mr Arnold, first of all, are you comfortable being here? If not please say so and we will move.'

When the man nodded his agreement, he went on, careful to keep his questions gender-neutral again. 'Thank you. Now, I want you to focus on where the suspect was when you first saw them, and if there is anything more you can remember about the figure you saw.'

'He definitely came out of the newsagent down there, now that I see the scene in context. He had to step round someone standing on the pavement staring at their mobile phone. That's the moment when he lifted his head and I briefly saw that his face was white.'

'Could you describe the features at all?'

'No, it was just a fleeting glimpse.'

'And now we're here, can you remember what it was that first made you think the figure was female?'

'I really don't know now. Just something about the way they moved, perhaps? I can't quite bring it to mind. I'm sorry.'

'Please don't apologise, Mr Arnold, you're doing brilliantly. Just one more thing. Are you able to gauge at all the height of the person, or could you get any impression of their build?'

He started to shake his head again but Ted continued, 'For

example, if I were to go down there and come out of the shop, do you think you'd be able to gauge the height of the figure you saw against my height, for comparison?'

Ted thought he'd better buy something while he was in the shop. He didn't want the shopkeeper reporting him for suspicious behaviour if he just went in and lurked. He was sure the PCSO up the road would love an excuse to come and exercise his 'any person' powers of arrest to get him taken away. He picked up a packet of Fisherman's Friend and paid for them. He went through them at quite a rate.

He was lucky that there was someone standing staring at their mobile as he came out of the shop so he was able to sidestep them without having to stage it. It was becoming such a common feature of modern life.

When he got back to the car and slid into the rear seat, he asked, 'Did that help you at all, Mr Arnold? Could you say whether the figure you saw was taller or shorter than I am?'

'You're not very tall for a policeman, are you?' Arnold observed, his tone conversational. 'What are you, about five four, five five?'

'You have a good eye for judging such things, Mr Arnold. I'm five four.'

'The lad was definitely shorter, but I wouldn't like to have a guess at how much because that's all it would be, just a guess and I'm sure that's no use to you. Same for his build. In those baggy clothes, he could have been any size.'

'DC Eccles, can you nip down to the newsagent and find out if they have CCTV from last week, if it's not already been done. Also ask if they remember anyone relevant in the shop on the morning of the incident. Any hoodies, anything that can help us. I'll drop Mr Arnold off then see you back at the station.'

Once again, it was Ted who brewed up. He didn't need to be reminded how Eccles took his tea. He sat down opposite the

DC and asked for his thoughts.

'First off, no CCTV for the day in question. They only keep tapes a few days before they record over them. Secondly, they don't remember any hoodies or anyone who stood out that day. Mostly regular customers, people they recognised.'

'Now, this context reinstatement stuff,' Eccles began. 'And that going backwards thing ...'

'Reverse temporal order of recall,' Ted grinned. 'Impressive, eh? Works well, too.'

'Is that the sort of stuff you do on one of these courses?'

'That's part of it. If you're interested, once we get this case done and dusted, I can look at the budget, crunch a few numbers, and see what we can do for you and DC Winters. I think DS Rakale has already done the course. So, back to our driver. Did we learn anything new?'

'Short, skinny, white lad. Fits Jake Dolan's profile exactly,' Eccles replied triumphantly.

'Mr Arnold didn't say skinny. He said he couldn't tell because of the baggy clothes. And his first impression was of a female, don't forget.'

'You don't seriously think this was a girl?'

'I'm not ruling anything in or out at this stage, Charlie. Do you ever read crime fiction?'

Eccles had trouble with keeping up with the way the DCI's thought processes seem to jump about all over the place. He shook his head.

'I do sometimes. Ian Rankin mostly. I read the reviews about them, too. Readers are always saying how easy it was to guess who the murderer was. Well, we can't guess, unfortunately. We just have to plod along methodically on the information we get. Let's just say, I want to keep all avenues open in this case.

'With that in mind, I want to have a full briefing on both cases with everyone present, from both teams. At Stockport, tomorrow. Eight o'clock sharp. Can you let Graham and the DS know, please. And Charlie, make sure you're on time.'

He said it with a grin, but it was still a reminder. When they'd first met, on a previous case, Eccles had tried boundary-pushing by turning up late for a team briefing.

The office was quiet when Ted got back to his own nick. He'd picked up a bagel on his way back and planned on a working lunch. Océane was working at her computer, and Jo was in his office, so Ted put the kettle on and invited him to join him for a catch-up. Jo nodded in response to being asked if he'd eaten yet, but gratefully accepted the offer of a coffee.

'So, make my day and tell me you've solved our case while I've been up the road.'

Ted had left Jo behind while he was up at South Manchester himself, although Sal had gone over there and was lending a hand.

'Can't do that, boss. Good Catholic, remember. If I lied to a senior officer, I'd have to go to confession and that would be an awful lot of Hail Marys and Hail Holy Queens. How did you get on?'

'What would you say if I told you Charlie had actually asked to be sent on a cognitive interview technique course?'

'I'd say do you want to borrow my rosary to do your penance, if you don't have your own. Because that sounds like a big whopper, to me.'

Ted laughed.

'It's actually true. We managed to get a bit more out of the bus driver using context reinstatement, and it seemed to impress him. The driver was able to remember that the suspect was white, which no one else has said before. Also, interestingly, he remembered that his first fleeting impression was that it was a girl, not a boy.'

Jo looked at him questioningly.

'So you're thinking ...?'

'Nothing involving jumping to any conclusions, at the

moment. I'm just saying we should keep an open mind in looking for suspects. I want to call a full team briefing tomorrow morning first thing, for both teams. Because we do now have two apparently motiveless killings, each with a suspect who is small and possibly female.'

'And you're seeing a connection?'

'Far from it. It's too soon. I'm just focusing on two cases where we don't know for sure the gender of the attacker in either of them, so I thought it would be a good idea to kick some ideas around together, all of us.'

When Jo had gone back to his office and Ted had finished his lunch, he typed up his own notes from the morning and emailed them to Leona to keep her in the picture. He added a note to make sure she knew about the briefing the next day. He still didn't trust Eccles sufficiently to pass the message on about the briefing.

Just then his mobile pinged with a text message, from Trev.

'Sorry can't talk today. At a shoot location in the wilds and signal is dire. Hopefully tomorrow. Hugs to the pussies. Love you loads. Tx. PS Not stoned today, officer.'

Ted laughed fondly as he read it, although he was disappointed they wouldn't get to talk. He knew he relied on his partner too much for moral support. Trev was the more gregarious of the two. On the rare occasions Ted left him on his own, he'd seek out company with Willow and Rupe, Ted's mother, any of his biker or karate friends, or even Professor Nelson, who was a big fan of Trev, and an even bigger one of his Triumph Bonneville.

Ted would see his mother at the weekend as she'd insisted on making a welcome home meal for Trev, knowing her son was busy working two murder cases. He'd agreed, but only if he bought all the ingredients. But he wouldn't normally look for her company just because his partner was away. Until Sunday, it would be just him and the cats – and work.

# Chapter Thirteen

'What we're going to be discussing this morning stays in this room. No leaks, please. None. Clear, everybody?'

Ted began the briefing the following morning with a word of warning. They were going to be kicking around some ideas which, if they got out into the public domain, particularly to the press, wouldn't help their investigations and might start panic.

Even DC Eccles joined in the general head nodding and murmurs of 'sir'. He was actually starting to show something of an interest.

'Jezza has already mentioned that she thought the figure from the CCTV could be female. Now the driver of the bus which killed Mrs Murray has said that his first impression of the suspect was of a girl. He amended that afterwards, though. He became convinced it was male.

'I am not at this stage trying to make a link between the two cases. I want to stress that, and that's why I want this discussion to stay under wraps. However, we do now have two unsolved murders with no apparent motive.'

'Three, boss,' Jezza put in. 'I've turned up nothing at all on the jealous scholarship rival angle in the Luke Martin case, so we still have no motive for that one. And there's another thing I thought of ...'

'Can we talk about that afterwards, Jezza? Let's deal with the other two first, then DS Rakale and her team can get back up to their own nick and carry on. Liaise with Jo before you leave, Leona, about extra bodies if you need them.

'So, as well as ambiguity over the gender of the killers,

there are some superficial similarities from the little information we have on them, mostly to do with size. The footprints at the scene where Tyler Bradbury was killed were small, and the youth seen pushing Joan Murray under a bus is also small. Smaller than me, according to the bus driver.

'I'm not convinced about Jake Dolan, the suspect DC Eccles and I interviewed, although we have a difference of opinion there. But he is certainly small and slight. We got his name from a tip-off, but it could just be that someone wants him off the streets. So, do we have any likely contenders for either case?'

'We've still got no leads at all for anyone seen with Tyler, boss,' Mike Hallam told him. He'd been coordinating the phone calls and door to door interviews. 'We knew it was a long shot, as there's such a short window between him going missing and the time of death. It just seems no one saw him at all, other than his killer.'

'What's the word on the street, Virgil?'

Virgil was liked and well respected within the black community, seen as a fair officer, not judgemental, always willing to listen.

'I had to smooth a few ruffled feathers, boss. There's just a feeling we're doing more for Tyler than we did for Luke Martin. I put them straight.'

That must have been especially hard for Virgil to take. He'd actually been working the Luke Martin case when his wife lost their first child. He'd even come in from compassionate leave to help with the case, a move which had nearly split his marriage apart.

'For our case, can't we do an identity parade, with Jake Dolan in it, see if the driver or anyone can pick him out?' Charlie Eccles asked. Not being from the Stockport team, he hadn't picked up on the sudden tension the previous remark had caused for a moment.

'It would be the logical next step, but other than a few

dubious tip-offs saying it sounded like Dolan's sort of thing, we have no description at all. Just the driver saying the figure was short and white, and he's the only witness to have given any kind of a description. If we tried to make a case out of that, any half-decent defence lawyer would, pardon the pun, drive a bus through it. Reasonable doubt? Too much of it even to take a punt at it, I would say.

'DS Rakale, perhaps you can haul in anyone else whose name's been suggested, see if they seem any more likely, and see what their alibis are like. Jo, perhaps if you go over and give a hand with any interviewing? I have things to do here.

'Anything else?'

The briefing was just breaking up when Virgil grabbed his phone, which must have been set to vibrate only, from his pocket, looking stricken.

'Sorry, boss, it's the wife. She wasn't feeling too clever this morning ...'

Ted waved away his apology. Virgil's wife was approaching her due date and they were both more anxious than most expectant parents, having lost their baby the last time.

'Hello, love, are you ... Okay, don't panic, I'll be right there ... Right, well you go in the ambulance, I'll go straight to the hospital ... yes, I'm leaving now. Don't worry, honey, I'll be there ...'

Virgil ended the call and looked at Ted.

'Boss, I need to go. She's gone into labour. It's too early. It wasn't meant to happen yet.'

None of the team members were surprised that it was Maurice who went to Virgil first and put a comforting arm round his shoulders.

'Don't worry. Babies come when they're ready. It'll be fine. The twins were early.' Then he too looked at Ted as he said, 'Boss, he can't go on his own. He's not safe to drive, worried like he is.'

'Of course. Go, both of you. Keep us posted.'

Jezza gave Virgil a brief hug as he headed for the door, Maurice close behind him. The rest of the team called encouragement and Megan Jennings added, 'Felix was early, too, and he was fine. Hope everything goes well, Virgil.'

'Right, we're two down for now. Jo, can you liaise with Leona and sort out who needs to be where as a result of that. Jezza, come and tell me what it was you wanted to talk to me about.'

Ted didn't bother putting the kettle on. He'd arranged to talk to the Ice Queen after morning briefing and that meeting would involve decent coffee. It was time they had a catch-up. He'd also called Jim Baker and asked him to be there. Briefing both of them at once would save time, and he needed to bring them up to speed with his latest thinking.

He and Jezza sat down facing one another.

'Trophies, boss,' she began. 'I can't find any reference anywhere to the missing violin bridge from the Luke Martin killing. Batman hasn't turned up yet and ...'

'Whoa, hold your horses, Jezza. I agree, it is something to consider, but you're making a leap by connecting two cases which we don't yet know are connected. If a dog ran off with Batman, he may yet turn up. The missing toy may have nothing at all to do with Tyler's killer.'

'And the old lady's purse, at South Manchester? Has that turned up yet? Or did a dog run off with that, too?'

Jezza had a sarcastic turn of phrase sometimes, especially when she was trying to argue a point and felt she wasn't making the ground she should be doing.

'Let's not get ahead of ourselves, DC Vine,' Ted said, his tone a reminder that she needed to keep control of her tongue.

'But, boss, there are killers who always take a trophy from the crime scene. I just wondered if it was worth going through old cases, and ones from other areas, for a killer who's done that before? Just in case it is the same person in all three cases.

Or even four cases. What about the garden gnomes from the arson? Were any of those missing?'

'I don't know if there was any inventory done of the gnomes. You'd have to look in the files. I doubt anyone would know for sure. I think you're in danger of getting ahead of yourself there, too.'

'But it does give similarities between all four killings, if trophies were taken from all. They're all motiveless at the moment.'

'I don't entirely agree with that. The arson case had a motive, of sorts. The deceased had been the target of a lot of ongoing abuse from local youths, simply because he was different. It's not an acceptable reason, of course, but it is a motive in a way.'

'And here's another idea.'

Once Jezza got into her stride, there was sometimes no stopping her, as Ted knew to his cost.

'Let's say that it's not the same killer in each case. That there are two killers. Or even more. Suppose it's some kind of a challenge between them? What if they're, I don't know, scoring each other on their killings? Does an old lady get more points than a little boy? Is someone with learning difficulties too soft a target to score much?'

Ted leaned back in his chair and looked at her. She had good ideas, but some of this was verging on the far-fetched. Still, he'd long ago learnt never to overlook any possible line of enquiry in murder cases.

'Right, do some digging, but don't spend too much time on it, unless you get anything more to go on than your intuition. I'm not dismissing that, it's often good, but with so much on our hands, and now an officer down with Virgil on paternity leave, we need to concentrate our resources where the strongest leads are.

'I know Jo wants to get Steve out of the office a bit more, so if you need any help with computer searches, ask Océane if she has some time she could throw at it. We need to make good use of her while we have her. As the Super keeps reminding me, the way the budgetary axe keeps randomly swinging, it could be a case of here today, gone tomorrow. And keep me informed.'

Ted just needed a bit of desk time before he went down to meet with the Super and the Big Boss. He wanted to catch up on emails and paperwork, to stay on top of both. Come what may, he planned to leave early to get to the self-defence club. He was keen to hear if any of the children had any feedback for him on bullying in their schools. He was giving his personal therapy sessions a miss for the time being, with so much going on. He felt reasonably together, not allowing himself to get too discouraged by lack of progress. He knew Carol would always find time to see him at short notice if he ever needed her help.

The main office was quiet when Jezza left the boss's to go back to her desk. Only Océane was there, working on her computer. Jezza decided to take the opportunity to talk to her about some computer help, should she need it. She also wanted to have a word with her about something else. She hadn't really got to know their new CFI, but she wanted to mark her card for her.

She explained the sort of thing she was looking for. Océane nodded and promised to find some time to at least start the searches during the day. Jezza was going straight out so wouldn't have the time herself.

'Oh, and about Steve,' Jezza said, as she turned to go. 'I'm very fond of Steve. He's like my kid brother. Just don't mess him about, all right?'

Océane's look in return was analytical. She studied Jezza rather as she might a piece of intriguing software.

'Jezza, you have a kid brother. And it's not Steve. Almost everyone on the team treats Steve as if he's some sort of wet behind the ears boy. He isn't. He's a man, and a very intelligent one. Highly regarded in gaming circles. A brilliant tactician. Have you any idea how incredibly sexy that kind of high intellect is?

'I'm really into Steve. I doubt I'll marry him and have his babies, and he probably feels the same way. But while it lasts, it's excellent. And we are both adults. About this, and about everything. Not that it is any of your business. But thanks for your concern.'

It wasn't often that Jezza was at a loss for words, but she was this time. Much as she hated to admit it, what Océane had said was perfectly true. She did tend to think of Steve, and to treat him, as another kid brother. She was surprised to hear a different side to him. She made a mental note to try to treat him better in the future.


Jim Baker had already arrived when Ted went downstairs to the Ice Queen's office. Once the coffee was served, Ted set out for the two of them what he had discussed with the expanded team at the morning briefing. He was quick to stress that he was not at the moment linking the two cases, only that it was something they were considering.

'Bloody hell, Ted,' Jim Baker growled. 'I'm not sure which of all of those possibilities appeals the least. Copycat killers? I don't like the sound of that one, in particular.'

'And there's still a distinct possibility that the killer or killers may be teenagers or children? I find that aspect particularly disturbing,' the Super put in.

'There's also these animal torture cases the RSPCA are working on. I've seen some sights in my time, but they were pretty harrowing in comparison. And they've all taken place in and around the park. Which gives them at least a geographical link with the arson from four years ago, and with the Tyler Bradbury case.'

All three were silent for a moment, thinking about the implications.

'We certainly don't want any of this leaking out to the press too soon,' the Ice Queen stressed. 'You have reminded the team once again about discretion? And you're still happy you can trust them?'

'My team, yes, one hundred per cent. I don't, of course, know the South Manchester three that well yet. Leona Rakale appears to be an exemplary officer; I'd be surprised if she gossiped outside work. DC Winters was good on the last case we worked on together. DC Eccles would be the weak link, if there is one. He's making an effort, but he still has some bad habits to get out of, a legacy from the old days. I have reminded him though. That's as much as I can do for now.

'Oh, and DC Tibbs' wife went into labour this morning, slightly ahead of her time. So he's gone off to the hospital and will be on leave for a couple of weeks, hopefully the proud father of a healthy baby.'

The Ice Queen hadn't been in post long enough to have heard of his history. At her questioning look, Ted filled her in briefly on the background.

'I do hope everything goes well. Please send him and his wife my best wishes when you hear from him. And please do let me know when you have news.'

Despite her frosty professional front, the Ice Queen could show a compassionate side to officers under her command. It never lasted long and was quickly replaced with the brittle formality which was the shield behind which she hid.

Maurice appeared back during the morning. There was nothing to report, he told Ted, but Virgil's mother-in-law had turned up. Unlike in some marriages, son-in-law and mother-in-law seemed to get on well together, so Maurice had left them supporting one another and caught a bus back to the station.

Ted was surprised to get a call during the afternoon from Mrs Atkinson, the foster mother of the boy Flip, one of Ted's most enthusiastic students at the self-defence club.

'I'm sorry to bother you when you're probably at work, Inspector,' she began hesitantly. She would have no reason to have heard of Ted's recent promotion. 'I'm afraid Philip won't be able to come tonight. He's had some trouble at school with an older boy and he's been injured. In fact, I was calling … I know this is a bit of an imposition, and I'll quite understand if you're too busy … I just wondered if you might be kind enough to pop round after the club tonight? Just to have a word with him? Only he seems to have got hurt trying to do some sort of detective work or something. He'd listen to you. If it's not too much trouble?'

Ted was quickly calculating time-scales in his head. He was committed to teaching the club, with one of the other members of the adult judo club to help in place of Trev. But he was in desperate need of his own judo session afterwards, especially if he was skipping his therapy. His cases took a hefty personal toll and Ted's form of release was his martial arts. It was never the same without Trev to spar with, but it would be something, at least.

'Would eight-thirty be too late to be convenient for you? I could be there by then, if that helps?'

When he got home to change into casual clothes and grab his kitbag, Ted received another text from Trev.

'Still no signal. Still stoned. Still horny. Can't wait for Sunday! Say hi to the kids for me tonight. Love you xx.'

He fired off a quick reply, hoping his partner was receiving them all right if the signal was that bad. He was also looking forward to their reunion on Sunday.

It was quickly followed by another text. A picture of a beaming Virgil smiled up at him, cradling a tiny, but clearly healthy baby in his arms. His message read: 'I'm a daddy. Meet Daisy May. Mother and baby doing well.'

Ted smiled as he forward the message to the Ice Queen and Jim Baker. He knew Virgil would have circulated it round the team already.

The club went reasonably well. None of the children present had anything to report about bullying in their schools. Ted reminded them all again that an important part of self-defence was not to put oneself in danger to start with.

After his own judo session, which was tame by comparison to how it was when Trev was there, he took a quick shower at the gym and got changed before going round to where Flip lived with his foster parents. He was shown into the front room where Flip was sprawled on the settee, watching television. He had a few bruises visible and one wrist was in a plaster cast which extended up his forearm.

He looked up and beamed when Ted walked into the room. Flip had a serious case of hero-worship where Ted was concerned and seemed determined to follow his example by joining the police force. He instinctively jerked his head in a flicking motion to clear his rebellious fringe from his eyes before he spoke.

'Hi, Ted! You should see the other bloke.'

He moved his feet out of the way so Ted could sit down next to him.

'So, Flip, what have I told you about never putting yourself in danger? What were you doing?'

'There's this older boy in our school, right. Thinks he's a right hard case. Picks on the little kids all the time. Robs off them, smacks them about a bit. I thought I'd try keeping a bit of an eye on him, like. Then I could give you a good witness statement.'

'But even with the training you've had so far, you were taking a huge risk, going up against a bigger boy.'

'Oh, he ain't bigger, just older. He's a right little squirt. Not much bigger than me.'

# Chapter Fourteen

'Right, before we get down to the serious stuff, we have a baby's head to wet. I suggest we finish the week with a drink in the The Grapes, after work tomorrow. I don't suppose for a moment Virgil will be free to join us but someone please let him know we'd love to see him, even for ten minutes.

'Now, I've got some fresh information which might just give us a new angle. From one of the kids who comes to self defence. You all know about Flip.'

Ted told the team everything he had learned from Flip the previous evening. The team, except for the new members, knew about him from an earlier case where a murder victim had been Flip's friend. Ted had got details of the older boy involved in the recent incident, and had been told that he was currently suspended by the school.

'Where are we up to with checking all the schools in the area for anything similar? Steve, you were working on that, weren't you?'

'Yes, sir. I've spoken to them all, with not much to show for it. They all seem to have quite robust anti-bullying policies in place. If they are still having problems, they didn't flag anything up.'

Was it Ted's imagination or was there a new assurance about their youngest team member?

'Well, there was clearly trouble at Flip's school two days ago, and from what he told me, it's been going on for some time. I'll go to the school first, then I want to go and talk to the boy who's been suspended. It may just be coincidence, but he's apparently quite small as well. I don't want us to get carried away seeing connections where there aren't any, but I will get Jezza just to outline her theory about the possibility of different killers but with a connection between the cases, nonetheless.'

Jezza looked pleased to be allowed to air her idea and was careful to present it as a credible possibility.

'So you're saying this is some kind of sick game? Bloody hell, in my day we thought Dare, Command, Kiss, Truth, Promise was going it some,' Maurice grunted.

'It's all only conjecture at the moment,' Ted reminded them. 'But, for that reason, we do need to start looking into similar cases in other parts of the country, just in case.'

'Sir, we need to be looking internationally.'

Steve was definitely getting braver. He was speaking up without hesitation and wasn't going quite as red in the face when he did so.

In response to Ted's querying look, he continued, 'Everything is done via the internet now, especially with younger people. They're all into social media of some kind. If this is some sort of competition, there will be a group somewhere behind it. After all, what's the point of pulling off a high-scoring killing if you've nowhere to boast about it? I wouldn't mind betting we'd find something, if we started digging.'

'When you say we, I imagine you mean Océane?'

She replied before Steve could answer.

'With respect, boss, this is much more up Steve's street than mine. I can get any computer to give up its innermost secrets to a degree he couldn't do. But when it comes to any kind of online game-playing, Steve's the reigning champion. Although I'd be happy to give him a hand.'

A coarse chuckle from Maurice.

'I just bet you would, bonny lass.'

'Maurice,' Ted said warningly. He wouldn't allow remarks like that during a briefing.

'And you think we need to look outside the country, Steve?'

'Yes, sir. If there is something going on online, then it means literally anyone from any country in the world could be taking part.'

Ted paused for a moment, while he took in the enormity of what Steve was saying. It was so far outside his knowledge that he was having difficulty getting his head round it.

'You certainly know far more about this than I do, Steve. So that's settled. You and Océane are on this and only this until further notice. Whatever it takes, see what you can find out. And I just hope you're wrong. The alternative doesn't bear thinking about. Let's start by circulating an information request through Europe, see if that throws up anything.'

'America too, boss, definitely.' Steve was even starting to sound assertive. 'I'm not being judgemental here, but there is documentary evidence that these things can spread like wildfire in the States. It's a language thing, principally. I would seriously start with the major English-speaking online communities first.'

Ted was amazed, but impressed. What Steve was saying made perfect sense, but it was so unusual for him to speak up with such confidence. He would normally have come quietly to Ted's office, tapping hesitantly on his door to put his theory forward.

'Maurice, you need to work with them as back-up, from the cold cases. Anything at all which could have a link. I'm thinking particularly of items missing from a crime scene, which could have been taken as trophies. Garden gnomes, Maurice.'

'Garden gnomes, boss?' he queried, then, seeing the look Ted threw at him, he sighed and nodded. 'Garden gnomes. Got it.'

'There's just another thing, boss, if I may.'

'Yes, Steve. You're on a roll. You most certainly may.'

'I'm pretty sure I've read somewhere that sometimes trophy

killers don't keep what they take. They leave it at their next crime scene. So we also need to look at unexpected things found at a crime scene, as well as missing things. For example, let's say we had a crime after the arson and a garden gnome suddenly appeared on that crime scene. I'll do some more checking on that, but it's something we need to consider.'

'Good. Excellent work, all of you. Lots of new angles to run with, so let's get on with it. And with the trophy idea in mind, I want to arrange for South Manchester to search Jake Dolan's house for anything out of place. That way we can rule him in or out, and I'll try to do the same for Flip's attacker, Max Newman.'

'Meanwhile, Jo, please sort out who's on what for now. Megan, are you free to come with me to the school, then to go and see the little charmer who broke Flip's wrist for him, despite his self-defence training?'

'Happy to, boss. Shall I go and get your car?'

Ted phoned ahead to make an appointment to see the headteacher of the school. He never liked visiting school premises. His own school years hadn't been good. Luckily, their visit was not to the school where he'd been a pupil. He still felt as if he was about to be put in detention when he was shown to the head's office.

Ted introduced them both as they showed their ID, then the head invited them to take a seat. He looked young to be the principal of such a large establishment, Ted thought, as the man composed his features into what was clearly his 'I'm listening' expression.

'As I mentioned, it's to do with the incident between two boys which resulted in injury to one and suspension of the other, as I understand it?'

'Sadly, yes. Young Philip seems to have taken it into his head to do some detective work of his own, spying on an older boy, Max. Max admits he was trying to take a biscuit from a younger pupil, which is clearly not acceptable. But it seems Philip has been having Kung Fu lessons and decided to wade in, which led to things getting out of hand.'

'Not Kung Fu, Mr Mitchell. Philip attends the same dojo as I do, learning judo. He also studies self-defence. I'm his *sensei*. I've already had a word with him about putting himself at risk. But in fact it was me who asked all the children who attend the club to inform me of any instances of bullying they observed. I did not, however, tell him to go ahead and try to deal with it himself.'

The man looked surprised.

'Oh, I see. I'm sorry, I misunderstood. We don't have a bullying problem at this school. We're constantly on the look-out for any signs of trouble, and we deal with it rapidly if and when it does arise.'

'Yet attempting to steal something, even a biscuit, from a younger pupil is certainly bullying, wouldn't you say? Not to mention theft. And breaking someone's wrist is a serious assault, of course.'

'Yes, yes, quite so. I'm sorry, I didn't mean to sound as if I was belittling the incident. We do take it most seriously, which is why Max was immediately suspended.'

'And what are these two pupils like, generally speaking? Is this kind of behaviour typical of either of them?'

The head pulled some paperwork towards him and consulted it briefly.

'Young Philip, as I'm sure you know, is in foster care, with an adoption application under way. He's generally a quiet, trouble-free pupil, with consistent mid-grade marks in most subjects. There have been one or two incidents with Max, I note. This is apparently not his first suspension. You must appreciate that with a school of this size, I don't know every single pupil individually.'

'Thank you for your time, Mr Mitchell. We'll go and visit Max now, see what he has to say for himself. We're particularly interested to hear of anything involving bullying or any kind of violence between older pupils and younger ones, in connection with an ongoing enquiry. Here's my card. If you do hear of any such thing, perhaps you would be kind enough to get in touch.'

As they got back into Ted's official car, with Megan at the wheel, he grinned apologetically at her as he said, 'I couldn't wait to get out of there, sorry. I hope it didn't show too much. School was not exactly a happy memory for me.'

He was interrupted by his mobile phone. The screen showed it was Bizzie Nelson calling.

'Morning, Edwin,' came the booming voice, so strong that he had to hold the mobile a short distance from his ear.

'Good morning, Professor.'

'You're not alone, I gather. As we've not met over any bodies recently, I wondered if you would like to come round this evening for a catch-up? I'm under strict instructions from young Trevor to make sure you're not lonely in his absence.'

Ted smiled his pleasure. Both he and Trev were fond of the rather eccentric but highly intelligent Professor. He enjoyed her company and, as a Home Office pathologist with many years' experience, she would be useful to talk to about his current cases. She may even have experienced something similar.

'That would be very nice, thank you, although I can't guarantee what time I'd get there.'

'Absolutely no problem at all. Come whenever you're ready. I'm a truly appalling cook but I'm sure I can find something in Marks and Spencer's which even I can't ruin too much in heating up.'

Megan was busy concentrating on driving, negotiating her way through some roadworks which had been causing major delays for some time now. Ted took the opportunity to fire off a quick text to Trev.

'Going on a hot date with a woman tonight x.'

It wasn't long before his phone pinged with a reply.

'Good! On way back to coast. Will try to call later but you may be in bed. Then I can think about you ...'

Ted hastily stopped reading and put the phone back in his pocket, worried he may be going pink and Megan would notice.

'This is us, then, boss,' Megan announced, as they pulled up outside a small end-terrace, with an untidy front garden.

A man came to answer the door and looked suspiciously at the warrant cards which were being held out to him. His T-shirt was not particularly clean and he looked as if he could have done with a wash and a shave. He didn't smell all that fragrant.

'Mr Newman? We're here about an incident Max was involved in at school. May we come in and talk to him, and to you, please?'

'A bit of a ruck between two school kids? How's that got anything to do with the filth?'

'More than a bit of a ruck, Mr Newman. The other boy has an arm in plaster. So, can we come in?'

With not much good grace, he turned and jerked his head for them to follow him, then led the way to a compact kitchen at the back of the house.

'Is Max in?'

'Bloody right he is, little bleeder. He's grounded, good and proper. Up in his bedroom sulking, playing with his little friend.'

The man sat down at the kitchen table, where there was an open newspaper, and a half-drunk mug of tea. Ted and Megan waited patiently for an offer to take a seat, which was not forthcoming.

'Has Max been in any trouble before, either at school or with the police?'

'He's a teenage lad, and he's no choirboy. 'Course he gets in trouble, it's only normal. He gets picked on, not being a big lad, so he sticks up for himself.'

'This would seem, on the face of it, to be a bit more to it than that, Mr Newman. We need to talk to your son, and we need you to be present, as an appropriate adult, while we question him. Would you mind asking him to come down to talk to us. This friend of his. Does he have a girlfriend, or is it another boy?'

The man snorted derisively.

'Are you asking if my lad's a woofter? Well, he bloody isn't. There is a lass he hangs round with. One of those, what do you call them, wears black all the time?'

'A Goth?'

'Summat like that, only she has pink hair sometimes, and different coloured make up. No, he'll be with Boris now.' His voice went up several decibels, without warning, so that both Ted and Megan winced involuntarily. 'Max? Bloody well get down here. Now.'

Ted always tried not to make judgements and assumptions. Nevertheless, he had formed something of a mental image of the teenager they had come to interview. They knew the boy was fifteen and Flip had described him reasonably well, giving an approximate idea of his height. What Ted was not remotely prepared for was the fact that he came into the kitchen with a large snake draped round his shoulders. The colour drained from Megan's face and she instinctively took a step behind Ted.

'This is our Max. And that's Boris,' the father sneered. 'Bloody thing. Eats us out of house and home, and there's only the wife working at the moment. I got laid off when the machine shop where I worked closed down. Production gone to bloody Poland or somewhere instead.'

'Boss, sorry ...' Megan said quietly, a note of desperation in her voice. Ted could tell immediately that she wasn't going to cope with an interview with a snake in the room, certainly not one of that size.

'Hello, Max, I'm DCI Darling, this is DC Jennings. We'd

really like to talk to you, but it might be better all round if you could put Boris somewhere safe while we do.'

The boy's father was laughing scornfully now.

'He's not poisonous, our Boris.'

'Perhaps you could show me where you keep him, if that's all right with both of you?'

This gave Ted the ideal point of connection before beginning the interview. Something which may catch the teenager off guard, get him to lower his defences. Bonding over what he imagined to be a python was not quite what he had in mind, but he wasn't afraid of snakes so he was willing to give it a go. He could tell that Megan was dangerously close to hysterics and he needed to manage the situation. It would also provide him with a perfectly legitimate reason to see inside the youth's bedroom, in case anything caught his eye at first glance.

The youth was as wary of Ted as Megan was of the snake, but after they'd been together to see the animal safely returned to its tank, they had at least exchanged a few civil words, Max telling Ted that Boris was a royal python.

When the two of them went back downstairs, the father finally nodded at the two officers to sit down, although he stopped short of offering them a brew.

'Max, tell me about this incident with the younger boy, Philip. What happened exactly?'

The boy's eyes kept darting warily towards his father as he started to speak, looking as if he was expecting a clip round the ear at any moment.

'He kept following me round, the little sod. Spying on me, like.'

'And what were you doing?'

'I was just asking a kid for some of his biscuits. He was stuffing his face and I were starving. I spent me dinner money on food for Boris. He bloody likes his grub, our Boris.'

'Asking him, or just taking?'

'All right, I just grabbed a couple of biscuits. Big deal. Then this little kid, this Flip, or Flipped more like, starts jumping around and like karate kicking at me. I had to protect myself, so I just shoved him. He fell over and, like, bust his wrist or summat. I didn't mean to hurt him. Honest.'

'You been nicking off other kids, you little bastard?'

The father raised a threatening hand but stopped abruptly at Ted's warning.

'Mr Newman, no. Certainly not in my presence.'

The tension was broken by Ted's mobile phone. He took it out, glanced at the screen, then said, 'Excuse me, please, but I do need to take this.'

He listened carefully then replied briefly, 'On my way. Mr Newman, Max, you must excuse me, I have to be somewhere. I would like to come back later and talk to you both at length.'


As they were walking out to the car, Megan said shamefacedly, 'So sorry about that, boss. I can honestly cope with most things, but snakes? Ugh, no. My worst nightmare.'

'I hope you really do mean that about coping, Megan. That call was the RSPCA. Sally, Rob's fiancée. They've got another animal torture case, in the park again. I want to go and look at the scene myself, just in case there is a connection to our enquiry. I've seen the files on the others and they are horrific. Sally tells me this is the worst one to date. If that's true, feel free to stay in the car. Sadly, I don't have that option.'

# Chapter Fifteen

'It really is all right to stay with the car if you want to, Megan,' Ted assured her as she locked the Ford up in the car park.

'It's fine boss, it's my job. As long as it isn't another snake, I'm sure I'll survive. But thanks.'

'Have a lozenge,' he offered, holding the bag in front of her. He'd already started on his first one, at the mere prospect of what lay ahead.

She shook her head.

'I'm not very keen on them, thanks.'

'I'm not really,' he confessed. 'I just find they help. And they remind me of my dad, so they're comforting in times of stress.'

As they walked across the park, following the directions Sally had given Ted over the phone, they could see that there was a uniformed police presence, as well as RSPCA officers, on site. An area in the trees had been cordoned off with incident tape. Sally saw them coming and walked over to meet them. Ted introduced her to Megan.

'Hi, Ted, thanks for coming so quickly. I phoned the nick to ask for some help to preserve the crime scene, especially in case there was any connection with your enquiry. Luckily it was found by one of the maintenance crew, who called it in straight away, but we have got a rather stroppy Jobsworth Joe Public over there, sticking his neb in.'

She nodded across to where a man in a cap and overcoat was looking across at the crime scene, his brows drawn down in a frown.

'I'm not interested in him for now, unless he was a witness. Tell me what we're dealing with.'

'It's a cat, Ted. Or what's left of one. And I know how you do love your moggies. We will, of course, be scanning for a microchip to see if we can trace an owner to let them know what happened. Naturally, we won't be going into any detail.'

Almost unconsciously, Ted put another lozenge in his mouth, although he hadn't yet finished the first. Then he and Megan followed Sally as she ducked under the tape and led the way into the trees, stopping only to slip on shoe coverings.

Ted had seen some sights in his years in the force. As a former firearms officer, he had witnessed bodies literally ripped apart by high velocity bullets. He knew some officers would have been unmoved at this atrocity because it was a cat, not a human. Not Ted. He loved his cats. They were part of his family. The idea of anyone doing anything like this to them or to any other feline filled him with horror. Megan managed a quick look but then had to excuse herself and turn away.

'Was it alive when ...?'

'We think the skinning was started while it was still alive, yes, going on the amount of blood. The plastic bag would have suffocated it as it struggled and the noose would have eventually strangled it. Sadly not immediately.'

'How sick does someone have to be to do something like that? What are we looking at here, Sally, in your opinion? Some sort of strange Satanic ritual? A cult thing?'

'I've no idea at the moment, Ted. We've not had anything quite like this lot on our patch before, not on this scale, at least, so I'm asking around other areas. The thing which is most worrying is, now we start to check back, we think other, earlier episodes - though nothing like as bad as this - may actually be connected.'

'How far back are we talking about?'

'Again, we're not yet really sure. We could be going back about five years or so. Some of the earliest were so mild in comparison they would have been considered as just random one-offs. Nasty, but sadly, not that unusual in modern life. But this...? This is taking it to a whole different level. That's why I thought you should perhaps look at the scene to see if there are any links to what you're working on. I know the little boy was drowned, but you did ask to be kept informed of any incident in the park.'

Ted was already carefully scrutinising the scene, to see if anything stood out. The ground was wet underfoot, churned up where someone had walked, but probably too soft to hold a good form when it came to footprints. He wasn't taking any chances on missing vital evidence, though. Time to call in Crime Scene Investigators to see if they could find anything which might help.

'Megan, while we're waiting for them to arrive, can you go and find the witness who discovered it and get a full statement, please? Just check what brought him here in the first place. Bit off the beaten track, for a groundsman, I would have thought.'

'He's over by the vehicles. One of my team always has a flask of tea in his van so he's giving him some. He was pretty shaken up, as you can imagine. I'll carry on with photographs for now, but I'll try not to trample over everywhere.'

Ted decided to withdraw a few yards, too. He'd seen more than enough, and there was nothing he could usefully do until the Scene of Crime investigators arrived to do their work. He wasn't sure whether he wanted them to find a link or not. He kept thinking about Jezza's theory of some sort of a challenge circulating on the internet. This one would surely have scored high points.

The man in the cap headed towards him as soon as he reappeared from the comparative darkness of the thick trees and bushes. He was probably in his early seventies, medium height, stockily built and with a bearing which immediately made Ted think he might be ex-forces.

'Have you seen that? Bloody disgusting, it is,' the man said without preamble. 'Wasting police resources, with those officers here, and I'm told it's just some dead cat. Pity they don't put as much time and effort into finding the swine who killed that little boy here last week. No signs of much going on with that, is there?'

Ted sighed to himself as he reached for his warrant card.

'As it happens, Mr…?'

'Sugden. Arthur Sugden.'

'Mr Sugden. I'm DCI Darling, the Senior Investigating Officer on that murder case. I'm here because I've asked to be kept informed of any and all incidents in this park, so it was reported to me by an RSPCA inspector. I can assure you that all available resources are being used on the murder case.'

The man looked him up and down dubiously.

'You're a police officer? You don't look tall enough.'

Sometimes, just sometimes, Ted felt like using his not inconsiderable martial arts skills on the next person who said that to him. Especially on a day like this, having recently seen what he had.

He didn't think the day could get much worse. When he saw a familiar figure striding across the park through the persistent drizzle, he realised it probably just had.

'Hello, Ted, I didn't expect to see you here. I didn't think this was anything for you; just some old dead moggy strung up in a tree.'

Pocket Billiards' annoyingly nasal voice, grating on his nerves, seriously risked being the trigger which pushed Ted beyond his usual polite calm, if anything did. Even with his raincoat on, Ted could see that the reporter's hand was working away at its usual activity. It made him feel slightly more sick, if that were possible.

'There is a little bit more to it than that, Alastair. And as I have just been explaining to Mr Sugden, I have simply asked to be kept informed of anything at all which happens within the park. I would hate you to read – or more importantly, to write –

too much into my presence here.'

He hoped the warning note had not gone unnoticed. He was relieved to see the first of the scientific team starting to arrive already, which gave him a good excuse to move away. As he did so, he heard Sugden turn his attention to the reporter, clearly in his element.

'Are you from the local paper? It's a bloody disgrace. All this for a dead cat, and what are they doing about that little boy, eh?'

In Ted's mind, Capman died a dozen deaths at his hands, none of them pleasant. The name just sprang to his mind for the annoying type in the cap. He realised how much the missing Batman toy was preying on his thoughts. He was particularly annoyed to think that there would undoubtedly be a critical report in the paper, beefed up by quotes from the interfering onlooker. And that meant the Ice Queen would be jumping up and down on Ted, as she would get leapt on from further up the chain of command. He would need to brief her as soon as he could get away. Forewarned was forearmed.

He went over to inform the investigators of what his particular interest was, anxious to know if there was any trace of their perpetrator at the scene. When he'd done that, and had a final word with Sally, he and Megan were ready to leave. There was no sign of the reporter; he'd already gone. Ted decided he'd better give him a call in what he suspected would be a vain attempt at damage limitation. If he did so, he could at least tell the Ice Queen, with a clear conscience, that he had tried.

'Sorry I didn't have time to talk much, Alastair,' he told him as Megan drove them back to the station. 'You know that as soon as I have anything for you, you'll be the first to hear.'

As he ended the call, he said to Megan, 'It's past lunchtime, I suppose, but make sure you take a break.'

'Funnily enough, boss, after that I suspect I've got about as little appetite as you have. That and the snake.' A shudder ran through her body at the memory. 'But that really was

143

something else, back there. It has to rank up there beyond the worst I've seen so far. It's worrying to think we have someone of that mentality working on the patch.'

'Even more so if, as Steve suggested, there may be more than one of them and some sort of sick competition going on.'

Ted was anxious to get his meeting with the Ice Queen over as soon as possible. She was always encouraging him to play nicely with the reporter. Ted hated eating with him at the best of times. If he was forced into inviting him out for a late lunch, after what he'd just witnessed, he doubted he could keep his stomach contents under control. He'd also find time at some point to phone Jim Baker and fill him in. He was answerable to both of them, in different roles. But the Ice Queen first, as she was near enough to breathe down his neck as a physical presence.

'That was an unfortunate coincidence. A tip-off from someone?'

'Certainly not from our side. I got the call directly while I was out interviewing a witness and went straight there, so only Megan and I knew, from our team. Sally had called the station, though, for back-up from Uniform, so I'll have a word with Kevin Turner. Of course, the leak could have come from anywhere. From the RSPCA, from the maintenance crew. Possibly even from the interested bystander at the scene.'

He described for her his meeting with the disgruntled member of the public in the flat cap, mentioning how pleased he had seemed to have a chance to talk to a reporter. It was always possible that he was the one who had called the local press.

'I do wish the public realised that we actually do more than our best on their behalf, given the budgetary restraints we're constantly facing.'

She sighed as she got up and went to her coffee machine, which was always on.

'I know you don't usually like a caffeine hit in the afternoon, but you do look like a man in need of something stronger than green tea.'

Ted smiled to himself. They were slowly becoming easier in each other's company. She had spent much of her early days trying to convince him that she was not his enemy. He doubted they would ever be friends, as he was with Jim, but they were certainly becoming colleagues with a strong mutual respect. Amazingly, it had been to Ted she'd instinctively turned in times of recent trouble in her private life.

He brought her up to speed with all their thinking while they sipped their coffee.

'I know you're doing everything possible, Ted, and I meant what I said about the budget. But, of course, it's only a matter of time before I come under pressure for results, especially from a financial point of view. Keep me up to date with anything you get. It helps me to fight your corner for you, and that's what I'm here for.'

Kevin Turner was also in his office. He seldom escaped the paperwork long enough to get out and about these days. Ted had to wait while he finished chewing the ears off a young officer. He recognised him as the latest new addition to Uniform, Gavin Jackson, when he came scuttling out of the office, looking suitably chastened.

'Honestly, don't they teach them to write these days, Ted? What use to me is a report which is barely above text speak. Tea?'

Ted shook his head as he sat down.

'I've just taken coffee with She Who Must Be Obeyed. Something of a pre-emptive strike in case my loathsome news-hound so-called friend drops me right in it with his latest piece.'

He told Kevin about his morning visit to the park. He spared him the worst of the details, just painted a broad brush-stroke of what he'd seen.

'Jesus Christ, Ted, you don't think there is any connection between all these cases? Mind you, which is worse? One seriously sick killer, or a bunch of them, working in competition with one another? I'll remind all of my officers yet again about confidentiality. Most of them know already, but I'll just mark all of their cards one more time.'

Ted found himself looking forward to spending the evening with Bizzie. He suspected she was as lonely as he currently was. Her ancient faithful canine companion had recently, as she'd told him, crossed the Rainbow Bridge. He'd thought it strange, coming from a woman of science. But he knew how devastated he and Trev always were at the loss of any of their cats.

He'd made time to go and see to his feline family before he went off to Davenport, where Bizzie lived. He seemed to be doing nothing but apologising to the cats for how little time he was currently managing to spend with them.

He fed them all, cleaned out litter trays, made a fuss of each in turn, talking to them all as he worked. Each got an extra cuddle, after what Ted had witnessed earlier. He often wondered what the team would think of him if they could see him asking the cats' advice.

'I'm sorry I have to go out again, boys and girls, but I really need to go and talk to Bizzie. Do you want me to leave the telly on for you? I could find a foreign film, like you watch with Trev. Freddie, what do you think? Mercury, don't get in the sink, please, I don't really want wet paws all over everywhere. Try to behave while I'm out. I'll leave a light on for you. Queen, you're in charge.'

He decided to walk down to Davenport. It wouldn't take him long and he was in need of some brisk exercise. He phoned Bizzie to let her know roughly what time he would get there. When she opened the door, he thrust a bottle of wine at her. He was a non-drinker but had chosen something he knew

Trev liked so he hoped it would do.

Bizzie was wearing what looked like some sort of shapeless tracksuit, underneath a blue and white striped apron. There were good smells coming from the kitchen.

'Ah, Edwin, thank you so much, that's delightful. Please do come in. I'm just endeavouring not to incinerate our supper. You'd think that with a Cambridge degree I should be able to follow simple instructions on the packet of a ready meal, but I'm afraid it's always rather hit and miss. I thought, as it's just the two of us and rather informal, that we could eat in the breakfast room, if you wouldn't mind?'

Bizzie's house was large, rambling over several storeys, with cellars underneath. It was one of the few in the road not yet converted into multi-occupancy flats. Ted would have been quite happy to eat in the kitchen, which was about twice the size of his.

For a ready meal, the food was excellent and came with side dishes and dessert. Bizzie opened the wine Ted had brought and looked set to finish the bottle. She'd bought sparkling apple juice for Ted, remembering his preference.

Ted desperately wanted to pick her brains about his current cases but was polite enough to wait until after the cheese board. He refused the offer of coffee, which would leave him too wide awake late at night. He wanted to be able to stay awake until Trev phoned, but needed to be certain of getting some sleep after that.

'You've considered the sexual aspect, of course?' Bizzie asked him, without preamble. 'As pathologists, we occasionally find evidence of killers masturbating on their victims. Not to mention occasional cases of necrophilia. And of course, you know only too well that there are killers who like to strike at the point of ejaculation.'

Ted did indeed know that, from a past case, one which had cost the life of an excellent officer on his team.

'The torture element, if that is connected to your killings, might well suggest that. There are those who find death and everything about it highly sexually stimulating.'

Ted thought about her words as he walked briskly home through the still, damp night air. If she was right, the case was taking on an even more disturbing aspect. He fervently hoped that she was wrong.

There were three youths waiting to cross the A6 at the same pedestrian lights Ted had chosen. His trained eyes automatically gave them the once-over. Two white, one black, ranging in height from tall and lanky to about his own height. All were wearing sweat tops with hoods up, with baggy pants and trainers.

'Got the time, mate?' one of them asked Ted.

The oldest trick in the book. Ted didn't always wear a wristwatch. If he had been wearing one with a metal bracelet, it might have saved his wrist and arm from serious recent injury, grappling with a knife-wielding sex attacker. He would certainly not have revealed it if he had one. Nor did he get his mobile phone out to check the time. Much as he hated to pre-judge, the first rule of self defence was always to avoid putting oneself in danger.

'Sorry, I've not got the time on me, but it's about half twelve, I think. Haven't you got mobiles?'

The light had changed to green and the four of them crossed the road together.

'Don't carry them, with what we do,' the middle-sized youth who had spoken told him. Seeing Ted's querying look, he grinned as he said, 'Freerunners, mate. Rule number one – don't carry anything on you that might injure you if you fall on it.'

Ted smiled as they jogged off in the opposite direction to the one he was taking. He knew Kevin Turner's officers fought a constant battle with the freerunners, who used any building and obstacle they could for their training. Members of the public were always phoning up to complain about them. Ted preferred them to be doing any kind of disciplined sport rather than getting up to the sort of things he had seen earlier in the day.

He decided to wait up for Trev's call, so he could spend a bit of time with the cats. He put a news channel on and sank into the sofa, his body immediately occupied by purring, kneading felines, glad of his attention at last.

When it came, his contact from Trev was a text, not the hoped-for phone call.

'Gone to a pargyhu won't phone. Is billirant. a abit pisse3d Talknm tomorrrow. Love you lotsxx Tx xcxx'

He chuckled at all the typos, which took him a moment to figure out, although he got the gist of it. But he was glad his partner was out partying and clearly having fun, even if he missed the chance to talk to him. He was pleased there were only three more days to go before he would see him again.

# Chapter Sixteen

'Well, it could have been worse,' the Ice Queen said in her most encouraging voice.

Ted didn't really see how, but he was grateful for her efforts to lift morale.

The two of them had arrived in the car park first thing, both early as usual. She had suggested they go straight to her office to check the local news website together to see what, if anything, the local reporter had made of yesterday's events.

Mincemeat, was Ted's impression. It stopped short of a total hatchet job, but it was a critical piece, beefed up with the anticipated quotes from the busybody bystander, enjoying his moment of glory. There were also rather more graphic details than either of them would have preferred from the council workman who found the scene.

Ted was mentioned by name, with heavy emphasis on him being the SIO on the murder case, from which he had apparently taken time out to investigate the death of a cat. Pocket Billiards hadn't approached him directly for a quote but had instead quoted him third hand, with the witness saying he'd been assured that all available resources were being used to find the little boy's killer.

'It's something and nothing really,' she continued.

Ted wondered which of them she was trying to convince. It was not what he needed at the best of times, and certainly not nearly two weeks into a murder enquiry with not a lot to show for it.

'You'll just have to butter him up a bit more. Perhaps buy

him a drink to thank him for a moderate article. We really do need to keep him on side as much as we can.'

Ted decided the remark on the tip of his tongue about putting powdered glass in the reporter's lager top might not be well received. Instead he made noises of assent without much conviction about them, then went upstairs to see the team for morning briefing.

He ran through with them the details of what he and Megan had seen the previous day, without going into too much detail. He was quick to stress that he was not yet connecting the different cases, still at the stage of looking at the similarities.

'Steve, this internet competition idea. Has it got legs or is it as far-fetched as it sounds?'

'For the killings, I'm not yet sure, sir, I'm still looking into it. For the animal abuse, sadly, it is a possibility. There are some very sick groups out there, even on moderate social media sites like Facebook. They soon get reported and taken down, but they often start up again quite quickly in a new guise.

'There is one way I would be able to find if there's a local link, but that would require me having access to the RSPCA photos of the animal victims. Then I could check to see if any photos similar to those had ever appeared anywhere on the internet.'

'They're not pleasant,' Ted warned.

'I appreciate that, sir, but surely it would be better to rule this line of enquiry out as soon as possible, if it's not relevant? And I could do that fairly quickly, with access to the photos.'

Ted had never heard him so assertive, certainly not in a team meeting before. He was pleased. He'd always had high hopes for Steve, if he could overcome his timidity. It seemed as if he was doing so.

'I'll get them forwarded to you for checking. I'm sure I don't need to say it, but they're not for general consumption. Your eyes only for now.'

Ted spoke to the team at length about Professor Nelson's theories on a possible sexual motive for the animal torture and, by implication, if the cases were connected, for the killings. He was hoping he might have results from Forensics before much longer on anything from either scene. They had details of the footprints from the Tyler Bradbury case but it hadn't yet advanced them far. A top-selling branded trainer, marketed simply as a youths' style. Depending on its colour, it could well have been worn by a male or a female.

'Boss, do you want me to carry on with the Luke Martin case for now?' Jezza asked him.

'Yes, definitely. I'm just bracing myself for the next round of accusations that we didn't do enough with that case. I don't want anyone thinking we value the life of a black teenager any less than that of a little white boy. We all know that's not true. Incidentally, I'll just pass on from the Super that she acknowledges that we're doing all we can with the ongoing cases. She just, naturally, wants us to do a bit more.'

Ted was planning a full briefing for Monday morning, if they didn't have any kind of a breakthrough over the weekend. He wanted to widen the range of house-to-house enquiries and was going to draw up a new list of questions to be asked. He planned to talk to Kevin Turner later in the day, and to get him, some of his officers and some of the PCSOs to attend on Monday. It was high time to take the investigation up to another level.

'Is it worth trying another reconstruction on the Luke Martin case?' Jezza suggested. 'I know it produced nothing last time, but perhaps memories may just be jogged. If nothing else, it would show we're still working on it. And what about a reconstruction on the Tyler case?'

'That would be tricky to do. We don't know enough of the circumstances to make it accurate. We don't know at what point Tyler ran into his killer. If we just show a little boy on his own running across the park, it might be completely the wrong image. It's something to keep in mind if we keep coming up blank, though.

'Jo, I'm leaving you pretty much in charge of South Manchester for now. Shout whenever you need more bodies on that. And I really want to know what happened to the missing purse. I know we've searched everywhere for it, but let's search some more. I'm not dismissing Jezza's trophy theory yet.

'Mike, CCTV from further afield, for the Tyler case. And before you ask, no, I don't know who or what we're looking for. Just get anything available gone through meticulously. Anything at all unusual, no matter how seemingly insignificant, flag it up and let's check it out. Jo, same for South Manchester, please.

'Right, family and friends. You all know that murder by complete strangers is comparatively rare. There's usually a link to someone known to the victim. Maurice, you help with the digging on that. Start with a deeper background check on the mother and all her known associates than we've done before.'

Tyler's mother was not a suspect. But the team knew all too well that there had been cases where a spurned lover decided to exact the ultimate revenge by taking the one thing that was precious beyond measure to their former partner. It was an extreme theory for a motive, but they had all heard ones even more far-fetched.

'Rob, I'm putting you in charge of that for the Tyler case. Anyone and everyone with knowledge of the little lad to be checked out thoroughly, please. Jo, the same for South Manchester. And Rob, first job for you is to check out the girlfriend of Max Newman, the school bully. Take someone with you.'

Seeing the anxious look on Megan Jennings' face, he said reassuringly, 'You're excused, Megan, just in case she's another snake charmer. Rob, ask Inspector Turner if you can borrow one of his officers. If at all possible, I would like a sample of the nail varnish the girl wears for comparison to the trace that was found in the scratch on Tyler's body. See if she'll agree voluntarily. If not, we'll need to look at bringing her in and making it a bit more formal.

'Let's hope this is the day for some real progress. Whatever happens, we'll be raising a glass to Virgil and his wife, and Daisy May, after work.'

Back in his office, armed with green tea, Ted set about trying to pull together everything they had so far, which didn't amount to much in any of the ongoing cases. So often in modern policing, CCTV provided the first lead, but they had nothing at all for Tyler or Luke, and what they did have for the South Manchester case hadn't proved to be of much use. That and the lack of a vehicle in any of the cases. Sometimes a random sighting of a number plate on CCTV footage started the ball rolling.

His office door opened and Kevin Turner came in, clutching an evidence bag which he tossed on to the desk in front of Ted with something of a triumphant gesture. Kevin didn't often venture upstairs. There were days he barely got out of his office.

'A friend of yours, I think, Ted,' he said, taking a seat. 'One of my officers found it just now and brought it straight in.'

Inside the bag was the missing flying Batman toy, slotted into the launcher and all ready for its next flight.

'It was found not far from the mangled moggy scene. I'd flagged it up as of importance which was why it arrived back here pronto. And yes, I will have a brew while I'm up here, just none of your foul green stuff.'

Ted was so absorbed with looking at Batman through the clear plastic that he hadn't even offered.

'Teeth marks, you see? Sharp teeth, like a dog. Bobby the dog was right when he was helping me.'

Ted looked up over the top of his reading glasses and saw the look Kevin was giving him. He laughed.

'Sorry, I was getting a bit carried away there. One brew coming up. But this is an important advance. I'll need to speak to the officer who found it for full details and a report.'

Kevin grunted towards Ted's turned back as he went to brew up for his visitor.

'Good luck with that. It was young Gavin, so don't be surprised if his report contains a few "soz" and even a "LOL" or two. But at least he found it and had the gumption to bring it straight in. He's trying very hard to redeem himself and win a few Brownie points off me.'

Ted handed him his drink and sat back down opposite him. It was a good chance to update him on the various theories they were turning over, and to fix up the expanded briefing for Monday morning.

Ted's desk phone interrupted them. Kevin took the opportunity to stand up to leave as they were about done. Watching Ted's face react to what he was hearing, he picked up the evidence bag and waved it in front of him. Ted understood the message and nodded his thanks, leaving Kevin to send it off to forensics for him.

'Ted? Bill,' the familiar voice of the sergeant on the front desk. 'I have Luke Martin's parents here. They're insisting on seeing you. Won't take no for an answer. As you can imagine, they've seen Pocket Billiards' latest piece of slander and they're not happy.'

He was speaking quietly, although Ted knew he would have positioned himself so the visitors couldn't hear what he was saying. Ted groaned to himself. He should have seen this one coming. He had been promising the couple for two years now that he wouldn't rest until he had justice for them and their son. Reading that he'd been spending his time investigating dead cats would inevitably have been upsetting for them.

He went down to the front desk himself. He wouldn't dream of delegating the task. He asked Bill to find someone to arrange drinks for them and led them through to a vacant interview room.

The couple seemed to have aged since he saw them last. Mr Martin had more grey hair than Ted remembered, and his wife was looking ten years older than her actual age. They had been to hell and back, and their journey was not yet over.

They had always been a reserved and dignified couple, tender and supportive to one another. They were staunch churchgoers and their faith seemed to have been some sort of comfort to them through their ordeal.

Ted couldn't begin to imagine how upsetting the news article had been for them. Despite it, they remained calm and polite. It was Mr Martin who spoke, his tone patient and reasonable.

'Inspector Darling, I must say at the outset that you have always treated us with kindness and compassion, and we've never lost our faith in you. You've always said that you would find whoever killed our boy and we have always believed you and trusted you. But this, Inspector. This. Is it true that you've been dealing with the case of a dead cat, whilst our boy's killer is still out there, free?'

Ted measured his words carefully before he said anything. He knew that this interview could go badly wrong if he didn't, with potentially disastrous consequences. He didn't want to be delivering platitudes but at the moment, that was about all he had. Above all, he was anxious to reassure the parents that he and the team worked to the maximum on all cases. None was given more attention than any other.

'Mr and Mrs Martin, I've just come from a team briefing. I have new members on my team now, ones who were not here at the time of Luke's death, so they're looking over the case with fresh eyes in the hopes of uncovering any angle which we have not yet explored.

'Your son's case is still very much open and we're still doing, and will continue to do, everything in our power for all of you.'

The boy's father looked intently at Ted who held his gaze unflinchingly. Whatever he saw in Ted's hazel eyes appeared to satisfy him, for now.

'Thank you, Inspector. Please rest assured that my wife and I have no intention of going to the papers. Our private life has already been picked over far too much in the media in the wake of Luke's death. We have no wish to throw any more fuel on that particular fire.'

When Ted went back upstairs, he found a nervous-looking PC Gavin Jackson lurking about outside his office, clearly waiting for him.

'Sir, Inspector Turner said you wanted to speak to me and I should come and find you.'

'Yes, thank you, Gavin, come in and take a seat.'

The young officer looked surprised. He had clearly expected to be left standing to attention in front of the senior officer. Almost everyone in the station was taller than Ted so he liked to make it less obvious by having them sit in his presence when he could.

'I believe you found Batman. Well done for that, and for bringing him straight in. Can you tell me where and how you found him?'

'It was about fifty metres from where the cat was, sir. Further on, in some more dense undergrowth. We'd been asked to help search for anything, and I found the toy.'

'Tell me exactly how you found it. By that, I mean what position was it in? What was the first thought that came into your head when you saw it?'

The young PC hesitated, clearly thrown by the question.

'You're my eyes on the scene, Gavin. I wasn't there to see it for myself, so I need you to talk me through it. Don't worry about how it sounds, just tell me what you saw and what you thought. You already know I work in some eccentric ways.'

'Well, sir,' he was still hesitant, but Ted nodded

encouragingly. 'It was propped up against the stump of a tree. It looked as if it had been put there like that for some special reason. I don't know ...'

He shook his head, but Ted encouraged him to continue.

'I know it sounds daft, sir, but it reminded me of a religious statue. Propped up against an altar.'

He was fishing for his mobile phone as he spoke. He scrolled swiftly and skilfully through its contents then held the screen up towards Ted.

'I took some photos of it, sir, and the area where it was, before I touched it. I'm sorry, should I have left it there and called you to see it?'

Ted took one of his cards out and slid it across the desk to him.

'You did absolutely the right thing, Gavin. Good work. Can you send copies of all the photos you took to my mobile. I agree with you. It makes me think of some sort of shrine. Just one more question. Is there any chance, do you think, that it could have ended up in that position if an animal, say a fox, or a dog, had been carrying it and had dropped it?'

'No, sir, not at all. It was sort of pushed a bit into the soil to make it stand up straight. It couldn't have been like that by accident, I don't think.'

'Excellent work, Gavin. Now, footprints?'

The young man's face regained its earlier anxiety as he admitted, 'Sorry, sir, I wasn't thinking about that. I just walked in and picked it up, in a bag so as not to contaminate it.'

'Don't worry, everything else you've done has been exemplary. We can work round that. Right, I'll need to get Forensics over there sharpish to see what they can uncover. So can you make yourself available to show them where you found it?'

By the time he'd wrapped up all the loose ends, Ted felt he'd made a bit of progress, at least. After taking the time for a quick drink with the team and with Virgil, who popped in to show his face, he was once again late home and facing a chorus of reproach from the cats. He'd picked up a takeaway, too tired to think of cooking, but that would have to wait until they were all seen to and settled down for the evening.

He hoped Trev would call rather than text. He wouldn't talk about work with him but it would be nice to hear his voice at the end of another long and testing day.

He realised he'd actually nodded off in front of the news channel when his ringtone jerked him awake.

'Hey, you,' Trev's warm voice was just the balm he needed. 'How was your day?'

'Oh, you know, same old policeman stuff. I bet yours was more fun. Tell me.'

'Mine? You'd hate it! Sunshine, parties, wine. I won't have time to phone tomorrow. There's a massive wrap party and I intend to make the most of it. But I'll see you on Sunday, and I can't wait.'

'What time are you flying back?'

Nothing so mundane as a scheduled flight for the fashionistas Trev was with. They were travelling in a chartered jet.

'I'll let you know as soon as I know. See you soon. Love you.'

# Chapter Seventeen

'Right, everyone, listen up.'

It was how Ted often started his morning briefings. This time, the expectant faces looking up at him were all feline. Blue, amber and green eyes studied him in fascination. The reason for their rapt attention was that he was busy opening sachets of gourmet cat food which smelt tasty, even to him, and putting the contents into six clean bowls.

'I'm going to be out all day today and I might be late home again. So here's some special treats for breakfast, and I'll leave you plenty of crunchies. Look, Roger, trout and sardine. That's your favourite, isn't it?'

Sapphire eyes looked in disdain from the dish to Ted, the chocolate-coloured nose and dark-tipped cream whiskers twitching in disgust.

Ted sighed.

'No? Well, it was last week. There's plenty for everyone so just sort it out between you. I promise I'll be home early tomorrow because Trev's coming home and I want to get the house looking ship-shape. Then we'll all be all right again. Everything will be back to normal.'

Ted intended to spend a chunk of his day at his desk once more. But first, he planned on revisiting the scenes of all the current crimes they were investigating, including the historical arson, in case there did turn out to be a link.

He'd been back to Hallam's Passage countless times since Luke Martin's tragic death there. There was nothing to see.

Nothing to mark the spot where a bright and talented young man had lost his life. Often Ted would walk the length of the curving passage, with its high, red brick walls, as if he could somehow absorb something, some tiny grain of a clue, by his mere presence. But there was nothing, and never had been. Officers had done a painstaking fingertip search the entire length of the passage and the surrounding roads, but they had not uncovered a single item to advance the enquiry.

Ted went first to the park where, at his request, the area where the Batman toy had been found was still taped off. It wouldn't keep the curious out, but at least it made it easier for him to identify the place where PC Jackson had found it.

The forensic team had been all over the site, on Ted's instructions, taking casts of any footprints, collecting soil samples for analysis to allow for cross-checking between sites. There was no need for Ted to cover up; it no longer mattered if he contaminated the scene. He simply ducked under the tape and made his way into the trees. He couldn't resist a glance round the park first, half expecting to see the same nosy man in a cap. It was still early and still drizzling. Only a few hardy souls were out and about. A couple of dog walkers, some younger teenagers on bikes, a solitary jogger.

Using the photos Gavin had forwarded to him, Ted was easily able to find the exact spot where the toy had stood, in front of an old and partially rotten tree stump. The indentation in the soil and leaf mould was still distinct. He could clearly see what Gavin had been getting at. It was almost as if the tiny clearing had become a shrine to something.

The most important thing Ted needed to know now was when did Batman reach his final resting place? Was he left there the day of Tyler's death, put there by the killer in some macabre ritual? Or was it more recent than that? The day of the cat's death? And if so, did that point to a connection between the two cases? Was Tyler's killer also the animal torturer?

The fact that Batman was attached to his launcher when

found suggested a direct connection to Tyler. From his own experience of playing around with the toy, Ted found he had kept the launcher in his hand whenever he went after Batman. So had whoever left Batman here taken the launcher out of the boy's hand, and had Tyler been alive or dead at that point?

It wasn't far to walk from where he was across the park to Shadwell Drive, where the arson incident had occurred. That death had not been treated as a murder. In the absence of evidence indicating intention on the part of whoever had put the firework through the letterbox to harm the person inside, rather than to cause some degree of criminal damage, the inquest jury had returned an open verdict.

Ted didn't know himself if he suspected a link between the arson and the other cases. It was just one more incident in the same area that he wanted to check out for himself once again. After four years, clearly there were no remaining traces of what had happened at the small mid-terraced house. There were certainly no gnomes gracing the front garden now. Much of it had been covered over with tarmac to provide additional parking, with just a narrow border round the edge.

There was nothing to see, as he'd expected. All the visit told him was that it was not far across the park to where Tyler had died, to where the cat had been so brutally killed, and to where Batman had been found. He added to his mental list the need to find out who lived in the road and get someone to do some digging into their backgrounds.

He drove via Heaviley on his way up to South Manchester, for another walk along Hallam's Passage and back. It wouldn't achieve anything, he knew, but at least it made him feel as if he was doing something. They had nothing from forensics, no CCTV, no sightings of a vehicle they could check out. None of their usual informants had heard anything. It was as if the killer had simply been walking past, decided to strike, then gone on their way unconcerned. Their only new lead to date had been Jezza picking up that the bridge was not with the other parts of the smashed violin, and had not been found in the search of the surrounding area. Was that now lying in some other sanctum somewhere? And how could they begin to find out if a gnome had been taken from the garden where the arson took place?

Ted remained convinced that it had been one person working alone who had killed Luke Martin. From experience, he doubted if, had there been more than one person involved, it could have been kept quiet for two years. Someone would have said something to someone else. A loose tongue was about the only way they were going to make much progress on the case.

Jo was up at South Manchester. He was in the office with DC Graham Winters when Ted arrived there. Leona was out chasing up leads. The teams in both stations were working longer hours, staggering their days off, if they got one at all. Ted hadn't asked them to. They'd all offered, all of them as stung as he was by the implied criticism in the press that they were not putting equal effort into every case. The Ice Queen was still being supportive over the budget and the extra hours. There was no guarantee that it would last, before the money managers higher up started to make noises.

'Why haven't we found the purse yet, Jo? Most snatchers just keep the contents then throw the bag or the purse away. Get rid of the evidence. So why hasn't it turned up? Were the litter bins searched?'

Jo had gone over the case notes so he had the answer to most questions off pat.

'Not all of them in town, boss, clearly, and not the ones close to. The killer legged it away pretty sharpish, so they weren't going to stop to do that. But Uniform have poked and prodded into every nook and cranny they could in the direction the suspect ran off in. Are you still thinking of Jezza's trophy theory? We could circulate a description of it, see if it turns up?

And does that mean you are now thinking of a link between the cases?'

'I still don't know what I'm thinking at the moment, to be honest. I don't want to make a thing of it yet, in case there is a link and it alerts our killer that we're on to them. Ask Leona and the team to come to the Monday morning expanded briefing and we'll at least float the idea of a link, see if it advances us any. I'm going to go through all the witness statements myself one more time. There must be something we're missing. I'll see you on Monday.'

If Ted was hoping for a lightning strike of inspiration from studying the files, he was out of luck. All he could do was to compile endless lists of what still needed checking and draw up a plan of action for Monday morning's briefing. Jim Baker was going to be in attendance, just in case there was a link and they could possibly be looking at a serial killer, which would come under his remit.

He'd warned the cats he might be late and he was, by the time he'd finished. Another rushed takeaway, another evening of nodding off in front of the news. At least this was going to be his last night on his own. Trev would be back tomorrow and, whatever happened, Ted was determined to get back from another trip in to work in good time to make sure the house was clean and welcoming, pick up his mother's culinary contribution, and make a pudding himself. He just prayed there would be nothing to interfere with his plans.

Trev had clearly enjoyed his party as there was no word from him on Saturday. Ted had hoped for just a brief text, but he heard nothing until mid-morning on the Sunday, when he was at his desk; a quick call to let him know when they would be leaving, and a promise to message him as soon as they landed at Manchester Airport.

Once he'd done as much as he could at work, Ted called in

at a supermarket for the ingredients to make a pudding, plus a single red rose, his special gesture, a nod to his favourite film, *Blazing Saddles*. Then he made a quick trip to his mother's to pick up their evening meal.

'Do give Trevor my love, won't you? You're so lucky, Teddy *bach*, to have found yourself such a lovely young man. The two of you always seem so happy together.'

Ted thanked her for the meal, gave her a brief peck on the cheek, promised to spend more time with her soon, and drove home to start attacking the cat hair with the vacuum cleaner.

The cats could sense his barely-concealed anticipation, prowling round, investigating whatever he did. He issued a stern warning when he'd finished.

'I want it to look nice when Trev gets back, you lot. So no dragging in dead animals, or throwing up fur balls or anything, all right? And be careful where you flick the litter. I don't want that all over the floor, thank you.'

Once he got the text that they were clear of Manchester airport and on their way, Ted couldn't even sit down with his mounting excitement at seeing his partner again. He felt like a teenager and laughed ironically at himself. He had a ridiculous notion that everything, including his current cases, would be so much better once Trev was home. He knew he relied on him too much, but couldn't help himself.

Willow and Rupert would be dropping him off and Ted had to fight the urge to stand at the window, waiting for the sight of Rupert's sleek, low, black sports car purring down the cul-de-sac in which Ted and Trev lived.

He was in the kitchen, fussing once more over the table setting, when the doorbell rang. He wondered why Trev hadn't simply used his key to let himself in. Perhaps it was at the bottom of his bag and not accessible.

For a brief moment, his heart jolted painfully in his chest when he opened the front door and saw Willow standing there, alone, Rupert still at the wheel of the car in the road. Then Willow's face broke into a wide smile as she said, 'Special delivery for Ted Darling,' and Trev burst into view from round the corner of the small porch where he had been concealing himself.

'Hey, you,' he said, as he engulfed Ted in a bear hug which threatened to crack his ribs.

He looked more stunning than usual, incredibly tanned, still dressed for Mediterranean weather in a collarless linen shirt and cropped trousers, his bare, brown feet in leather sandals.

As soon as Ted could pull free enough to remember his manners, he invited Willow and Rupert in for a drink, or at least a cup of tea, before they went on their way, but she laughed off the suggestion.

'Honestly, Ted, it's so sweet of you but we've had to put up with Trev pining and drooling about you all week. You seriously don't want the two of us cramping your style.'

'I do not drool! I admit to the pining, but that's all.'

She kissed them both, waved away Trev's effusive thanks, but promised to take him up on his offer of cooking them both a meal before too long.

Rupert, at the wheel of the black car, had his eyes hidden behind mirrored sunglasses and looked more like a gangster or a drug dealer than a male model. The policeman in Ted couldn't help but wonder what the neighbours would think.

The car had barely purred its way out of sight before Trev shut the door and grinned provocatively at his partner.

'I've had the most amazing time. But I can't begin to tell you how much I've missed you. So I guess I'll just have to show you.'

He was already peeling off his shirt as he started up the stairs, two at a time. His sandals, crops and underpants followed shortly, dropped in a negligent trail as he made his way to the bedroom. Ted followed him without need of persuasion. Even he resisted the urge to stop and tidy up his partner's clothes on the way.

'Oh, my God, look at you,' Ted said admiringly, as Trev did a shameless twirl. 'You're bronzed all over, no white bits at all.'

Trev laughed delightedly.

'Oh, Ted, stop being a boring old fart. I've been to the south of France, living on a yacht. You know, skinny dipping, nude sunbathing, wild parties. All the things you'd curl up and die if I did when you were with me. So, are you just going to stand there admiring the tan, or are you going to show me how much you've missed me?

Afterwards, as they lay back, damp with perspiration, breathing and heart rates slowly coming back down to normal, Trev put an arm round Ted and pulled him closer.

'So tell me how you've been getting on. Have you caught the bad guys yet?'

'Not yet, but we're still trying,' Ted said evasively. He didn't want to break the mood. He wasn't keen on talking about his work with Trev. He certainly had no intention of telling him about the RSPCA case he'd been called to. He just hoped his partner didn't look on the local news website for any reason and see the story there. 'I can't get over how good you look with an all-over tan. You must have put some of the models to shame.'

Trev laughed delightedly.

'Well, Laurence did include me in some of the shots, but only in the background, as scenery,' he said, pronouncing the name with a flawless French accent.

Ted turned his head and looked at him quizzically.

'Laurence?'

'One of the photographers on the shoot. We got on really well. It was one of those "you couldn't make it up" things. We've lived in some of the same cities and it turned out we'd even been to a couple of the same international schools, though not at the same time. We're going to keep in touch.

'But now, I want to go and take a long shower, after just now, and travelling before it. And we're both going to be in deep trouble with the cats, especially as you shut the bedroom door in their faces and I haven't even said hello to them yet.'

'I'll go and sort out the supper. My mother made you that chicken in cider you like. It'll be ready when you are. And I've made a pudding. No idea if it's any good, though.'

Trev stretched like a contented cat.

'I couldn't have had a nicer homecoming. I'll be down in a minute.'

Ted picked up his partner's clothes and sandals on his way down the stairs, put the footwear neatly in the hall and collected his travel hold-all. He might as well put a wash on while he waited to eat supper. Despite the all-over suntan, he was still surprised by how few clothes Trev had got through in ten days, knowing how fastidious he was about his appearance.

As soon as he heard Trev finish in the shower, he had the meal plated up and ready, which earned him another hug.

'I've had an amazing time, but it really is nice to be back to being spoilt rotten. Yes, hello, you lot, I'll give you all a proper cuddle later but I'm starving now,' he told the cats.

They were busy swarming round his legs, backs arched, upright tails twitching, purring loudly. Trev was the one who usually fed them and spent time with them. They clearly considered Ted a poor substitute.

They'd just finished the first course when Trev's mobile rang. He looked at the screen and smiled.

'It's Laurence. Sorry, do you mind if I take it?'

When Ted nodded, he picked up the call, his voice warm and affectionate as he began, '*Salut, toi,*' which Ted understood, but after that it was just a stream of rapid-fire French which went right over his head.

*He stood up to clear the plates and produce the pudding he had so lovingly prepared. It suddenly seemed inadequate.*

*'Oui, oui, toi aussi, gros bisous, bye-bye, ciao,'* Trev ended

*the call with a lot of kissy sounds then looked apologetic. 'So sorry about that. Wow! Is this syllabub? And did you make it? That's so sweet.'*

'I remembered you'd ordered it when we went out for a meal one time, so I thought I'd have a go. I used apple juice instead of wine, so I can have some. It's probably not very good, though.'

Trev took a big spoonful, savoured, then swallowed it, his eyes rolling in appreciation.

'Oh yes, that is seriously good. Yes, yes, yes...'

He threw his head back as he went into an Oscar-winning performance of the famous scene from *When Harry Met Sally*.

Ted laughed, in spite of himself. Despite thinking he was sharing the meal, the moment, and his partner with Laurence.

# Chapter Eighteen

They were using the large ground-floor conference room for the Monday morning briefing. With so many extra officers attending from across the various branches of the enquiry, it was the only room with space enough to accommodate them all.

Both the Ice Queen and Jim Baker were present, as well as Kevin Turner and some of his officers, but it was Ted's baby. He was in charge. For once, he wasn't perching on a desk but standing in front of the white boards which displayed all the details they needed for the briefing.

One of the forensics officers was present. Ted hadn't yet had chance to catch up with the scene of crime reports. The lab had been working flat out all weekend on the samples from where the cat was found, and from the clearing in the woods where Batman had ended his days.

Ted singled him out to begin. Depending on what his team had uncovered, the forensic evidence could alter the way the briefing needed to go.

'Doug, thanks for coming. What have you got for us?'

'Well, you already know that the footprints from by the river where the boy was found are a youths' trainer, size 33 European. The prints were not good where the cat was found; it was wet underfoot and they didn't hold their shape well. However, we are confident they were left by the same type of shoe and the same size.

'We can't tell you if the same person was involved, just that the shoe size and type is the same. And that soil analysis indicates that the same shoes were worn at the cat site and where the toy was found. From the shoe size and the depth of the imprints, we believe that the wearer was small and slight, not weighing very much. We can also tell you that they are left-handed and a County supporter.'

Seeing the looks of disapproval from all the senior officers present, he went on hastily, 'Sorry, that's just dark forensic humour. Totally inappropriate and I apologise.'

'All right, we all have different ways of dealing with difficult cases, but let's please all remember why we're here. Take a good look at the photo on the board. That is Tyler Bradbury. A little boy who should have been starting school later this year, and no doubt getting up to all the stuff small boys do. He won't now,' Ted reminded them.

Suitably chastened, Doug continued, 'I brought a pair of the exact make of trainers in question, which we used for comparison. We've finished with them now, so I thought they might help. They're marketed as unisex, so I suppose it would depend on the colour whether a lad or a girl would wear them. Just a note which might be useful to the enquiry. They're high end, pricey, and in that size, according to my missus, who knows about these things, you won't find them in your average shop. At best they could order them in for you. We bought online but again, not all the stockists we looked at had them in; they were sometimes a special order.'

He took a pair of white trainers out of a carrier bag and passed them over to Ted who held them aloft for everyone to see.

'They definitely look a bit girlie in white, boss. I'd never get Felix to wear those. But in a different colour, red, maybe, I could see him wanting a pair. It is just possible they could be worn by a woman, an adult. I have a friend who takes that size, even though she's quite generously proportioned everywhere else, apart from her feet and hands. She's not tall, either.'

'Thanks, Megan, that's helpful. It does mean we're probably

still none the wiser about the gender of our killer, or their age, it seems. At least not from their shoes. But it looks probable that our killer is also the animal abuser, at least in the last case, and was involved in putting Batman where he was found. The fact that Batman was back on his launcher when found does suggest contact with Tyler. It's likely that he was holding the launcher, after Batman had flown off out of the garden. But I must stress that's only conjecture.

'Doug, are you able to tell us how long the toy was there?'

'We would date the footprints where it was found to between twenty-four and thirty-six hours, but that's not exact. So, more recently than Tyler's death, and seeming to coincide with the cat killing.'

'Thank you. Right, this is probably the moment to get Jezza to mention again her theory of a trophy killer, and also the possibility – slight at this stage – of a link to the Luke Martin case. Jezza.'

Jezza laid out her theory, succinctly and factually. She mentioned the fact that the missing violin bridge had been overlooked at the time of the initial investigation, without hinting at blame. The team had been busy enough looking for what items they could find, not concerning themselves with what might be missing from the scene.

'So that's the interest in finding the purse in our case, boss?' Leona asked. 'You think there's a possibility of a link, of another trophy taken?'

'It is only a possibility at this stage. I can't stress that enough. So what did the search of Jake Dolan's house reveal? For those not yet up to speed with all the details, Jake was our first possible suspect for that case, from a phone tip-off. You've got all the info in the hand-outs, to catch up on.'

'Nothing more than a bit of skunk, boss. Not even enough to make an issue of. Definitely personal use quantity, unless you want me to take it further? But no signs of a purse or anything else untoward. Wherever he keeps the drugs he sells, it's certainly not at his place. And his feet are too big to fit our killer's prints. We checked out all his shoes.'

'Thank you. Maurice, talk to us about garden gnomes.'

Maurice first briefly outlined the circumstances of the arson attack and its proximity to the park.

'There are plenty of photos of the garden after the fire, and you can see a load of gnomes in the front garden. There was no inventory or anything taken of them; they weren't seen as significant.

'But boss, can I just say, if it's a youth we're looking for, and there is a connection to the animal abuse cases, going from the notes you circulated, they must have been very young at the time those started happening, surely? Possibly even at the time of the arson case.'

'There may well be no connection. It's just worth flagging the arson up as a case which was never solved, and it is near to the park, which is also where the animal abuse has taken place. And there is the slight possibility that a trophy may have been taken from the arson site. I admit it is only a tentative link at this stage. But I wouldn't let age put us off. We all know that juveniles have been responsible for some dreadful things in recent years.

'Right, Rob, how did you get on with Max Newman's girlfriend? Again, if you're not up to speed yet, Newman was flagged up as bullying younger children at his school so he was worth checking out in connection with Tyler. His feet are also too big for the footprints at the scene, but he does have a girlfriend, who's a Goth or an Emo who possibly wears purple nail varnish, and a trace of something similar was found on Tyler's body.'

'I went to see her, boss. First off, she's a tall, rather lanky girl with big feet. Her main interest in Max Newman seems to be his pet snake, and that's not a euphemism. She loves reptiles, but her parents won't let her have one of her own. She was pleasant, cooperative. Happy to give us a sample of her nail varnish, which I've sent off to the lab. I don't know if there are any results yet?'

'We've been going full throttle all weekend,' Doug responded to the question. 'As far as I know, no, not yet, but hopefully shortly.'

'Fair enough. But in any event, she has a watertight alibi for the day Tyler died. She was on a field trip with the school.

'As regards friends and family, boss, we've got a lead on a former boyfriend of Tyler's mother, from a while back, but we haven't yet had time to go and find him. Peter Harrison. He has form.'

'We certainly know him, if it's the one I'm thinking of,' Kevin Turner put in. 'Decidedly dodgy. Buys and sells anything, no questions asked. He's got form for assault, too, but mostly drunken pub brawls, as far as I remember. But he is a nasty piece. I could see him going after the little lad just to spite the mother, if he felt she'd treated him badly. As I remember him, though, he's a big bloke. It couldn't be his footprints we have, unless he has a small accomplice. A kid of his own, perhaps.'

'I'll make it a priority today to track him down and talk to him, boss.'

'Good, thank you. Now, back to the animal abuse cases. Steve, what have you found out from the various groups online?'

Even with his new-found self-assurance, Steve went slightly pink in the presence of so many people, particularly the senior officers. But he presented his findings clearly, and his voice was audible to all.

'I can't find any trace of photos of the latest incident appearing online anywhere. I've also searched on other, previous images, and for anything coinciding with any of the dates the RSPCA gave us. Nothing. So either our animal torturer doesn't share their images with anyone, or they're posting them somewhere I haven't yet found. But I will carry on looking.'

'Thank you, Steve. Now, if anyone has anything else, anything at all, do feel free to chip in. We need ideas from all of you. Don't, whatever you do, think your idea, or the information you've come across, is too far-fetched to be relevant. I hope you all know by now that I'm approachable. If it's something you don't want to raise in a public briefing, please feel free to come and talk to me in private. Someone, somewhere, knows who's behind these crimes. So let's find them and get some justice for the families.'

Jim joined Ted for a drink after the briefing. If there was a definite link between the cases, they would come under his remit, as overall head of Serious and Serial Crimes.

'I know you're as on top of it as you can be, at this stage, Ted. But don't be afraid to ask for help if you need it. I'm with Debs on this one. To hell with the budget. Let's get the bastards behind these cases off the streets. Leave her and me to worry about the costs and face the consequences.'

Another frustrating day of pen-pushing followed for Ted. Even with the support of both his senior officers, he still needed to balance the books and the hours. More so, with no suspects in sight. They were the ones who would have to justify the budget. They relied on him to keep the books in order to allow them to do so.

It was late afternoon when Mike Hallam stuck his head round the door to ask, 'Do you want to come and look at something on the CCTV, boss? It may be entirely unrelated, but I'd like to see what you think of it.'

Sal and Océane were at their desks, working together on the Sabden House enquiry once more. There was still a long way to go on the paperwork with that one, in order to present CPS with a hopefully watertight case. Jezza had just come back in and was settling at her desk to write up notes of her day so far. Jo was still up at South Manchester, so Ted and Mike had the old Big Boss's office to themselves.

'What am I looking at?' Ted asked, as he sat down in front of the screen.

'This is from earlier in the day of the cat incident, boss,' Mike told him as he started the footage.

It was grainy and indistinct, but Ted could see a solitary figure walking along a road near some shops. It wasn't possible to tell if it was male or female because their hood was up, effectively masking their face. Their hands were stuffed into the kangaroo pockets of a hoody, and they appeared to be wearing tracksuit bottoms with it. The baggy clothes rendered the figure genderless.

'Hempshaw Lane?'

'Yes, boss. Whoever it is is walking down from the Offerton Fold direction. Like I said, it may be unrelated. But they don't look very big, and it is the day of the cat incident.'

He ran it again, at Ted's request. It was no clearer the second time. It had been a damp and dismal sort of day so there was nothing strange in someone walking along with their hood up and their head down.

'Let's get Jezza in, see what she thinks. See whether she reckons it's male or female, for a start. She has a good eye for that. Without saying anything first, of course.'

Mike went to the door and called her in, telling her simply that he needed her to view some CCTV footage. She went to stand behind the boss, leaning over his shoulder to look at the screen, the tall figure of Mike Hallam looming over both of them.

Jezza asked to see it through three times before she gave her verdict.

'Honest answer? I just can't be sure if that figure is male or female. I'm still convinced the South Manchester one is a girl but this time I can't be certain. Slouching along like that it's hard to tell. Sorry.'

'That's fine, Jezza, I appreciate you being candid. No point in guesswork.'

Jezza went back to her own desk to finish up as Mike asked, 'Are we going to release it, boss? Perhaps say we think it's someone who was a witness to something and ask them to come forward, or anyone who knows who it is.'

'I'm not sure at this stage whether it would help or hinder. If it is our cat killer and they did also kill Tyler, we risk pushing them underground if they know we're looking for them. I'll sleep on it, then I'll talk to the Super and the Big Boss before I decide.'

Ted had sent a text to warn Trev that he might well be late back and not to wait to eat if he was hungry. When he got back, his partner was ironing the few holiday clothes he had worn, which Ted had washed for him, in front of the television. He had his mobile phone tucked between his shoulder and his ear. The conversation was in French, so Ted couldn't follow it, but it sounded intimate, and there was a lot of laughter going on.

He wound it up as soon as Ted came home, with a few blown kisses, then turned to exchange a kiss with his partner.

'Laurence?' Ted asked, careful to keep his tone neutral.

'Laurence, officer, good bit of detection,' Trev laughed as he put the phone down. 'How was your day? Are you hungry? It won't take me a minute to heat yours up, whenever you're ready to eat.'

Ted sank gratefully onto the sofa, yanking his tie loose and undoing his top shirt button. He knew it was a mistake. As soon as he got comfortable, the cats swarmed over him, purring and treading with their paws and he knew that, if he so much as closed his eyes, he could happily doze off.

'It's been frustrating. I've not made the progress I would have liked. I'll perhaps have a quick shower and get changed then eat, if that's okay? Have you eaten?'

Trev was about to answer when his mobile phone rang.

'Hi, Shewee,' he greeted his younger sister, Siobhan, by her school nickname. 'To what do I owe the honour?'

Ted could only hear one side of the conversation. He had no reason not to listen, trying to fill in the blanks.

'Of course you can come and visit. You're welcome any time, you know that. As long as you're not nicking off school.'

'Friday evening should be fine. I'll cook. Ted will try to be here, but you know there's no guarantee with his job.'

He was looking towards his partner for confirmation and Ted nodded in agreement.

'How are you travelling? Do you want picking up from somewhere?'

'You have a boyfriend? Do the Olds know? With his own car? How old is he? What happened to concentrating on the eventing team?'

'You do know Ted will have him arrested if he drives irresponsibly, and I will karate kick the crap out of him if he messes about with you in any way?'

There was a much longer pause while he was clearly listening to reassurances from his much younger sister.

'All right, just take care and don't let him drive too fast. Text me on the way, to let us know when to expect you. *Bisous, frangine.*'

He was laughing as he rang off.

'Well, that's a surprise. Kid sister has landed herself a moneyed boyfriend, double-barrelled, no less, although she insists they're just friends. He's invited her up to his parents' place near Prestbury for the weekend, so she wants to bring him here first, to show him off, I imagine. They've got eventers and polo ponies and all sorts, so she's going to be playing some polo.'

'He's going to think we live in a garden shed, if they live out Prestbury way,' Ted commented, looking round their modest home. 'What's a *frangine*?'

'It's a bit like sis. Shewee speaks fluent French, too, she spent some time living with the Olds in Paris. Are you all right with them coming to visit? You will try and get home in time, won't you?'

'If I remotely can, I will, but you know what it's like. Right, quick shower and change, then I'll eat something, but I think I'm definitely ready for an early night.'

'That sounds good to me.'


The insistent muted buzzing of his mobile phone, moving about and lighting up on his bedside table, woke Ted. The screen display showed him it was shortly after one in the morning. It didn't feel long since he'd gone to sleep. He took the call, speaking quietly, although he knew it would take nothing short of an explosion to wake Trev once he was sound asleep.

'Sorry to disturb you, sir, but we have a nasty one for you. Not far for you to go, at least. A woman's been killed in her house on Hillcrest Road. The teenage daughter apparently walked in on the attacker, who then knocked her out, bundled her into a car and took her hostage. She managed to get away and sound the alarm, so we sent a team round to the house and found the mother dead in the kitchen. Bludgeoned to death with a hammer, from the early reports at the scene. The daughter's been taken to hospital with a head wound, but it doesn't sound too serious. She was conscious and lucid, just very shaken.'

The duty sergeant gave Ted the house number. It was within walking distance but he decided to take the car as he would have to go straight in to the station from there to get things under way. He would have preferred to throw on some casual clothes but, as he had no idea when he would get chance to come back to the house to change, he reluctantly opted for his suit. He stuffed his tie in his pocket for now so he could at least put it on before he crossed the Ice Queen's path.

He phoned Jo and Mike next, giving them the address and asking them to join him at the scene as soon as they could. Once he'd assessed what they were dealing with, he'd decide who else to call in.

He checked his pockets carefully to make sure he had his lozenges. A murder such as the sergeant had described was not going to be a pretty sight.

# Chapter Nineteen

There was already a uniformed presence at the crime scene when Ted arrived, and the Scene of Crime team members were just setting up. Two PCs were taping off the area in front of the house, a neat and well-presented detached property. A few lights had gone on in neighbouring houses and curious faces were peering out of windows. One or two souls had braved the chilly night air and were in their front gardens, craning for a look at what was going on, alerted by the flashing blue lights of the police vehicles.

A taxi was just pulling up and Ted saw Professor Nelson climb out, pausing to pay the driver. He went across to greet her, surprised she had not come in her own car.

'Morning, Edwin. I'd had rather a generous nightcap just before the call came in so I thought it prudent not to risk an encounter with any vigilant officers on the prowl. Don't worry, though, I am more than capable of doing my job.'

Ted never doubted it for a moment. She was a competent and meticulous forensic pathologist with years of experience. Even with slightly too much good single malt inside her to pass a breath test, she was still the best person for the task ahead, one he could always rely on. She would be in charge of the crime scene from the beginning. It would be her decision as to when the body could be removed, but it would not be until she had found out everything she could on initial examination.

Ted left her to make a start. He would go in when she told him he could. It worked better that way if space was limited. In the meantime, he went in search of the first responding officers for all the background he could get. As soon as Jo and Mike arrived, he'd get them to start talking to the inquisitive neighbours, to see if anyone had seen anything. He knew there was no point sending Mike into the house. His DS had some excellent qualities, but a strong stomach was not one of them. And from the sounds of it, this crime scene risked being a messy one.

'Tell me what you know so far,' he asked the two PCs who had been the first on the scene, once he had located them.

'The call came in just after midnight, sir,' one of them began.

'Exact timings, please,' Ted interrupted him, but staying polite, as ever.

'Sorry, sir,' the constable consulted his notes before continuing. 'Seven minutes past midnight. A young girl, sounding hysterical, then she handed the phone over to an adult who was with her. She'd been found at the side of a road near Marple, with a head wound, and with her hands tied with cable ties. She said someone had broken into the house and killed her mother, then abducted her.'

He gave Ted the exact location where the girl had been found, before continuing with his account.

'We came straight round, sir. The front door was closed and there was no reply when we rang, knocked and shouted through the letter box. There was a light on at the back of the house, but no others showing. In the circumstances, we decided we needed to get in, so we managed to squeeze down the side of the garage by climbing on the fence. The back door was ajar and we could see someone lying on the floor in a pool of blood. I went in, to check for signs of life, but there weren't any, so we called it in and secured the scene.'

'Do we have an ID yet?'

'A Mrs Edwards, sir. The daughter is called Morgane. She's been taken to hospital but as far as I know, her head wound isn't serious.'

'Thank you. You'll need to get the rear taped off as well, in case anyone came in that way, and include some of the field at the back. Make sure you liaise with the investigators about your own footprints and DNA on site but well done, you did a good job.'

Jo and Mike had just arrived, from different directions, each in their own car. More lights were starting to go on and more interested faces were appearing at windows and front doors. Ted briefed them both on what he knew so far.

'Make a start with anyone nearby, find out who saw what, if anything. Get some of the uniformed officers on to it, too. Let's get all the information we can while it's still fresh in people's minds. From what the first responders have said, it's possible that the killer got in through the back door. There's a field behind and I think some of these houses may have garden gates which open on to it.

'I don't have any more details yet, but if the girl was found up near Marple, as I was told, there must be a vehicle involved. Mike, you're excused going inside, but make sorting out any CCTV a priority, please. Anything from the front here, but also round the back. That means Broadway, Parndon Drive, Morton Walk, if any of that is covered. Get someone round there as soon as possible, see if there's anyone about to ask if they saw anything. And check on coverage between here and where she was found, up Marple Old Road, near the junction of Marple Road and Torkington Road.

'Clearly someone will need to talk to the daughter as soon as possible. I'll phone the hospital and ask to be kept informed. I want to know who's with her, who's the next of kin. They'll need to ID the body, of course, poor sod. Oh, and I'll also want to listen to that 999 call, to hear exactly what was said.'

Jo and Mike nodded and got to work. There wasn't a lot Ted could do immediately, while he waited for the all-clear to go inside. He wasn't kept waiting too long before one of the crime scene officers, fully suited up and masked, came to the front door and called quietly to him, 'The Professor says you can come in now,' handing him coveralls at the door.

The suits were always too large for Ted's stature, making him feel like a small boy dressing up in his dad's clothes. Once he was fully covered, so he didn't transfer any of his own DNA to the crime scene, he made his way to the kitchen at the back of the house, already sucking greedily on the first of his menthol lozenges.

He paused in the open doorway, looking carefully round the room to take in the scene. As he had feared, it was not pretty. There was a fair amount of blood, on the floor and splashed on the kitchen cupboards and work surfaces. Ted's keen eyes noticed immediately that there were a lot of footprints, the blood trail trampled about, going through into the hall.

Bizzie Nelson was bending over the body of a woman which lay on the floor. Ted could see that there were extensive injuries to her head. A hammer, already in an evidence bag, was sitting in the middle of the table.

'There's your murder weapon. Our killer conveniently left it for you. Numerous blows to the head. I'll be able to give you chapter and verse on them from the post-mortem findings, but that might have to wait until Wednesday morning. We're backed up with the multiple fatality crash from the ring-road. Part of the reason I was paranoid about not driving, after dealing with the shocking aftermath of a drunken driver.'

'It looks like there's been an awful lot of to-ing and fro-ing in here.'

'I noticed that immediately. But I would imagine that whoever found her like this may well have panicked. I heard it was the teenage daughter, and that she was abducted?'

'That's the initial information we have, but none of it is confirmed yet. She's been taken to hospital with a head wound. I'm going to phone to see when I can talk to her. Clearly, the sooner I can do that the better.'

'We'll need her DNA, of course, as soon as possible, to help us untangle the crime scene and its secrets. I can already tell you that the body was moved. You can see that the wounds are principally, but not exclusively, towards the back of the head, so the victim was facing away from her killer. Over there is where the initial attack took place, but this is where she was found.'

'Moved rather than crawled?'

'Oh, I think so, definitely. The traces here in the blood would tend to suggest she was pulled along the floor. There's no sign of her having moved by herself. And over there, on the edge of that work surface, there's a bit of blood and some hair traces. The surface looks like granite, so it would be quite hard to impact against. There are some blonde hairs sticking there which, at a first superficial glance, are too light and too long to belong to the deceased. Possibly the origin of the daughter's head wound?'

'It goes without saying that I need every inch of the house and garden gone over with a fine- tooth comb, but I know you and the team will be on it thoroughly. I'll go for a mooch round outside, see what Jo and Mike have found so far. Call me if there's anything else of interest.'

'Hand your overalls in before you disappear, please,' the investigator who had let him in told him, although he knew there was no need. Ted knew the overalls he'd worn would have to be checked to see if he'd picked up any vital evidence and that if he needed to come back in, it would be in a clean set.

In the end, Ted decided it would probably be as quick to drive round to the hospital for news of the daughter's condition than to waste time phoning. If it was a busy night, there'd be no one free to talk to him and if he happened to land on a Jobsworth, he could spend precious, frustrating minutes getting nowhere fast. At least in person - even if, at his size, he didn't look particularly impressive - he could wave his badge.

He parked his car, put the Police sign on the dashboard, and headed for A&E. Even at this hour of the morning, there were plenty of people waiting. A young woman was staffing the reception desk and phones. Her smile was welcoming enough, even when Ted produced his card.

'DCI Darling. I'm enquiring about a Morgane Edwards who was brought in earlier with a head injury. It's in connection with a police enquiry.'

'Darling?' she smiled. 'That must cause you a few problems. Oh, I'm sorry, that was a bit tactless. Morgane has been taken through to cubicles to be examined. I'll see what I can find out for you. That's her father, over there; he's also waiting for news.'

Ted looked in the direction she was indicating and saw a man who looked to be in his early forties, shifting impatiently in his seat, constantly crossing and recrossing his legs and glancing up at any sign of movement. He was solidly built. Ted thought he wouldn't look out of place on a local rugby team.

'Is there somewhere I could have a quiet word with him, while we're waiting for news?'

'Yes, you could take him to the relatives' room. I'll make sure someone knows where to find you. I think it's free at the moment.'

Ted went across to the man, still holding his warrant card, which he showed him discreetly, not wanting to draw attention to either of them or to the reason for their presence there.

'I wondered if we could have a quiet word, please, Mr Edwards? They know at reception where to find us, so they'll come and let you know as soon as there's any news of your daughter.'

Ted led the way to the relatives' room. He'd had to use it on various occasions in the past, so he knew where it was. He stood aside to usher the man in, then invited him to take a seat.

'First of all, I'm very sorry about your wife.'

'Ex-wife,' the man corrected him automatically. He looked shell-shocked, clearly unable to take everything in.

'I apologise, we don't yet have much information. So, does your daughter live with her mother?'

The man nodded then said, 'I don't even know how she is. I only saw her very briefly when they brought her in. She looked awful. A lot of blood...'

'Please try not to worry, Mr Edwards, although I know it's hard. They do know where we are and someone will come and find us as soon as there's any news.

'So did your ex-wife work? What did she do for a living?'

'She's ... she was a solicitor. Criminal law. You've probably seen her in court, or maybe at the police station.'

Ted frowned. The name meant nothing to him and he hadn't been able to recognise the battered figure he'd seen at the house.

'She went back to her maiden name. Mason. Stephanie Mason. Morgane is Edwards.'

Someone had got their wires crossed early on, Ted thought to himself. He'd need to update the whole team with the correct information. He also made a mental note that they would need to look into the possibility of any disgruntled clients, ones the victim hadn't managed to save from a conviction, especially from a custodial sentence. He did remember her. A formidable defence solicitor with a good reputation for winning tricky cases.

'I'm sorry to sound as if I'm prying, but I do need to know facts as soon as possible in the enquiry, to have the best chance of getting justice for you, for Morgane and for your ex-wife. Was she involved with anyone else, since the divorce? A new partner, anyone she was seeing?'

The man shook his head wearily. He looked utterly bewildered by everything which was going on, a reaction Ted had seen so often in his career.

'Tell me about your daughter. What age is she? Still at

school?'

Edwards nodded. For a moment he smiled with pride.

'She's sixteen. Doing really well at school. She's very good at art and design. Hoping to go on to Loughborough.'

'And what about friends? Boyfriends? Who does she spend her time with?'

A noise like a derisive snort.

'I can tell you don't have a teenage daughter, Inspector. She doesn't tell her dad that sort of thing. There is a boy she's friendly with, she told me, but it's mainly because he has a snake and it really fascinates her. The colours and textures, she says. She's drawn it, based a piece around it. But why are you asking about Morgane? She's the victim here, as much as Stephanie.'

'It's often helpful to form a picture of people connected to the victims in some way. Cases like this involving total strangers are comparatively rare, so we would always begin by looking at anyone in the immediate circle of family and friends. Can you remember the name of the boy with the snake?'

He shook his head, looking completely overwhelmed.

'Not really. Mark? Matt? Max? Something like that.'

At that moment, there was a brief knock on the door and a nurse came in.

'Mr Edwards? We've finished with Morgane for now and she's asking for you. She seems to be fine but we're going to keep her in for a few hours yet, just to monitor her condition. That's routine with a head injury, so try not to worry too much. If you'd like to come with me, I'll take you to her. Just you at the moment, I'm afraid,' she added to Ted.

The man leapt to his feet in evident relief. Ted rose as well and handed him one of his cards.

'We will, of course, need to talk to Morgane as soon as possible. And we'll need her clothes, please, for forensic examination. Will you be taking her home with you when she's discharged?'

When he nodded, Ted went on, 'Then please let me know as soon as we can come and talk to her. The sooner she can tell us everything she can remember, the more helpful it will be to the enquiry.'

Ted's mobile beeped to announce a text message as he was walking back to his car. He was surprised to see from the screen that it was already gone eight o'clock. He realised he was feeling hungry and looking forward to a cup of tea, as soon as he could lay his hands on one. The text was from Trev.

'Wow! Just saw it on the news. Nice neighbours we have. You ok? Go catch the bad guys! Txx'

Ted reached his car and slid into the driver's seat. He decided to give Trev a quick ring.

'I'm just taking five minutes so I thought I'd call. It's a grim one. I've no idea what time I'll get home tonight. I'll text you when I know. Sorry.'

'Don't be daft. It's your job. I understand that. I'll see you when I see you. Just take care of yourself.'

'We're all right, aren't we?'

'Of course we're all right. Silly sod. Go get the baddies. Love you.'

Ted decided to call at a café on the way back to pick up hot drinks and bacon rolls for himself, Jo and Mike. They'd done nearly a full day's work already and there was still a lot of ground to cover. At some point, they needed to get back to the station and bring the rest of the team up to date. Ted had already phoned Rob O'Connell to put him in charge until they got back. He also called Jim Baker to fill him in.

'Anything so far to link it to any of the other cases?'

'Nothing concrete yet. Just a slim coincidence in that she apparently knocks around with the lad with the snake sometimes, her father told me. I haven't been able to interview the daughter yet. They're keeping her in hospital for now, to make sure she's all right. The father will phone me as soon as she's released, then I'll go round there and get a statement from her, see what that throws up.'

He phoned Mike before he left the café, to let him know he had breakfast for all of them, suggesting they walk down the road and meet him in Broadway for a short break. He didn't want them to be sitting in front of the house munching bacon rolls. It wouldn't give a good impression and he didn't want any more bad publicity. He guessed, from what Trev had said, that the press pack would be there already.

Mike arrived first. He'd been doing door to door, talking to anyone he could find, asking standard questions, taking notes. No one he had come across had seen anything at all suspicious, but he had mostly been speaking to people who lived on Hillcrest Road itself. If the killer had come in the back way, across the field, they could conceivably have passed unnoticed. Mike hadn't gone round that way onto the field itself, not wanting to trample where the attacker might have walked before the investigators had had a chance to check for footprints.

Jo came slightly later. He'd been helping to coordinate the search of the house, so he would have had to change out of coveralls before leaving the scene. He opened the rear door, slid on to the back seat and gratefully accepted the cardboard cup of hot coffee and the delicious-smelling roll, oozing grease through its paper bag, which the boss handed to him, between the two front seats.

'Marvellous, boss, thanks. My belly thinks my throat's cut, despite looking at all the gore in there. You did well to avoid that, Mike. Oh, and boss, I have something for you in return.'

He pulled a clear plastic evidence bag out of his coat pocket and passed it to Ted with the triumphant air of a magician who'd just found the correct card.

Ted looked at it, then looked at Jo, who nodded.

'Yes, boss, I think you'll find that that's the bridge off a violin. It was propped up on a bookcase in the lounge back there. Looking for all the world like a trophy on display.'

# Chapter Twenty

Ted decided to leave his car where it was for now and walk back to the house. He wanted to touch base before leaving Jo to manage the crime scene. He and Mike would go back to the station to brief the rest of the team.

As he walked the short distance, he saw a familiar, unwelcome figure lurking about amongst the small crowd of onlookers and cameras standing near the taped-off area, craning his neck to see what was going on.

'I wonder if I can arrest our favourite news-hound for being in possession of offensive teeth?' he joked quietly to the other two, then forced a smile as he said aloud, 'Alastair, fancy seeing you here.'

'Morning, Ted. You're on this case, then? Not been called away to deal with any dead bunny rabbits or poorly parrots?'

Ted gritted his teeth at the inappropriate humour, but there were too many people about for him to risk the response he felt like giving.

'I'm SIO on this case, Alastair, and it's receiving my undivided attention, like all my cases. Now, I'm just off back to the station, where I'll see to it that you're the first to get a press release on this. In the meantime, if you have any questions, I'll leave you in the capable hands of DI Rodriguez.'

He knew Jo would be more than a match for the reporter. He went to the front door once more and asked for Professor Nelson to come out to him, to save him dressing up again. He asked her to keep him posted on when the body was being removed, and when the post-mortem would be. He could have sent Jo to that, as he was currently managing the crime scene, but he preferred to take it himself.

'I'm leaving Jo Rodriguez in charge here for now, so if there's anything you need, he's your man.'

'I do like your gold-toothed friend. So very charming.'

Ted chuckled to himself as he walked back to the car. He wondered if there was any woman anywhere that Jo wouldn't try flirting with. He'd probably made the Professor's day, coming on to her. Ted was one of the few people who knew that the inspector with the wolfish smile, which revealed the gilded tooth, was all talk and definitely no action, thanks to a feisty Spanish wife who ruled the roost at home.

Ted had arranged to talk to the Ice Queen after the briefing, and Jim Baker would be coming over to sit in on both meetings, then to catch up with Ted afterwards. The way this case was going, they were going to need to expand the team, so Ted was anxious to talk to both his senior officers, the purse-string holders.

'Right, we now have our first possible link to the Luke Martin case,' he told his team, at the start of the morning briefing.

He held up the bagged violin bridge found at the scene, which he would be sending off to the lab shortly. He wasn't sure if the forensics team would be able to match it exactly to the violin, but he hoped they would get something from it which would be of use to them.

'This does give more weight to Jezza's trophy killer theory. Jo found it on a bookcase at the Hillcrest Road crime scene. You'll get the photos of it *in situ*, but he did say it was on display there, rather like a trophy. So it is just possible that the killer brought it with him to leave at the scene. We shouldn't overlook the outside chance that it was already there, for some reason; also that it's not connected to the case in any way. It might not be the same one, but it is a coincidence and I don't like coincidences.'

'Steve, I want you to continue trying to find out anything you can online about trophy killers and their motivation, particularly those who take something from one scene and leave it at another. Now, there's something of a time-lag here, if it was our killer who left it. They've had it for two years before they left it somewhere. Is that unusual?

'Maurice, anything at all in the files you've been looking at, on people who do that kind of thing? Let's check if there's anyone on our patch with form for doing something similar. Any cases where something was taken from the scene and never found? I want it all recorded and flagged up.

'As soon as I get word that she's fit to interview, I want to go and talk to the daughter in this case, obviously. She might have vital information for us. Megan, I might need you with me on that one, please.'

He mentioned the possible link to Max Newman, the owner of the snake. It was an angle that would need investigating.

'Rob, what news of this ex of Tyler's mother? Have you tracked him down yet?'

'Yes and no, boss. I know where he is. He's in Germany, working, and has been for the past year, from the information I have so far. I've got a phone number for where he's supposed to be working, so I'll give them a call and hope I can manage to find someone who can *sprechen Englisch*, as those are about the only two words I know.'

'If you get stuck, Trev's German is fluent and he'd be happy to help. It would save me a few quid on the budget that way, too.

'For now, we need to continue to treat each case as a separate entity, while keeping in mind the possible link. We're going to need extra bodies, though, and that's one thing I want to talk to the Big Boss and the Super about. I'll go and do that now, unless anyone else has got anything, so you know where to find me, if you need me urgently.

'Just a timely reminder to everyone, though. Check and

double check everything, please. We nearly got off to a false start this morning because someone had assumed that a mother would automatically have the same surname as her daughter. Of course, that's not always the case.'

As they headed downstairs together, Jim told Ted, 'You're going to need more manpower on this, clearly. You can't run four separate enquiries yourself; it's not humanly possible. And if they are connected, you still need more bodies. I'll come over and base myself here for a bit. Then I can at least man the fort and run the paperwork while you do the legwork.'

'I can handle it,' Ted said, sounding stubborn.

'Ted, you're not Superman. You don't wear your bloody pants outside your trousers. Accept some help, before you're forced to do so from higher up than me.'

'I do want an FLO on the case though, as soon as possible. Can you get me one?'

A Family Liaison Officer could work with Morgane and her father to deal with what they'd been through, and might help the daughter to remember details she may have suppressed. They were also trained in helping to manage the press intrusion that would inevitably follow a case which was bound to attract a lot of publicity.

'I've got the perfect person for you, and I happen to know she's just finished a big case, so she's free. DC Kate Jones. She'll be ideal for this. A good officer and a mother of two. I'll make the call.'

He was still on his mobile phone as the two of them went into the Ice Queen's office. As they sat down, she got up to serve coffee.

'Right, you'll have Kate tomorrow morning by ten, when she should have finished writing up her reports on the previous case. Just let me know what other reinforcements you need and I'll sort them. Morning, Debs; sorry, I should have said that first.'

Jim took the seat she indicated, the chair creaking in protest as he lowered his bulk onto it, and gratefully accepted the coffee she placed in front of him.

Ted quickly went over what he'd already told the team, then Jim joined in.

'This is either Serious or Serial or both, so without wanting to tread on anyone's toes, I'm planning to install myself here for the foreseeable. Ted thinks it means I don't trust him,' he said with a sideways glance at his colleague and friend, 'but in fact it's because I trust him too much. I know he'll work himself into the ground if I don't keep an eye on him.'

'Quite so.'

Ted looked from one to the other of his senior officers, as they seemed intent on discussing him as if he wasn't there.

'I am here, you know.'

'And you must realise we're both responsible for your welfare, as you are for your team's. I can see you're itching to get back to your enquiry, so Jim and I will talk budgets and leave you to it.'

'I'll be happy to use a corner of the desk in your little cubby hole, Ted. No need to turf anyone out to make room for me. You won't even know I'm there.'

Ted was anxious to speak to the uniformed officers who had attended the scene where Morgane Edwards had been found. He'd phoned Kevin earlier to ask to see them when he'd finished morning briefing. Kevin had kept them back for him, writing up their reports of the incident, so it was fresh in their minds when they spoke to Ted.

He knew both of them to be experienced officers who would give him all the details he needed without any omissions or oversights. The more senior of the two did most of the talking, her partner just adding the odd detail or clarification as she spoke.

'The call came in at seven minutes past midnight. A young girl, who identified herself as Morgane Edwards, Morgane with an E, said her mother had been murdered at their house in Hillcrest Road. She quickly became hysterical, so the phone was taken by a person who was helping her, a Mr Taylor, who gave us the address where they were.

'One unit was despatched to Hillcrest Road; Karen and I went to the house in Marple Old Road. Mr Taylor let us in. His wife was looking after a young girl who was bleeding from a head wound. She was still slightly hysterical and just kept repeating that a youth had broken into the house and killed her mother with a hammer. She said he'd thrown her against a work surface, where she injured her head, then had forced her to go with him to a car across the other side of the field at the back of the house. She said she'd managed to jump out of the car and run away.

'Mr and Mrs Taylor had already gone to bed when she turned up. It seems they'd left a light on by accident, which is what Morgane saw. They were woken up by someone ringing the bell on their front gate and screaming for help. Mr Taylor went out and found Morgane in the lane outside, clearly distressed. Her hands were tied in front of her with cable ties. He helped her into the house and called his wife, who came to help.'

'What happened to the cable ties?'

'Mr Taylor cut them off with a pair of kitchen scissors and yes, sir. We did think to recover them. We bagged them and brought them in.'

Ted heaved a silent sigh of relief. There could be valuable DNA on the ties, hopefully from their killer. They'd need a sample from the good Samaritan who had taken the girl in, to eliminate him, as he'd handled them.

'Thanks, Tricia. Sorry to interrupt your flow.'

'We didn't try to question Morgane too much. She was really too shaken up and we didn't want to press her until she'd been seen by a doctor, not with a head wound. We just got her to confirm what she'd said on the phone. She did tell us that she managed to jump out of the car at the lights by Seventeen Windows where the traffic was on stop. She said she ran up Marple Old Road and shouted for help at the first house where she saw a light on. Mr Taylor had already called an ambulance, which arrived not long after we did and took Morgane to hospital. She gave us her father's number so we could contact him. He said he'd go straight to the hospital.

'We got statements from both Mr and Mrs Taylor, and we also spoke to some of the neighbours who had come out to see what the commotion was about. The elderly lady next door confirmed having heard someone screaming outside but admitted she was too frightened to do anything. She saw the Taylors helping Morgane into their house, but that was all.'

'Did anyone see or hear another person, or a vehicle or anything?'

'Nothing, sir. We did ask everyone. It is one way, of course, so if Morgane ran up from the lights, the car would have had to do a U-ey then either chase her the wrong way up the road, or drive round to the top end, by which time she would probably have been safely in the house.'

'Excellent work, thanks, both of you. Just one small detail. The mother wasn't called Edwards. She was Stephanie Mason. Somewhere along the line, we got the wrong info to start with.'

His next job was to listen to the original 999 call. Transcripts and second-hand testimony could only tell him so much. He needed to hear it for himself, to listen for any tiny nuance, each little hesitation, which might indicate something to him.

He listened to it three times in succession. It appeared to be nothing more than what he had been told. A young girl's voice, sounding frightened, confused and hysterical. Asked which service she wanted, in response to her call, she started gabbling frantically.

'Oh, God, I don't know. Police! No, ambulance! Both of them! Somebody help me, please. He's killed my mum.'

The operator's voice; calm, professional. Asking her to slow down and give her name and address.

'I'm Morgane Edwards. Morgane with an E. Please help me! Someone broke into the house. He's battered my mum to death. Then he abducted me, in his car. I managed to escape.'

The operator again, still patient and reassuring, asking for the address.

'Mum's house is in Hillcrest Road. I'm ... oh God, I don't even know where I am.'

There were muffled sounds as the phone was clearly passed to someone else. Then a man's voice, speaking in an even tone, without panic.

'We're in Marple Old Road. Morgane turned up outside our gate just now, tied up. She has a head wound which is bleeding heavily so we will need an ambulance, please, urgently, and whatever you need to send to her mother's house.'

Ted could hear an exchange in the background, the man asking the girl for more details. Then he came back on the line and gave exact addresses for both properties, with clear instructions of how to find his house.

The operator asked the man to stay on the line while she put him through to ambulance control. Another calm voice took over, asking him questions about the girl's condition and making suggestions of what to do whilst he waited for the ambulance to arrive. They stayed on the line with him until he announced that the ambulance was there.

Nothing untoward there. Nothing other than what he would have expected to hear. But it was always worth checking out for himself. He headed back upstairs to his office, which now felt even smaller than usual with Jim Baker installed at a corner of the desk. Ted was starting to feel like a man who'd been on duty since one o'clock in the morning and it was barely lunchtime yet. He was in urgent needed of a brew.

'Kettle's just boiled,' Jim told him, clearly having read his mind. 'I'll leave you to make your own green gunge. I've no idea how you like that stuff. I don't even know how you can drink it.'

He gave Ted a searching look and asked, 'You look knackered. Have you eaten yet?'

'I had a bacon roll and a coffee earlier on.'

'Well, you and I will take a stroll round to The Grapes together as soon as we get a moment. Get some proper scran inside you. You're no use to the enquiry if you keel over. And before you start to protest, that's not a suggestion.'

'Jo and Mike have been on duty as long as I have.'

'Yes, but it's you shouldering the responsibility. The three of you need to make sure you get away at a decent time today; get plenty of rest to come back at it fresh tomorrow. We've made Rob up to DS so he can sub for Mike when necessary. And if you think I'm not capable of doubling for you and Jo then I might just be offended. So, what have you got on that's going to stop you taking a bit of time to catch up on sleep and come back looking slightly more human tomorrow?'

'I want to interview the daughter as soon as she's released from hospital. The earlier we get her statement, the sooner we can crack on.'

'If she's being kept in hospital after a head injury, you won't get to interview her today. Next?'

'I'm just waiting to hear when Bizzie Nelson can do the PM ...'

As if on cue, his mobile phone rang and it was the Professor.

'Your victim is on her way now, Edwin, but as I said, I can't fit her in today. It will have to be first thing in the morning. Are you still coming yourself?'

'By first thing, you mean...?'

'Six o'clock sharp, if that suits you?'

Ted groaned inwardly but readily agreed.

'That was Bizzie. The PM is early doors tomorrow. Six o'clock.'

'Right, so as soon as you know when you can interview the girl, you can go and get some rest.'

In fact it was much later in the afternoon before Ted got the call from Morgane Edwards' father to say that she was going to be discharged. He asked if, in the circumstances, Ted could delay visiting her until the following morning as she was still shaky and looked as if she just needed a good night's sleep. The father didn't sound too clever himself, but he mentioned he'd been called to the hospital mortuary to formally identify his ex-wife. Ted sympathised, although he knew Bizzie's team would have made her as presentable as they could first.

'Morgane's fretting, wanting some of her own things from the house ...'

'Not possible for now, I'm afraid. The house is now a crime scene, of course. Does she have anything at your house?'

'Flat. Shoebox, in fact. Yes, she does, she always keeps a couple of changes of clothes here for when she visits. But she left her mobile phone at the house and she'd really like that, if at all possible.'

Ted made non-committal noises. Everything within the crime scene would need to be checked so there was no way he could promise early return of even personal effects.

'Fair enough, I understand. I also just wanted the chance to have a quick word with you first, without Morgane around to overhear. It's not a secret that the divorce was not a particularly amicable one and that, being a solicitor, my wife took me for every penny I had. That gives me something of a motive, I imagine, for wanting her dead.

'I didn't kill her, however, and I certainly didn't abduct my own daughter. Nor did I pay anyone to do so, in case that was going to be your next question. Luckily, and this is the part I don't want Morgane to know about at this stage, I'm seeing someone else. And last night I was in bed with her, at her house in Holmes Chapel, when I got the call from the police to tell me what had happened.

'I'm more than happy to give you her contact details, but I'd be grateful if you didn't tell Morgane. I'd prefer to do that in my own time. After everything she's been through, I worry it might upset her. She likes to pretend she's very grown up but in some ways she isn't. No doubt she'd deny it furiously, but she is a bit of a daddy's girl. She wanted to come and live with me, but my blood-sucking ex had made that impossible, financially speaking.

'So I'll see you tomorrow, but I would be very grateful if this could be on a need to know basis, as far as Morgane is concerned.'

# Chapter Twenty-one

Despite Jim Baker's best efforts, it was no earlier than usual when Ted finally admitted defeat and headed for home. He had to accept he'd done all he could for one day. The next day risked being a full one, with the early PM, a new team member joining them, and his first chance to interview the second victim in his latest case.

He'd sent Trev a text to let him know roughly what time he'd be back. He'd gone past the stage of being tired now, feeling wide awake and scratchy, but he knew he needed to get some sleep before his early start the next morning. He had to be on top of his game with this case.

The weather was fine and mild for once, a change from the recent succession of damp and dismal days. He found Trev out in the garden, his camping mat on the lawn while he went through his fitness routine on it. He was encircled by silent cats, watching his moves in fascination. He was doing effortless stomach curls, his muscles standing out under his tanned skin, when Ted appeared in the garden.

Ted was struck with the familiar emotions he experienced whenever he saw his partner – overwhelming pride and admiration, tinged with feelings of inadequacy and incomprehension at what Trev saw in him.

Trev finished his exercises then sprang lightly to his feet, picking up a towel to wipe perspiration from his face before greeting his partner with a kiss.

'How was your day? It's been a long one. What time did you go out this morning?'

'About one o'clock. You were fast asleep. Before I forget, I doubt I'll get to the dojo tomorrow, certainly not in time for self-defence. I really need to, though. I need a proper workout. And I need to get to my Krav Maga club, too, sometime soon. Can you sort the kids tomorrow? Oh, and if Flip turns up to watch, tell him I asked after him. How was your day?'

'Playing with big bikes all day? What's not to love! I got to test ride a real beast of a new one Geoff is thinking of stocking. Best of all, I got to practise my Japanese. The rep couldn't answer everything we wanted to know so I phoned Tokyo for more details.'

He was grinning his enthusiasm as he spoke. It sounded like a better day than Ted's.

'I'll just go and grab a shower and get changed before we eat, if you don't mind. I'm really sorry I'm not much company at the moment. You know what it's like, with a case like this.'

'Luckily I live with you for the sex, not your sparkling repartee,' Trev laughed.

He was teasing him, Ted knew. Trev's sense of humour and fun was just one of the things Ted loved about him. Somehow, feeling tired and a bit preoccupied, the comment worried him more than it should have done. Certainly more than it was meant to.

'I am sorry. We are all right, aren't we?'

'Of course we are, you muppet. Why wouldn't we be? I know what your job's like, after all this time. Just promise me you really will try to get back on time to eat with Shewee and her boyfriend on Friday. I need your policeman's intuition to know whether or not I can trust him with my kid sister.'

'There's something rather interesting about the pattern of wounds,' Bizzie Nelson told Ted next morning at the post-mortem examination on Stephanie Mason, their latest murder victim. 'Do you notice anything?'

Reluctantly, Ted leaned closer, studying the damaged skull,

sucking hard on his customary menthol lozenge.

'They look rather more precise than I would have expected for what we first took to be a frenzied attack.'

'Precisely!' The Professor laughed at her own joke. 'Let me go through it in more detail for you. This blow to the back of the head, almost central, and delivered with considerable force, would most probably have been enough to kill her, though possibly not immediately. It was made from behind and would undoubtedly have felled the victim. But then, and I know you don't like conjecture any more than I do, the pattern of the other blows seems to me to be almost experimental.'

Ted looked at her quizzically, not quite grasping what she was getting at.

'From the precision with which the blows were placed, it's as if our killer were experimenting with what damage each subsequent blow would inflict. The back of the head – smash! Like a boiled egg, hit with a spoon. Very satisfying. Then what about the temple? Thwack! That splits open quite nicely. The crown of the head? The skull is a little harder there, not quite so good.

'You and I have seen plenty of frenzied attacks where the blows fall randomly, with no sense to where they land. But these look different. My report will let you know, in detail, which of the blows were made after death had already occurred. The body was certainly moved. At some point she was turned over and dragged and this wound here, to the other temple, is quite different. It's made from lower down and again with considerable force. In fact, it rather puts me in mind of a golfer lining up for a tricky putt.'

Her words preyed on Ted's mind as he drove back to the station to brief the team on what the PM had shown so far. He didn't like the idea of the kind of cold detachment which would be necessary to carry out a killing such as Bizzie was suggesting. She'd stressed that she was largely speculating, but that it was based on the evidence of the wounds. A frenzied attack with a hammer was bad enough, but imagining someone staying dispassionate enough to deal the kind of injuries Bizzie had shown him spoke of an altogether different profile for their killer.

It was Jezza who first voiced what was at the back of his mind, after he'd described the initial PM findings to the team.

'Boss, does that kind of behaviour fit the profile of our animal abuser? They seem to have been honing their craft with increasingly sadistic acts.'

'I don't want us getting ahead of ourselves,' he warned. 'But yes, on the surface, there's a similar element. Drowning a small boy, even pushing an elderly person under a bus, could conceivably be spur of the moment actions. But from what the Professor was saying, there's a certain degree of cold-blooded detachment in this.'


On the dot of ten o'clock, Ted got a call from Bill at the front desk to tell him that his new FLO, DC Kate Jones, was there. He went down himself to welcome her. He was not the sort of senior officer to send his team members running errands for him. Jim was with the Ice Queen so at least the office wouldn't feel quite as overcrowded as it did with his presence. He put the kettle on to boil before he went down. It would be nice to welcome the newcomer and bring her up to speed with a brew, and he was about ready for one himself.

He liked what he saw on first impressions. DS Jones was pleasantly smiling, in her thirties, auburn hair in a jawline bob. She was casually dressed in jeans and a zipped sweatshirt. She held out a hand to him in greeting.

'Morning, sir. I'm Kate Jones, your new FLO. I'm looking forward to working with you.'

He smiled as he shook her hand.

'Likewise, Kate. Please don't worry about the sir, we're quite an informal team. Would you like to come this way?'

He showed her to the stairs and fell into step companionably alongside her.

'I hope I'm not too informally dressed, boss? Only, I thought that if I need to make a connection with a teenage girl, I might look better like this than in my usual work suit.'

Ted turned and grinned at her. His grin was that of a naughty schoolboy. It was his most disarming weapon. It made him look nothing like a policeman and had lulled many people into relaxing their guard in his company. The fact that he was completely oblivious to how attractive it made him was even more appealing.

'I'll let you in on my guilty secret. By choice, I'd be in jeans myself. It's just that the Super is quite strict on dress code for her officers. I honestly don't mind what you wear, as long as you're doing your job.'

He showed her into his office and invited her to take a seat.

'The kettle's just boiled, if I can interest you in a tea or a coffee?'

He went over to make the drinks himself but she stopped him.

'Boss, would you be offended if I asked to make my own coffee? It's just that people never believe me about how strong I like it and how little milk I take.'

'Let me guess – just a cloud of milk? I can do that, if you trust me. It's how my partner Trev drinks his tea.'

Ted's reputation for being relaxed and informal was widely known in the force. She'd certainly never had a DCI brew up for her before, and he'd almost got her coffee right. He'd just been a bit generous with the milk, although it was nearer to her taste than most managed to make it.

They chatted for a few moments as they drank. Kate had been doing her homework on her new temporary boss and had heard a lot about him, particularly his love of cats. She told him about her large ginger tom, Garfield. The DCI was certainly easy company, even when he switched into professional mode to tell her what he needed from her. She didn't often encounter senior officers who said please and thank you when briefing their team.

'We're going to go and question Morgane at eleven o'clock. She's currently staying with her father in Bramhall, and this is my first chance to meet her and see what she has to say. Whatever we get from the interview, she and her father are going to need support in the days ahead, which is where you come in.

'Statistically, you know as well as I do that there's a strong possibility that whoever did this is known to the family in some way. It might be someone related to a criminal case Stephanie Mason had worked on, so not necessarily someone Morgane would recognise. I need you to get close to her, please, find out if she knows something without realising that she does. Maybe her mother talked to her about some of her cases. I also need to know if there's a boyfriend on the scene. For either of them. Her father told me she doesn't talk to him about such things.

'When I interview her, I'd like you just to observe and take notes for now, please. If I miss anything, ask her later on. Find out what she knows, and how reliable a witness she is. If you've finished your drink, we should make a start. Do you want to take your own car, so you're independently mobile?'

'Do you need me to come back in at the end of the day for a catch-up? I shouldn't need a car during the day, should I, so I could leave it here for now.'

Ted shook his head.

'Phone me if there's anything urgent, otherwise come in for morning briefing tomorrow and fill me and the team in then, before you go back to Bramhall. If you're not taking your car, I'll take my official one. Would you mind very much if I asked you to drive, please? I'm always getting told off for not using it enough and for not having a driver.'

She decided she liked him even more when he settled happily into the front passenger seat and chatted informally as she expertly handled the car through the traffic, heading out towards Bramhall.

As they turned into the road where Morgane's father lived, Ted added, 'I'd quite like the chance to talk to the father on his own at some point. If I give you a nod, can you perhaps take Morgane out to make a brew or something while I do so, please?'

She was still smiling at the number of pleases since she'd first met him as she went with him up the drive to the ground-floor flat in a large detached house which was Mr Edwards' home. Most of the front garden had been sacrificed to make room for cars belonging to residents of the multi-occupancy. There was room for Kate to park on the driveway. Ted imagined most of the residents would be out at work at this time of day.

They found the right bell push for Edwards' flat and the man came to the door himself to let them in.

'Good morning, Mr Edwards. This is DC Jones, your Family Liaison Officer. She's going to be spending a bit of time with Morgane, and with you, to give you any help and support you need.'

'Please call me Kate,' she said as she shook his hand.

'Are you taking time off work at the moment, Mr Edwards? If there's somewhere you need to be, Kate can stay with Morgane.'

'I work from home, fortunately. I design and build websites for clients, as well as doing some graphic design for them, any marketing material they need. Morgane gets her artistic side from me. Please, come in. Follow me. It's a bit narrow in the hallway, where they split the house into flats. This is mine, on this side. Do come in.'

He led the way into a modest-sized living room with a bay window which housed a desk and a computer. There was a gas fire, which was on high, inset into the chimney breast. A leather armchair alongside it faced a flat-screen TV in a corner of the room. Opposite the fire was a sofa, which was where Ted got his first look at Morgane.

She was small, blonde, her hair long and slightly frizzy as if from a recent shampoo, loose around her shoulders, falling forwards to partially mask her face as she bent over an artists' sketch book, working away with quick and confident pencil strokes. She looked up when the two police officers followed her father into the room. Her eyes were wide, a striking light blue. She was wearing pyjamas under an over-sized fleece jacket, despite the warmth in the room, which looked as if it belonged to her father. Her feet were encased in big fluffy slippers in the shape of lions. She looked more like twelve than sixteen; vulnerable, innocent.

'Hello, I'm Morgane,' she said. 'Morgane with an E.'

Ted remembered she had said the same thing in the 999 call. She trotted it out almost like a mantra. Comfort in the familiarity of it, perhaps.

'Hello, Morgane, I'm DCI Darling. This is DC Kate Jones. She's your Liaison Officer. She's going to be spending some time with you. She's here to help you.'

The girl's father indicated to them to sit down. Kate sat next to Morgane on the sofa, Ted took the armchair opposite. Edwards turned his work chair round from the desk to sit facing them all.

'Sorry it's so warm in here,' he said. 'Morgane can't seem to thaw out at the moment. I suppose it's the shock.'

'First of all, Morgane, I know that this is difficult for you and you may not find it easy to talk about what happened. Please just take your time, and tell us anything you can remember, in your own words. There's no rush; don't feel under any pressure. If you think of more you want to say after I've gone, Kate will be staying on and you can tell her anything - anything at all - that you think will help us. Kate's going to be taking some notes, if that's all right with you?'

The girl nodded, and turned over a page in her sketch book,

her pencil going to work once more. Ted let her carry on. If it helped her to feel comfortable, he didn't mind what she was doing while she spoke to them.

'Just tell me everything you can remember of Monday night, please.'

'My mother and I had a row. Another one. I keep thinking that the last time I spoke to her, it was angry words. And shouting.'

She kept glancing up at him from time to time as she spoke, then her eyes would return to whatever it was she was doodling or drawing.

'What was the argument about?'

'Oh, you know, the usual mother/teenage daughter sort of stuff. Do your homework, tidy your room, you should help round the house more. I'm out at work all day and you don't even load and unload the dishwasher. Get a sensible career. You're not going to make any money out of art.'

Her father opened his mouth to speak but Ted held up a hand to silence him. He wanted to hear the daughter's words, not his.

'In the end, I'd had enough. I did the whole stomping off in a temper thing. What mum always calls me being a stroppy teen. Flounced out of the back door, slammed it shut and went out the back way, through the garden gate onto the field. I'm not supposed to go out that way at night. Mum likes to keep it locked, in case someone comes in that way.'

This time, when she looked up, her eyes were full of tears and her lips were quivering.

'I keep thinking that this is all my fault. I left the back gate unlocked and he must have come in that way, mustn't he? I was a complete cow to my mother, the last time I saw her, and I let her killer into the house.'

Kate silently handed her a tissue and gave her hand a gentle squeeze.

'Please try not to think like that, Morgane. It doesn't help, and it might not even be true. Just focus on telling us everything you can remember,' Ted told her encouragingly. 'Where did you go? About what time was this?'

'I don't really know. About ten o'clock, perhaps? I'm not sure. I was so angry I just went off without my mobile and I don't wear a watch. I walked for ages, trying to calm down. Then I thought I'd better go back and make it up with my mum. We were always having rows about nothing, but we always made up before bedtime. We'd both say we were sorry, we'd have a cuddle, then we'd both go to bed happy and everything would be fine for a few days. Until the next time.

'But now I can never do that, can I? I can't tell my mum how sorry I am and get a cuddle from her. Never again.'

This time, as she looked up, she let the tears spill from her eyes, dripping from her face onto her sketch pad. Kate instinctively moved close enough to put a comforting arm around her. Morgane gratefully fell into her arms, her shoulders shaking with the violence of her sobbing, clearly overwhelmed by her feelings of guilt and loss.

# Chapter Twenty-two

'Are you all right, sweetheart? Do you want to take a break?'

Edwards got up and went anxiously to his daughter, hovering about ineptly. Clumsily rubbing her back as she sobbed against Kate Jones, who had come well-armed with tissues and was handing some to Morgane.

'It's fine, Mr Edwards, it's quite normal, don't worry,' Ted said quietly.

He didn't like to appear heartless but he needed information only Morgane could give him to make any progress with the case. He had experience and endless patience in carrying out similar interviews, and he knew already that he could rely on Kate for exactly the support Morgane needed.

'Morgane, we can take a short break any time you need to, but you will understand that I have to ask you these questions to help us catch whoever did this. The sooner I get your answers, the sooner my team can go to work.'

She sniffed a few times, blew her nose, then sat up and looked at him.

'I understand. I'm sorry, I just had a little wobble. I'm all right to go on now.'

Her father still hesitated, looming over her, but at a gesture from Ted, he went back to resume his seat.

'And you can't remember where you walked, Morgane, when you left the house? You can't remember anywhere you went?'

The question seemed to surprise her. She looked at him for a moment, her eyes dry now.

'I, er, no, I'm not really sure. I can't remember. I just walked about for an hour or so, I suppose it must have been. Maybe longer.'

'That's fine. Don't worry about anything you can't remember. Just tell me what you can. Now, and I know this is going to be hard for you, can you please tell me about when you went back home. Tell me what you saw, what happened then.'

'I went back in through the back gate. It wasn't locked, so Mum hadn't closed it. She was probably waiting for me to get home first. The light was still on in the kitchen, but the back door was partly open. I remember slamming it shut when I left, so I thought Mum must have come outside looking to see if I was back yet.

'I went up to the back door and I could see straight away that something was wrong. My mum was lying on the floor, not moving. I thought perhaps she'd fainted or something so I ran indoors. Then I saw the blood. Oh God, there was so much blood, everywhere.'

She paused, screwing her eyes up tight. She'd stopped sketching for the moment and was clutching her pad and pencil to her chest. Her father made a move to get up again but Ted motioned towards him and shook his head gently. He needed to let her speak, to recount her memories. Kate was there to support her and she was doing a good job.

After a moment, the girl reopened her eyes, let out a long, slow breath, and started to sketch again.

'I didn't know what to do at first. Mum was making a sort of moaning noise in her throat. It was awful. I went to her and tried to wake her up, to make her talk to me. It didn't seem right, her lying there on the hard tiles. I thought perhaps if I could move her onto the carpet in the hall, she would be warmer, more comfortable. I wanted to call an ambulance but I couldn't see my phone anywhere. I couldn't remember where I'd left it. I started to go into the hall to use the landline, but then I was afraid to leave her.

'I tried to make her wake up. Like they do on the TV. I shook her gently by the shoulders. I kept asking her if she could hear me. But she couldn't. She couldn't. I think I knew then that she was dead. That the sound I'd heard her make was her last breath. I just wanted to cuddle her. One more time. I didn't know what else to do. I hugged her and hugged her. I kept telling her how sorry I was. But she didn't wake up. She wasn't responding at all. I knew really that she'd gone.'

She broke off, a small choke in her voice as she sniffed back more tears. She put her pencil down and took another tissue from Kate to pat her eyes and blow her nose again.

'Are you all right, treasure?' her father asked her.

She nodded resolutely, once more picking up her pencil.

'I need to do this now, while it's still fresh in my mind. I don't suppose it will get any easier to go through, just by waiting any longer.'

'Tell me what happened next, Morgane,' Ted told her encouragingly. 'You're doing really well. Just tell me what you remember next in the sequence of events.'

'He came into the kitchen then. This lad. It really scared me. Even though I could tell now that my mother was dead, I didn't think there was anyone else in the house, so I jumped a bit when he came in and I think I screamed. He seem startled, too, like he hadn't realised I'd come in, or something, even though I hadn't been trying to keep quiet especially.

'When I saw him and realised who he must be, I panicked and tried to run out of the door. He grabbed me by the back of my hair, pulled me back, then slammed me against the cupboards. I think I slipped in the blood because I fell and hit my head hard on the edge of a work surface. It hurt a lot and it was bleeding. Then he grabbed me again and tied my wrists together with one of those plastic things. You know, they make like a loop and when you pull it tight it somehow locks itself and you can't pull it open again. He pulled it really tight. It cut into my wrists and hurt a lot.'

As she spoke, she stopped sketching for a moment and with her pencil hand, she rubbed subconsciously at her other wrist. Ted could see that there was still a red mark where the cable tie had clearly bitten into her flesh.

'Where did it come from? The cable tie, I mean?'

Again, the question seemed to take her by surprise. Her eyes narrowed slightly, then she said, 'He took it out of his pocket. He must have had it with him.'

'And the hammer, Morgane? What can you tell me about that? Had you ever seen it before?'

Another tear squeezed out of the corner of one eye and he could see that the memory of the murder weapon had caused her pain. She put the pad and pencil down and wrapped her arms round herself, for the warmth and comfort. She still looked frozen.

'That was ours. Mum's, I mean. Well, probably one of Dad's he left behind when he moved out. I got it out ages ago. I'd been on at Mum to put up some of my drawings. She didn't want me to do it myself. I don't think she trusted me. I kept asking her to do it and she kept saying she would when she had time. It was another thing we were always rowing about. I could have done it easily enough but she wouldn't let me.'

'Now think back to the youth you saw come into the kitchen. Tell me anything you can remember about him. What was he wearing?'

'He had a hoody on, with the hood up, and, like, baggy tracky bottoms, I think. I noticed he had those blue gloves on. Plastic ones. Like they wear on television in hospital dramas, police series, that sort of thing. And he had plastic bags on his feet, over his shoes. I remember thinking that looked strange, but then realising it meant he wouldn't be leaving any clear footprints or any traces of himself.'

'What about his height? In comparison to you. Could you estimate how tall he was?'

She was looking at Ted appraisingly, pausing in the sketching she'd resumed.

'You're not very tall, are you? Could I stand next to you, just to get an idea?'

Ted obligingly stood up and waited expectantly. She moved her pad and pencil aside, got off the sofa and came to stand next to him, quite close. She was about four inches shorter than he was. She lifted her hand as she said, 'He was about up to here, I think.'

As her hand made contact with the side of Ted's face, there was a crack of static electricity that made him flinch involuntarily. He thought he saw the pupils of her light blue eyes dilate suddenly and for an absurd moment, he thought she was flirting with him.

'Oh, I'm sorry,' she said, flustered.

'It's fine,' he assured her. 'It's the fleece. It happens to me all the time with my cats when I'm wearing a fleece, especially in a warm room. So you're saying he was a couple of inches shorter than me?'

She nodded, then turned to go back to her seat.

'You're doing brilliantly, Morgane, but I think we could all do with a short break and a drink now. Why don't you take Kate and show her where everything is so she can make us all a brew? Mine's tea, white, two sugars, please.'

He nodded imperceptibly to Kate. He wanted Morgane out of the room for a moment so he could talk to her father. Kate got the message and stood up, ushering the girl out of the room, asking her to show her the kitchen and the kettle. The sketch pad lay face down on the sofa next to where the girl had been sitting.

Once they'd left the room, Ted turned his attention to the father.

'How do you find her, Mr Edwards? You know your daughter better than anyone. How is she bearing up, would you say?'

'She's amazing,' he said, unmasked admiration in his voice. 'I don't know how she's coping so well. Morgane has always been a very strong individual. She's very much her own person, never mixes with the crowd. Likes going around by herself. Very self-sufficient. But I'm amazed at how she's handling things so far.'

'How old was she when you and your wife got divorced?'

'She was nine when I left home. The divorce happened a couple of years after our so-called trial separation.'

'And can I ask what the cause of the marriage break-up was?'

'Not me playing around, in case that's what you were thinking. No, I just didn't measure up to Stephanie's expectations in many ways. She was always ambitious. I wasn't, so I didn't fit her purpose.'

'And what will happen to Morgane now? You mentioned there's not really enough room for her to live here on a permanent basis. What about the house in Hillcrest Road? Who gets that? If Morgane inherits, would you move back there to look after her?'

The questions were all posed with Ted's usual disarming candour, but the man's eyes narrowed at the implication behind them.

'In other words, you're asking me if I killed my ex-wife, or arranged for her to be killed. So not only would that stop her bleeding me dry for child maintenance and the like, but I'd then get my daughter back, and the family home to live in.'

He reached for a piece of paper, lying face down on his desk, and handed it to Ted.

'I knew you'd need to check out my alibi, so I've written down the name of the woman I was with, and her address and phone numbers, as well as my mobile number. I know you have a way of tracing where a phone is whenever it makes or receives a call. The police phoned me to tell me what had happened, so I assume you'll be able to verify where my mobile, and therefore where I was, at the time I took the call. Like I said to you on the phone, Morgane doesn't yet know about Carla so I'd be glad if it could stay that way for now. I think she has enough to deal with at the moment, don't you?'

'Thank you, Mr Edwards. I hope you appreciate that it is my job to ask these questions. I'm here to get justice for the victims and their families. I wouldn't be doing my job properly if I didn't investigate every possible angle.'

Edwards nodded his understanding. He looked weary, worn down by the whole affair. Ted strongly suspected the man hadn't slept much more than he had since it had happened.

'As far as the house goes, my wife being a solicitor, and she having taken the family home as part of the divorce settlement, I imagine she'll have made provision for Morgane in her will. I suppose I better contact her lawyers and find out, on Morgane's behalf. Then I would need to discuss it with her to see what she wants to do. I can't imagine her wanting to carry on living in the house where her mother met a violent death.'

'Thank you. And can I just take your first name, please?'

'It's Clive. Another thing Stephanie didn't like. It wasn't quite trendy enough for her.'

They broke off conversation as the door opened and Morgane and Kate came back in, each carrying two mugs of steaming drinks. Morgane had Ted's drink and brought it over to him. He instinctively tried to avoid contact with her hand as she handed it to him. He'd found the static shock surprisingly unsettling and was keen to avoid another one which he risked as she was still wearing the fleece.

The girl sat down, moving her sketch pad to the side table next to her end of the sofa. She lifted her slippered feet up onto the seat in front of her, then pulled the fleece down over her knees to cover her legs. It may never resume its former shape, but she seemed to be seeking warmth and comfort wherever she could find them.

Ted allowed time for them all to have some of their drinks. He was watching the girl closely over the rim of his cup as they drank. Once he judged that she had thawed out sufficiently and relaxed a little, he started his questioning again.

'Going back to the youth, Morgane. Did you know him? Had you seen him before?'

Still clutching the mug with both hands, blowing on its contents then taking sips of the hot liquid, she shook her head.

'No. No, I don't think so. I didn't recognise him, at least.'

'Can you describe what he looked like?'

She put down her mug and picked up the sketch pad, turning back a page.

'I can do better than that. I've drawn him for you.'

She held up the sketch pad, facing towards him. Ted was careful to try not to react in any way. It was an incredible piece of drawing. Even for a quick sketch, it was better than some old Identikit pictures he'd seen done. Her father was beaming proudly.

'I told you she was artistic. She's brilliant at portrait sketches. I keep telling her she could be a court artist. If ever she needs to earn a few bob, she could make a fortune as a street artist, maybe in a tourist town.'

'How accurate would you say your drawings are, Morgane? How close would you say that is to the youth you saw?'

Her smile had a hint of self-satisfaction about it as she replied, turning back to the page after, which she held out.

'I thought you might ask me that, so I did this.'

The second sketch she showed Ted was a stunning likeness of himself. In a few quick strokes of her pencil, she'd captured the essence of him. His overall expression was serious, in policeman mode, but his mouth was showing a smile of encouragement. It was so realistic, in such a short time, that there was something almost disturbing about it.

'That's excellent, Morgane, thank you. Very helpful. If I

may take the one of the suspect? We may well still need you to come into the station at some point to help make up a computer composite, but this is a great start.'

She tore it carefully out of her pad, then removed the other one.

'I did it for you, hoping it might help. Here, have them both.'

Ted thanked her, then asked her to continue her recollections, starting from the point where she said the youth had tied her hands.

In between swallows of her drink, she told him everything she could remember. She spoke clearly and without hesitation. Ted merely prompted her gently from time to time, asking for more detail. She told him that the youth had forced her out of the house by the back door and through the garden gate onto the field behind. It was dark and there was no one around. He'd pulled her hood up, she thought so that it would disguise the fact that she was bleeding.

She said he had an arm around her neck as they walked, which could, at a distance, have looked like a possessive hug. But he'd told her that he had a knife in his pocket and he would use it if she made the slightest sound or sign to try to alert someone to come to her aid.

They saw no one, she said, as they crossed the field into Broadway, and he then steered her towards a side road where there was a car parked, which he opened with the keys, then forced her into the back seat.

'Do you remember which road it was?'

'I'm not really sure. I was so scared by this time. I knew he'd already killed my mother and I thought he might do the same to me if I didn't do as he said. I didn't know if he was going to kill me. Or to take me somewhere and rape me.'

She made direct eye contact with Ted as she said that, her expression earnest. Her father shifted uncomfortably in his seat at that moment.

'I think it might have been the road with the funny name. Mum and I always used to make a joke of it and call it Kippersley so I can never remember what it's really called.'

'Knypersely Avenue,' Ted told her, as much for Kate's benefit with the note-taking as anything else. 'When you went out walking earlier, did you happen to go that way, after you crossed the field?'

Her face screwed up in a frown as she tried to remember. Then realisation dawned and she looked horrified.

'You mean he might have been there earlier on, watching and waiting for me to leave?'

'I'm not saying anything, Morgane. I'm just asking if you can remember where you walked when you went out earlier.'

No, she couldn't remember. No, she couldn't tell him what make or model the car was. She wasn't interested in cars, only in people, so she wouldn't be able to draw the car for him. She thought it was black, certainly dark in colour, and remembered it had a loud stereo system playing Rap, she thought it was, although it wasn't her thing. The car wasn't very big, she remembered.

'He told me to keep right down on the back seat. I was really dizzy by now, my head was spinning, so it's all I really wanted to do anyway. I couldn't tell which way we were going really, but I tried to look out at one point and I recognised the end of Lisburne Lane as we were going past.

'I kept trying to untie my hands with my teeth but I couldn't, the strap was too tight. Then before we'd gone all that far, he stopped and I could see traffic lights on red. I thought I'd take a chance. I pulled the back door open, jumped out and ran as fast as I could, in the opposite direction. Then I ran across the road as soon as I could, to get away from him.

'Then the lights must have turned to green because I heard cars beeping their horns, then tyres squealing as if he was pulling away quickly. I ran up a road I came to until I saw a house with a light on, then I started screaming for help.'

She took a welcome large gulp of her drink after talking so much. Ted decided it was time to wind up the questioning for now. He thanked her for her help and was just about to think up a reason to ask Kate to walk out to the car with him when she clearly read his mind.

'Boss, before you go, can I just check in the car to see if I left my other notebook in there?'

As they reached the car, she looked at him shrewdly and asked, 'You recognised her sketch, didn't you? Of the killer?'

'Alleged killer,' he corrected automatically. 'You're very observant. And yes, I did, and it's rather shaken things up a bit. It's the spitting image of Max Newman, the lad with the snake.'

# Chapter Twenty-three

Before he left to go back to the station, Ted asked Kate not to mention Max Newman's name to either Morgane or her father. He knew he didn't need to. He'd seen enough already to know that she was a thoroughly professional officer who knew her job. He just liked to cover all bases.

He realised he was suddenly hungry. He hadn't risked breakfast before the post-mortem, meaning to grab something afterwards, and realised from the way his stomach was rumbling that he had yet to do so. He remembered the bacon rolls of Monday and decided the short detour to the same café was worth it to line his stomach with a couple of those. His eating patterns became so erratic when working a difficult case that he often wondered how he'd escaped the ulcers which plagued others he knew of, like Kevin Turner.

The office was relatively quiet, with many of the team out. Rob was in charge of things, with Jo at the Hillcrest Road crime scene and Mike still coordinating house-to-house near to Tyler's home. Ted asked Rob to contact everyone and pull them in for an update at five. He wanted to arrange to bring Max Newman in for further questioning the following morning. He'd ask Kevin Turner to send a couple of his officers round to get him and his father up first thing. Nothing like an early morning visit from the boys in blue in an area car to emphasise that things were serious.

Jim Baker was in their shared office. Ted headed straight for the kettle for something to wash down his second bacon roll. He'd already devoured the first one hungrily on his way.

Jim shook his head at the offer of a drink, indicating his own half-full mug on the desk.

'So, how was the girl? A good witness?'

Ted sat down with a smile. He carefully unrolled the sketches she'd given him, trying not to get bacon fat on either of them, then handed the one of himself over to Jim.

'Bloody hell, Ted! That's uncanny. She did this? She's certainly very talented. Any particular reason for drawing you?'

Ted held up the other sketch as he said, 'She did this one of the youth she said killed her mother, then she did the one of me to convince me of its accuracy.'

Jim took it and scrutinised it carefully.

'Is he known to us?'

'He's known to me. I've already interviewed him. It's Max Newman, the lad with the python, or someone who's a dead ringer for him. I'm going to pull him in first thing in the morning and question him further. I didn't much like him for the Tyler Bradbury case and his feet are too big for the footprints there, but he's going to have to go some to talk himself out of this.

'I want to get some incident boards in place up around Seventeen Windows, asking for the public's help with anything at all suspicious they may have seen. From what the girl told me, it's very likely that at least one driver will have seen her jump out of the car at the lights.'

'You heard what Debs and I said, Ted. Whatever it takes, let's do it. Sort it out with Kevin. And do me a favour, will you? Don't bring bloody bacon rolls in, while we're sharing an office. Bella's got me on a bloody low fat diet and I could just murder half a pig between two loaves of bread.'

Once the team were all together, Ted brought them up to date with everything he'd learned from his interview with Morgane. He'd put her drawing of the person she claimed was the killer up on the white board. Megan recognised it straight away.

'That's Max Newman, isn't it, boss? The boy with that creature I refuse to name? Or if not, it's someone who's strikingly like him. How accurate is it likely to be, though, after all she's been through?'

Ted unrolled the sketch of himself and held it up for them all to see.

'She did that one of me in a few minutes, while I was talking to her. She said she'd done it so I'd know how accurate she was. I've arranged for Max Newman to be brought in first thing and I want to interview him again myself.'

'Boss, just one thing,' Jezza began. 'A teenage girl, going out without her mobile phone. I'm finding that a bit hard to swallow, I have to say.'

'I must say I tend to agree with Jezza, boss,' Jo commented. 'My two eldest, George and Sophie, are fifteen and fourteen and they have to be surgically removed from theirs. I'm forever having to read them the riot act for texting at the table. Her phone was found in her bedroom, so she did genuinely leave it behind, and it's gone off for testing. And talking of her bedroom, there's a rather interesting development there.'

'Sorry to interrupt you, Jo, but just so I don't forget. Can you chase up forensics on that phone, please? We need it as soon as possible, if not sooner. Once they've finished with it, Océane can you get it to give up all its innermost secrets? I want to know about any and all calls, especially recently, and where she was when they were made. We need to be concentrating on people known to the family and until Kate can gain Morgane's confidence and find out about any boyfriends or whatever, that's our best way. Right, Jo, carry on.'

'Said bedroom was incredibly tidy. Almost obsessively so, I would have said. I'd love any one of my mob to keep theirs looking like that, yet you say she claimed she and her mother rowed over the state of her room. So perhaps she'd made a special effort.

'Anyway, whatever the reason, it was pristine, the bed

made, the bedspread neat and tidy, without a crease. However, a pile of her underwear had been tipped into the middle of the bed and from the stains on those, which are being tested, of course, it looked as if someone had, in the words of the confessional, been pleasuring themselves over her smalls.'

Ted was never sure how much of what Jo said about his Catholic background was true or just part of the role he liked to cast for himself.

'So we possibly have the killer's DNA?'

'We have someone's, boss, for sure.'

'Boss, there's something else that doesn't sit quite right with me.'

Jezza again.

Ted nodded to her to go ahead. Her ideas were often helpful.

'Morgane gave the officers who attended her father's mobile number to contact him.'

Seeing blank looks, she went on, her tone impatient.

'Who knows phone numbers off the top of their heads, these days? Tommy does; memorising numbers is just one of the things he likes to do. But honestly, could all of you say you know your next of kin's mobile number without looking at your own phone to find it? Hardly anyone dials phone numbers any more, they're all saved on speed dial.'

'I know Trev's,' Ted said without thinking, then saw the grins of his team. They all knew how close the boss and his partner were. 'All right, maybe not everyone does, but where does that take us? What are you suggesting, Jezza? That Morgane is somehow involved in killing her own mother?'

'I'm not suggesting anything, boss, I'm just flagging up a couple of things which don't sit quite right with me.'

'Which is what we need. Jo, we'll get a DNA sample from Max Newman in the morning, as soon as we can, and get that sent off for checking against that found in Morgane's bedroom. We'll see if we can get the lab to rush it through for us as it's clearly our most important lead so far. Morgane's father did mention that she knew a boy with a snake and that he might have been called Max. I think it's a bit too far-fetched to imagine we have two teenage boys called Max who both keep pet pythons and who both live on our patch.

'I also want CCTV from the route the car would have taken to go from Broadway, or a road just off it, passing Lisburne Lane and finishing up at Seventeen Windows. Luckily, that limits the likely routes. Mike, can I put you in charge of that, please? I can't tell you much about the car, I'm afraid, just that Morgane said she thought it was small and black, or at least dark-coloured. I'll chase up the Professor to see if she can narrow the time of death down for us. That will at least save us time looking for the vehicle before the event. If we can clock the car leaving, we can work back from that moment when we need to. There's going to be hours of tape which needs viewing, so let's try to narrow it down as much as possible from the start.'

'What exactly are we looking for, boss?'

'Ah, that's the million dollar question. Let's concentrate on what we know, or at least what we think we know. Morgane said she was in the back seat, so probably a car rather than a van. She also said it was black and, being an artist, I don't imagine she'd get the colour wrong. So let's start off with dark-coloured cars. Ignore vans and anything light or brightly-coloured for now. She thinks she went out at ten and came back an hour or so later, and she was found just after midnight. She could be wrong in her earlier timings, so try looking initially between nine o'clock and midnight.

'Right, I'll be interviewing Max Newman early. I've asked for him to be brought in at eight o'clock if that's possible. I'm hoping, if he's still half asleep, that he won't have had time to think up an alibi, if he is involved. So the Big Boss is in charge of morning briefing,' he said, nodding towards Jim Baker. 'Jezza, are you able to get in for eight? Can you sort out childcare for Tommy? I'd like you in on this if possible. You're good at picking up on anything that's not quite right.'

Jezza nodded. 'No worries, boss, I can sort that in a phone call if you give me five minutes.'

'Fine, come and find me when it's sorted and we'll talk about how I'd like the interview to go.'

It was not long after he'd finished his discussion with Jezza that Ted's mobile phone rang. Kate Jones, with an update.

'Morgane and I chatted for a bit after you left, boss. Nothing too detailed, I didn't push it. I want to gain her trust before I start asking too many probing questions. Anyway, she was clearly very tired so she's gone to bed for a snooze. I thought I'd try talking to her father now, see if he says anything useful when it's just me and him. Anything in particular you need me to ask about?'

'Try to find out about friends, of Morgane and of her mother. Ask about relatives, too. Let's get full details of the close family circle. Oh, and we're going to need. ..'

'The clothes she was wearing when she found her mother.'

Not so much interrupting him as finishing the sentence for him, showing him again how on the ball she was.

'I already asked about those, but they've been washed. Morgane stuck  them straight in the washing machine, once she got home from hospital, before she'd even showered and changed.'

'And her shoes?'

'She binned them, boss. Said they'd never clean up to the point where she'd wear them again so she threw them in the bin. And it's been emptied since, I checked.'

'We're going to need Morgane's fingerprints and DNA, and get her father's too, please, as soon as you can. We'll need to know exactly who handled what in the house.

'About washing the clothes so quickly. I did mention to her father that we'd need them. Is that normal, from Morgane, would you say, or a bit hasty?'

'Perfectly normal, I would say. Her dad said she spent ages in the shower, too. I can imagine it must be awful to have yourself and your clothes covered in your mother's blood. Also she doesn't seem to have many things here so she'd be thinking of having a clean change of clothing. I doubt she'll feel much like going out shopping at the moment. Is it worth bringing the clothes in to see if any traces of anything are left?'

'I think anything's worth a shot. Can you drop them off here? I know you're not mobile ...'

'I'm getting my partner to taxi me, so I'll bring them in when I leave here. He works sensible hours so he's free to help, and my children are with their doting granny, who loves any excuse to babysit them for as long as possible. If you've already left, I'll see you in the morning for the briefing, boss.'

Ted highly doubted he would have left by then. He intended spending some time going through the notes of his interview with Morgane before he left for the evening. He'd already resigned himself to missing his martial arts session, although with regret. Jim Baker, though, had other ideas.

When he stood up and started to gather his things together, he told Ted, 'Time you were making a move, too, Ted. Isn't it your judo night? You look as if you need something like that. Sitting here half the night isn't going to make any difference in the greater scheme of things.

'I'm going home to Bella and a nice home-cooked meal. You should go and spend some time with Trev, while you can, doing whatever it is you do. And no, I really don't need to know. Just go and burn off some energy. You look like you need to. I'll see you here in the morning, bright-eyed and bushy-tailed.'

Put like that, Ted had to admit it sounded inviting. And Jim was right. He could sit here for another few hours looking through CCTV images but he'd not really be any further forward with the enquiry until he had the results of the semen stains found in Morgane's bedroom. More importantly, until they'd been checked against Max Newman's DNA, which they wouldn't even have until the following morning.

'Is that an order, boss?' he asked with a grin.

'I can make it one, if it means you'll get your backside out of here at a decent time and go and have some fun.'

For once, Ted didn't need telling twice. He was going to be too late for the children's self-defence group, but he could at least now do his own judo session and was eager for some fast and furious randori with Trev. Despite Trev having the height and weight advantage, Ted had the speed and technical skills to beat him every time, especially fired up as he was by the current case.

He knew their coach, Bernard, would always put him with Trev when he could see that Ted was wound up by work. He was looking forward to it, an unexpected bonus, as he'd resigned himself to not getting there. But he knew that meant he was pushing his luck if he hoped to get away at a decent time to eat with Siobhan and the visitor she was bringing on Friday, as he'd promised to try to do.

He went home first to pick up his kit bag and change into sweats. He was immediately accosted by the cats, looking accusing and shamelessly claiming to be starving, although Ted could see that Trev had already given them food and cleaned up after them.

'It won't work, you lot, I don't believe a word of it. I can see that you've already eaten. I'm going out now, but I won't be long. Oh, and make yourselves scarce when we get back. I want to spend a bit of time with Trev without competing with you for his attention.'

Ted found he was suddenly in an extremely good mood. Jim had been right; he needed to let off a bit of steam and spend some time with his partner. When it came to music, both he and Trev were big fans of Queen. But alone in his car, as he was now on the way down to the dojo, he indulged his ill-kept secret love of country music. Kenny Rogers, at full throttle, singing '*We've Got Tonight*' with Dolly Parton, his preferred version. Ted joined in with his more than acceptable tenor voice, drawing some odd looks whenever he stopped for traffic lights.

Trev had just finished with the juniors by the time Ted had got changed into his judogi and gone into the dojo. The way Trev's face lit up when he saw his partner never failed to make Ted's heart race. Trev was encircled by adoring youngsters but he extricated himself skilfully and came over immediately. They were always discreet in front of the youngsters but for anyone who could read body language, the chemistry between them was obvious.

'Hey, you, I didn't think you could get here. I'm glad you did.'

'You may not say that when I've finished with you,' Ted said huskily, his voice low enough so the juniors couldn't overhear him.

Trev laughed delightedly. He was just about to reply when Flip bounded up to them, his face beaming almost as much as Trev's. His arm was still in plaster, although the bruising to his face was fading fast.

'Hi, Ted; Trev said you weren't coming tonight. Can I stay and watch you train? Please?'

He looked hopefully from his hero to his foster mother. Ted hadn't really wanted an audience. As wound up as he was, he sometimes got a bit carried away and Bernard had to step in to calm things down. But seeing how eager Flip was, he hadn't the heart to say no.

More than ever, Ted was yearning to get to his Krav Maga club soon. He hadn't had time to go recently and it was there more than anywhere that he could burn off pent-up energies and frustrations. In this dojo, under the watchful eye of Bernard, and now the adoring gaze of young Flip, he would have to keep control of himself.

Even so, both he and Trev were sweating and out of breath when they'd finished the session.

'Shower here, or when we get home?' Trev asked as they went to the changing room to put their outdoor clothes on.

'I think at home would be safest, don't you?' Ted asked him with a suggestive smile. 'What about food? No doubt we'll want something later.'

'I put a casserole in the oven before I came out, on a low light. It'll be fine, until we're ready for it.'

The shower turned out to be a long and an interesting one. Afterwards, Ted realised that with the bacon rolls a distant memory, he was ravenous. Once he'd finished eating and sided away both their plates, he sat for a moment, smiling at his partner.

'We're more than all right, aren't we? I sometimes worry that we're not. But we are.'

Trev laughed.

'If you still have doubts after that, then I don't know what I can do to convince you.'

# Chapter Twenty-four

Max Newman's father looked bleary-eyed and disgruntled when Ted and Jezza went into the interview room where he and his son were waiting. He was unshaven. He'd pulled an unbuttoned shirt on over his dirty T-shirt which looked and smelled as if it had not been washed since Ted had last seen him in it a week ago. His body odour was tempered only in part by that of stale beer and cigarettes.

His son, sitting next to him, looked smaller than Ted remembered, clearly ill at ease. His eyes were travelling ceaselessly from the two officers to his father and back.

'Is all this bloody fuss still over him nicking a few biscuits from another kid and shoving that other lad over when he tried to attack him? It's a bit of bloody overkill, isn't it? Sending a squad car round for all the neighbours to see?'

'I just need to ask Max a few more questions, Mr Newman,' Ted said patiently. 'Max, you're not under arrest, but I have to ask you a few more things, in connection with a rather more serious matter. Your father is here as an appropriate adult to ensure that your interests are protected because you're under the age of seventeen. Do you understand that?'

Max nodded warily, as if worried about what he might be agreeing to.

'Max, can you tell me if you know someone called Morgane Edwards, please?'

The expression in the boy's eyes changed as if iron shutters had clanged down. He shook his head emphatically but didn't speak.

'You said you did, you little git,' his father said to him. 'When it came on the telly, about her mam being murdered, you said she was at your school.'

'Please allow Max to speak, Mr Newman. Your role is to support him, nothing more.'

'Yeah, well just tell them the truth, then we can get out of here.'

'So do you know her, Max?'

The boy shrugged.

'I know she's at the same school as me, but there's hundreds of pupils. I don't know 'em all. They announced it at school, what happened. I'm not in the same class or nothing.'

'Do you know how to drive a car, Max?' Jezza put in at this point.

She and Ted had agreed between them who was asking what questions, and at what point.

Again the shrug.

'I've messed about with cars a bit with me mates, nothing more than that.'

'Do you have access to a car? Do either of your parents have a car?'

The boy's father opened his mouth to reply but Ted cautioned him not to.

'It's Max we're interviewing, Mr Newman. Please just allow him to speak. If you think he doesn't understand a question at any point, then you can help and advise him.'

'We ain't got a car. Me dad had to sell it when he lost his job.'

Ted took over the questioning again.

'Max, we're going to ask you if you would consent to us taking your fingerprints and a saliva sample containing your DNA, so that we can eliminate you from our ongoing enquiries. Would you be happy with that?'

Now the father was looking as wary as the son.

'Do we need a lawyer or something? What's he done that

you need to do all this stuff? How can I advise him if I don't know what he's supposed to have done?'

Again, the boy was darting suspicious looks from one to another of them. He had muddy brown eyes. They finally settled on Ted's face with a look that was something like an appeal.

'I want to talk to you. Just you. No one else. Not me dad, not another copper. Just you and me.'

Ted was taken aback but trying not to show it. He measured his words carefully as he replied.

'That's not really going to be possible, I'm afraid, Max. There has to be an appropriate adult present at all times when I interview you ...'

'Not an interview. I just want to tell you summat and I don't want anyone else to hear it. Especially not 'im.'

He jerked his head towards his father as he spoke. The older man's brows drew down in a frown as he looked at his son, clearly about to say something else.

'Max, I'm going to have to go and take some advice on the best course of action. There are rules I have to follow when I'm talking to a young person, and I'm not someone who breaks rules. DC Vine will stay with you for the moment and I'll find someone to bring you some refreshments while you wait.'

He looked at Jezza and she gave a barely perceptible nod. Message understood. The boss didn't want Max left alone with his father in case there was any undue pressure brought to bear on the boy, especially any threat of violence.

It was to the Ice Queen that Ted went first. She was overall in charge of everything which happened in her station. If Ted did anything out of order, her head would roll first, fractionally ahead of his.

'You have no idea what he wants to talk to you about? It's not likely to be a confession to killing the girl's mother?'

'At this stage, I don't really know, but I get the feeling we're not going to get very far with him unless I do let him speak to me first. I think he's wary of his father. I had to stop him raising a hand to Max when I first spoke to him last week.'

She was shaking her head.

'I don't like the sound of it at all. You could find yourself in a compromising situation if we don't handle this very carefully. Would he speak in front of another appropriate adult, do you think?'

It was Ted's turn to shake his head.

'I get the feeling he wouldn't. He and I did have a chat together when he was putting his python away, when Megan and I went to the house last week to talk to him about bullying. We got on all right. Maybe he thinks we bonded a bit.'

'Is Superintendent Baker in the building?'

'He should be by now, I imagine. He's taking morning briefing while I'm questioning Max.'

'I think DI Rodriguez is perfectly capable of taking over from him for that, don't you? I think the best course of action would be for you to talk to this Max in an interview room away from his father, but have the Superintendent Baker watch via the camera. Then at least you have a witness to what is said and done.'

'I'll have to tell Max, if he asks if anyone is watching or listening.'

'Of course. But you can tell him it's that or carry on as you are, with his father in the room. Or his mother, if he has one and if he prefers her. I think that's the best way forward.'

Once Ted and Max were alone in the room, the boy's eyes travelled round every inch of the walls until he spotted the camera, high up near the ceiling in the corner.

'Is someone watching and listening?' he asked shrewdly.

'It's that or nothing, I'm afraid, Max. It's my boss, and it's as much for my protection as yours. You could make allegations about me if we were alone.'

'Is it a bloke?'

'Yes, it is. He's called Baker. Detective Superintendent. Are you happy to go on? I could ask him to come into the room, if you would prefer that.'

There was a long pause while Max appeared to consider his options.

'Okay, I trust you. I don't mind if he listens. I just don't want him sitting there looking at me, while I'm talking. Not face to face, like. It's … it's not easy to talk about but I'll tell you. This lass, this Morgane. I do know her. I done 'er, but only the once. Well, twice, but on the same day.'

'When you say you done her ..?' Ted asked for clarification.

'You know. Slept with 'er. Had sex, like. But only one time.'

'And when was this?'

'Couple of weeks ago, about.'

Ted sat back in his chair to give himself time to think. This was certainly an unexpected turn. He couldn't continue this any further as an informal conversation. He was going to have to make it official and record the interview. And for that he was going to have to find an appropriate adult Max would be happy to talk in front of.

'Max, what you've just said has serious implications. I'm going to have to interview you formally, under caution, and you need to have an adult with you, one you're happy to talk in front of. What about your mother, if you don't want it to be your father?'

'Bloody hell, no!' he snorted. 'I'm not talking about stuff like that in front of me mam.'

'Fair enough. And there's no one else? It needs to be someone over eighteen.'

When the boy shook his head, Ted continued, 'Then I'll see if I can arrange for someone from the Youth Justice Team to come and represent you. In the meantime, we can get you something else to eat and drink while you wait, if you'd like. Did you have any breakfast, before you were brought in.'

Max shook his head. Ted wondered if he got enough food at home.

'So, you were thinking he might be the one having a J. Arthur over Morgane's undies and he's admitting to sleeping with her instead?' Jim asked, as he and Ted sat in their shared office, waiting for YJT to send someone over.

Jo was just winding up the morning briefing and team members were starting to leave to get on with their appointed tasks. Kate Jones had been in, as requested. Ted took a moment, before she left, to draw her aside and let her know what he'd learnt so far, promising to update her as soon as he had more details.

'Again, don't mention Max's name to Morgane, please. Just see if you can get her to open up a bit to you about friends and particularly any boyfriends.'

Jezza had sorted out taking fingerprints and DNA swabs then had seen Max and his father installed in a corner of the reception area with drinks and sandwiches, under the watchful eye of Bill, on the front desk. He would see to it that there was no intimidation of Max going on from his father, and no danger of either of them absconding before the formal interview could take place.

'That's about the long and the short of it,' Ted told Jim. 'Certainly unexpected. Not at all what I was anticipating. I thought he might admit to a bit more petty theft at school, something like that, but this? This is something else.'

'Does it put him in the frame for the killing, though? If the DNA matches, it puts him at the scene, but what about the rest of it? From what I saw of him briefly, just now, he didn't look like someone who was expecting a murder charge.'

'You've seen him in the flesh now so you can see for yourself how accurate Morgane's drawing is, if it's meant to be him. I'll have to see what more we can get out of him, and, of course, wait for the DNA results. I'll call the lab and ask for those to be a priority, then I'd better get together with Jezza again to decide how we're going to question him from here.'

'I'll make myself scarce so the two of you have a bit more room to talk. I'm surprised you didn't grab my old office when you had the chance. It was always a bit poky in here. I'll go and talk to Debs. Her coffee's better than that cheap instant stuff you serve.'


He may have been right about the coffee. Jezza opted for green tea, like the boss, when they sat down to catch up. He told her everything Max had said to him and waited to see if Jezza, with her usual keen mind and intuition, would go straight to the part of the story which troubled him.

'Hang on, boss, rewind. Morgane said the lad she saw in the house had gloves on and plastic bags on his feet, to leave no trace. But then he goes and ...' She was about to use coarse slang then, knowing that the boss was old-fashioned, thought better of it. 'He stops to masturbate on her smalls, conveniently leaving us with a sample of his DNA after all. That doesn't make any sense.'

'Perhaps he just couldn't control his base urges? The Professor did suggest to me a sexual motive in all of this. It's not uncommon in cases of torture and killing.'

He was interrupted by his desk phone ringing. It turned out to be someone from the Youth Justice Team, apologising, but saying they had no one free until the following morning. They explained that Max was a low priority since he had parents, even though he refused to speak in front of them. They were currently busy trying to protect the rights of other young people who had no family.

Staying polite as ever, Ted thanked them and arranged a time for the following morning when someone could sit with Max while he was questioned. When he put the phone down, he muttered, 'Damn,' which was about as strong as it got in front of any of his team.

'Problem, boss?'

'Problem. YJT haven't got anyone spare until tomorrow morning, so we'll have to send Max and his delightful father home and get them back tomorrow. Maybe his dad might even manage a wash and a clean shirt before then.

'Do something for me in the meantime, Jezza, please. Check out if Max is known to social services. I have a feeling the father may hit him and he looks as if he doesn't get enough to eat. If he is known, there's an outside chance we could get a social worker to be an appropriate adult, so we could question him sooner.

'One more thing, please, when you've done that. Can you go round to the hospital, to A&E, and find out everything you can about Morgane's injury. All available details.'

'You're thinking there may be more to it than she's said so far?'

'I'm not thinking anything at this stage, just that I'm going to look a complete idiot if there is something not right about it and I haven't checked it out early on.'


Ted knew there was little point pestering Bizzie Nelson for a shorter time-frame for the death of Stephanie Mason. She'd already narrowed it down as much as possible. But he was in the mood for leaving no stone unturned.

'Up to my elbows in entrails, as usual,' she replied cheerfully, when he asked if she was busy, then, when he told her the reason for his call, 'You and I have had this conversation before, more than once, Edwin. I always narrow it down for you as much as I possibly can. Any more than that and we would be into the realms of guesswork and I know that it's no more use to you than it is to me. As I keep reminding you, real life is not like a television series, where everything has to be wrapped up in an hour, so there's always some way the pathologist can pinpoint the exact time of death. Like the conveniently broken watch the victim was wearing, which stopped at the exact time of death.

'Of course, that sort of thing is old hat these days as those who do wear watches tend to have shockproof ones. When I get a moment, I'll try to have another look at my notes and see if I can help you any further. Is the time critical in some way?'

Ted explained that with the prospect of looking through endless CCTV footage, it would help enormously if they could pin it down at all. He went on to ask her if he would be likely to get a DNA match from Max's saliva sample compared to the semen stains before the following day when he would be interviewing him again.

'Unfortunately for you, Edwin, yours are not the only bodies occupying both me and the lab at present. You could try giving Doug a ring and seeing what he can do for you. I gather your bosses didn't altogether appreciate his gallows humour at your briefing. He's a cat fancier – did you know that? Goes to shows with his British shorthairs. Perhaps you could try some feline bonding before you ask for special treatment.'

It was worth a try. Ted was prepared to do whatever it took to move the current case along. Max's words to him had rather turned the enquiry on its head. If what he had said was true, Ted wondered why Morgane was putting him in the frame for killing her mother, unless he had done so. But Jezza had put her finger on exactly what was troubling him. If the killer had gone to the trouble of wearing gloves and shoe covers, why leave semen stains which would inevitably confirm his presence at the murder scene?

He spent some time chatting about cats with Doug at the forensic lab. Ordinarily, he would have enjoyed it, but he was itching to get on with the case. When he decently could, he steered the conversation round to the semen stains and said that they had sent off to the lab a sample from a potential suspect. He said he was interviewing him the following morning and would really appreciate knowing by then if his DNA was a match.

'That's pushing it, especially with everything else we have on at the moment. But I'll do my best for you, seeing as you're another cat lover. One thing I can tell you from what we've found out so far from the scene. Almost all the traces we've found belong to the mother or the daughter. We've already checked out the daughter's DNA, even before we had your samples. She had her own *en suite* so we used samples from her toothbrush and hairbrush.

'So far, the only trace from anyone other than those two appears to be the semen stains.'

It was late once more when Ted got home. He'd warned Trev in a text that he intended to work on, in the hopes that he could get far enough ahead of himself to justify leaving in good time the following evening to eat with Siobhan and her friend. He'd told him to go ahead and eat whenever he was hungry; he'd grab something when he got in.

Trev was talking on his mobile. French, so Ted assumed it must be Laurence again. The conversation sounded warm and cosy once more. Ted wished he knew enough to grasp a bit of what was being said.

Trev had been watching a film and had clearly hit pause to make or receive the call. Ted glanced at the screen while Trev was winding up his call with lots of kissy noises. He recognised the film. Trev was someone who could happily watch a favourite film endless times without ever tiring of it.

The frozen image showed a small figure in a red coat with the hood up, against a backdrop of stone steps and damp-looking walls, with a canal in the foreground.

'*Don't Look Now*?' he asked his partner as Trev ended the call and leaned across to kiss him as Ted sat down. 'Do you want to watch the end? Shall I un-pause it?'

'You know it always scares me. Even though I know by now who the killer is, I can only watch it from behind a cushion. Switch it off, if you like. I'll go and sort you some food out, if you're hungry?'

As Trev went into the kitchen to prepare the food, Ted used the remote to restart the film. He'd seen it almost as many times as Trev had, but this time it was making him think. Especially when the figure was revealed to be someone other than the child the audience was expecting to see.

# Chapter Twenty-five

'A film Trev was watching last night reminded me of something. We're focusing on young people, teenagers at the moment, but we mustn't overlook the possibility that our killer, or killers, are adults who are below average size and have particularly small feet.

'While I think of it, Kate. Do we know yet what size shoes Morgane takes? We'll need to know that to eliminate her footprints from the scene.'

'I've only seen her in those big fluffy slippers so far, boss, but I'll find out for you today and let you know. Is she a possible suspect?'

'I'm like Poirot at the moment with this one – I suspect nobody and I suspect everybody. She was, after all, definitely at the scene where her mother was killed and she's made no attempt to conceal that fact.'

'Speaking of Morgane, boss, something interesting from the hospital,' Jezza put in. 'On the face of it, nothing I wasn't expecting. I spoke to the registrar who'd seen to her who told me that she'd cleaned up the wound, applied butterfly stitches and arranged a precautionary scan.'

'I sense a but?'

'I pressed her a bit more on the cleaning up. She told me she removed something which could have been a bit of soil or grit from the wound. So where do you get soil or grit from a granite worktop?'

'If someone's been preparing fresh veg or salad and not wiped the edges?' Megan suggested.

'Perhaps she fell over, running up Marple Old Road,' Ted put in.

'Oh, come on, boss, you and I both know about falls from martial arts. How do you fall over and land on your eyebrow, which is where the wound is? There were no defensive marks on her hands or arms; I asked the registrar. There was just the head wound. And if you tripped and fell, you'd automatically put your hands out to save yourself, especially if they were tied in front of you.'

'Right, let's not get too carried away with Morgane as a suspect at this stage. I need to hear more detail from Max. He's admitted sleeping with her, a couple of weeks ago, so now we have to work out what possible motive Morgane would have for making him the prime suspect for her mother's killing.

'Kate, over to you on that one. Again, don't mention him by name to her yet, until I know what he has to tell me. But please keep on trying to gain her trust, see what you can find out. Try and get her to show you any of her other portraits. It just occurs to me that she may, for some reason, have produced Max's face because it was familiar to her, but out of context. They are at the same school, after all, even if what Max has said isn't true.

'Maurice, I'd like you and Steve to start checking previous offenders for anyone of particularly small stature. Anyone who's ever come to our attention for any reason. If there's nothing local, check nationally.

'We'll have a get-together again at five, everyone, please. Kate, you too. By then I should know what Max has to say for himself and, with any luck, we'll have the DNA comparison to tell us whether it was him in Morgane's bedroom that night.'

Ted hadn't realised how on edge he was, waiting for the DNA results. It was only when Jim threw a screwed up ball of paper at him from his end of the crowded desk that he realised he was tapping his pen constantly as he read through his notes.

'Whatever it is that's bothering you, Ted, get it sorted, man.

If you keep on tapping like that I might have to arrest you.'

'Sorry, Jim, I'm just impatient for those results. It's going to make a lot of difference to how the interview goes with Max.'

'You're sure it's just the case? There's no trouble in paradise between you and Trev?'

'No!' Ted's tone was so emphatic that Jim gave him a shrewd look. They'd known each other a long time.

'Are you trying to convince me? Or yourself?'

'It's nothing like that. It's just the usual work versus personal life stuff. I just wish I could spend more time with him. Do the kind of things he likes doing a bit more than I manage to do. You know what it's like.'

'Well, if you ever do want to talk to someone about anything, you know you can talk to me. I may not be much good at the relationship counselling stuff. But I can listen, and pat you on the shoulder, and say 'there, there' in all the right places, if it helps.'

Ted was relieved when his mobile phone rang. Jim was a good friend, but he couldn't imagine that him wanting to talk about his personal life with Trev would ever be comfortable, for either of them.

The caller was Doug, with the results he was waiting for.

'We have a match. The semen samples match the DNA sample you supplied from your Max Newman. There were a couple of things of note, though ...'

The desk phone rang and Jim answered it. He caught Ted's attention and gestured with one hand, pointing downwards. Ted understood the message. Max Newman had arrived, and hopefully his representative from YJT.

'Doug, thanks for that, I really appreciate you pushing it through. But I need to go now. Said suspect has just arrived and I want to crack on. I'll call you back as soon as I can.'

Ted couldn't wait to get started with Max, now he had the results. He could place him at the scene of the latest murder and he was eager to hear his explanation of that. He strode into the main office to collect Jezza.

'Anyone who's free, I want a full background check on Max Newman and everyone connected with him. Parents, any siblings. Any convictions anywhere, even fixed penalties, I want to know. Particularly dig deep into the father's background. I didn't much care for him, and not just because of his personal hygiene issues.'

Max's father was sitting waiting in the reception area, his expression truculent. He stood up to accost Ted as soon as he saw him.

'I want to know what's going on. Max won't tell me owt and he's gone off with some woman. I'm his father. I should know what's going on.'

'Mr Newman,' Ted said quietly, not wanting their conversation to be overheard. 'Max has said he would prefer to speak in front of someone impartial and we have to respect his wishes. As soon as I know anything, I will tell you more. But I'd just ask you to wait patiently for now, please.'

He and Jezza went through to the interview room where Max was sitting talking to a woman from YJT. It was not someone Ted had met before, so he introduced himself as he and Jezza sat down opposite the two of them.

'Aditi Padmanabhan,' she told him. 'Please feel free to call me Aditi. I've had a brief opportunity to talk to Max. He's not at all keen to speak in front of a woman, but I've assured him that I'm impartial, here to support him, not to judge him.'

'The same goes for DC Vine, Max. She's here to take notes of what you say. At this stage, I just want to talk to you about Morgane Edwards. You've already indicated that you want to tell me something about her. Are you happy now to go ahead and do that?'

'I 'spose I'll have to be. It's gotta be better than talking in front of me dad.'

He shifted uncomfortably in his seat, then locked his eyes

with Ted's and began. As Ted suspected, once he started, he barely paused for breath.

'You know I've got this snake, right. Boris. A royal python. I tried to draw him at school once for a project but I'm crap at drawing. The art teacher, Miss Lake, asked about him. When I said he sheds his skin a few times a year, she told me to bring some in and try working with that. That was okay. She asked if she could give some of it to some other students to work with and I said yes.

'This girl, Morgane Edwards. She's older than me, in a higher class. She's good at art. She had some of Boris's skin. She come up to me in the corridor one day and said she'd like to meet Boris, draw him live. She showed me some of the stuff she'd done with some of his skin. It was awesome. Anyway, I wasn't keen. Royals don't much like being handled and gawped at a lot. They're quite shy.

'She asked if she could come and watch him feed one time, draw him eating. She was, like, really interested in what he ate and how he ate, all that stuff. He usually eats about once a week. I generally give him a small rat, sometimes day old chicks. We fixed up a day when I was going to feed him, when I knew my dad would probably be out. I didn't really want Morgane seeing him. Me dad, that is.'

He paused to drink some of the water which had been provided for him. His eyes were still on Ted, ignoring the two women in the room as much as he could.

'She turned up and asked to see Boris, do some sketches of him, before he ate. She can draw really quick, so that was okay. I explained about putting him in a different tank to eat. You shouldn't feed them in the vivarium.

'Anyway, as soon as I moved him into his eating tank, she reached in her pocket and brought out a baby rabbit. She said it was a present, for Boris. But it was still alive. The poor little sod was petrified. I told her I couldn't give it to him. You're not allowed to feed them live prey and anyway, it could be dangerous for him, in case he got injured. Even from a littl'un like that, maybe kicking him or summat.'

He paused to take a long breath, looking more ill at ease than ever.

'She just laughed and chucked the little bleeder in with Boris. Some royals are real fussy eaters, but he's a greedy sod. He wasn't going to say no. They wrap themselves round their prey, crush 'em and swallow 'em whole.

'When she saw him doing this, she went, like, crazy, man. I mean hot as hell crazy. Horny.'

Now he was turning red and risked a quick look at Aditi, then at Jezza. They both remained impassive in the face of his growing embarrassment.

'Her eyes went all wide and wild-looking, like she was getting really turned on by it. The little bunny started screaming when Boris got 'im and that seemed to fire her up even more.'

This time he looked pointedly from one woman to another then back to Ted, his expression pleading.

'Look, mate, this is really difficult to talk about, especially with women here. I want to tell you my side of things, in case she tells you and it's summat different. But it ain't easy.'

'You're doing well, Max, and you are doing the right thing. I can assure you we're all professionals here. I understand that it isn't easy, but you can tell us anything. Aditi will advise you if at any point she thinks you should stop.'

Max paused to drink more water, to buy himself some time as he weighed up his options. It was clear that he didn't want to talk about it but realised that it was in his best interests to do so and to be as frank and honest as possible.

'I was standing next to her. She suddenly grabbed me. You know, down there,' his eyes dropped briefly to his lap, then locked once more with Ted's. 'She started saying stuff about wanting to see my snake in action next. She pulled me over to the bed and just, like, pulled my pants down and ripped hers off. She must have planned it. She brought condoms and shoved one on me really quickly. Then she went totally wild. I've never known anything like it, and she weren't my first. I'm not a kid.'

He paused for a moment, glancing warily from one to the other of them, clearly looking for judgement in their expressions. He found none. All three stayed impassive, Jezza just writing quickly, trying to keep up with everything he said. He took another drink of water before he continued.

'She'd brought some cans with 'er; vodka and summat fruity. We drank those after, and she sketched a bit. As soon as I could, you know, get it up again, she was at it again, like a bloody rabbit. Then she just got dressed, grabbed all her stuff, her sketch book, the cans an' that, and she went. Not spoke to me since. If I try and talk to her at school she just blanks me.'

Jezza turned to Ted. He could see she was dying to ask a question but wanted his permission. He imagined it was the same one that was on his mind. He nodded briefly.

'Max, what happened to the condoms you used? Did you dispose of them?'

He seemed surprised by the question, frowning in response.

'I dunno now. I can't remember.'

'You must remember, Max. You surely wouldn't want to leave them lying round in your room, in case your mum or dad saw them. Or is it something you do so often they wouldn't say anything?'

'Bloody hell, no. Me mum'd go mental. Now you mention it, I didn't find them, so she must have taken them for some reason. Wouldn't surprise me if she'd made, like, one of her art pieces out of them. She is seriously weird.'

'Max, I appreciate your apparent honesty up to this point. I know this hasn't been easy for you to talk about. I'm going to ask you a question now and it's very important that you answer it as truthfully as you can. Where were you on Monday evening, say between about eight o'clock and midnight.'

'Can I just interrupt you there, Inspector?'

It was Max's representative who cut in at that point.

'I'm assuming you're asking Max to provide an alibi for himself for the time of death of this Morgane's mother. If so, it's only right that I advise him that he doesn't, at this time, need to answer your question.'

'You're quite right, of course. I apologise, Max, I should have made that clear myself. You are under no obligation to answer that, or any other question at this time. However, it would help enormously if you don't mind answering it, and also if you'd mind telling me if you've ever been to Morgane's house.'

'Bloody hell, no.' He looked outraged by the mere suggestion. 'She lives up Offerton somewhere, the posh end. I don't even know where. I wouldn't go up there. I don't mind telling you about Monday, I got nothing to hide. I was at home. Me dad's grounded me, cos I got suspended from school so I just stayed in. Don't want any more trouble.'

'Can anyone verify that?'

'Me mam was at work, as usual. Me dad was ...' He hesitated for a moment. 'He were out doing a job for a mate, he said.'

Ted left Jezza to find an empty interview room to talk to Max's father while he sprinted upstairs to find out what had been discovered about the man's background.

'He's got a bit of form for petty theft, but nothing serious. A suspended sentence, spent now. But he's on the radar, suspected of doing a bit of driving for others who've been up to worse than that,' Maurice told him. 'If his lad said he was doing a job for a mate, I'm betting he doesn't mean he was helping him with hanging wallpaper.'

His suspicions were confirmed when Jezza reported back that Newman had been reluctant to say where he'd been but would only say he wasn't at the house the whole evening. Max could have gone out without him knowing, he said, although he doubted it because 'he knows what's good for him', as he told Jezza. He also said that his wife would have been back from work around ten o'clock so could account for Max's presence in the house then, which she did, when Ted sent Jezza round to the hospital where she worked, to talk to her.

It gave him a lot to feed back to the team at the catch-up briefing later on. It meant they could place Max's DNA at the murder scene, but only through the semen stains in the bedroom. There was no sign of his presence elsewhere.

'So it's just possible that the two of them were at it in her room when the mother came home,' Maurice suggested. 'They had a massive row when she caught them, they chased her downstairs and one or other of them killed her?'

'But then why has she shopped him? Unless she's trying to clear herself and she was involved?' Jo put in.

'I want to talk to Morgane again tomorrow. Kate, are you able to work tomorrow? Have you got childcare sorted? At least for part of the day? I'd like you to be there; just tell me what time suits you best.'

'I'm at your disposal whenever you need me, boss. Granny and my partner have a full programme of fun and treats planned already for Bella and George, just in case I was needed. I doubt I'll be missed.'


Ted managed to get home just as Trev was seating his guests at the table in the living room. It meant he had no time to shower and change, but at least he'd made it, as promised. He leaned down between Trev and his sister to plant a kiss on each of their cheeks, then turned his attention to Shewee's boyfriend, who had leapt to his feet as soon as Ted came in.

'Henry Baillie-Douglas, sir; I'm very pleased to meet you,' the young man said, holding his hand out to shake Ted's.

He was tall, nearly the same height as Trev, almost as sun-tanned, well-spoken, thick, blonde hair and dark blue eyes. He was casually dressed in chinos and an Oxford shirt that even Ted could tell had cost a fortune and had probably come from Jermyn Street.

'Ted is fine, Henry; even my team don't bother with the sir, unless they've done something wrong. Please sit down. Sorry I'm on the last minute, as usual, but at least I made it.'

He was stunned at the transformation in Shewee since he'd seen her last. She was always so fashionably turned out, mature, confident, looking far older than her actual years. This time she was wearing no make-up and her shiny black curls were pulled back into a severe pony tail tucked through the strap of a baseball cap with a polo logo. She wore a hooded jacket several sizes too large, with baggy sweat pants. The look was completely androgynous.

Nor had Ted or Trev ever known her so quiet. She barely got a word in. She simply sat there looking at Henry in something like awe. He was busy trying to persuade Trev to go and join them for the polo match the next day, promising to furnish him with ponies.

'I haven't played polo for so long I'd probably fall off and disgrace myself,' he laughed.

'Well, come and watch us play tomorrow. Stay to dinner, then stay over and you can ride out with us on Sunday. We've still got some hunters up. Father doesn't turn them all away, so there's always something for me to ride when I go home.'

'It sounds like fun,' Trev admitted, always eager to ride whenever he could. 'Would you mind?'

'Of course not,' Ted told him immediately. 'It will be great for you, and I'm going to have to work for a good part of the weekend, so it would ease my conscience.'

As Ted and Trev stood on the doorstep, each with an arm around the other, to wave their guests off, Ted watched the sleek, sporty, silver car purr demurely up the road then asked, 'Do you think Shewee knows about Henry?'

'That he bats for the same team as us?' Trev laughed. 'I doubt my sister has yet acquired a finely tuned gaydar. Most of us have done it. Taken the token girl back to show the parents. I know I have, and even slept with one of them, as you know. You were lucky you didn't need to, with an understanding father.'

'No wonder he likes her turned out like that. I kept thinking that without the make-up and the feminine clothes, she could pass for a lad at a distance.'

# Chapter Twenty-six

Ted was pleased that Trev would be having fun while he would be working most of the weekend. It made him feel better about the hours he intended putting in.

Trev was still fast asleep when Ted left for work, as usual. He left him a note on the kitchen table, telling him to enjoy himself but to take care riding big horses. They all seemed terrifying to Ted, although he knew Trev had grown up with them and was an accomplished rider. He weighted the note down with the sugar basin and sternly told Queen, who was watching him with interest, not to interfere with it.

He was going into the station first thing. He wanted to phone Kate Jones to brief her in advance on what he intended to talk to Morgane about. In particular, he wanted to brief her on how he intended to play things. He was impressed with her so far but he needed to be sure they were both singing from the same hymn sheet when it came to a small deception he planned to introduce.

The team were still doubling up on their usual weekend numbers, with so much extra work to cover. Jo and Mike were in their shared office, Maurice and Jezza were in the general office together. Just as Ted went in, Jezza was hurling a hefty book at Maurice's head. She grinned guiltily as the boss walked in.

'Sorry, boss, but that cheesy grin and incessant humming was driving me mad.'

Ted could see what she meant about the grin. He suspected the reason behind it.

'I'm glad things are going well, Maurice. As ever, leave the personal stuff at home, please. You're grown-ups, your personal life is your own. But I don't want to have to start putting you and DC Jennings on separate shifts.'

He went to find Jo and Mike, who had been wading through CCTV footage near to the Offerton murder site.

'Nothing of any use to us at all so far, boss,' Jo told him. 'Are we sure Morgane couldn't be wrong about the car colour? We've not yet found anything likely that's dark-coloured and small going in the right direction at the right time, apart from a couple which we've already traced and eliminated. Unless he took a very strange route.'

'I'd be surprised, with her art background. But being kidnapped, traumatised and presumably terrified might do strange things to someone's powers of perception. I'm going to talk to her again later this morning, so I'll see if her story stays the same.

'Any calls yet in response to the incident boards up near where she was found?'

'Nothing, boss,' Mike told him. 'Not even timewasters. That's strange, of itself. Could she have got confused about which end of Marple Old Road she ran along? I mean, a bang on the head like that, and everything else, she might not have been thinking straight.'

Mike's comment set a bell jangling in the back of Ted's mind, a couple of things he'd made a mental note to look at again and hadn't yet done so. He went to his own office and put the kettle on. He'd go through his notes and the various statements once more before he went to talk to Morgane again.

He remembered that Doug from the forensic lab had wanted to talk to him further about the semen stains. Ted hadn't yet had time to call him. He knew some of the scientific team would be working over the weekend and hoped Doug might be one of them. Unfortunately not, and no one he spoke to knew anything about it, so Ted left a message to say he'd called and would try to call again the following morning, when Doug would be back at work.

Next, he turned to the crime scene report and the mention of the blood and blonde hairs on the edge of the work-surface. Those hadn't yet been matched against Morgane's, but what interested Ted most was the detail that there was not much blood. Yet he'd made a note of Morgane's father telling him that when she'd been brought to the hospital, there had been a lot of blood. Then there was the question of the dirt in the wound. As Jezza had pointed out, it rather suggested that she'd received a second injury between leaving the house and being found, and he needed to find out where.

There was one person who could help him with that line of enquiry, one he knew wouldn't be likely to have anything planned for a Saturday evening and may well jump at the chance to join him for supper.

'Bizzie, I'll come clean at the start and admit this is a dinner invitation with strings. I need to pick your brains and, as Trev is away playing horses, I wondered if you'd like to come round and share a takeaway while I do so? Come in a taxi and I'll drive you home afterwards, then you can enjoy a glass or two of wine.'

The professor laughed delightedly.

'Edwin, it sounds like just the tonic I need for this evening. I'm going to visit Mummy this afternoon, never my favourite activity, so I'd love some company afterwards.'

They arranged a time, a menu, and Ted checked on her preferred drink to accompany it.

Kate met Ted at the door when he arrived at the flat in Bramhall. She led him through the kitchen to a tiny sun lounge at the back of the house, overlooking a pleasant garden, which was clearly well-tended. There was a small shed down in the bottom corner, in front of a high fence which effectively screened the back of the house and the garden from nearby properties.

There was a small dining table and four chairs, as well as a compact bamboo sofa, all of which made the space feel crowded. Morgane, looking brighter, but still in pyjamas, was sitting at the table with her sketch pad. This time she was wearing a large sweatshirt over the top, its kangaroo pockets pulled well out of shape by having fists thrust into them. Her father was sitting next to her.

After preliminary greetings, Ted sat down opposite Morgane and took out the photocopy he'd made of her sketch of the person she said had abducted her and killed her mother. He placed it on the table in front of him, looking directly at Morgane.

'Morgane, do you know someone called Max Newman?'

'I don't think so. The name doesn't ring a bell.'

This time, Ted didn't stop him when her father interrupted her.

'Isn't he the boy you told me about, darling? The one with the snake?'

She looked surprised.

'Mad Max? Is that what he's called? I know about him, through school, but everyone just calls him Mad Max.'

'Have you ever been to his house?'

She looked at him in something like horror.

'His house? Good grief, no, I don't even know where he lives. Why would I?'

'But you've done sketches of the snake?'

'No, not really. I mean, I know Mad Max brought in some of its skin when it moulted, or whatever they do, and Miss Lake, the art teacher, gave us some to work with. I loved the patterns, so I looked up online about them. The pattern's called desert ghost, which I really liked, so I did some sketches of the ones I found online. I used those, and some of the skin, to create something for a big course work project I was doing. Daddy, would you mind getting that from your room to show to the inspector, please?'

Her father was beaming in evident pride.

'It's stunning. But not everyone likes snakes and it is very vivid, so I keep it in my room. You'll see what I mean. I'll go and fetch it.'

'I call it Metamorphosis. It's a fantasy piece. I got an A+ for it.'

Ted did see what her father meant. It was, in equal measure, possibly the most striking and the most disturbing piece of artwork he could remember seeing. It started at one side of the frame with serpent's coils, increasing in size, beginning with actual skin from Max's python and continuing through intricate pen and ink sketching. It erupted to a climax just off-centre of the piece with a 3D representation of a dragon's head which exuded a feeling of evil that was almost tangible. Ted had watched *The Hobbit* at the cinema with Trev, a fantasy lover. Morgane's piece made Smaug the dragon appear about as menacing as one of Ted's purring cats.

'You see?' Edwards asked proudly. 'Stunning. She's so talented, my princess.'

'And has Max ever seen the finished work?'

'Good heavens, no, why would he? I only know about him because of the skin, and because people at school talk about him. Everyone thinks he's weird because he keeps a snake in his bedroom. I mean, it is a bit freaky, you have to admit.'

'And you can't think of anything else, anything at all, which might help us further, Morgane? Anything other than your sketch? Something about the car, perhaps? You're sure it was dark-coloured?'

She shook her head then winced slightly, her hand going to the wound on her eyebrow as if the movement had caused her pain.

'Are you no further forward with catching the killer? I haven't seen Morgane's sketch anywhere, not on TV or in the papers, asking if anyone knows who it is. Is there a reason for that?'

It was Morgane's father who posed the question, but Ted kept his eyes fixed on the daughter as he answered smoothly.

'We're not quite ready to make the sketch public yet, Mr Edwards. We want to make absolutely certain we have a good case against anyone before we bring them in. I'm sure you know, through your ex-wife's work, that we only have a limited time to hold someone on suspicion, so we like to have more to go on. Our main problem is that we haven't found any traces of the killer's DNA anywhere, which makes our task difficult.'

Morgane's eyes made a movement so rapid that it was barely detectable. But Ted had seen and recognised it. She'd been surprised by what he said.

'Nothing anywhere?'

It was again the father who asked the question, but Morgane was studying Ted avidly, waiting for his response.

'Well, as Morgane says, he appears to have been wearing gloves and shoe coverings. Sadly, killers being obliging enough to drop one of their cigarette ends at a crime scene with their DNA on is something which only happens in crime fiction.'

'Talking of crime fiction, Morgane, why don't you show the Chief Inspector those sketches you showed me earlier? See what he thinks. They're really very good,' Kate Jones put in.

Ted knew she would have a good reason for interrupting the flow, since this was not something they'd discussed earlier.

Morgane started to protest with a show of what Ted suspected was false modesty, then eventually pushed her pad across the table to him. He started to go through the sketches from the beginning. As she'd said, there were a few of coiled pythons, highly detailed in capturing the intricate patterns of their skin. But most were portraits, some of which Ted did recognise.

'This one is very good. It's Idris Elba, isn't it? Do you like crime fiction, Morgane? Do you watch series like Luther?'

'I love stuff like that. I started watching it because of my mum's work. You know, as a solicitor dealing with criminal cases. And my dad saying about me maybe being a court artist.'

'Who's your favourite character in Luther?'

'Alice!' she said emphatically.

Ted raised his eyebrows.

'It doesn't bother you that she murdered her own parents? And killed the dog?'

'Oh, yes, of course, that was terrible. But I just love the way she outsmarts the police all the time. She's a bit like some sort of a spy. A spook. I think she's cool.'

Kate walked out with him to the car when he'd finished his questioning.

'She's certainly unusual, Kate. What do you think about the relationship between her and her father? Normal, or a bit unhealthily close?'

'I've been wondering about that a bit. He might just be over-protective of her, after all she's been through. She is strange, though. And she certainly seemed to react when you said you'd found no DNA anywhere, although she hid her reaction well.

'She doesn't really seem to have any friends. I know she's not got her mobile at the moment, but no one's tried to make contact with her. No one from school, I mean. We've had the press pestering a bit but I keep sending them packing, but no friends or anything. Surely someone would have been in touch? And no signs at all of any boyfriends. I've tried asking her outright and she just says she's concentrating on her art for now, to get good enough grades for her first choice of university.'

'Any other family that you know of?'

'There's a grandmother, her father's mother. Morgane seems close. She lives in Wythenshawe. She phones often and Morgane chats away quite happily to her. Apparently she usually visits her at least once a week.'

'Wythenshawe?' Ted echoed. 'So there's a South Manchester connection? And we have the other case over there, with some similarities.'

'Oh, God, boss, Should I have made the connection and flagged it up? Sorry.'

'Don't worry, it's fine. You're not involved on that case so you weren't to know. Anyway, it may be no more than a coincidence. Up to now, Morgane hasn't been a suspect.'

'And now?'

'Now, I have no idea. Now I need to go back and talk to Max again and I need Forensics in his room turning it inside out for any trace there of Morgane's presence. One of them is obviously lying, but which one? In the meantime, you need to get her to show you as many of her sketch books as possible. I'm particularly interested in any which show a python feeding. Especially one feeding on a baby rabbit.'

Ted was relieved when he phoned Max's home and a woman answered. He'd quite like to meet the mother, who told him that her husband was out for the day. He'd feel reassured to know there was at least one parent looking after Max properly, even if she was out at work a lot of the time. His gut feeling told him Max was not the killer, but he couldn't go off his instinct alone.

He'd need a warrant to get the house searched for traces of Morgane's presence there, unless Max and his mother consented, and that was going to be tricky. Max might be afraid of being linked to her by forensic evidence. But if tests showed she had been in his room, she had lied and Max had apparently told the truth.

When he arrived at the house, Ted was at pains to explain to Max's mother that her son was not under arrest and it was not a formal interview. He could see that the youth was uncomfortable with the whole idea of saying anything in front of his mother, but Ted needed answers.

'Max, love, you need to tell the truth. Whatever you've done, you know I'll stick up for you. I'm your mam. If your dad doesn't need to know, he'll never hear it from me. Please, just tell the inspector what he needs to know.'

'Max, you've admitted to me that Morgane Edwards has visited the house and has been in your bedroom.'

His mother's hand went to her mouth and she looked anxious.

'Mrs Newman, please don't worry. You're probably imagining the worst, but Morgane is sixteen. Anything which may have happened between them is not my main concern at the moment. Max, this is very important. Did Morgane touch anything? Boris's tank, for instance? Could she have left fingerprints anywhere?'

'I keep Boris really clean. I look after him proper.'

His concern genuinely seemed to be at implied criticism of how he took care of his pet, rather than anything more serious he might be facing.

'He does, Inspector, Max is really good with Boris. His tank is always spotless. Max, love, if you've had a lass in your room, that's all right, that's normal. I won't tell your dad. Just please answer the inspector's questions. I don't want you in trouble with the police.'

'I clean the vivarium every day. He only uses the feeding tank once a week or so, and I do clean that too, but it's possible she may have put her hand on the glass when she was putting the rabbit in there.'

'Good, thank you. Now this is really important, both of you. I need proof to show if Morgane has been in your room. I know you've told me she has, but I need concrete evidence. Now, I could apply for a warrant to search it thoroughly, and in the meantime you could clean up any trace. Or, you could give me your permission, Mrs Newman, for me to bring forensic officers in to check for prints.'

Max was looking at his mother, his eyes appealing for her help and advice. She reached out and took his hand.

'Oh, I don't know, Max, love. I don't know what to do for best. Should I phone his dad, Inspector? Do we need a lawyer? What's best for Max?'

'I can't advise you of that, Mrs Newman. All I can do is to assure you that I'm not someone who would ever intentionally allow an innocent person to be charged with any crime. It's a question of trust. If you trust me, then you can give your consent. But only you can decide, I'm afraid.'

She looked searchingly at Ted, then her glance went between him and her son and back again.

'Dear God, I hope I'm doing the right thing, but all right. Yes, you can bring your people in to search his room.'

Ted waited around for the Forensics team to come and take fingerprints in Max's room. There were plenty on the outside of both tanks, around the edges where Max had clearly missed with his cleaning cloths. It would be some time before he got any results, after detailed comparisons were made, but if Morgane had been in the room, then she had lied to him and he didn't like that. It made her an unreliable witness for anything she told him, one the CPS wouldn't be keen to put up as a main witness for the prosecution in any future trial.

He left himself enough time to call for a takeaway on his way home, Indian, at Bizzie's suggestion. He somehow wasn't surprised that she'd asked for a Vindaloo, the hotter the better, and with extra chillis. He wimped out and opted for a milder Biryani, never being keen on burning his digestive tract in the guise of enjoyment. He also picked up the Tiger beer she'd asked for with the meal, and a bottle of a decent red to follow.

Flushed with proud success at his recent attempts at syllabub, he bought the ingredients to make another one. The cats were pleased when his efforts resulted in a fair amount of splashed cream, as his attention wandered for a moment and he lifted the hand whisk out of the bowl before it had stopped rotating.

'This is incredibly kind of you, Edwin, and very fortuitous. I'm sure Mummy gets more irascible every time I visit. Lately it seems I can't do anything right. A good passage-clearing curry is just what this doctor ordered.'

Seeing his look of alarm, she laughed and reassured him.

'Nasal passages. Sinuses. Nothing like it for clearing the head.'

They ate first and, only when they had retired to comfortable chairs with their coffee and the after dinner mints Bizzie had arrived clutching, did Ted bring the conversation round to the head wound, the dirt and the amount of blood.

'Scalp wounds tend to bleed quite alarmingly. Generally, eyebrows not quite so much. There certainly wasn't a lot of blood where the wound was probably caused. From what you've said, I would say there was a second blow, later, at the same area of the head. Very strange, but there is a hypothesis.

'For reasons best known to herself, the young lady wanted to look even more dramatic when she was found. So, as she trotted in search of help, she picked up a handy rock and bashed herself on the same place on her eyebrow. Splitting it open like that a second time would explain the more dramatic bleeding, and also the trace of dirt. But I have absolutely no suggestion to make as to why she would do that.'

'So how would I begin to prove that that's what happened, if it did?'

'You'd need a specially trained blood detection dog, but I'm not sure the GMP Tactical Dog Unit has one. I think you'd need to ask South Yorkshire. But I don't know how easily you'd get one, as they're in high demand, especially on such a tenuous theory as this. And whether it could find you anything with the time lag involved since the incident, I have absolutely no idea.'

# Chapter Twenty-seven

It was late by the time Ted had run Bizzie Nelson home and got back himself. He'd half hoped to hear something from Trev but realised he was probably having the time of his life. Polo matches and dinner parties were much more his style than Ted's.

Ted fired off a quick text, hoping Trev would remember his own inebriated typo from before and appreciate the joke.

'Hope you're having a billirant time. Enjoy your ride tomorrow. Don't fall off! See you afterwards. Love you. Ted x'

He was tired but his head was buzzing so much he doubted that he would find sleep easily. It was one of the rare times he almost envied colleagues who would have opened a bottle of wine before bed to help them to relax. But Ted had watched his father die an alcoholic and was determined not to go down the same road himself. The only thing he occasionally took was a strong antihistamine, which seldom failed to knock him out.

He was in early the following morning, reading through case notes once more, killing time until he could phone the lab and talk to Doug. In fact it was Doug who phoned him, earlier than Ted expected.

'These semen stains, boss. Don't take this the wrong way, but it's a bit of a speciality of mine. And I'd far sooner talk to you about them now, over the phone, than in a team briefing, with ladies present. I know we're both men of the world so you'll understand my points.'

He went on to explain that Investigators found semen stains

not infrequently at all sorts of crime scenes, including burglary, and that he had been given the dubious honour of becoming the lab's expert on them.

'Now I'm sure I don't have to explain the mechanics of ejaculation to you and I'm relieved not to be doing so in public. But there are a couple of things about these particular stains which don't quite sit right with me, based on my experience. Not for what we are clearly expected to take them for, which is someone masturbating over a girl's underwear.

'First is the quantity of ejaculate. Less than I would have expected. Much less than average. But there could be all sorts of reasons for that, like a medical condition. Secondly is the actual pattern of the stain. If someone was standing there masturbating, we would expect to see something like a splatter pattern.'

He broke off and chuckled.

'Sorry, but I'm just imagining my toes curling up if I was having to explain all of this in front of young DC Vine in particular. But I expect you know what I mean. These traces were different. If I had to make an educated guess – words you never thought you'd hear from a scientific type – I would say the semen had been wiped on to the underwear.

'In the old days we could have checked for spermicide to see if a condom had been involved. Someone might have wiped the contents of one onto the underwear, for instance. But it's being phased out now. Modern brands don't always have it.

'Oh, and another thing, in case you've not seen the report yet. The cable ties, from the girl's wrists. The only DNA we found on those was hers. No traces of anyone else's. And teeth marks.'

'As if she'd been trying to get them off?'

'Possibly,' Doug's voice was hesitant. 'This must be my day for wild guesses, but as they were near the pointed end of the tie, I would have said more as if she'd been pulling them tighter. But of course I've no idea if that was the intention or not. In the back of a moving car, she could just have been desperate and trying whatever way she could to escape.'

Kate came to the door once more to let the boss in. He'd sent a text ahead to let her know what time he hoped to be there. They took the opportunity to exchange a few words in the front garden before going inside to talk to Morgane again.

'No more sketch books, boss. She says the others are at the house. She's keen to get them back, as well as some more clothes, and her phone.'

Ted frowned. He didn't remember any mention of sketch books in the inventory from the house. He made a mental note to check again.

Morgane and her father were in the front room, which was again warmer than Ted found comfortable. He slipped a hand through his tie to loosen it and undo his top button. He again produced the photocopy of Morgane's sketch and held it up to her.

'Morgane, I just need to ask you once more if you know who this is?'

'Why do you keep coming round here harassing her?'

The father's tone was truculent, his face darkening.

'Morgane's the victim in all of this. She's lost her mother and been frightened half to death. Yet you seem intent on interrogating her as if she was a suspect. I think it's time I called my ex-wife's law firm and had someone to represent her interests.'

Ted gave him his most disarming smile.

'I'm sorry if you feel that way, Mr Edwards. And Morgane, I hope you understand that I'm not in any way trying to upset you further. I'm just trying to establish facts so we can make some progress with this enquiry.'

Kate had sat down next to Morgane, tissues at the ready, sensing that this could be a difficult interview. Clive Edwards was sitting at his work desk, his feet planted wide apart, hands resting on his open thighs. He still looked angry.

Ted kept his voice quiet, the tone gentle, as he probed with questions.

'My problem is this, Morgane. Your sketch is a striking likeness of Max Newman. The boy with the snake. You deny knowing him. He tells me you do know each other. That, in fact, you've been to his house. I have to ask you now if that's true?'

Her father was clearly building up to say something, but Ted's eyes were looking at the girl intently, watching for her reaction. Slowly, her lower lip started to wobble. Fat tears appeared in her eyes. Then she threw herself sideways, burying her face in Kate's lap as ragged sobs shook her body.

'I did go there. I did. To draw the snake. For my art project. But then he...he...he raped me.'

Edwards sprang to his feet, covered the short distance between him and his daughter and dropped to his knees in front of her. She pulled away from Kate and flung her arms round his neck, her face against his chest, as her crying became more hysterical. He just kept repeating meaningless endearments, stroking her soft blonde hair, his own voice thick with suppressed tears.

Ted exchanged a look with Kate and the two of them got to their feet.

'We'll give you both a moment, Mr Edwards. It's been a shock for you. Take your time.'

He and Kate withdrew quietly to the kitchen, where she put the kettle on.

'Well, what did you make of that performance, boss?'

'You think it's a performance then? You're not buying it? I must confess, I have my doubts.'

'She must have known you would talk to Max at some point. You mentioned his name to her. One of them is lying.'

'She's clearly highly intelligent. She must know a rape allegation is hard to prove or disprove, especially some time after the event. And she's already said she likes watching crime series. She could have this all worked out. Let's assume, just for a moment, that Max did rape her. For whatever reason, she didn't want to go to the police. She didn't recognise the person she claims killed her mother and kidnapped her. So why not set Max up for it? See him go down for something, at least.

'Let's take these drinks through, see if she's calmed down enough to tell us her version of events. I have some updates from forensics but I'd prefer you to listen first and see what opinion you form.'

Edwards looked up as soon as the two officers went back into the room. From his expression, he had gone up a notch from angry to fuming.

'I'm going to be making a complaint about your conduct. It's unforgivable, treating my daughter like this, after all she's been through.'

'That is your right, Mr Edwards. I'll give you contact details for my senior officer, of course.'

Ted had already decided he'd put him on to Jim Baker, rather than the Ice Queen, anticipating such a move. Jim was fair, but he'd far sooner take a bollocking from him, if necessary, than the frosty Ice Queen. He still hoped he could smooth things over so it wouldn't come to that.

Kate handed out the mugs then she and Ted resumed their seats. Kate sat on the opposite end of the sofa to Edwards, who now perched on the arm, still holding his daughter.

'Morgane, I appreciate this is very distressing for you. I just want to make it clear that we need you to tell us exactly what happened, on both occasions, as honestly and accurately as you can.'

She lifted her head and made direct eye contact with him. There was something in the expression of her eyes which he couldn't fathom. Something almost as unsettling as her artwork.

She told her story calmly and concisely. In some ways, it differed little from Max's account, except in one crucial area.

Max had said she was the instigator. According to Morgane, Max had grown increasingly aroused at the sight of the snake feeding. She was sitting on the end of his bed, sketching. She could see his growing erection pressing against the tracksuit bottoms he was wearing, she told them.

'I started to get a bit worried. I mean, I could see he was getting, you know, a stiffy, looking at the snake feeding. I thought I'd better get my things together and get out of there. I thought perhaps he just wanted to...he might just be going to...'

She looked anxiously between the three of them, picking her words.

'I don't know how to say it politely,' she said, making a motion with her hand as she spoke.

'You thought his intention was to masturbate?' Ted supplied calmly. 'And what happened then?'

'I just wanted to get out of there. I didn't want to watch that. As soon as I tried to leave, he grabbed me and threw me on the bed. He said he had a knife and would use it if I struggled. He said he'd get the snake out and it would wind itself round my neck and strangle me while he was raping me. I was terrified. So I just let him. As soon as I could, I got up and ran out. It wasn't him who killed my mother. I didn't really get a clear look at who did. But I just saw my chance to get my revenge on Max for what he did to me. I'm so sorry. It was stupid of me, I know that now. I'm really sorry for wasting your time.'

'Morgane, this next question is very important. Did he use a condom?'

'Yes,' she said quickly. 'That's why I didn't think it was worth reporting. He wouldn't have left any trace and it would just have been his word against mine. I'm so sorry.'

'This has been difficult and upsetting for you, and for your father. I'm going to go now and leave you with Kate. When you feel up to it, perhaps you'll tell her any details at all that you can remember about the real person who abducted you. I'll come back tomorrow and perhaps we can talk some more.

'Mr Edwards, I wonder if you'd mind seeing me out, please?'

At the front door, he took out one of his cards and a pen.

'I'm noting the contact details of my senior officer, Detective Superintendent Baker, for you. Please feel free to get in touch with him if you feel my conduct has been in any way inappropriate. It was certainly not my intention.'

Edwards took the card and studied it.

'So what now? Are you going to arrest this Max boy for what he did to Morgane? I'd no idea she'd been through anything like this, and now losing her mother as well. How is she ever going to get over it all?'

By the skin of his teeth, Ted managed to get to the shop before it closed. He'd been impressed with the meal for two for a tenner deal, including a bottle of wine, which he'd had enjoyed when he'd been to Bizzie's house and wanted to get the same thing for when Trev got home. He'd have no time to cook anything himself and he didn't want Trev to have to. He added the customary single red rose, their little shared joke, so it would hopefully be a nice welcoming touch.

He made sure he was back in good time to have everywhere tidy and the cats fed and cleaned out. Trev had only been gone overnight but he'd missed him. He needed him.

He'd brought paperwork home with him and worked on that until he heard Trev's Triumph motorbike turn into the drive, then the sound of the garage door opening and closing as he locked his precious baby safely away.

Ted heard him stride into the hallway. The familiar soft thud as he put his motorcycle helmet on the hall table. The sound of him slipping out of his leathers and boots as he called out, 'Hey, you. I've had the most amazing time. I've got some fab video to show you of me jumping.'

He strode into the kitchen and headed straight to Ted, giving him a brief hug and a kiss. His mobile was in one hand

and he was flicking the screen.

'I'm just sending the videos to Laurence. Yet another horse-lover. You're surrounded by them. I really must teach you to ride one day, then you can join in. Here, look. I rode one of Henry's father's hunters, a big grey tank called Hector. Pulled like a train but jumped his heart out for me. You can see. Shewee filmed us.'

Ted felt an unexpected pang of jealousy that the mysterious Laurence had seen the film before he had. He sternly told himself to stop being petty and ridiculous. Of course Trev would share it with knowledgeable horse people. Ted could only look in awe and admiration, watching Trev and the enormous grey horse hurtling over seemingly huge hedges at alarming speeds.

'I'm glad you had fun,' he said, wondering if it sounded as lame as it felt. 'I got us a ready meal. I haven't had time to cook and I didn't want you to have to.'

Trev flopped down in a kitchen chair.

'I'm still stuffed, to be honest. I've been very well looked after. A huge breakfast before we rode, and an enormous lunch afterwards, which went on and on. Oh, and Shewee did brilliantly in the match yesterday. Scored a couple of goals. I was really proud of her. I've got some film of that here.'

At that moment his phoned pinged with an incoming text. Trev looked at the screen and laughed delightedly.

'Laurence. Green with envy.'

His fingers flew expertly over the keyboard as he fired off a rapid reply, smiling to himself as he did so. Then he looked up at Ted and asked, 'So how has your weekend been?'

Ted sat down next to him, pulling his chair closer, needing the warm presence of his partner to bring some normality back into his life.

'Oh, you know. Playing mind games with a teenage killer. Same old, same old.'

Trev reached out and took hold of his hand, giving it a

sympathetic squeeze, just as Ted asked, his tone anxious, 'We are all right, aren't we? You and me?'

'Of course we are! For goodness sake, Ted, why do you keep asking that? I've been having fun, doing the kind of stuff I like. I know it's not your thing and that's fine. We've never been joined at the hip. You've got your Krava Maga and your work. I've got my bikes and my horsey stuff. It's always been like that.'

'I just worry, you know, that I'm a bit dull for you. You've been having some fun, then you have to come home to me being preoccupied with work, as usual ...'

'I don't have to come home. I come home because I want to. I understand about your job. I've been with you long enough. I can appreciate you may feel anxious when I'm away. But if every time I go off and have some fun I'm going to come home to a police interrogation, it takes the edge off it. We're fine. At least, I think we are. If you have to keep asking if we're all right, then perhaps it's you that doesn't think we are.'

'I'm sorry. Really. It's a difficult case. I know it's not easy living with a copper.'

'I didn't walk into the relationship with my eyes closed. I trust you. All these long hours you put in, it never occurs to me that it's anything other than work. You weren't my first, not by a long chalk, and you know that. But none of them ever loved me like you do. Which is why I trust you.'

They'd always been honest with each other about their previous liaisons. Trev had told Ted his first time had been with a much older spy-master friend of his parents. A real screaming old queen in a Cashmere overcoat, as he described him, with a penchant for innocent, unspoilt boys, the younger the better.

'You're acting suddenly as if you're jealous, and I don't understand why. I came back from France with an all-over tan and you behaved as if you thought I'd been taking part in wild naked orgies or something. Surely the fact that the first thing I wanted to do when I got home was to rip the clothes off you should tell you that wasn't true. Now I go away for one night and it's the same again. What do you think I did, jump into bed with Henry to help him decide on his sexuality?'

Trev was starting to sound angry and that was unusual. He had one of the sunniest natures of anyone Ted knew, except where his parents were concerned.

'Why don't you tell me what's really bothering you?'

The ideal moment. Perfect timing for Ted to ask the question which was burning a hole in his guts, tearing his heart out of his chest. But how to ask a question to which you feared the answer?

'I think our relationship is wonderful. The sex is amazing, and you're my best friend. I've never cheated on you, Ted, and I never would, if that's what's worrying you. But it hurts me, more than you can imagine, that you might even think that.'

Trev stood up, pushing his chair back with a clatter on the kitchen tiles. Queen, in her familiar place on the table, arched her back and hissed warningly, not appreciating the raised voice. Barcelona, the most timid of the cats, shot out through the cat flap like a small, black, ballistic missile and didn't stop running until she reached the sanctuary of the thick bushes at the bottom of the garden.

'I'm sorry,' Ted said again, aware that it sounded even more empty after so much repetition. 'I trust you. Of course I do. Come on, sit down, let me make you some tea. Or a glass of wine, perhaps?'

'Oh, I need more than wine. I'm going out. I've no idea how long I'll be. I shall undoubtedly get thoroughly pissed so don't wait up. I'll sleep in the spare room tonight.'

With that, he slammed out of the house, sending the rest of the cats, even Queen, scurrying for cover.

In a rare loss of self-control, Ted slammed his fist into the kitchen door, punching with such force that the panel splintered. He was too hyped up even to feel the pain, but the blow split the skin on his knuckles. He lifted the hand to his mouth, licking the blood away.

He didn't know what to do with himself. Had no idea what he could do to make things right. He felt a desperate urge to seek out a partner for some violent, uncontrolled Krav Maga, but he desperately wanted to be in when Trev got back. He was in his sweats, so he took himself out into the back garden to start on a vigorous karate kata, hoping that would work it out of his system. But nothing seemed to help.

He went back into the house, picked up his mobile and called a number.

'Mam?'

Ted had never called his mother anything since she'd come back into his life. Certainly not that.

'Mam, can I come round and talk to you, please?'

'Oh, Teddy, *bach*, of course you can. You don't have to ask. Come now, *bach*, I'll put the kettle on.'

He stopped only to drape a towel around his neck. Then he ran flat out all the way to his mother's house at the most punishing rate he could set himself. He arrived feeling his lungs were on the point of exploding and his heart was in overdrive.

As a child, after she'd left, he'd spent endless nights crying himself to sleep for his mother. Now, suddenly, she was the one person he wanted to be with, to talk to.

It was late when Trev finally rolled in, very drunk. Ted was sitting at the kitchen table, paperwork spread out in front of him. As soon as he heard the front door, he went out into the hallway.

'Don't start, Ted. Just, you know, don't. I'm going to bed. In the spare room.'

He turned to start lurching up the stairs but Ted went to stop him.

'Let me sleep in the spare room. That bed's far too small for you. You take our bed.'

Trev whirled back to face him, almost falling over with the sudden movement.

'For God's sake, Ted, will you stop being so bloody reasonable. I'm the one who's completely pissed. I'll sleep in the bloody spare room. And don't wake me up in the morning.'

# Chapter Twenty-eight

Trev groaned loudly from under the covers as Ted sat on the bed next to him and gently shook his shoulder.

'Sod off, Ted, it's the middle of the night.'

His voice was muffled as he pulled the duvet further over his head.

'I'm sorry to wake you early when you said not to. I behaved like a complete prat last night and I just wanted to make it right before I go to work. I brought you some coffee.'

Trev was trying to burrow back down into the bed. It was too narrow for him to sleep as he usually did - spread out, with his long limbs everywhere.

'If I say I forgive you, will you go away and leave me to die in peace? I have the hangover from hell.'

'I brought you some water, too. I thought that might help. And some wholemeal toast, in case you wanted something to eat.'

More low moaning, but slowly Trev lowered the duvet from his head and opened one cautious and bleary blue eye.

'Sadist! Do you want me to throw up?' but at least his tone was mellowing, less hostile.

'I just want you to know how sorry I am that I pushed you to it. I've got one hell of a morning in prospect. I've got to sell Jim an idea that'll probably see him put me on restricted duties. But I promise that, as soon as I possibly can, you and I are going to do something together, something really special. Just to show you that I know I'm a right pain.'

Trev's long sigh turned into a wince as he tried to sit up,

blinking rapidly.

'All right, all right, I forgive you. Now give me the coffee and go.'

Ted bent down to plant a kiss on his cheek, then stood up to go.

'God, you haven't even shaved. It's like being kissed by a hedgehog. Watch out for the Ice Queen, she'll have a hissy fit if you go in like that.'

Then, as Ted reached the door, smiling again now that things seemed to have been smoothed over, Trev added, 'I know you love me, Ted, and I love you. Just please don't smother me.'

His words preyed on Ted's mind as he drove in to work. His mother had said something similar to him the evening before and he knew it was true. He was a mass of insecurities. He couldn't help himself. But he made a mental promise that he was going to change. He'd start by going back to Carol for some more counselling sessions to help him. That would please Trev. It would show he was committed to getting their relationship back on track.

Ted was always in early. This time he'd made sure he was even earlier, not wanting to run into the Ice Queen. He knew he looked rough. He'd barely slept, just a couple of snatched hours on the sofa in between paperwork. He hadn't shaved because his right hand was painful and swollen where he'd punched the door and he was shaking slightly with the combined effect of too much strong coffee through the night and not enough sleep.

He'd managed a shower and a clean shirt, but his tie was at half-mast and his collar button undone. He had too much to worry about and he never bothered much about his appearance, until forced to.

Although Ted was early, Jim Baker wasn't far behind him. Nobody could ever accuse the Big Boss of slacking. As he walked into the office, he glanced at Ted, sitting behind his desk, and went straight to put the kettle on.

'Christ, Ted, you look rough. Have you not slept? A breakthrough on the case?'

'I do have a theory I want to run past you. But first, I want to ask you a favour. A big one.'

Jim was busying himself making the drinks.

'Name it,' he said, then added, 'I'm making you a proper strong coffee, none of that green weasel's piss you usually drink. You look like you need it.'

He plonked the mugs down on the desk and took his seat at the end of it. Ted looked warily at the foul blackish brew in his mug and wondered if his heart could take much more caffeine without going into palpitations.

'I'd like to get away at a decent time if I can tonight. I behaved like a right dickhead to Trev last night. We had something of a row. I need to make it right.'

Jim was looking shrewdly at Ted's damaged hand, but thought it best not to mention it. He could be surprisingly tactful, at times.

'When did you last take a day off? And why do you think you're so indispensable that me, Jo, two DS's and the rest of the team can't hold the fort for a couple of hours without you?'

'Point taken. When you hear what I have to say, you might send me home anyway, never to return.'

He paused for a gulp of the coffee, wincing at the strength of it.

'I want to make Morgane Edwards a prime suspect for her mother's murder.'

Jim continued to slurp his coffee, seemingly unconcerned. Then he said, 'All right, very funny, ha-ha, but it's not April Fool's Day. What's your real idea?'

'I'm serious, Jim. The more I see of her, and the more digging I do, the more I'm convinced she's the killer. And I also think she may be involved in at least one of our other cases.'

'Tell me what evidence you have.'

'Ah.'

Ted's stock stalling tactic expression. The one he always used when he knew that what he was going to say next was not going to go down well with the person he was talking to.

'At the moment, next to nothing. Which is why I want a warrant to search the father's flat. Every last inch of it. And I want to contact South Yorkshire for a trained blood sniffer dog. I want to find the rock I think she hit herself with after she left the house to make the wound look worse.'

'Is this sleep deprivation talking?'

'I'm serious, Jim. We've found no trace at all of anyone else at the crime scene, only the semen stains. And according to Doug, at the lab, they look like a clumsy attempt on someone's part to plant evidence. If no one else was there, how did the bridge from Luke Martin's violin get there? And the lab have confirmed it is the same one. We've also found no trace at all of this mysterious youth in the dark car, no sightings by the public, nothing on CCTV. Let me outline for you what I think happened, then you can tell me whether you think the idea has legs.'

Jim listened impassively, drinking his coffee, saying nothing, as Ted laid out his theory.

'I thought at first that it could have been the argument she admitted having with her mother, which simply got out of hand. Except for the semen stains. They make me think that this was, in fact, a cold-blooded, pre-meditated crime, planned a couple of weeks in advance at least.

'Morgane goes to see Max, on the pretext of sketching the python. They both admit having sex, the only difference is on the subject of consent. Both say a condom was used. I think Morgane took the condom, or condoms, depending on the version, with her and stashed them somewhere. In the freezer, perhaps. I'll have to ask Doug. She'd decided, for whatever reason, to do away with her mother, and now she had the means to put Max in the frame by leaving his DNA at the scene.

'After she's killed her mother, she hits her own head against the work surface. Enough to split the skin but not enough to incapacitate her. With a hood up, it wouldn't show much, if anyone saw her. She jumps on a bus up towards Marple. Gets off somewhere before Seventeen Windows. She's got the cable ties in her pocket. She puts one on, pulls it tight with her teeth. She goes into Marple Old Road from the top end, which is why no one saw anything at the lights where she said she got out of the vehicle. There simply never was a youth in a car.

'Now she needs to have a bit more blood, to make it look dramatic, so she picks up a stone somewhere, smacks herself on the same place, chucks the rock under the bushes. And appears on the doorstep as a poor little victim of a terrible crime, bleeding impressively from a head wound.'

Jim finished his coffee and put the mug back down on the desk.

'So you want a specialist sniffer dog to find a specific rock when you have no idea where it might be or even if it exists? Have you any idea what that's going to cost us? And what if it can't find it? Or the blood traces have been washed away by now? Dammit, Ted, you do remember who her mother was and which firm she worked for? The girl's father is bound to instruct that firm and if you've got this wrong, they'll hang us all out to dry.'

'We've got a connection to South Manchester, too,' Ted ploughed on, ignoring his objections. 'Her grandmother lives in Wythenshawe. Morgane visits her often. I want search warrants for anywhere and everywhere Morgane might stash things. I want to see all of her artwork. I've seen some of it, Jim, and it's disturbing. That's why I also want a psych evaluation of her. I want someone with experience of dealing with disturbed young people to tell me if what I think I see in her is right. I'll even work with a profiler on this one if I have to.'

'Blimey, if you're going to let me bring in a profiler, then I'll have to start taking you seriously. That's a bloody first.'

'It's her, Jim, I know it is. I just need to find a way to prove it. Starting with checking CCTV on all the buses she could have caught.'

'Ah, yes, that old inconvenience of having to prove what we think we know,' Jim said dryly. 'And this is definitely what you think? It's not just clutching at straws because you're over tired and there's no one else in the frame?'

Ted shook his head emphatically. He was tired, he'd be the first to admit it, and arguing with Trev had unsettled him. But he knew he was right on this. He just needed Jim to trust him enough to let him have the resources necessary to prove he was.

'What about the lad with the snake? Has he got an alibi for when Morgane's mother was killed?'

'His mother says he was at home at ten o'clock when she got back from work. I know she's not going to be the most convincing witness, being his mum. But he does use his phone to chat in various online groups about reptiles, he told me. We can check his phone, and pinpoint where it was at the time of the murder.'

'All right, I've trusted you before and you've never yet let me down, although it's been close at times. Let's run with this for now. I'll sort out search warrants, you talk to South Yorkshire, see if they have a spare woofer this side of Christmas. I just hope to God you're right, Ted.'

All of the team were in early, all anxious to push on with the enquiry. Ted had asked Leona and her team to join them even before he'd known he would have important news for them. Océane was always in earlier than the hours she was paid for. She seemed to love her work. So far the relationship between her and Steve was causing no problems in the workplace and had certainly done wonders for his self-esteem. She indicated to Ted that she had things to say, so he asked her to say her piece, as soon as he'd finished outlining everything he'd already said to Jim Baker.

What he had to say caused a few raised eyebrows amongst the team, but they knew him well enough by now to trust his instincts.

'This mobile phone, boss,' Océane began. 'Are we sure this belongs to a teenage girl? And are we sure it's her only one? There is so little on it that it's positively boring. Hardly any friends, very few messages, no photos to speak of.'

'She couldn't just have deleted everything?'

Océane's tone was patient enough as she explained that she had already checked for anything which might have been dumped, but that the phone was squeaky clean.

'Right, so, when we get search warrants, which the Big Boss is going to arrange, we're looking for a possible second phone. Rob, I'm going to put you in charge of getting the father's flat searched and I want a thorough job. Nothing missed, please. I particularly want that 3D dragon art piece, from her father's room, and anything else like it you find. I want whoever does the psych evaluation to see it. This may well be tomorrow, by the time we've got warrants and sorted out bodies to do it all.

'Kate, I don't want Edwards getting wind of it in advance, of course, not until Rob puts the warrant in his hands. When they arrive, I want you to take the father and Morgane out somewhere. We'll sort out where. Maybe get a hotel room and take them there. He isn't going to like it one bit, so prepare for protests. He needs to leave when you tell him to. He can get his lawyer to join you later.

'Jo, we now have a Wythenshawe link. I want you and Leona to check out the grandmother. Find out about when Morgane goes there, if she has any friends over that way. If she keeps any stuff at her gran's house. Sketch books, art work, anything. And find out if she visited her grandmother on the day Mrs Murray was killed.

'Jezza, can you get round to the school, check on attendance records for both Morgane and Max for the day of the bus death. I don't think Max is involved, but let's make a proper job of this. Also ask around a bit more for any information you can find out about Morgane. Does she have friends? Who are they? What's her attendance and conduct like? You know the sort of thing. And before you go, I need you in my office for five minutes, please.

'Megan, can you talk to Max's Goth friend? Ask her more about him. See if she knows anything about Morgane. If she and Max are close there's just a remote possibility he's talked to her.

'Charlie and Graham, we'd better do a thorough in-depth background check on Jake Dolan. I don't think he's in the frame for any of this but we need to be certain. Check his alibis for the Hillcrest Road murder, and also the Luke Martin case and Tyler Bradbury. All of you be aware that the defence in this is quite likely to be Stephanie Mason's old firm and they don't take prisoners. We need to anticipate every spanner they're going to throw in the works on this case and have an answer for it.

'Another thing, Kate. You've probably already thought of it, but just to flag it up. If the press get the slightest whiff that we're investigating Morgane, you're going to be under siege at the flat. I'm going to talk to Inspector Turner about some extra bodies to keep it under observation round the clock. In particular, I don't want Morgane going out anywhere, hiding or destroying anything.'

'I can arrange to stay over, if it helps, boss?'

'Thank you, but I'd prefer to avoid that. There is one thing I have to mention at this stage. Up to now, Morgane has been considered as the second victim in this case. I may, of course, be completely wrong. But if I'm not, it means that we're dealing with an incredibly cold-blooded killer, even if she is young and looks innocent. And that means, Kate, that you could be in danger.

'I don't want to pull you out, at this stage, nor do I want to put someone else in with you, either of which would raise suspicions. But your safety is my responsibility, and it's an issue we need to address. Make sure you have your spray with you, to hand, at all times. And just watch out for the father turning possessive. I'm still not sure about their relationship.

'Right, let's get on with it. And Kate, take care, and stay in contact. Jezza, five minutes, please, and Boss, I need a witness.'

'This sound intriguing,' Jezza said as she followed Ted and the Big Boss into their shared office.

Ted pulled some cable ties out of his pocket as he said, 'I need to see how easy or not it is for someone to put these on their own wrists. I need someone with smallish hands and slim wrists, similar to Morgane. Also someone who wouldn't think I was making them some sort of strange proposition, asking them to tie themselves up.'

It took Jezza a matter of moments to do it, deftly using her teeth to pull the end of the tie to secure it tightly round her wrists.

'I think we've just shown clearly how easy it was for Morgane to tie herself up, probably just before she arrived at the house for help. And Jezza's obligingly shown us why the teeth-marks were on the end of the strap only,' Ted said, as he took out a pocket knife and carefully cut Jezza free. 'My bet is she also hit herself with the stone at the last minute. That's where I'm going to ask the dog handler to start.'

Trev was surprised to find Ted's car already in the garage when he got home from work. As he went in through the front door, Ted was waiting for him in the hallway, grinning excitedly, dressed in his walking gear.

'I promised I'd find time for us to do something together. Well, we're going camping. Right now.'

'Have you been suspended? How can you get away in the middle of a big case?'

'We're not going far, and it's only for one night,' Ted said, grabbing his arm and pulling him through the kitchen and out of the door leading to the back garden.

He'd put their tent up on the lawn. There was a light drizzle, so he'd added an awning, with their camp kitchen underneath it. Food was laid out ready next to the portable gas stove.

'Is it all right?' he asked anxiously. 'I bought venison sausages. Not too crazy an idea?'

'It's totally mad,' Trev laughed in delight. 'But I love it! What larks, Pip. I'm not hungry yet, but drag me to your tent and I may just work up an appetite.'


'Inspector?'

An anxiously quavering voice called out from the other side of the high garden fence later on.

'Is everything all right? Only I heard a strange noise, coming from your garden. It was very loud. I could hear it from my kitchen.'

Ted sat up guiltily, putting a gentle hand over Trev's mouth to keep him quiet as he convulsed into giggles.

'Sorry to have disturbed you, Mrs Adams. Everything's fine. We were just, er, trying to catch one of the cats to worm him.'

Trev was nearly hysterical at this point. Ted kept his hand firmly in place.

'Would you like me to come round and help you? I'm quite good with cats.'

'No! No, thank you, Mrs Adams, that's really kind but I've got him cornered now. Sorry again to have disturbed you.'

He'd never been more grateful for the high wooden fencing, topped with wire mesh, which they'd put up to try to keep the cats from straying on to nearby busy roads. From outside her back door, the elderly neighbour couldn't see into their garden and Ted knew that she slept in the upstairs front room, keeping the back room as a guest room for family members who only visited once a blue moon.

'Well, if you're sure ... Good evening to you then, Inspector.

'Good evening, Mrs Adams, and thank you again for your concern.'

Trev was crying laughing by this point. Ted looked at him fondly. It was good to see that his crazy idea seemed to have put things right between them.

'Right, where were we? And if you have to make so much noise, at least try to sound like a cat being wormed.'

# Chapter Twenty-nine

The boss was back on form. The whole team had noticed the difference in him the previous day and been concerned by it. This morning was business as usual. They could see the familiar energy in him. His suspect was now within his sights and it boosted the morale of all of them. They could sense they were nearing a conclusion.

They had a quick early catch-up, but Ted had scheduled the main briefing of the day for later on, when he hoped they might finally start to have some results. He had an appointment himself with a man and a dog and he chose Maurice to go with him to drive his official car.

Ted had got lucky with the dog section from South Yorkshire. He'd had a long conversation with a helpful sergeant who told him that their top blood dog, who had a one hundred per cent success rate, was in high demand and was currently on secondment in another part of the country. He did, however, have a young, eager dog, fresh out of training and ready to face his first challenge.

'It'll cost you less, too, sir. I can't guarantee you a result, especially not with everything you've told me. But we'll give it a good go for you.'

Kevin Turner had sent some of his officers to close off Marple Old Road from either end while the dog worked. Ted was pretty certain that, always assuming he was right about Morgane, she would have injured herself as close as possible to the house she had selected to ask for help. She would need to have hit herself hard to have the right effect. He couldn't imagine her taking the risk of doing it too far away and not being in a fit state to make her dramatic entrance.

The dog handler arrived promptly and got out of his van with a small and lively black and white springer spaniel. It had a grinning face and frenetically wagging tail, straining at its lead and clearly dying to get to work.

'Morning, sir. Simon Archer. We spoke on the phone. And this is Tally.'

Even Ted didn't feel too wary faced with such a friendly-looking dog, especially now he at last understood the reason for his long-term fear of dogs.

'Thanks for coming, Sergeant. I appreciate it's a long shot, especially for a young dog. But it really would help us enormously if Tally could find what we're looking for.'

'Like I warned you, he's young and inexperienced. He's done well in training, but this is a big ask for him. We'll do our best, that's all I can promise you.'

Ted and Maurice stood back out of the way while the handler let his dog off the lead and sent it on its way with words of encouragement.

Handler and dog made one pass down the road, to well beyond the house where Morgane had called for help. The dog was clearly searching the whole time, its tail never still, nose glued to the ground. They then crossed the road and worked back up the opposite side to their starting point.

Nothing.

Ted felt his heart sink. He'd been so sure his theory was correct, but the dog had found nothing. His disappointment must have shown on his face as the dog handler gave him an encouraging smile.

'Don't worry, sir. I told you, he's young and inexperienced. Don't expect miracles. He doesn't yet know enough to get into every bush and thicket we've gone past. We'll have another couple of passes and see how we get on. Just be patient.'

It was on their third attempt that the dog squeezed itself

right into the hedge next to the house then gave three excited yelps.

'That's his tell, sir. He's found something with blood on it. I just hope it's what you were looking for.'

He went up to his dog and threw a tennis ball to distract it. The springer bounded after it, all thought of work gone from its mind now it had a toy to play with. The handler had gloves on. He struggled into the hedge, the gap not so accommodating to his bulky figure as it had been to the dog, and scrabbled about with his covered fingers.

'Is this what you were looking for, sir?'

He held up a fist-sized stone, which glinted in the weak morning sunlight. It looked like a small piece of ornamental alabaster. Ted noticed there were other similar pieces along the hedge-line. He stepped closer and held out an evidence bag for the handler to drop the stone into.

'Sergeant, I think it just might be,' Ted said, looking closely at dark stains on the white rock. 'It's clearly had some protection from the elements, thankfully, so we may just get identifiable traces from it. I can't thank you enough. Or Tally. Would he let me stroke him?'

Maurice, who had known the boss long enough to know his fear of dogs, looked surprised.

'He'd let anyone stroke him, sir, he's a right softy. And if you throw his ball for him, you'd be his friend for life.'

He whistled his dog and it shot eagerly back to his side, sitting looking hopeful, dropping the ball from its jaws when ordered to. Ted held out a still hesitant hand and an eager pink tongue licked at it, the power of the tail wagging moving the dog's entire rear end as it hovered, rather than sat, full of expectation. Ted picked up the ball and got ready to throw it.

'Thank you, Tally, you've really helped me. Good boy.'

'Wow, boss, you touched a dog,' Maurice chuckled as they walked back to the car.

'After a breakthrough like that, Maurice, I nearly kissed

him. Let's just hope it's a day when all the cards are finally stacked in our favour. Next stop, the flat in Bramhall, please. I want to see how Rob's getting on.'

Rob and his team were looking despondent when Ted and Maurice arrived for an update.

'Nothing, boss. We've turned the place inside out but we've not found anything of any use. We've got that dragon picture you asked about and I see what you mean about that. I wouldn't like that leering down at me from my bedroom wall, for sure. But apart from that, nothing.'

Ted wandered about the flat, poking and prodding into corners, although he knew Rob would have done a good job. He'd just been so sure that they would have found something. He was convinced Morgane had a cache somewhere, possibly with a second phone and more of her drawings. They hadn't found it at either of her parents' homes, so they would have to look elsewhere. But where?

He stood in the small sun lounge, looking out into the garden. The early promise of sunshine had now given way to a light rain once more. Ted was remembering the great night he'd spent with Trev in the tent in their own garden. It hadn't taken much to put things right between them. Just a bit of time and imagination.

'And the shed?'

There was an awkward pause and Rob's face fell visibly.

'Shit, boss. It never occurred to me. I didn't realise it belonged to this flat.'

'It might not, but you should have checked,' Ted said mildly. 'Never mind. It was just inexperience. You won't make the same mistake again. I've done worse, believe me. Shall we go?'

Ted and Maurice were pulling on blue gloves as they walked down the damp lawn to the green wooden shed. The door was padlocked. Ted indicated to one of the uniformed constables with them to spring the lock. As the door swung open, Ted went in first and looked around.

It was a neat and tidy space, gardening tools carefully cleaned and put away. DIY tools lined the shelves down one side, plastic milk bottles converted to hold nails, screws, staples. There was a pair of green Wellington boots, a man's large size and, next to them, dwarfed in comparison, a pair of small, stained, white trainers.

'So, Morgane, you didn't throw them away, after all,' Ted said, half to himself.

Rob was also inside the shed, carefully looking through the items on the shelf. He picked something up and handed it to Ted.

'Boss.'

Ted took the tartan purse he was holding out to him. He snapped open the fold-over flap and looked at the card inside the clear plastic front pocket.

'A bus pass, in the name of Mrs Joan Murray. Very interesting. Let's see what Morgane has to say to this.'

Rob followed the boss out of the house as they were leaving. Even Maurice could do tactful when he saw the need so he strode on ahead, making some excuse about starting the car and getting the heater going so they could dry their feet from the damp grass.

'Boss, I'm really sorry about that...'

'Seriously, Rob, there's no need. Once this case is wrapped up, you and I will have a quiet half hour in The Grapes. You can buy me a Gunner and I'll tell you some of the things I did as a new DS. Then you'll understand when I say don't sweat it. Learn from it and move on. Wrap things up here, and we'll see you back at the nick. It's been a good day for discoveries. Let's hope we're on a roll now.'

Ted knew he was likely to be in for a long day. After the briefing, he and Jim would need to get together with the Ice

Queen and put her in the picture. They'd have to decide at what point they needed to show their hand and think of bringing Morgane in for questioning under caution. They certainly needed to liaise with CPS early on, with such a potentially difficult case to bring.

As Maurice drove them back to the station, Ted sent a text to Trev, warning him that he might be late and telling him to eat when he was hungry. There were still plenty of sausages left. Ted had bought enough for an army.

'Don't mind how late you are if we can sleep in the tent again. I'm sure another cat needs worming. Txx'

Ted hid a smile but it was not lost on Maurice.

'Is everything all right at home, boss? Only, I couldn't help but notice the hand ...'

Ted knew he wasn't prying, just genuinely concerned.

'Absolutely fine, thanks, Maurice. I just did a daft thing. Nothing to worry about.'

'If ever you need someone to talk to, Ted, away from work, you know you can trust me.'

Maurice was the team member who'd known the boss the longest so he slipped sometimes into first-name terms. He was also the one who'd seen him nearly lose it on one occasion, and seen him at possibly his lowest ebb.

'I know that, Maurice, and I appreciate it, thank you.'

'Boss, we need another search warrant,' Jezza said at the end-of-day briefing, as soon as Ted had updated the team on progress so far. 'Morgane has a locker at school. They wouldn't give me access to it, without a warrant. We need to know what she's stashed there, and as soon as possible, in case she tries to go after it herself. And according to the school, she's a real loner, no proper friends, seemingly no interest in making any. Loves her art, shines at it, other than that, an average pupil.'

Ted had arranged for Morgane and her father to spend the night at a local hotel. He didn't want her knowing too soon that they'd found the purse and her trainers. Those had gone straight off to the lab for testing, with instructions that they were top priority. The hotel was under observation. There was no way Morgane or her father could leave without being seen, but it had freed Kate up to come in and report.

'Mr Edwards is now spitting tacks, boss. He's beyond incandescent. He's spent most of the day on the phone to his solicitor and as you suspected, he's using his ex-wife's law firm. Morgane, on the other hand, seems to be perfectly calm, just sits there sketching all the time, as if none of this concerns her.'

'That's why I want to get a psych evaluation of her early on. Her behaviour seems very bizarre to me. I need to make sure we can go ahead and interview her under caution. I don't want her entire testimony ruled as inadmissible if the other side's psych says she's suffering from post traumatic stress, or something.

'Jo, what news from the granny?'

Jo reached down and produced a carrier bag from by his feet. He carefully lifted out something in an evidence bag and held it up for all to see.

'Meet Gordon, the mooning garden gnome. We lifted it from the garden, with Mrs Edwards' permission. She said it was a birthday present from Morgane, about four years ago, she thinks. She's never liked it. She finds it a bit rude, but she kept it on display to please Morgane because she'd spent her pocket money on it. Or so she said. Although I think we could take a guess about where Gordon may really have come from.'

The ceramic gnome had its trousers pulled down to expose naked buttocks and was leering over its shoulder at anyone who approached it.

Jim Baker was shaking his head in disbelief.

'So you're saying that this young lass, what age is she, sixteen? That she's killed three people, including her own mother? And the arson case was four years ago, when she would have been, what, about twelve?'

'I think she's killed five, boss. Luke Martin's violin bridge was found in her house. And I wouldn't mind betting that, once forensics have finished with her trainers, we can put her at the scene of Tyler Bradbury's murder, too. You can see now why I want that psych evaluation, and soon. I think we're possibly looking at a psychopath the likes of whom I've not seen before. And if I'm right, don't forget, that also means she's our animal torturer, too.'

'This is almost beyond belief,' the Ice Queen said, with the suggestion of a shudder. 'Hopefully it's only once in a lifetime we come across something like this. Between us, we must have more than sixty years of service and it's a first for me. We absolutely cannot afford to make any errors.'

'That's why I want the psych evaluation as soon as possible. And why we need to gear up to oppose bail when we finally do charge her.'

'I can definitely arrange the evaluation. But we're going to need the father's consent, unless we charge her first. And have we yet got enough to do that with any certainty?'

She and Jim were drinking coffee. Ted had refused and instead opted for water. He'd had far more caffeine in the last couple of days than he liked.

'I'm only guessing but I think he'll consent, and his legal team will back him. I think they'll do it expecting it will rebound on us, show that we're going after a poor young girl in shock after losing her mother. But I think a psych assessment will show an entirely different side to our Morgane.

'I also want to search her school locker first thing. If she's hiding anything, that might well be the place. There may be a second phone, and we need that.'

'If Debs can sort out the shrink, I'll sort the warrant for you. I'm sure you've got more than enough on your plate without that.'

'I'll need to get a team out in Shadwell Drive asking if there are still any neighbours from the date of the arson who might remember Gordon the gnome. It's tentative, and I doubt we can prove anything, but it's worth a try.'

'When are you going to talk to the girl again?'

'After we've looked in her locker. I want all the ammunition we can find before I start. But I don't want to do anything with her before that psych evaluation.'

Things were starting to move quickly. Ted had his warrant to search at the school by mid-morning the next day. He and Jezza went there together and were once again shown in to see the headteacher.

'Mr Mitchell, we have a warrant here to search Morgane Edwards' locker, and also anywhere else she might keep personal possessions.'

Ted handed the document over and the head studied it in detail, as if checking its authenticity. He was clearly not used to the police turning up at his establishment wanting to search through pupils' personal possessions.

'I would also very much like, if it's at all possible, to talk to her art teacher. A Miss Lake, I believe?'

'I'll arrange that for you. May I ask what this is about? I thought Morgane was a victim in this case?'

'I'm afraid I'm not at liberty to discuss it with you. If we could just see her locker, please? And is there anywhere else she might keep her things, on the school premises?'

'No, nowhere that I'm aware of. I'll take you to the lockers myself. I'll get my secretary to arrange for Miss Lake to be available as soon as possible.'

He was clearly keen to hang around while Ted and Jezza carried out the search. Ted firmly but politely asked him to leave them to it. He promised they would come and find him as soon as they had finished.

Jezza had brought evidence bags and a holdall, in case they

found anything of interest.

'Bingo,' she said as her groping hand found something at the back of the top shelf inside. She withdrew a gloved hand, holding up a pink mobile phone. 'Now it'll be interesting to see what Océane can find on this one. I'm betting it won't be quite as sweet and innocent as the one which was left conveniently for us to find at the murder scene.'

The locker also yielded up several sketch pads. A quick flick through them showed their content to be rather different to those they had already seen.

'Can you get that phone to the lab for fingerprinting as a matter of urgency, Jezza, please? And tell them I want it done and passed on to Océane yesterday, if not sooner. Take the car and get this art stuff back to the station. We'll need to go through it all. I'll hop on a bus when I'm done here.'

The Head's secretary showed Ted to the art room where Miss Lake was waiting for him. She didn't currently have a class so the room was free for them to talk in.

'Thank you for making time to see me, Miss Lake,' Ted began, showing her his warrant card. 'You'll know, of course, that Morgane's mother was killed last week. I'm the Senior Investigating Officer in that case and as part of my enquiries, I'm trying to build up more of a picture of Morgane, if you'll excuse the pun. I understand she's a talented art student.'

The woman was mid-thirties, studiously Bohemian hippy styling, with a distinct whiff of patchouli. She had a myopic-looking way of peering intently when she was spoken to.

'Very talented, a very unusual style. She's produced some quite striking and sometimes disturbing pieces. Have you seen her Metamorphosis?'

Ted nodded.

'I have to confess I wouldn't want to look at it too often. It would give me nightmares. Do you have any more of her work here, in the classroom?'

'Oh yes, one or two of her pieces are on display as they're

really very good. She draws portraits quite brilliantly,' she was indicating one on the wall behind her, an unmistakable likeness of herself. 'She also loves to work experimentally with other media, like the snake skin.'

She led the way across the room towards something hanging on the wall. To Ted, it looked like an angry mix of blood reds and black which didn't immediately mean anything to him.

'Here she's used some faux fur she found on the market, together with some items she found lying about. It symbolises chaos. Quite disturbing, don't you think?'

Ted was looking closely at the black fur. He took out his reading glasses, put them on and studied the work more closely.

'And what do you think this is here? These silvery-grey slivers of something?'

'Ah yes, very intricate work, there, painstakingly done. She shaved slivers off pigeon feathers she'd found while walking in the park, she told me.'

'Miss Lake, those are not from feathers. They're cat claws, or parts of them. And this isn't faux fur. It's real animal fur. If I'm not mistaken, that is also from a cat. I won't know until we've tested it, but I'd take an educated guess that the red is animal blood.'

He put his glasses away and took out the warrant. The woman was now looking decidedly queasy.

'I'm going to need to take this away with me, for detailed examination. I wonder if you'd be kind enough to find me something to wrap and carry it in?'

She was so eager to find him something that it was obvious she couldn't wait to get the now offending item off the wall. Ted strongly suspected that as soon as he left, the art teacher might be about to lose her breakfast.

# Chapter Thirty

Virgil was back with the team, after his paternity leave. Ted couldn't believe how quickly the last two weeks had flown by. He caught him yawning widely at his desk, trying to catch up with the current cases.

'Sorry, boss,' he said guiltily. 'I optimistically hoped all the horror stories I'd heard about sleep deprivation with a new-born were exaggerated. I think they're actually understated.'

'How is little Daisy?'

'Completely gorgeous, of course, but she definitely has the lung-power of a potential opera singer.'

Ted headed for his office and the kettle. He'd got off the bus a stop early so he could pick up a sandwich on his way in. It looked like being another long day. Jim was at their shared desk but refused the offer of a drink. The kettle was still hot from the one he'd recently made himself.

Ted had the wrapped collage, done by Morgane, under his arm. He put it down carefully while he made his drink then sat down.

'Another exhibit?'

'Something I collected at the school, along with the sketch books which Jezza brought back. Have you eaten, or are you just about to? You might not be so keen to after I show you this one and tell you what it is.'

He put gloves on before he stood the canvas upright and carefully unwrapped it.

'I give you Chaos, by Morgane Edwards. I want to show this to the shrink when I talk to him. Any news on that front?'

'He was seeing her this morning, but I don't know if he's done that yet. He promised to come in and find us once he'd finished. So, what am I looking at here? It just looks like a bloody mess to me, but I'm not remotely artistic. Bella despairs of me. She likes going to art galleries and stuff like that. I'd rather eat my own eyeballs.

'Oh, and before I forget, Doug's been trying to get hold of you for the last half hour. He says he has some results for you.'

'I'll call him in a minute, then. And what you're looking at here is precisely that – a bloody mess. I'll need Doug to confirm it for me, after I've shown it to the psych, but unless I'm much mistaken, this is cat fur, and I do have six of them, and these, down here, are cat claws. So I'm guessing that the red is cat's blood, or possibly from another animal.'

Jim looked at him in horror.'

'Christ, Ted! So you're saying this young lass skinned that cat alive and pulled its claws out to make a painting?'

'I think you call it a collage,' Ted said dryly. 'You should go to those galleries with Bella. You could learn a thing or two.'

'Piss off, Ted,' Jim growled, but his tone was good-natured. They were old friends, both away from the office and at work.

Ted grinned at him as he got his phone out to call Doug. Sometimes it was a bit of banter between friends which provided the antidote to the dark side of human nature which confronted them almost daily.

'Doug. Make my day and tell me you have good news for me.'

'I have good news for you, boss,' he responded dutifully. 'Morgane's prints identified on the python's tank, so you have her there. Yes, semen can, and is, regularly frozen, for things like artificial insemination, without it degrading, although it's not usually done in a home freezer, so I need to investigate further and see if there's any way we can show that. And finally, because I know you're up against it on this one, I'm going to surprise you with another best guess.

'We're still working on the prints we got from the mobile phone this morning to get a reliably accurate match to Morgane's. But we've lifted them and I'm biking the phone over to you so your CFI can start digging into its innards as soon as. What I will say is that the prints on it are a definite match for the ones on the python tank and for many we found at the house. I'm within a cat's whisker of telling you we can definitely place the phone in Morgane's fair hands.'

Ted gave an involuntary shudder at the mention of cats' whiskers after what he'd seen that morning.

'Speaking of our feline friends, once I've spoken to the psychologist, I'll be sending over to you one of Morgan's collages which we lifted from the school. I want you to identify all the substances used in its construction, please. And Doug, this may possibly be something you would prefer to pass on to a colleague to work on. I know you're a professional but I'll admit, it's something I'm struggling with a bit.'

It was mid-afternoon when Bill called up from the front desk to tell Ted his visitor had arrived and he was sending him up with a PC to escort him. It was young Gavin Jackson once again who tapped on the door to show the man in. Ted thanked him and stood up to introduce himself. They had the office to themselves. Jim was downstairs, balancing budgets with the Ice Queen.

'Ted Darling. Thanks for doing this so quickly, I appreciate it.'

The man was tall, gangling and thin. He looked about mid-forties but his hair was more silver than grey, its style haphazard. He was wearing comfortable cords, gone baggy at the knees, with an open shirt and tweed jacket. He looked like an actor who'd come to audition for the part of a mad professor, Ted thought, as he invited him to sit down.

'Anthony Hopkins. Yes, really. Like the Hannibal Lecter actor. The only difference is that I pronounce the Th and he doesn't, and I don't usually eat people's livers, with or without fava beans. So I imagine we can begin by bonding over difficult names, growing up.'

Ted smiled. He liked him already.

'I usually begin by offering my visitors a drink. Can I offer you a tea, or some coffee?'

He stood up to put the kettle on. Hopkins turned to look at what was on offer.

'Ah, green tea would be very Zen after the morning I've had,' he said, shaking his head to sugar or honey.

Ted put their drinks in front of them and sat down, his notebook ready to make jottings.

'So, our Morgane. What did you make of her? What can you tell me about her?'

'May I call you Ted? Do please call me Anthony. Let me say at the outset, Ted, that I am not someone prone to exaggeration or drama. I've worked with young offenders for most of my professional career. I didn't think there was anything left which could shock me.

'I have to tell you, Ted, in all seriousness, that Morgane Edwards scares me. I could tell you she was a psychopath with sociopathic tendencies. Or vice versa. Nowadays, all such recognised conditions are somewhat lumped together as Antisocial Personality Disorder, which sounds rather benign, doesn't it? I can tell you without hesitation that there is nothing whatsoever benign about Morgane.'

'Is she insane? Can her defence enter an insanity plea?'

'Ah, *mens rea* and all that. What a legal quagmire that is. Most courts would certainly find that sixteen is well within the age of discretion and therefore she would be presumed by law to be sane and to be accountable for her actions, unless the defence can successfully prove otherwise. Personality disorder is a clinically recognised mental disorder, so they would have some leeway there.

'Is she insane? No, probably not. Is she able to recognise

right from wrong? No, absolutely not. I hope you have a watertight case against her, Ted, as this young lady is, in my professional opinion, extremely dangerous and very likely to offend again. My personal advice, for what that's worth, is you should attempt to remand her in custody, to a secure children's unit, as soon as possible.'

'I don't yet have a strong case. Will she confess in interview, do you think?'

'Confess isn't quite the right word. It implies some acceptance of culpability. I'm serious when I say she won't recognise that she has done anything wrong. She will be able to justify her actions to herself and will expect others to accept that justification, too. However, she might well tell you what she's done. She might even be proud of her actions, especially if she thinks she's been cleverer than anyone else.

'There's something else I should mention, Ted, although you may well have picked up on it already. There's likely to be a strong sexual element in this. It's highly probable that Morgane was sexually precocious and is promiscuous. She may well get sexual gratification from her acts. Indeed, that may be her main motive. I had the distinct impression throughout that she was trying to flirt with me.'

'I had exactly the same. It made me uncomfortable.'

'On that subject, although there is no reason why there would be a connection, I just wondered about her relationship with her father? She did talk about him rather a lot and in a way which I found a little unsettling and, I would say, a bit immature for her age, if you understand me?'

'We have a Family Liaison Officer with them. She and I have both remarked on the same thing. He won't, of course, be able to be present for any further interviews now as he may well be called as a witness by either side.

'I've got this collage she did. We think it links her to a series of animal torture cases the RSPCA are investigating.'

Hopkins gave it barely a glance before replying, 'Wouldn't

surprise me at all. That would also fit with the sexual element.'

'What about emotions? I thought psychopaths didn't have any, or didn't show them. Yet she's broken down in tears several times when we've been talking to her.'

'Ah yes, I had that treatment, too. She won't actually feel the same emotions as others, but she will have learnt to produce the actions normally associated with them. By watching other people, or perhaps watching telly, she will have learnt that in such and such a situation you might produce tears. They won't be genuine, though.'

'What about pain? We think she inflicted the head injury on herself, twice over, and that must have hurt, surely?'

'She will feel pain, in all probability, but she will see it as a means to an end, nothing more. Don't forget, she is someone extremely calculating, highly manipulative. Which is what makes her so very dangerous.'

'Thank you for all of this, it's been most helpful. Am I right in thinking, based on what you've said, that there is no reason why I don't now interview her under caution? The defence aren't going to jump all over me claiming she was unfit?'

'Oh, they will certainly try to. So it will just come down to their psychologist and me, in court, trying to prove who has the most impressive one.'

It was clearly an old joke he used frequently as, after a staged pause, he smiled and winked at Ted.

'Qualification, that is.'

Another late night for Ted, yet another snatched meal, and the prospect of an early start again. Trev had broken their camp in the garden and put everything away. He felt Ted deserved to return to the comfort of the bedroom.

'With a bit of luck and a following wind, we'll have our prime suspect safely locked up before the weekend so if we do, I promise we'll do something special together. Maybe some real camping? We could go to the Lakes? Or Snowdonia?

Whatever you fancy.'

'That sounds wonderful. Billirant, in fact. Especially this weekend. But don't make promises you can't keep, Ted.'

'No, really, I'll do it. I'll officially book myself off. I'll even leave the phone behind, if it makes you any happier. Jim keeps telling me the team can manage without me, so I'll put them to the test. I just have tomorrow to get through first, and it's likely to be tough. I'm interviewing our prime suspect, and both the psych and I think she's a serial killing psychopath.'

'Ah, yes. Tomorrow. Well, you know what they say. We've got tonight. Who needs tomorrow?'

Ted kissed him quickly, before he could start singing and massacring one of his favourite songs.


Ted had brought the morning briefing forward half an hour. He wanted to be fully prepared for his first formal interview with Morgane. Kate had told him the defence team were ahead of him on the appropriate adult issue. Her solicitor didn't count as such, so she would be accompanied by her godmother, her late mother's secretary.

Kate was taxed with keeping the father out of harm's way. He was insisting on accompanying them to the station, but Ted wanted him well out of the way. He and his daughter were still staying at the hotel so he was sending an area car to pick Morgane and her godmother up from there.

Ted's plan was to allow Morgane to be released on police bail after interview, but to offer a strong objection to continued bail once she was charged and put up before magistrates the following day. With the psych evaluation, they could hopefully show enough possibility of the risk of re-offending for her to be remanded in custody.

He'd just finished the briefing when his mobile rang. The screen told him it was Willow calling which surprised and alarmed him in equal measure. Jim was busy talking to Virgil and being shown the baby pictures, so he took the opportunity of an empty office to go in there to take the call.

'Hello, Willow, this is an unexpected surprise. To what do I owe the honour?'

There was a pause before she said, 'You really have forgotten, haven't you? Ted, I've just been speaking to Trev and he's a bit upset.'

Ted felt his heart do some sort of a flip, or perhaps it was his stomach dropping down from where it should have been. He groaned.

'Oh, God, it's today, isn't it? His birthday? Shit! I'm so, so sorry. I know it sounds lame, but it really is this case. It's driven everything else out of my head. I'll call him now. Thanks, Willow.'

Trev's reply was more terse than usual. He clearly was upset.

Ted started to sing softly. Stevie Wonder. Not *Happy Birthday;* that would have been too obvious. *I Just Called To Say I Love You.*

After the fourth line, Trev gave in and laughed, the warmth back in his voice.

'I am so very sorry I forgot. Honestly. I can't promise anything for tonight, but I'm going to spoil you rotten at the weekend. I'll get back as soon as I can tonight. Love you.'

As soon as he'd finished the call, Ted went back into the main office and looked around. He hated to use his team members as gophers but desperate times called for desperate measures. Megan was still at her desk and always seemed approachable so he went over to her.

'Megan, I'm really sorry to ask, but I am deep in the do-do with Trev and I need a big favour, if you're going out at all today?'

'Of course, boss, no worries. What can I do for you?'

'I forgot his birthday. I need you to get me a nicely wrapped single red rose.'

She looked at him and smiled.

'Last of the big spenders, eh?'

'No, it's a joke between us. But you're right, dammit. Get three. Three red roses. And thank you.'

He got his wallet out and handed her a note.

'I'd also appreciate you keeping this quiet. I'll never live it down otherwise.'

'Your secret is safe with me, boss.'


Morgane was sitting serenely at the table in the interview room, between a matronly older woman in a fluffy cardigan and the person Ted knew to be her solicitor. She was a formidable defence lawyer, a real street fighter. Her impeccable designer suit was so sharp it almost constituted an offensive weapon.

Ted had chosen Jezza to accompany him. Her keen perception could be useful to him. He introduced her and himself, got the formalities out of the way and started the tapes running. He asked the other three to identify themselves for the purpose of the tape.

He'd brought a bag in with him and put it down at his feet. He reached into it and took out an item in a plastic bag, which he laid on the table.

'Morgane, do you know what this is?'

'Is it off a guitar?' she asked, reaching out to pick it up, then looking to him for permission to do so. He nodded.

'No, not a guitar,' she said, examining it closely. 'A violin, I think. We did some still life studies of musical instruments in art. I thought it was boring.'

'Do you know where this one came from?'

'No idea. From a violin, I suppose,' she replied, with no apparent trace of irony.

'And what about this?'

He lifted out the purse which had been found in the shed.

'Oh, that. I found that in a waste-paper bin, not far from my gran's house, in Wythenshawe. I don't know why I kept it really. I just saw it sticking out of the top of the bin.'

Her solicitor interrupted her smoothly.

'Don't forget what I told you, Morgane. You don't have to answer any of these questions at this stage, if you don't want to.'

The girl looked at her in surprise, her blue eyes widening.

'I don't mind. Why would I? I'm just trying to help them to find out who killed my mum.'

'And what about this?'

The mooning garden gnome made his bare-bottomed appearance alongside the other items. The girl laughed delightedly, as if at the sight of an old friend.

'Oh, that's Gordon the garden gnome. I got him for my gran, ages ago, for her birthday.'

'Got him or bought him?' Jezza queried, picking up on the turn of phrase.

For a moment, the expression in Morgane's blue eyes changed. There was a flash of something like anger. Or contempt. She looked annoyed by the interruption.

'Bought him, of course. From a garden centre. Why?'

At that moment, there was a quiet knock and a PC in uniform put his head round the door.

'Sir, sorry to interrupt. Can I speak to you a moment?'

Ted nodded to Jezza to follow procedure with the tape, then stepped out into the corridor.

'There's a message from your DI upstairs. He needs you to go up and he says it's worth interrupting you for. And not to shoot the messenger, sir.'

'Thank you. Please could you arrange drinks for everyone in there, and please tell DC Vine I'll be back shortly.'

He took the stairs two at a time, eager to see what was so important that Jo had called him away from the interview.

The first thing he noticed was that Steve was crouching down next to Océane's desk, a protective arm around her. She was looking pale, wiping at her mouth with a paper handkerchief. Jim Baker was looming over her, making what were clearly intended to be consoling noises. Jo and Mike Hallam were standing behind her, looking at her computer screen.

'Sorry to interrupt, boss, but you really do need to see what Océane's just found on Morgane's second phone. It's not pretty, though.'

Ted strode across the office, feeling bad that he hadn't warned her that any images she found were likely to be graphic. The screen showed the skinned cat incident in the park, blown up to full size. Even though Ted had seen the real thing, he somehow found this image of it even worse.

'Océane, I'm really sorry, I should have warned you. Are you all right? Do you want to go home?'

'I'm sorry, boss, it was just a bit worse than I was expecting. I only just made it to the ladies' in time. But I would say that just about everything you need is on here.'

'Why don't you take a short break? Go and have a cup of tea or something?'

He looked around the office for someone to send with her. Megan was out, Jezza was downstairs. But Maurice was there, and he was the obvious person to send.

'Maurice, can you go with her, please?'

'I'll go, boss,' Steve said, standing up and looking eager to do something to help.

'Sorry, Steve, we need you here to work this thing for us. One of us may break something, or wipe vital evidence. Océane, you're in safe hands with Maurice. Take as long as you need.'

As they went out of the office together, Ted told Steve, 'Right, please show me everything you found on the phone. Can you print some of it off for me? I'll tell you which ones.'

He looked round the office for someone else.

'Virgil, please can you nip down to the interview room. Tell Jezza to make it a formal break for about fifteen minutes.

If you were to happen to let slip in front of Morgane and her brief that I've been called away to look at some important new evidence which has just come into my possession, that would be excellent.'

Virgil grinned at him.

'Understood, boss.'

Ted turned back to the screen, looking in horror at what unfolded there. In the end, he got Steve to print off just two, for now and took them downstairs with him, asking Jim to join him for five minutes, with the Ice Queen, to discuss strategy.

'I think we now have enough here to charge her with Tyler's and her mother's murders to be going on with. I'd like to do that, shortly, but I'm changing my opinion about bail. Depending on how the next part of the interview goes, I favour going for overnight custody in a secure unit, youth court in the morning and an application for continuing custody.'

Morgane was still looking completely unconcerned, sitting chatting to her godmother, with the occasional aside to the solicitor.

Morgane, I'd like to show you a couple of photos now.'

First, he slid across the table the picture of the Batman toy, propped up against the tree trunk.

'How did you find that?' she asked, frowning.

'How, Morgane? Not where?' Jezza again pounced on the question.

'Detective Constable, you're putting words into my client's mouth,' the solicitor cut in.

Ignoring both of them, Ted pushed another photo towards her. It was of Tyler Bradbury's semi-naked body, floating at the edge of the river. To his astonishment, she pointed at it and started laughing.

'He's showing his bum, just like Gordon the garden gnome. I thought he'd sink like a sack of spuds, but he kept floating back up to the top, no matter how long I held him under.'

'Morgane, you mustn't say anything, nothing at all,' the solicitor cut in sharply, her expression suddenly one of distaste but trying to stay professional and look after her client's interests.'

'And your mother, Morgane? What happened there?'

The solicitor tried again to intervene but the girl made direct eye contact with Ted and smiled, her expression one of innocent flirtation.

'I thought the first blow would do it, but it didn't. She just kept gurgling. I had to hit her a few times.'

The godmother had turned white and looked in danger of sliding off her chair.

'Morgane, you're going to be taken now and formally charged with the murder of your mother, Stephanie Mason and that of Tyler Bradbury. I have to warn you that additional charges may be forthcoming.'

Then, for the benefit of the lawyer, who was still trying to find words, 'We will be opposing bail. Quite vigorously.'

# Chapter Thirty-one

It was not as late as he feared when Ted got home. He still felt bone-weary. The interview with Morgane had left him feeling wrung out. He'd dealt with plenty of heartless killers in his career, but he'd never come across anything like Morgane. It was made worse by the fact that she was so young and looked so angelic.

He'd sent Trev a text with an idea of when he'd be back and asked if he needed to pick up a takeaway. He felt bad that, not only had he forgotten Trev's birthday, but he hadn't been able to take him out for a meal. Come hell or high water, he intended to do something nice for him at the weekend.

Trev was in the kitchen and something smelled good. Ted realised he was ravenous. He remembered having bought a sandwich but he had no idea what had become of it.

Ted held out the roses with a smile of apology.

'Oh, thwee wed woses, how twiply womantic.' Trev laughed, adapting the line from the film. 'I'll put them in water. Supper's ready when you are.'

It was only then that Ted noticed a huge, extravagant bouquet in a vase on the table. Beautifully wrapped, full of fragrant blooms swathed in ribbon, it must have cost a fortune. As Trev was fussing over Ted's offering, pathetic in comparison, Ted couldn't resist a sneaky look at the card which was still attached.

'Mille baisers. Laurence.'

He had no idea what it meant. He didn't want to know what it meant. He felt totally inadequate in the face of such competition.

'Have I time for a very quick shower? I feel totally tainted by the interview.'

Trev moved the big bouquet out of the way and gave Ted's gift pride of place on the kitchen table, which was set for them to eat at. It made Ted feel worse, somehow.

'As long as it is quick. I spoke to Shewee. She's still enthusing about Henry's place and his parents. I think she's mentally already marrying him and having his babies, poor lamb. She doesn't know I told him that if he's just using my kid sister while he decides on his sexuality, I will break every bone in his body. Slowly. Which is a bit hypocritical of me, considering I once did the same thing. Ironically, now I come to think of it, with a girl called Henrietta.'

He realised Ted was not paying a lot of attention to him. He was leaning against a work surface, scowling, his arms folded. His brain was working overtime, turning *mille baisers* round in his head, looking for a meaning. A thousand something, but what? He'd sneak a look on his laptop as soon as he could.

He could just ask Trev. He should ask Trev. The trouble was, he wasn't sure he wanted to know the answer.

'Planet Earth to DCI Darling. Hello?? Hey, you, go and get that shower, if you're going to. I'm starving, even if you're not.'

'Yes, sorry, I was miles away. I won't be long. Sorry again that I forgot your birthday. I'll make it up to you at the weekend. I suggested hiking but it's your birthday, so you choose. Whatever would make you happy.'

'Fab! We can fly to Paris for the weekend. Shopping, art galleries, maybe a flea market.'

'If that's what you'd like,' Ted told him, groaning inwardly.

Trev laughed.

'Oh, Ted, you're no fun to wind up, it's just too easy.'

He called after his partner as he took the stairs two at a time, heading for the shower.

'And you can make it up to me later, when we've eaten. In bed.'

'It's fine, Ted, honestly. It happens to everyone occasionally. It's not surprising, given the stress you're under. I put too much pressure on you.'

Ted had sat up and swung his legs out over the side of the bed. He was leaning forward, his shoulders hunched, the picture of abject misery. When Trev went to put an arm round his shoulders, he shrugged it off. He looked to be poised ready for flight.

'Ted, really, it's fine. Come on, come and lie down with me. We won't do anything. Just hold me. Talk to me. Tell me what's troubling you.'

Trev knew his partner better than to try putting the light on. If Ted would talk to him at all, indoors, it would only be in the dark, and only if he felt safe, not vulnerable.

Slowly, reluctantly, Ted slid back into the bed and lay awkwardly on his back, not moving. Trev propped himself up on one elbow to look at him in the semi-darkness, the only light that of a street lamp shining faintly through the thick curtains.

'Talk to me. Please.'

Ted took a deep breath.

'I just keep thinking. About you and Laurence. And wondering how I can match up.'

Trev rolled silently onto his back, putting a forearm over his face. His shoulders and upper body started to shake with emotion. It took Ted a while to realise that his partner was crying with laughter.

'Are you laughing at me?'

'Oh, Ted, you silly sod. I should be angry with you, for not trusting me. But it's funny. It's priceless. Honestly.'

When he got his breath back, he sat up and leaned over Ted.

'Laurence is French. It's a woman's name in France. Laurence is a woman. My new BFF. You know, my latest fag hag. I am so, so sorry you didn't realise that. It never occurred to me that you might think she was a man. I honestly thought you knew me better than that.'

Feeling increasingly stupid, Ted asked warily, 'And what does *mille baisers* mean?' hoping he was pronouncing it correctly.

'It means a thousand kisses. She's very flamboyant. She's a French woman, with a gay best friend. She thought she was doing something nice for me. And I never realised you were eaten up with jealousy thinking she was my new lover.'

'I should have asked you, shouldn't I?' Ted's voice was sounding more miserable than ever.

'You should have trusted me, Ted. That's what the issue is here. A lack of trust. And if you were worried then, yes, you should have asked me. But you do have to see the funny side of it.'

'Maybe one day,' Ted said glumly. 'Now I just feel a total prat for ruining your birthday and making a complete fool of myself. I'm sorry.'

'Let me just explain it to you, one more time.'

Trev's delivery became staccato as he punctuated each word with a kiss.

'I. Love. You. And. Only. You. Goodness knows why; you can be the most annoying bundle of angst and low self-esteem. But I do. Very much.'

Ted turned on his side to kiss him back.

'Well, Mr Policeman. I may not be a clever detective, like you are,' Trev said, 'but I do think your self-esteem is rising again.'


Morgane Edwards was due to appear before the youth court at ten o'clock the following morning for remand. On a charge of murder, her case would have to go before the Crown Court for trial at a later date. Ted had an early morning briefing arranged with Jim, the Ice Queen, and someone from CPS to discuss the grounds for opposing bail.

Before it was due to start the Ice Queen drew Ted aside for a quiet word.

'This is your golden opportunity to gain maximum points from your reporter friend. The press and media will be all over this like a rash, of course. They'll know already and you can't give him any real information before the hearing. But you could at least phone him on the pretext of making sure he knows about the hearing and drop hints that the identity of the accused may well surprise a few people.

'Ad lib, keep him on side. Give him a sweetener. We may need to use him again in the future.'

She was right, Ted knew, but he never contacted him with good grace. It went against the grain.

'Morning, Ted, you saved me the bother of having to call you. So, who have you got in custody?'

'You know I can't tell you that, Alastair. I just wanted to make sure you had the timings and details of the hearing. What I will tell you is that it's going to surprise a few people.'

'It can't be the ex-husband, if it's youth court. So is it the daughter? It's more likely to be family than a stranger.'

'You'll know at ten o'clock. I just wanted to give you the heads up.'

'I've got news for you, as it goes, Ted. I'm moving to Liverpool. Getting a bit same old, same old round here. I needed a change of scene and a better job came up. I'll miss our little chats in The Grapes, though, I must say.'

'Yes, me too,' Ted said, crossing his fingers for the lie. 'Good luck to you, Alastair. Do look me up if you're ever this way again.'

Then he added, without really knowing why, 'As a leaving present to you here's something that you're the first to know, but keep it quiet for now. Although our suspect will appear on two counts of murder this morning, I'm hoping there will be more to come. But that's all I can say for now.'

The news of Pocket Billiards' departure put him in a surprisingly good mood. He hoped it was just the first in a series of good news for the day.

'I come with fresh and surprising news for you,' the Crown Prosecutor told them as he accepted coffee and sat down for the pre-hearing meeting. 'Our accused has undergone a change of legal representation overnight. We understand that her late mother's law firm no longer wishes to represent her.

'The father is apparently livid and threatening them with all sorts. But we all know they've built their reputation on winning tricky cases. They don't want to handle one which looks like a complete lost cause from the start, based on what they've seen of their young client so far. The official line is that they fear a conflict of interest, defending the daughter of a late colleague. But I think we all know that that's a load of bull. It's quite heartening, too. If their side is already seeing it as not worth fighting for, it looks more promising for us.

'You've talked to her, Ted. Do you think she'll confess? I mean a proper confession, not what she's said so far. I can't see even a third rate legal team letting her enter anything other than a not guilty plea.'

'As Dr Hopkins explained it, it wouldn't be a confession, as such, as she doesn't recognise that she's done anything wrong. But she may well tell us all about it when I next question her. I'd say there's still a possibility we'll get a guilty plea. I intend to put more charges to her. Mrs Murray, the bus victim, quite probably Luke Martin and possibly the arson fatality, from four years ago.

'I don't want to get Mr and Mrs Martin's hopes up, but I might tell them that we do, at last, have a suspect for Luke's death. It's high time we put that one to bed.'

'You really think she did that one? A random stabbing in

an alleyway?'

'From talking to her, and from Dr Hopkins' assessment, I think she's capable of anything. Once we get the rest of the forensic results, we'll charge her with the animal tortures, too. We'll be looking for life with a recommendation that she's never released.'

'Do we have any idea of motive?'

'Read the psych assessment. I suspect if I asked her why she killed any of them, she might say why not?'

Kate was now *persona non grata* with Morgane's father. The enemy. Worse, the enemy within, who had been in their lives only to seek to frame his precious daughter. He was refusing even to entertain the idea that Morgane might have committed the crimes with which she was now charged.

He'd been advised to stay at the hotel until the last minute as the press pack currently had his flat under siege, waiting for his return. They'd be on him like hyenas at the court.

It was more a quick get-together than a morning briefing and Ted had called it slightly earlier than usual to prepare for court. He wanted to remind the whole team, including those from South Manchester, that in line with tradition, he would be in the chair for the first round at The Grapes after work.

They might have their prime suspect in custody but there was a long way yet to go to build the case, especially with the other charges still to be brought.

'Kate, I want you at court and I want you keeping an eye on Mr Edwards, please. I know he thinks you're the enemy now but if Morgane is remanded in custody, and it's likely that she will be, until a trial date, he's going to need someone he knows to support him, if necessary. I'd just like to take the opportunity to thank you for your work. Do please join us in The Grapes at the end of the day. I'm buying.

'Right, I need to get my files together and get myself sorted out. Well done, everyone, good job. Make sure all your notes are up to date. Jo, you're in charge. Let's build solid cases for Tyler Bradbury and Stephanie Mason first, then see where we go from there.'

Trev had supervised Ted's wardrobe for the day as there was a good chance he would be appearing on television, if only locally. Youth court was not open to the public, but the press were allowed in, and cameras would probably be hovering outside hoping for some glimpse of human tragedy they could share with a public avid for such stories. Nothing could be said or shown to reveal the identity of the accused through the youth court process, although that could be changed when it went to Crown Court for trial. That was likely to be some time in the future, and Ted and his team would be working flat out until then to provide every detail CPS needed to get a solid conviction and the right sentence.

Morgane's father was there and was allowed to sit next to his daughter. She looked, if anything, even less concerned than before. The way she was looking about her, staring intently at faces, made Ted feel sure she was mentally drawing those present and, as soon as she had access to pen and paper, she would be capturing their likenesses.

Her new legal representative was a real come-down from the previous one. If her mother's colleague was Premier League, the young man with the cheap suit and unfortunate speech impediment who was with her for the hearing was from the subs' bench of a lowly town club.

The new defence team had clearly had no time to put together any kind of case for bail. Faced with the impressive report from Anthony Hopkins, they had simply rolled over to show their underbelly. Morgane was remanded for a week in secure youth custody. It was a pattern which would be repeated a few times before the trial, unless the defence could find the teeth to fight convincingly for her release on bail.

Ted could feel Edwards' eyes boring into him like lasers as

a composed and smiling Morgane was led away from him. He took Kate's arm to hurry her outside.

As they reached the doors, they were confronted by press and TV cameras anxious to get something, anything, they could use.

From behind them came a wordless bellow, more the sound of an animal in torment than that of a human being. Ted instinctively whirled to face whatever danger was approaching and to put himself directly in front of Kate.

Clive Edwards flew at him in a fury of whirling fists, inarticulate sounds of rage spilling from his lips, frothy saliva flying from his open mouth. He was stocky, heavier than Ted, and the earlier impression of a rugby player was accentuated by the head lowered into a thick neck, in which the veins stood out.

A passing uniformed constable stepped forward, drawing his baton, reaching for his spray.

'Leave it!' Ted said sharply.

When the younger man hesitated, he barked, 'I said leave it!'

Ted simply side-stepped neatly out of the way, his skills and timing at martial arts no match for an enraged hooker from a local club. He pushed Kate safely out of range then, almost gently, got Edwards in a restraining arm lock which saw him effectively immobilised but in no pain unless he struggled.

All fight left him in an instant. His face simply caved in on itself in a flood of grief, tears and snot. He made to turn and Ted let him, allowing him to collapse against his shoulder, his body torn by sobs. Kate moved closer, holding out tissues.

'Get him out of here, Kate. Take him back to his room. Make sure you're not followed. He won't hurt you. Stay with him until he's calm. Find someone to take care of him. I'll see you later.'

He was speaking quietly, aware that he was under the glare of the press cameras, hating the idea of what they might do with the incident.

As Kate led Edwards away, now meek and compliant, Ted used the tissues to wipe the shoulder of his good suit, glaring at the press but trying to stay polite as he asked them to move on, to respect the man's grief and to leave him in peace.

The constable was still hovering anxiously, not sure what to do. Ted nodded to him to accompany him as he turned and walked away. He knew every officer in the station by name. The young man had acted correctly; he just wanted to put him straight.

'Tony, you did the right thing. You were trying to prevent an assault on a police officer, and that's your job. Just next time I ask you to do something, please do it. First time. I had control of the situation. I didn't need you pepper spraying me by mistake. But you were right to try to intervene. I'm sure Susan's told everyone how she had to pack me off to hospital one time when I wasn't in control. Thank you.'

He went on his way leaving the PC feeling relieved. Some senior officers would have given him a public bollocking for not obeying an order. He knew Ted wasn't like that.

Ted's mobile pinged as he walked the short distance back to the nick. Trev.

'Don't be late tonight. We're going away for the weekend and it's a 3-hour drive. And remember. You promised! Tx'

Ted smiled to himself. He had promised, and for once, he intended to keep it. He was going to tell Jim, Jo and the Ice Queen that he would be off duty for the whole weekend. Morgane was safely off the streets in secure custody. If any other villains decided to kick off over the next two days, they could be somebody else's problem.

Until Monday, Ted was not a DCI in charge of Serious and Serial crime. He was an ordinary person, spending some quality time with the person he loved.

# Epilogue

Trev was tight-lipped and appeared tense about their destination for the weekend. All he would say was that he had a plan to deal with the trust issues they'd experienced.

As usual, he'd supervised Ted's wardrobe for the trip, packed for him, and laid out what he was to wear to travel in. Ted was relieved to see that it was an outdoor and smart-casual dress code. He'd promised Trev they would go wherever he wanted and he'd meant it. He was just glad that he was clearly not going to be expected to dress up like a dog's dinner.

They took the car. Ted drove, Trev navigated, as Ted resisted having a sat-nav in his personal car. He always said he hated being ordered to do things by a disembodied voice. All he knew was that they were staying in a high-end B&B near to Gloucester.

They arrived late but, far from a disgruntled greeting which would have been justified, given the hour, Trev was greeted almost deferentially. Their en-suite room was stunning, in the gable end of a converted barn, with huge windows, doubtless revealing a magnificent view in the daylight.

After an excellent breakfast, Trev, still quieter than usual, directed Ted a few miles away to a small village. They turned off a quiet road into an impressive driveway, which curved its way up to a large house. Trev leaned over to sound the horn and a tall, grey-haired woman in her sixties came to the door and stood smiling on the top step.

Trev bounded up the steps and wrapped her in one of his

famous hugs, then turned, indicating Ted, who was following him cautiously, no idea where he was or why they were there.

'This is Mrs Payne. And this is my partner, Ted.'

'It's nice to meet you, and so lovely to see Trevor again, after all these years. Do come in.'

The hallway was wide, imposing, mosaic-tiled, smelling of wax furniture polish. Trev led the way into a downstairs cloakroom which was bigger than their kitchen at home.

'Are you going to tell me where we are, and why we're here?' Ted asked anxiously.

'Trust, Ted, remember? We're here because we're going riding. And don't look like that. There is only one horse I would trust with your life, because she's one I've trusted with mine many times.'

Ted was looking at him with a mixture of surprise and horror.

'You mean ...?'

'That's right. Welcome to my humble ancestral home. Well, one of them, at least. Here, put these on; we always keep plenty of spares for guests.'

He'd been rummaging round on a shelf beneath the coat hooks and thrust a pair of leather half-chaps and a skull cap at him. He had his own holdall with him and he quickly stripped off his trousers, replacing them with his own breeches and boots, then strapped his crash hat on over his black curls.

'But isn't your horse retired? Won't it be frisky, if it's not been ridden for a long time?'

Trev smiled patiently.

'Trust, Ted. This weekend is all about trust. I thought that if I brought you to the last place on earth I ever wanted to come back to, then you'd know how committed I am to winning yours, once and for all. And she's kept in very light exercise. It's good for her joints. So no, she won't be frisky, she's too well behaved.'

They went back out into the hallway then along a

passageway, heading towards the open door of a large kitchen. Ted was dying to stop and look at the photos hanging there, looking for glimpses of Trev in his former life. He admitted to himself that he was also looking for stalling tactics. Getting on to a big horse was not his idea of a nice way to pass the weekend.

From the back door of the kitchen, they crunched over a neatly-raked gravel path, leading round the side of the house, under an impressive clock-tower, with stables on either side, and into a yard. A young girl, a groom, presumably, was standing there holding what looked like an enormous horse.

'This,' Trev said proudly, 'is Delta Fox. Foxy.'

Even Ted could tell that the horse was a venerable old lady. There was a powdering of white hairs on her face. But her eyes were kind. As soon as she heard Trev's voice, she raised her head, pricked her ears and made a low whickering noise.

Trev went to her and wrapped his arms around her neck, speaking gently to her. Ted could hear the emotion in his voice, see the tears in his eyes, at the reunion. He felt bad again, thinking only of his own fears, not of his partner's feelings in returning to his childhood home.

Trust, he told himself sternly. This was all about trust. But on a purely practical level, he had to voice his concerns.

'How am I even going to get up there?'

Trev was now adjusting the stirrups, gauging their length with an expert eye. He smiled gently.

'We never mount from the ground if we can avoid it. Bad for the saddle, bad for the horse's back. You're going to use a mounting block. I shall show off horribly by vaulting on.'

The groom had already positioned the horse in place, then she left them to it and went back to the stables.

With infinite patience, Trev got Ted safely installed, talked him through how to sit, how to relax. He'd tied a knot in the reins and handed Ted the buckle-end, showing him how to hold it.

'These are the reins. This, here, is called a panic strap, and that's exactly what it's for. When you feel anxious, you tuck your fingers under that and hold on. One thing you never do is pull on the reins.'

Ted was anxious again.

'Will she run off if I do?'

'No, but you'll hurt her mouth, and I know you don't want to do that.'

The groom had reappeared with another horse, a chestnut, the morning sunshine reflecting off the bright gold and henna highlights in his coat and mane. True to his word, Trev vaulted effortlessly from the ground onto the big horse and quickly adjusted his stirrups, then checked his girth.

'And this is George. Marsha here tells me he's the ideal steady Eddie for me. They keep him for non-riding visitors to have a plod round the old estate, which is all we're going to do. I'm going to be leading you. I'll have full control of both horses, so you'll have to trust not only Foxy but me too. Completely.'

The first stride the big mare took sent a wave of near-panic through Ted. The ground seemed an awful long way down. He tried to remember everything Trev had told him: Trust. Relax. Breathe.

The horses ambled companionably down a track leading away from the house. Ted found it wasn't quite as bad as he'd thought. The regular swaying of the horse's stride relaxed him more than he'd imagined it would. He felt an absurd desire to talk, to vocalise inner feelings, even things he'd thought were long buried.

Trev talked too. Things from his childhood he'd never previously mentioned. It felt relaxed and natural. Mutual trust. That's what it meant.

They turned off into a green lane which led towards a copse of trees on top of a small hill. The ground began to rise slightly with every stride. Trev clicked his tongue and the horses broke into a slow and sedate jog. At first it was bouncy, uncomfortable. Ted watched what Trev was doing then, with some vocal encouragement, he managed, hesitantly, to do the rising up and down which came so effortlessly to his partner.

Trev clicked again and it suddenly became much less uncomfortable. Smooth, rhythmic.

Trev was smiling in delight as he carefully slowed both horses back to a walk before they started blowing.

'Well, Mr Policeman, you just had your first little canter. How was it for you?'

Ted grinned.

'I think I'm enjoying myself. Can we do it again tomorrow?'

**The End**

Lightning Source UK Ltd.
Milton Keynes UK
UKHW011952300619
345321UK00001B/149/P